The Sound of Thunder

The Sound of Thunder

Kim Joo-young

translated by
Chun Kyung-Ja

▨ Si-sa-yong-o-sa, Inc.

The Sound of Thunder

ISBN : 0-87296-038-2

First printing 1990
Si-sa-yong-o-sa, Inc.
55-1 Chongno 2-ga, Chongno-gu
Seoul 110-122, Korea

Jacket Design by Kim Jin-pyong

Printed in KOREA

Preface

The Sound of Thunder (Chondung Sori) by Kim Joo-young was published in 1986 and immediately met with an enthusiastic reception from the Korean reading public. The author was born in 1939 in a small village in North Kyongsang-do. He entered Sorabol College in 1959 and graduated several years later after interrupting his studies to do military service.

Kim's first major work, *A Dormant Time* (Hyumyon-gi), appeared in 1970. In a satirical vein, the author depicts ordeals and disillusionments experienced by country folk upon migrating to the big city. The style is brusque and earthy—"naturalistic"—focusing on human passions and weaknesses that were to recur as themes in Kim's later offerings.

After producing a number of well-regarded short stories, including *A Woman on a Wooden Horse* (Mokmawiui Yoja), Kim moved to Seoul in 1976. The move brought some shifts in the form and mood of his narratives. The starkness and profane diction of his earlier style became subdued somewhat, and the thematic focus on nomadic lives began to be explored from the point of view of female protagonists, a refreshing change from most fiction at the time.

A progressively broader readership took note of the artistic talents of Kim Joo-young in the late 1970s. In 1982 his reputation was further enhanced when he was honored with a coveted Prize for Literary Prose. In 1983 he commenced serial publication of a massive *roman-fleuve* entitled *The Innkeeper* (Kaekju), of which seven volumes have appeared to date. This cycle, sat in the late Choson Dynasty, describes the decline of the old aristocracy, the abolition of the system of slavery, and the ascendancy of mercantile classes.

The novel here presented in translation, *The Sound of*

Thunder (Chondung Sori), is a story of homelessness. Set in the bedlam of the Korean War, the book probes beneath the surface of historical stereotypes to recapture the tragedy of partition from the perspective of a woman trapped by coincidence between the two warring camps.

It is a realistic tale of resilience and survival against great odds and in the face of terrible moral ambiguities. The author marks how a young widow is torn between the heavy burdens imposed on her by traditional Confucian imperatives of decorum, by unchosen motherhood, by ineluctable sexual passions, by all the insufferable visages of a cruel fate, and not least by the pointless guilt evoked by one insoluble dilemma after another.

The thunder of the title is a portent of many things—of bloodshed and birth, of rape and vengeful rage, of ostracism and reunion, of mindless wrath and the redemption of compassion. Whether thunderclaps are likely to be followed by a hail of bullets, a deluge of tears or a soft healing rain is not easy for the reader to foretell. This uncertainty, indeed, is one of the features that makes the book an often compellingly realistic work of art.

"Division literature"—the genre of novels and other narratives in which the sundering of the Korean nation in two is reflected—has in the past most often been written from a masculine point of view and with men as the leading characters. Here, by viewing the world through a woman's eyes Kim Joo-young broadens his readers' understanding of the tragedy of a conflict which not only annihilated hundreds of thousands, but also drove millions of Korean women into their own unique abysses of despair. The courage such women summoned from deep within themselves should be remembered, for in it may be found a dignity that silently denounces the atrocities men commit in the name of their vainglorious ideals.

Chun Kyung-ja

The Sound of Thunder

The Sound of Thunder

A Yoke

All day long the sky was ink blue. Not a trace of a cloud was visible the whole day. Then, as evening slowly settled over the Kalmoe hillside, engulfing the entirety of Woljon-ri in the grayness of dusk, a rumble was heard, as if huge boulders were sliding down a mountain slope. The sound might have come from somewhere far off behind Kalmoe hill, or maybe from Sokpori, a village about twenty miles distant.

Though initially startled, a discerning ear soon could make out that the rolling rumble was the sound of thunder. At that very moment, a woman was rushing at breakneck speed along the irrigation ditch that sliced down from Kalmoe hill into the rear of Woljon-ri. The ditch was broad, opening wider than the outstretched arms of a six-foot man. Yet not a soul witnessed the woman's flight as she raced along the mud banks of the watercourse, hair disordered, seemingly chased by the thunder past the even furrows of the cornfield.

From early that morning she'd had a feeling somebody might come to see her. There was no reason to think so, not a sign of any impending visit. The day's routine would be just as it always was, as it had been every day for the past nine years. One more day of her life would slip by uneventfully, no doubt. Nevertheless, a breathless anxiety had filled her heart since dawn and she couldn't say why. She kept checking her abdomen, drawing long, deep breaths. Her ears were trained to alert her to any signs of movement from outside the house.

The sun rose high in the sky and still nobody had come in past the servant's quarters into the yard. The whole morning through the only visitors were the beams of sunlight lingering outside. In this gloomy old house, haunt of two women oblivious to the passage of time, even a visit by Chom-gae could turn the morning into an event.

Ordinarily, upon passing the servant's quarters Chom-gae proceeded straight to the stable, but today he didn't so much as glance that way and instead crossed the yard and stood quietly on the stepping stones facing the main hall of the house. It was most out of the ordinary for him.

For some time the duty of leading the cow out to pasture in the morning and of bringing her in for fodder at nightfall had been entrusted to Chom-gae. But there had seldom been occasion for him to exchange words face to face with old lady Pak, just once or twice on a few of the monthly market days.

To be precise, it had been nine months since Cha Pyong-jo had taken leave of the servant's quarters and Chom-gae had undertaken sole responsibility for the livestock. At the time, when out of the blue Chom-gae had volunteered to look after the Choi family's cow and horse, the two women scarcely could find a pretext to refuse his offer.

Even though born an outcast, and at the age of forty still barely eking out a humble living as a butcher, Chom-gae was a man with his heart in the right place, mindful of the hardships endured by his neighbors and willing to help. Despite his lowly ancestry, the man was neither base nor vulgar, and old lady Pak had taken to addressing him with a modicum of respect rather than using the low forms of speech Chom-gae encountered from others.

On this particular morning, just as on the day nine months earlier when he'd first offered to tend the animals, Chom-gae came in and loitered out in front of the main hall, seemingly tongue-tied. It was not Kil-nyo inside, but old lady Pak in the room across the yard who first sensed someone's presence outside. More accurately, Kil-nyo had also felt his presence but decided to wait until the old lady opened the door of her room.

As the sliding door opened with a crack, Kil-nyo's old mother-in-law, Pak, wheezed in an asthmatic voice,

"Is that you, Chil-rye's father? What is it?"

Chom-gae's glance darted over to the heavy double door which was troublesome enough to open even halfway. Discolored by age, the sliding doors of the house looked awful. Under the bright sun, their wood panels were as wretchedly wrinkled as the old woman's jowls.

Abruptly bending over to pluck some weeds sprouting up between the stepping stones, Chom-gae said:

"I'd better be off to the market in town this morning, ma'am."

"To town? Is today a market day?"

"Yes, ma'am."

"Well, that's nothing I need to mind, is it?"

"I've been to the stable and the cow looked a bit strange."

"The cow?"

After some hesitation, Chom-gae appeared to have made up his mind, and went on, though his voice was strained,

"Well, the truth is, the cow came into heat, and I feel too sorry for her to just ignore it."

"Into heat, you say?"

Pak absent-mindedly echoed Chom-gae's reply, then suddenly slammed the door shut. After that, no instructions of any sort were to be heard. Standing beside the stepping stones, Chom-gae showed no particular unrest at receiving no orders. He turned his glance toward the main room and continued, though it was not clear whether he was addressing Kil-nyo or old lady Pak,

"It so happens that today is market day at Sokpo. If I take the cow to the cattle market there, I'll be able to find a bull before sundown."

The door of Pak's room flew open with a sudden sense of urgency, and out came the flushed face of Pak.

"Cattle market, you say, but it won't do. Nameless beasts they may be, but in the middle of the marketplace... before the eyes of a crowd... it just won't do."

The old woman unmistakably was angry, but Chom-gae feigned not to have noticed and said,

"We do have some so-called bulls in these parts, but not a one of them is a match for our cow."

"What are you loitering here for? To provoke me?"

A faint smile crossed Chom-gae's lips.

"In that case I'll be going, ma'am. Be back before long."

Listening to the vibrant bustling as the cow was led out from the stable, Kil-nyo felt a sudden dull ache in her abdomen. At the pain her heart instantly sank. The pain was fleeting, however, and a moment later she once more was seized by a sense of suffocation that threatened to curl up her fingers.

Kil-nyo bolted the door of her room and then slipped her hand inside her skirt, stealthily feeling around her waist. The tips of her fingers checked the smooth texture of the cotton wound about her belly. In silence she counted the days in reverse, then stopped herself and shook her head. It was just not possible, she told herself. She pulled her hand back out from her skirt and felt her forehead. The tips of her fingers were moistened with cold sweat.

In the end Kil-nyo realized she could no longer control her body. But no matter how hard she racked her brain, it just could not be possible. She may not have been too clever with arithmetic, but she surely was capable of figuring a rough estimate of the date it was due.

The rest of that day until the sun was heading down, Kil-nyo busied herself with the daily chores. She was extra-meticulous with the housework even though insufferable pains whirled through her whole body. She could not let anything about her motions betray her physical condition to her mother-in-law's eyes.

From the time she first discovered she was carrying a living seed inside her, Kil-nyo had been careful not to make a single false step in managing the household, so old Pak wouldn't have the slightest ground for suspecting her daughter-in-law was pregnant. Also from the outset she had bound her abdomen so tightly that even if Pak had been eagle-eyed, she wouldn't detect the doings of the past, not unless she had seen Kil-nyo stripped naked.

There were some things beyond Kil-nyo's power to conceal, however—the cold sweat soaking her forehead, that pallid complexion and the frightened look on her face. For nine years the two women had been living together within the same walls, yet rarely did Pak show her face in her daughter-in-law's room.

This reluctance on the old woman's part was not lacking a reason. Kil-nyo recalled several times that Pak had reminisced about her own past: how as a newlywed she had dreaded the sudden appearance of her loathsome mother-in-law in the couple's room. It was worse, she said, than having your hands stuck inside a beehive.

"As if confronting a moon on a sunny day, she used to scrutinize every single move I made, passing judgment on the new addition to the family. I felt like someone marched naked in public—most unpleasant it was."

It had been eight or nine months since Pak had last mentioned the subject. From then on her occasional visits to Kil-nyo's room for this and that had ceased altogether. How lucky for her that her mother-in-law had had such an experience herself! On the other hand, old Pak had from time to time had opened her double door and just stared with a bewildered expression on her face as Kil-nyo moved about the yard. That gaze, doleful yet not reproachful, made Kil-nyo feel terrible, as if screws were being applied to her joints.

Today, too, Pak's door stayed closed, once Chom-gae had left in the morning. But for an occasional rustle as the old lady turned about, she maintained an absolute silence like a body laid to rest in a grave. Like years before when she'd observed a full year of strict mourning for her own mother-in-law, old Pak uttered not a word the whole day.

By the time the sun set with a reddish glow trailing behind,

Kil-nyo knew she could no longer stay in her room enduring the pains. It had all at once dawned on her that the pains were a definite announcement of childbirth. Exactly how she got away from the house she didn't know herself. She only recalled casting a quick glance toward her mother-in-law's room as she passed through the gate. The door was shut as firmly as the mouth of a corpse.

Once out of the gate the pain in her abdomen shuddered upward at every step until her whole being was saturated with agony. She peered up at Kalmoe hill. Realizing she had that far to go, she gritted her teeth. For a moment she lost her sense of direction when she came to the point where the immigration ditch emerged from the village and started up the hillside. Her mind fled her body and she was so dazed she couldn't tell if she was going up the path away toward the hill or down it toward the village.

At that moment her eyes fastened on a building, a slaughterhouse that Chom-gae had once pointed out to her. Chongung it was called, he'd said. She had never been anywhere near it. From hearsay she remembered it was where a Japanese policeman, the resident official in Sokpo-ri, came for a drink of warm blood whenever Chom-gae butchered a cow.

The slaughterhouse stood beyond a crumbling stone wall, at the far end of the cornfield that ran alongside the irrigation ditch. One of the eaves of the building was collapsed half to the ground. Kil-nyo leapt over it without a thought and went in. The sound of thunder seemed quite close now. Each time the thunder rolled by, grating its way over the hillside of Kalmoe, clumps of earth broke off and fell from between the thin beams lining the roof above.

Leaning on the decrepit earthen wall, Kil-nyo sank to the ground. One of her hands grasped a pillar that by its looks was none too sound, and with the other she unwrapped the piece of cotton she had wound tightly around her abdomen. Thereafter, Kil-nyo fell into a befuddled state, with everything swimming before her eyes, and finally she fainted.

By the time she regained consciousness, the sky was teeming with stars and she was quaking from the cold like a tree in a gale. She crawled out of the slaughterhouse and propped herself against the stone wall, barely gathering enough strength to get to her feet. It was a mystery to her how on a day full of rolling thunder there could be so many stars in the sky.

She sat down beside the ditch where the rows of a plot of millet tapered away. Even under the starlight she could tell that the sticky substance smeared all over her hands was blood. It was past two in the morning when, having washed her hands and tidied her clothes, she arrived back home.

To her dismay, the light was on in her room. But her mother-in-law was not there standing vigil. Pak's room was also lit, but she seemed to be lying there quietly, as she had all day. Upon sensing someone outside, however, she opened the door. Her thin white hair, lit from behind, was shining like spun silver. Kil-nyo traversed the yard until she reached the stepping stones. Pak spoke first.

"I put the light on."

"I've been out for some air, mother."

Pak gazed up at the night sky.

"I heard thunder earlier, and now so many stars and so bright! Bright as the eyes of little children."

"Shall I come in and look after your bed?"

"No need, dear. The bed matters little for one my size, besides I can take care of it myself. But something is troubling me."

"What's that, mother?"

"Hwang is not back yet. Do you suppose he took to drinking at the market? I wonder...."

Kil-nyo was startled, having forgotten that Chom-gae had set off that morning with the cow in search of a bull at the market, or so he said.

"I'll walk out to the main road for a look, then, mother."

Pak hurriedly stopped her, waving her hand in the air.

"This is no hour to go out again, don't even mention it."

"It's not far, just a few steps."

"What concerns me is not that we can't trust Hwang, I'm just afraid something went awry with the business he was on."

"Well, let's wait a bit longer, then."

"Being late is always the way with market-goers. The night wind is not good for you, now hurry in."

The night was deep, but the stars were as bright as a waxing moon, and the old woman's worries about the brute were plain enough... so why was she so adamant about keeping Kil-nyo from venturing out when it was only a few steps? Perhaps the light had not been dim enough to hide the blood-stains on Kil-nyo's skirt. And even if she hadn't seen that, the odor of blood emanating from Kil-nyo was certainly noticeable. Yet, old Pak had uttered not a word about her daughter-in-law's suspicious behavior.

Once back inside her own room, Kil-nyo changed her clothes, combed her dishevelled hair and tried to recover the equanimity of a normal day, at least outwardly. She flopped down on a pillow. Had she severed the umbilical cord? She wondered. Only now did things occur to her that should have been considered.

Judging from the blood on her hands when she left the place, isn't it possible that she managed to cut it, even in the throes of utter despair and confusion? She focused on the ache in her belly, the bitter pain that a while before had felt like a gnawing vacuum. Again she clenched her jaws and gritted her teeth. No one must see her in this wretched state.

All that remained of the Choi clan was this desolate old house with weeds sprouting between the roof-tiles, and these two women ill-starred enough to have been widowed at an early age—two widows barely managing to stay alive, miserable though their existence was.

Upon joining the Choi clan, Pak had provided the family with an heir, an only son, albeit of an ailing constitution. For this sickly boy of hers she herself had selected a girl from Hamyang to be his bride. But where was he to find the energy to sire an heir when he wasn't even able to salvage his own life?

Day by day, his illness penetrated deeper and deeper into his very marrow. Less than six months after his wedding, Pak lost her son, carried off by an emissary from the other world. When you think of it, her past life had been as futile as a nonsensical dream one might have during a short nap.

Pak's mother-in-law, Kim, was the one who had brought to the Choi clan the reputation of being a family of virtuous women. Mindful of the honorable history and the great dignity of the clan, Kil-nyo simply couldn't return to her own family after her husband died, even though their bond had been broken by death after six short months. Besides, it was unlikely her family would welcome her back.

Thus, an aged widow past seventy and another barely twenty years old, still wet behind the ears, had for the past nine years been left entombed in this once fine old house. Often as not, they communicated by coughs and glances. Such was, if you like, the dignity of the Choi clan. Despite the worsening ill-repair of the house there was a constant pall of solemnity. No recklessness could break the still air of duty.

Even were it not for that air, Kil-nyo had felt no strong urge to flee over the past nine years. Nor had she paid frequent visits upon her own family. That this old house of the Choi clan in Woljon-ri was where she had to stay, this was all there was in her thoughts. Never once did any other notion, any thought leading to an impulsive wish for escape, intrude into her head.

Like a horse tethered to a spike driven into the earth, she knew only that she was stuck where she was, and had to remain there until she rotted. Perhaps, too, it might have been because her mother-in-law, old Pak, had been playing the role not only of companion but of overseer.

All the same, gentle streams have their vortices and mild breezes their wild whirlwinds, and Kil-nyo was not without intense experiences unknown to Pak. Even during the most deplorable period of the Pacific War, when the silverware was confiscated and every last handful of grain was seized, life in the

Choi household went on oblivious to the outside world. Never had Kil-nyo expected that a single night would come back to haunt her in the form of the present, most unbearably disgraceful, predicament.

As Kil-nyo gripped her abdomen once more, she heard the clang of a cowbell out by the servant's quarters. The dull thud of a man's footsteps passed along with the sound of the bell towards the stable, and Chom-gae's voice was heard quietly saying something to the animal. A moment later, Chom-gae crossed the yard and stopped at the stepping stones before Pak's room.

"I've just come back, ma'am."

As if anticipating a reprimand from Pak, Chom-gae spoke in a voice recoiled back into his throat. The door opened, and Pak spoke in a voice as faint as if it had issued from the other world,

"What's the time, now?"

"A little after three, ma'am."

"It's good you're safely back. Not that you'd have gotten into trouble in a strange place, but I couldn't sleep worrying you might have been drinking and hurt yourself on the way back."

"I'm awfully sorry to have worried you, ma'am. I did have a couple of drinks at lunch, but I wasn't so drunk as to lose my way."

"Your wife must be worrying about you."

"I stopped in at home on the way here, so don't worry, please."

"So, have you taken care of the business you went to do?"

"It gave me more trouble than I'd expected, ma'am."

"Trouble? You mean it didn't work out?"

"I did run into a bull all right. But the owner was such a complete idiot he had to make things difficult."

"Are you telling me you went all that way for nothing?"

"For nothing? No, it wasn't like that, ma'am."

"Then, you paid him for the service?"

"A few drinks would have done it, but the guy was firm about finding a buyer for his bull before letting me use the animal. So I had to wait almost till the market closed for the day."

"You've spent the whole day troubling yourself for our family. You must be exhausted, so hurry home now and get some sleep."

Chom-gae, however, wasn't in a hurry to depart. He lingered on. A closer look at him revealed a longish package wrapped in brown paper tucked under his left arm. What was curious was what he said as he stepped up on the step and placed the parcel on the edge of the wooden floor.

"Please, do take this in."

"What is it?"

"Dried seaweed, ma'am."

"Seaweed? Where on earth did you get this at this time of year? The season is long gone."

"It so happened there was a seaweed peddler from Cholla-do at the market, and it was from this past season and the price was not bad, so I bought a few bundles."

"If so, you should take them home with you. We don't have much use for it here."

"No, ma'am. I had this family in mind when I bought it, so I bargained for a bit extra."

"I said it won't do—you're doing poorly enough as it is, you can hardly afford to support others. I can't accept this."

"Please, ma'am. You shouldn't act this way."

"It's pointless to argue. If you were leading a life of luxury, I wouldn't feel too proud to accept it, but that's not the case. Say not a word more and take this back with you. It pains me that I'm unable to help you, knowing how badly off your family is. This is just too much of a turning of the table. I can't sit here and with any justice accept gifts from you, now can I?"

So resolute was Pak that Chom-gae picked up the package of seaweed and headed out through the gate. He was familiar enough with Pak's intransigent nature that he knew only too well she was not a woman who'd accept the thing quietly. He had made the attempt without thinking she'd be likely to be talked into taking it.

At dawn the next day, it turned out that Chom-gae was himself obstinate, too. His wife walked into the servant's quarters bearing a pot on her head, went straight into the kitchen, and sat the pot on the hearth. Then she went over past the main hall to the open door of Pak's room.

"Ma'am, I've brought some seaweed soup and left it in the kitchen."

"Seaweed soup?"

"My husband told me to bring some over, ma'am."

"I can't make any sense out of this. Last night he was trying to give us some dried seaweed, and this morning he sends over soup made from it."

"I don't know, ma'am. He's been pressing me plenty, and there's more than enough seaweed at our place, too."

"Do lower your voice. The neighbors might think we've been cursed with seaweed."

"Well, I'd better be off, ma'am."

"Your husband and his stubbornness! His heart is in the right place, and that's fine, but he shouldn't be as stubborn as a mule."

By this time Chom-gae's wife was already on her way out the gate. Now that Pak had given a half-assent, Kil-nyo couldn't help but serve up the seaweed soup for breakfast. What surprised her was not just the seaweed out of season, but the neatly sliced beef in the broth, beef that these days was as hard to come by as pure gold.

As tradition had it, no dish could be better than this for a woman recuperating from childbirth. Only then did Kil-nyo start to suspect the true intention behind this gift. Half-doubtful, she kept a keen eye on Chom-gae as he came and went morning and evening, but she could detect nothing suspicious about his behavior.

She was convinced nobody had seen her rush to the slaughterhouse that night, for the banks of the irrigation ditch were dense with fully grown stalks of corn. The view from the village was completely cut off. Anyhow, nobody in their right mind was likely to be out near the slaughterhouse at nightfall with heavy thunder rolling nearer. Besides, at that hour hadn't Chom-gae still been occupied at the Sokpo-ri market?

Despite all these reasons, she couldn't readily shake the vague suspicion that Chom-gae somehow had figured out what had happened that night. The only change she'd noticed in his behavior is that he seemed to be spending more time at the stable than usual. And if they ran into each other in the yard, he was the one who turned his glance away first.

When she thought it over, however, these seemed nothing more than minute changes in the usual routine. In the two months following that night, not a single sign was visible in the Choi household to bespeak the shameful deed she had done, a deed awful enough to disgrace the whole family. Still, Kil-nyo spent many a sleepless night tormented by nightmares.

Day by day she became visibly more emaciated. She couldn't even manage to get up at the normal hour to prepare breakfast. It had been her habit each day at dawn to drop into her mother-in-law's room and get some kindling for the fire, but even this small task had become too much to bear. August was approaching and the weather was unbearably sweltering, but she seemed unaware of the heat and stayed lying down shut in her room all day.

One morning when she went in to greet old Pak, the latter asked,

"You're looking more and more haggard lately. Are you going through some illness without saying anything?"

"No, mother."

"Don't be that way. Judging from your face, it's plain enough you need someone to look after your health."

"Maybe it's just the heat."

"Heat? It's not as if you've been working in the beanfield with the sun on your back, is it?"

Kil-nyo said nothing.

"That your health is suddenly failing is beyond me. Night before last, I could hear you ranting in your sleep from way over hear. I started over to your room, but you quieted down."

That night, Kil-nyo snuck out of the house again. She knew it was hopeless, but she already had paid three nocturnal visits to the slaughterhouse. When she went two days after the delivery, she discovered the baby had disappeared. Whether this was fortunate for her, or an omen of greater misfortunes to come, she found it difficult to say. But for the next few days, Kil-nyo felt her heart throb at the very thought that the baby's disappearance might mean it was alive somewhere.

Perhaps it was better that way, she told herself. No, it had to be alive, at all costs. In any case, the sheer uncertainty prevented her from calming down, and so she had returned to the place three more times.

It had happened on that night after she came back from the slaughterhouse. Seeing Pak's room dark, she went in and lit the lamp. Underneath the lamp she found an unfamiliar bundle. Without pausing she untied the dark purple kerchief, wondering if it had been placed there by her mother-in-law. But no sooner had she opened it than she suffered a shock that made her as dizzy as if she were suspended over an abyss.

There neatly folded lay the cotton cloth, stained with blood, that Kil-nyo had used to bind her abdomen. Before she knew what she was doing, she had stuffed the bundle in the closet. But as time passed, she realized she could no longer endure the terrible shock all alone. Maybe it was Pak's doing, she thought. She took the bundle out of the closet and clutched it to her chest. Then she went over to Pak's room. It was already past three in the morning, but her mother-in-law was awake. Pak rose from her bed and sat.

"Do sit down."

Oddly enough, Pak displayed no sign of surprise at her daughter-in-law's visit in the dead of night, bundle in hands. Trembling and pale as a ghost, Kil-nyo sat down with her back to the door and pushed the bundle across the floor toward Pak. For a long while, she didn't lift her head.

"I'd more or less guessed it, dear. But it wasn't me who brought you this bundle."

"Please, mother, you should...."

"How can I condemn you when the pain I've endured for seventy long years still pierces my heart. I, too, might have lost my lofty principles early enough if you, a young one, had not been here beside me, watching all the time."

Pak's face, speckled with age spots, began to twitch and tears welled up in her eyes. With a deep sigh of grief, she added,

"When will you ever be free from this yoke?"

"Mother, I deserve to die...."

"Don't even think of that. This is the evidence that your child is alive, isn't it? That this strip of cloth was so carefully folded and sent to you, wasn't that to let you know that your newborn baby is in the hands of someone who'll bring it up safe and well? Who knows the circumstances, but it looks like the person wanted very much for you to know that the child is alive."

"How can I live as a human being...."

"But up to now you've not been able to end your life. It's heaven's doing that you had neither the guts nor the shamelessness to bring the baby into this house. That child will have a long life."

"What can I do now?"

"Dragging my life out these seventy years, I've had too many problems I couldn't tackle alone. Go back to your room now and get some sleep. The father of the child must be somewhere nearby. Don't let him see you're withering away."

Pak said not a word more. Only a short sigh escaped her lips. Kil-nyo picked up the bundle once more and left Pak's room.

It had been some ten months before. The wind was biting for an early winter day. It had been around midnight, maybe past. Kil-nyo was afraid that unless she got some extra firewood for her mother-in-law's room, the old lady would catch a chill that night. After thinking twice, she finally got out of bed. Leaving her room, she crossed the yard and went over to the shed next to the servant's quarters. That was where the firewood was stored.

It was a moonless night and the inside of the shed was pitch dark. She looked over her shoulder and saw that Pyong-jo had the light on in his room in the servant's quarters. How strange it was! Why on earth had she tried to peep in through the crack in the door?

Pyong-jo was only a youth leading the life of a hired servant, but the mere fact that he was male made her cautious around him. Never before had the notion occurred to her of stealing a glance at him—and that is exactly what she did in spite of herself. The room was brightly lit by a lamp, but fortunately there was no sign of a man. Only the bed with its dirty sheet showed that a man had been there.

Just as she was about to move back away from the cracked door, she was startled from behind. As she uttered "My goodness!" a rake-like hand clamped her mouth shut. Pyong-jo lifted her up and carried her into his room.

"I've known for some time that you've had your eye on me."

It had been a little over year since the manless family had taken on Pyong-jo as a servant. He was an outsider who'd drifted into the village, but they hadn't bothered to inquire into his past. How could he do such a thing... Kil-nyo was furious, but by then she was already half-unconscious from being forcibly pushed into the room. His hand was still pressed over her mouth, but she managed to say,

"That's... not true."

"You're too young to sleep alone, that's nonsense. Peeping into my room at this hour... how long have you been doing this?"

"The shed was so dark... I wanted to see if there was a light... to borrow...."

"Is that lame excuse all you can think of? Your lucky you ran into me tonight. Must've been pining away for me all this time. But then I, too, have been waiting for the right moment myself."

"Let me go!"

"Let you go? What are you talking about? You came out here on your own and now you want me to let you go? If you walk out now, you think there'll be no trace of you left here? If I just take this ribbon off your blouse and keep it, that'll be enough to set the whole village abuzz. Needn't act prim with me."

Pyong-jo's hand crept inside her blouse and touched her breast. Her heart plummeted into a bottomless pit. There was a tearing sound as he ripped the ribbon fastening her blouse. By the time she opened her eyes, shocked by the sharp pain below, Pyong-jo's foul smelling mouth was pumping on her forehead.

The only male in the house. It wasn't as though there hadn't been times when she lost herself momentarily watching him move about. She even remembered one time when the sight of the sweat-soaked small of his back under a thin shirt fed a sudden impulse to throw her arms around him. But that had been nothing more than an evanescent instant, just airy foam that vanished seconds later in the stream of time. Never once had her heart been truly enthralled by him.

"Hell, there's nothin' that special about what's between your legs! What's all this fuss?"

These words spat out by Pyong-jo were barely audible, as if they were spoken in another far-off world. The sticky fluid from Pyong-jo's crotch was smeared all over her thighs. In a flash, Kil-nyo covered up her lower part and said,

"I'll kill myself."

"No need, I was going to leave this house anyway. And you shouldn't try to find out where I am. Yours isn't even as good as a winehouse girl's, so you can stop making such a fuss over it."

" . . . . "

"You'd better pay what I owe at the Chechon bar at the marketplace. If you don't, the owner will be out here after a month or so to collect the money, and that'll be a disgrace for you. Shit, turned out to be a pretty cheap screw, huh?"

Pyong-jo let her up, slapping her on the hip as he blew out the lamp. He said such things only because he knew very well that the family was in no condition to pay his wages, and he had decided to leave the next day without even giving them time to try to gather the money to pay him. That he berated her so vulgarly, insinuating that her body was defective in a critical way, was beyond Kil-nyo's comprehension. The next morning, sure enough, Pyong-jo's gruff voice was heard coming from in front of old Pak's room.

"Ma'am, I'm going now."

It took some time for Pak to open her door.

"Going where? To the marketplace again?"

"No, ma'am. I'm leaving this house for good."

"Leaving?"

"Yes, ma'am."

"What a bombshell to drop on us! What on earth do you mean by taking off all of a sudden like this?"

"That's just the way it is."

"Such an impudent tongue. Besides, winter'll be here before we know it."

"Winter or summer, it's all the same to me. I'm crossing over to Japan."

"To Japan?"

"Yes, ma'am."

"Why Japan of all places?"

"Something might come up if I head down South to one of the ports."

"Just how have you come to such a decision, at least tell me that."

Turning a fleeting glance toward Kil-nyo's room, Pyong-jo said,

"It's a long story, I won't go into it."

"Do come in."

"No need to, ma'am. A man bound to leave might as well hurry on to lighten the burden for those left behind."

"You talk as though you've been asked to leave."

At this, a faint grin appeared at the corners of Pyong-jo's mouth as he replied,

"To go is my wish."

"What do you mean it's your wish. Just yesterday afternoon you had no such plans, did you?"

"Isn't that what a man's lot is all about? A series of unexpected events?"

"I can't make any sense out of what you're saying."

"I'm not surprised."

"You're not?"

"Just how many times have you been outside these walls in your lifetime, ma'am? How could you understand the world when you don't even know what's happening right outside your own house?"

This time it was Pak who was at a loss for words. There was a pause before she spoke again.

"What about your wages?"

"I'll drop by later."

"When do you mean?"

"When an unexpected event pops up."

"What a way to talk!"

"I can't help it if you think I'm insolent. After all, I'll never be a son-in-law of the family, will I?"

With those last words Pyong-jo turned his back and was gone. About five days after his departure, Kil-nyo managed to settle what he owed at the Chechon tavern in the marketplace. To go there herself was out of the question. Through Chom-gae, she paid what must have been the price of a woman Pyong-jo had bought, though the bill said it was for liquor.

Even so, since becoming pregnant there were times when Pyong-jo's face flashed before her eyes—it was a mystery to Kil-nyo because the only feeling he evoked in her was shame, not the slightest warmth toward him. Abortion would have been against nature, a deed too outrageous for her even to consider. She just waited for the lump of flesh in her belly somehow to melt in secret. But the more desperate this ludicrous longing became, the larger her abdomen grew. Her only available means to battle her growing belly was to bind it up with strips of cotton. But perhaps this method was just what helped the fetus to thrive for eight months and take on human form, when otherwise she might have miscarried.

In all events, Pyong-jo's abrupt farewell ended up giving Kil-nyo a reason to postpone doing away with herself. Ever since she realized she was pregnant, every moment had been consumed by her fight against the bloody lump within her. There was no time to spare dwelling on the thought of suicide. And so she declined into her present dreadful condition.

Plagued now by the new problem of guessing who'd put the bundle in her room, Kil-nyo's illness quickly worsened and she grew paler than ever. The compassion in Chom-gae's eyes was unmistakable when now and then he rested his gaze on the visibly withering young woman.

Unusually frequent visits to the Choi house by Chom-gae's wife seemed due to Chom-gae's growing concern. No longer could he simply watch as she grew more emaciated with each passing day.

"A strange man, indeed," Pak had muttered three days earlier when she saw Chom-gae leaving the servant's quarters after hanging some blinds on Pak's door. Kil-nyo, busy wiping the floor of the main hall, kept her glance at the level of old Pak's knees, not daring to look her mother-in-law straight in the eye.

"I know he's an awfully good-natured man, but the way he dotes on us is not right. True, he's been our next-door neighbor for nearly twenty years, and neighbors ought to share and help each other out—that's why they say good neighbors are better than distant relatives. But we've never given anything to his family. It makes me wonder why he's so eager to give us a hand…. The whole village knows he's good-natured, all the same, there's something very odd about the way Hwang Chom-gae's been taking care of us."

"Maybe it's the calf on the way that makes him so devoted."

"That occurred to me, too, but to pour out heart and soul as he does over nothing more than an animal is just not natural."

Kil-nyo had not divined the real meaning underlying her mother-in-law's words. As for Pak, she was in no position to say anything more bluntly. Pak went on mumbling half to herself in a barely audible voice,

"Born a nobody... that he was born into the lowest of the low is the only problem, if it is one... but in today's enlightened world... won't be so long before he's freed from that burden...."

After a pause, Pak changed her posture and went on, "Haven't heard anything from the fellow yet?"

"...."

"I've just made a complete fool of myself by asking such a thing when you and I live here without a moment away from each other."

"Well...."

"Let's not dwell on it. I won't bring it up again, dear, never."

Pak picked up a jewelry box lying at the head of the bed. After rummaging through it, she at last took out a very worn old coin and showed it to her daughter-in-law.

"See this coin? Your husband's grandmother, who was renowned as a woman of virtue, kept it her whole life, and on her deathbed, she laid this coin in my hand. In the confusion of the moment, I just took it. I didn't know at the time what it meant. It was only a few years ago that I realized it was meant to be a yoke. Up to now I too have been unfaithful dozens of time in my heart, so who am I to reproach you? Especially when it happened without your consent."

Three more days passed. Near dusk Chom-gae hurried past the servant's quarters, crossed the yard and sprang over to the step outside Pak's room. He was nearly out of breath.

"Ma'am?"

There was no reply from inside.

"Ma'am, we've been liberated!"

Only then did the double door quietly slide open, and the silvery head of Pak craned out.

"Liberated? What in the world are you talking about?"

"I've been to town today, ma'am."

"So?"

"People were making a great commotion, everybody whispering about how we've been literated."

"If we'd been liberated, they'd be doing more than just whispering about it. Did they say what'll be happening now?"

"They say that with Liberation the Japanese at the resident office will all be kicked out."

"Then who'll be in charge?"

"We Koreans will, ma'am."

"I had a feeling something was brewing, it's been in the air, no wonder."

"Nothing is certain yet, so make sure you stay in the house."

"Have you ever seen me leave this house?"

"Everybody's worried to death!"

"Is that so?"

"Nobody really knows what the political situation'll be when the dust settles. Not a single grain of rice is left, they say."

Pak glanced over at the stable, and Chom-gae said in a low tone,

"Cow seems to suffer from morning sickness, just like a human."

"When she's not properly cared for...."

"You shouldn't even think about selling the cow, though things are getting hard. With a little one astir inside, we can't just hand her over to a stranger, even if she's only a beast."

"You're right," Pak responded, but in a voice lacking conviction.

If the truth be told, the word "liberation" carried no special significance for the Choi family. The two women had been living in retreat from the world for so many years, and undoubtedly would keep on living in isolation in days to come, that to them liberation was nothing startling. It only meant that the government office at Sokpo-ri, some miles off from their village, would no longer be run by Japanese.

Howsoever the world might have turned inside out, and whosoever might carry off on his back this decrepit old house, it seemed that the two women would never be parted from their familiar lair. That would have been something quite beyond their power.

Even if Kil-nyo resolved to rebel, the sheer weight of the old house easily would bury the rebellion beneath its dense shadows. Back when Pyong-jo unexpectedly abandoned the servant's quarters, the two women hadn't stirred the slightest, and though it was too early to say what sort of squall liberation might bring onto the house, that the two of them would be affected seemed unlikely.

It happened, however, that they were swept up by a whirlwind, and one issuing from a source they had never dreamed of. It was a least expected and most momentous turn of events.

Upon receiving visitors, Pak's habit was to open her door and remain seated in her room. Partly this was due to her feebleness in moving about, and partly it was due to her longstanding practice of staying indoors unless leaving the house was absolutely necessary. But on the day that Chom-gae came and announced that he intended to move away from the village, Pak was so astonished that she summoned Kil-nyo to help her outside.

For the first time in years, Pak came all the way over to the edge of the main hall and sat there.

"In the whole seventy years I've lived, never was I so shocked as I am now to hear the word 'leaving' from you."

Chom-gae stood there motionless before her, his head hanging down. Pak's wrinkled hands trembled visibly as they lay across her long skirt. Hiding her quaking hands under her skirt, Pak asked,

"Where will you go?"

Strangely, Pak made no inquiry about the reasons behind his decision to leave the village—it had been the same with Pyong-jo.

"I'll decide once I get to town, ma'am."

How could he have no destination? He just didn't want to mention it if he could avoid it.

"Where's the rest of your family?"

"They're probably to town by now. It wouldn't look good to the neighbors, so I sent them on ahead of me."

"The harvest will be starting in less than two weeks, won't it?

And it's not like we have nothing to bring in."

"To move at harvest time makes it easier to find work in a strange place."

"What about the butcher shop?"

"It's nothing to speak of, not worth much."

"Do you have to leave today?"

"Whenever I leave it'll be a 'today', ma'am. I may be lowborn and unschooled, but I'm not leaving this village with a carefree heart...."

Throughout this exchange, Chom-gae's eyes were riveted on the feet of Kil-nyo, who stood down in front of the hall. What was strange to her was that from afar she could hear the rumble of thunder, just as she had that day when she raced to the slaughterhouse.

"I wish I'd had the chance to see your wife off...."

"She kept telling me she wanted to say good-bye to you, but I told her to stop it. Her heart's in the right place, sure, but I had to give her a slap in the face to stop that sniveling."

"You've only daughters in your family, you ought to have an heir before you get any older."

Chom-gae said nothing for a time, then broke the silence, saying,

"I've kept it a secret till now, but my wife is pregnant—baby's due in a few months. If it's a boy, I'd hate for him to see his father working in a slaughterhouse, lugging cow's heads about in baskets. That's why I decided to leave Woljon-ri, though I don't really want to. Besides, everything's in such turmoil these days that if we settle in a new place nobody will be likely to dig out my origin."

"Don't go too, too far off."

There was a tremor in Pak's voice, but Chom-gae said nothing either way. As he started to turn around and head away, Pak suddenly raised both her arms to stop him. She pleaded with him to help her walk to the stable. Once there, Pak picked up the bridle of the cow and out the line in Chom-gae's hand.

"Take her with you."

Chom-gae just stood there, his face turned away.

"Ma'am, it's not right. I made up my mind never to touch this bridle. It's the fear of it that made me leave this place, you know."

"I've walked all the way here from my room. For me, that's a trip as long as the one you're setting out on. If you want to be liberated, it's only right for this cow to leave the Choi family, too. How are we two women going to look after this beast when you're gone?"

"She's carrying a calf."

"That's exactly why you should take her."

"Can't do that, ma'am."

"Do you want me to drop dead right here in front of your eyes?"

"What a thing to say, ma'am. Stop this nonsense, please."

"Well, then, say not a word when the calf is born, and when it's grown and able to wear a bridle, send us word, even if it has to be by a roundabout way."

Despite Pak's earnest entreaties, Chom-gae still made no reply. She did not blame him. And Chom-gae did accept the bridle from Pak.

"Gidd on."

That was the only thing Chom-gae said. For some reason the cow's eyes were bloodshot from that morning on. The cow ahead of him, Chom-gae trudged along the fence and was about pass out through a narrow lane when Pak, who was leaning on Kil-nyo, tapped her daughter-in-law on her back and said,

"You, luckless idiot, you! Hurry up and go after him. You might hear something more that he didn't want to say just now."

Only then did a certain notion flash through Kil-nyo's mind. As she was about to pull away from the old woman, suddenly she felt the weight on her arm increase as Pak seemed to collapse. Her face as white as a sheet, Pak was already on her way across the threshold of the other world. Her bloodless palms were etching circles in the air and Kil-nyo could not move a single step.

A Satchel

It was early winter in the year after Liberation that Pyong-jo returned to Woljon-ri. No one knew in any detail the sort of life he had been living for the past two and a half years since taking his leave from the Choi family. In fact, he had changed so dramatically that hardly anybody recognized him.

Although he had come back to Woljon-ri, his entry into the village was not direct. When he reached Sokpo-ri, still twenty miles from the village, he wasted several days loitering about an inn there. Like a rooster tactfully courting a hen, no doubt he was circling the outskirts of Woljon-ri to get a feel for the place. No longer was he the Pyong-jo of old, wearing rags and his worldly possessions in a bundle under his arm. He was not looking to stay in someone's servant's quarters. In other words, he had shed his old outer skin.

Having decided to pause for a while at Sokpo-ri, he took a room at the Changchunok Inn, which had a winehouse on the premises. Clad in a western suit and wearing a felt hat on his head, he was carrying a heavy satchel with a tortoise shell handle.

This was around the time that a good many men who'd crossed over to Japan or who'd been drafted were coming back to their home country and their hometowns. But neither Sokpo-ri nor Woljon-ri was Pyong-jo's hometown. From his clothes he looked like a man just back from Japan, but he'd headed for Sokpo-ri instead of his family's home.

Since his bearing was decent enough and his speech was somewhat urbane, the proprietress of the Changchunok Inn, a former courtesan, could not treat him too badly. During the several days he stayed at the inn, Pyong-jo did nothing much to speak of. Mornings and evenings he dressed himself up neatly and took walks through the town, returning before long to his room.

On the sixth day, toward evening, Pyong-jo set off for Woljon-ri. By the time he entered the village it was already so dark that the few people who knew him could hardly see enough of his features to recognize him. From a distance he contemplated the blue-gray tiled roof of the old house as dry stalks of weeds trembled in the early winter breeze.

The wind coming down off the mountain scattered the smoke of evening fires over the thatched roofs of the village. The whole world outside was buzzing like a beehive cracked open, but Woljon-ri lay somnolent beneath the mountain, still as a corpse.

Pumpkin vines, untouched during the harvest season, still were draped like rags over the earthen wall and the fences. The main gate of the Choi house was half open. They must have grown tired of the creaking from the wind, for a rock had been placed there to keep the gate from moving.

The wind blowing out through the gate from the yard felt colder than the wind from the lane beyond the house. The cords of straw twine hanging from the pillars of Pak's room, now a mortuary chamber, swayed in the wind. The manger in the stable was turned upside down.

The house was badly run down and mostly empty, yet there still were some signs of it being inhabited. The outside window of the mortuary had recently been redone with white rice paper, and a pair of rubber shoes, even whiter than the rice paper, were neatly set on the step in front of the main hall.

Pyong-jo walked across the front yard toward the stepping stones. Inside the rubber shoes was a layer of grayish-white dust. He cleared his throat a few times. The side door opened and Kil-nyo's face appeared. She scanned the stranger in a western suit standing below. Then the door closed again. There had been no change in her expression to indicate she had recognized the man. But then Pyong-jo heard the sound of the door being latched from the inside.

The way Kil-nyo's hair was parted struck him for some reason. In a quiet voice, as if to himself, Pyong-jo said,

"Nobody has seen me, so you needn't worry."

This alone was adequate evidence that the two of them were in no position to meet freely. Pyong-jo, however, removed his shiny shoes and stepped up onto the floor of the main hall. The door latch easily broke when he forced it and the way in was soon clear.

Kil-nyo was sitting up straight on the warm side of the room, her knees covered with a quilt. The shadows under her eyes were darker than the darkness of the room. Pyong-jo struck a match, lit the lamp and turned up the flame. The wick gave off a sooty smoke for a while and then burned cleanly. Through the back door came the murmur of falling leaves. The floor was cold. The woman looked far too small to warm this space with the heat of her body.

Kil-nyo was in mourning. Her eyes were nailed to the opposite wall, and Pyong-jo was staring at the part line running down the very center of her head.

"This is no way for a somewhat educated woman to greet an important guest."

Casting this criticism in her face, Pyong-jo picked up the broken door, propped it back in its place, and then flopped down in the middle of the room. The lamplight nearly was blown out, and it flickered wildly for a time before coming back to life.

"It's unlikely a woman who's been healthy and normal her whole life should suddenly have turned into a deaf mute. Shouldn't you say something, sweet if it's sweet or bitter if it's bitter, at seeing a man come back after some years away?"

Despite Pyong-jo's importuning, Kil-nyo stayed still with her mouth clammed shut. Seeing that though she was expressionless her figure was well preserved, he made a snide comment,

"I see you've managed to hang on to your life despite your unseemly state, so I guess the so-called aristocracy is no different from the commoners."

This remark jeered at the incident two and a half years earlier when he had forced her to surrender her chastity. But except for a barely visible flush on her face, Kil-nyo still made no response. Pyong-jo made no further efforts to berate her lack of hospitality, and after looking about the room, abruptly said,

"When did the old lady pass away?"

"A year and a half ago."

"Though she was in bad health, I thought her toughness of will would let her hold out much longer than that. Maybe the Lord of the Underworld got impatient waiting for her."

Pyong-jo rifled through the pockets of his jacket and took out a cigarette. The light of the match showed he was not a man who'd been eking out a livelihood from hand to mouth. The knuckles on his hands were smooth and even, and his face had lost its old copper color and was now clean and light.

Kil-nyo thought she had to say something to this man. Here she was, face to face with the man to whom she had more to say than to anybody else she'd ever met. But she just couldn't bring herself to open her mouth.

The only possible way to begin, whether her story turned out to be a counterattack or mere grumbles, was with the fact that she had borne a child fathered by him. But she dreaded owning up to the truth about the baby, and he was unlikely to believe the child was his when she wasn't even raising it herself.

Particularly to this man, who was being so flippant owing to that single unhappy incident of their flesh being mixed—just once long ago, she had no wish to bare her soul to him. And that only a few years before he had been a mere servant of the Choi family no doubt added to her discomfort.

Pyong-jo, who'd been puffing away on his cigarette, looked about and with a dreamy look on his face said,

"Let me see... how old would you be this year... about

twenty-nine, eh?"

Kil-nyo said nothing.

"So, how do like living with goblins in a house that reeks of rotting wood? After all, you are the very last woman of the great Choi clan, the great Chois whose name and power was feared far and wide in this part of the country. If you'd whelped an heir, then things'd been different, but now what's there to keep you here? Want to crumble along with the columns of this house? Is that why you've planted yourself here with that face of a ghost? If you don't object, tonight I might bless you with a child. But I'm not going to force you like I did before, so you needn't fear that. You see, I've become a man with a reputation of his own to think about."

Kil-nyo was counting the years backwards in her head. But for that one sinful episode with this man, for the past nine years she'd lived the life of a young widow. The only thing she'd gained from that nine years of life was remorse over what happened with Pyong-jo.

What on earth had she been expecting as she immersed herself in toil all the time, unwittingly conveying her state to the neighbors? Is it possible she'd been awaiting his return, in spite of herself? No, that was impossible. Then had she desired to recover the dignity of the decaying Choi family? For that she had neither the will nor the inclination, and though the motive would've been worthy, it was a mission too daunting for her even to attempt. That had been plain from the start.

Or might she have laid her own secret plans to latch on to a marriageable widower and so improve her lot? No, that was not it either. But what was it, then? Until now, she'd merely been drawing breaths. To stay alive—had such an absurd goal been her joy in life? Yes, that was possible. Kil-nyo kept on staring at the lamp. It barely flickered as the wick was consumed by the flame.

"You've lived in this house for almost ten years and should know by now it's too much for a woman to live here alone."

Pyong-jo blurted this out without warning.

At the sound of the wind rising out back, Kil-nyo clutched the quilt more tightly around her legs. An instant later Pyong-jo violently snatched the quilt away, rasping,

"What you've got under there isn't worth much, so quit guarding it like that... it's ridiculous!"

"Behave yourself, please."

"At the slightest provocation women are ready to yell 'I'll scream!' Go ahead, then. Scream if you want. But once the rumor is flying that Shin Kil-nyo of the so-called noble Choi clan has been dallying with some bastard who worked as a servant in her own house, whose reputation'll be ruined, yours or mine? Don't you see, it won't be Cha Pyong-jo, it'll be Shin Kil-nyo who dragged the Choi name through shit. Even when you and I did it, think it over, who was the one who came down to the servant's quarters in the dead of night? Who peeked into that room where a man was sleeping alone, huh?"

"It wasn't like I was hungry for a man."

"You can make excuses now, but who in their right minds will believe your story? Just go out and stop anybody on the road and ask. Who do you think people will say had the dirty notion in the first place, you or me?"

Pyong-jo, a rancid smell spilling from his mouth, made a sudden lunge toward Kil-nyo. His cheeks flushed deep red as he ripped at the bow on her blouse. As she saw his hand move hastily to loosen his necktie, Kil-nyo heard a roll of thunder like an enormous rock crashing down a slope. It was the same thunder heard in early summer three years before when she'd abandoned the newborn baby, that bloody lump, in the slaughterhouse at Kalmoe hill—the same thunder that had shattered every bone in her body. Again she was engulfed and her whole body was thrashed by it over and over. In a reflex Kil-nyo grabbed her thighs, but there came a terrible pain that felt as if one of her legs had been severed at the knee.

"Just because you're acting the prude, do you think I'll stand here and watch?"

"Stop it, please!"

"You stop playing the fool!"

Kil-nyo grit her teeth with enough force to crush her gum and clenched her eyes shut until they hurt. As Pyong-jo tried to pry open her mouth with his hands, she felt his hot breath right under her nose. How those minutes passed was beyond her. Pyong-jo was lying beside her, naked below the waist but fully clothed above, reeking of sweat. She was shaking all over.

"Don't be afraid. I'm leaving anyway."

When he spoke, Kil-nyo remembered how three years before he'd said something very similar after raping her. But those words that had left her cold three years ago, why did they have such an impact now? It was almost as though they had the power to stop her from breathing in her heart of hearts? "You mustn't go!," she wanted to wail. But she didn't have the nerve, for that was a plea of intimacy that only should pass between a man and woman whose love for one another has entwined them into one.

"This time matters are a bit different. I've got a few things to take care of before leaving. I mean, I can't just torch this house, can I? Then I'd have to do time in prison."

"What are you talking about?"

"Keep your mouth shut. A woman has no business nosing into the details. Just stay in your place and don't dare meddle with a man's doings."

Pyong-jo picked up his trousers and started putting them back on. Then for a while he attended to smoothing out the crumples in them, using saliva to fix the creases. After rearranging his outfit, he took his western-style hat from the hook on the wall and spent still more time setting it on his head so that it covered exactly half of his forehead. While absorbed in this task he muttered,

"You sure make a lot of fuss for a woman with nothing special."

Once the side door had been shut with a hysterical bang, Kil-nyo heard Pyong-jo grunting as he put on his shoes at the edge of the main hall. Then his footsteps were heard crossing the yard to the servant's quarters. His steps sounded too imposing and full of pride.

Kil-nyo was utterly drained and laid there for a long while before sitting up. She took down the lamp from its hanger and refilled it with kerosene. Then she began sewing back on the torn ribbons. That night passed without her getting any sleep at all. Did she have any moral duty to stay in this house? Wasn't there truth in what Pyong-jo had said, after all? She wondered.

Ever since she'd married into the Choi clan and her husband's death less than a year later, not even once in nine years had she posed to herself the question of moral obligation. Neither, in all probability, had her grandmother-in-law, that paragon of female chastity, nor had her mother-in-law, Pak, who'd drawn her last breath that day when Chom-gae left them for good. Like figures carved into the walls of a temple, they had set themselves down in a corner of this grand old house and just stayed there motionless until summoned to the other world.

It began to dawn on Kil-nyo that Pyong-jo's unexpected call the night before might not have stemmed from his lust to possess her body again, nor from any affection from the past, but to force her to reflect on this moral duty.

The sleepness night ran on into a new dawn, and even the wind that had thrashed about the whole night long died down with the new day. Late in the morning as the sun neared the middle of the sky, Kil-nyo regained her senses at hearing a noise outside the main gate. She slid the side door open halfway and peered out toward the servant's quarters.

Out of the blue a palanquin was being borne in through the gate. The bearers marched without pausing straight into the yard and set the palanquin down in front of the steps. The two men standing on either side of the litter were strangers. The leader bowed toward the half-open door and said,

"Madam, get on the litter, please."

These two men must have been lunatics, Kil-nyo thought, to ask her to get inside the palanquin. She hastily shut the door, saying,

"You must have the wrong place."

"Wrong place? Impossible."

"Just whose house are you looking for?"

"There's not a single man in these parts who doesn't know that this is the residence of the Choi family."

"But then who are you asking to be taken on the litter?"

"The daughter-in-law of the family, that is, you, I mean."

"That's what I meant when I said you'd come to the wrong place. I live alone in this house, so stop making a commotion and be on your way. You can ask directions once you're outside."

"No, ma'am. We can't be going until you get on this. You see, we've been paid already, paid plenty for this job, and you won't be getting rid of us very easily."

Though what the man said made no sense, there was a certain threat implied. Marking that the attitude of the bearers was oddly suspicious, Kil-nyo straightened her clothes and came out into the main hall.

Two outsiders suddenly appear in the front yard and refuse to leave—it was an unheard of ruckus. Kil-nyo scrutinized their faces and searched her memory but they were both totally unfamiliar. Judging from their general appearance they did not seem to be from any of the small mountain villages around Woljon-ri. Her heart sank.

Upon seeing her dismayed and irresolute, one of the bearers called up to her,

"Hurry down, please."

"I don't know who you are, but I must say your conduct is most regrettable here in a house where a woman lives alone."

"Most regrettable indeed is our position. For we may have to load someone on this litter against her wishes."

"This is worse than being struck by a bolt of lightning! Just what do you think you're doing?"

"If you waste much more time we'll have no choice but to carry you over and put you on ourselves."

Kil-nyo glanced quickly over at Pak's room. Only then did it occur to her that the whole thing could be some ploy concocted by Cha Pyong-jo. But she was not brave enough to pronounce that name in front of these two men. They must have been under strict orders, for they refused to divulge who was behind the whole unseemly matter. She felt her legs weaken as her eyes darted again to Pak's room.

"Hurry down, madam, please."

Muttered the second bearer, who until then had been silent, and then he took a few steps forward toward where she stood. Scared out of her wits, Kil-nyo said,

"I don't know who's responsible for this commotion, but go back and tell him never to try such an outrageous thing again."

At this, the two bearers changed their bearing and became impatient and menacing. The first bounded up the steps and put his hand on the back of Kil-nyo's neck.

"Don't be difficult ma'am. As I said before, if you don't co-operate we'll just carry you by force to the litter."

"How insolent you are! They say the world has gone to the dogs, but where are your manners?! How dare you speak of force!"

She thought she ought to return to her room and bolt the door, but her legs were quaking so badly that she couldn't budge an inch. Or perhaps her legs weren't actually trembling at all, and she only imagined that they were.

"See, what'd I tell you? Didn't I say it wouldn't be easy?"

In a flash, the other man leapt up from where he'd been standing and together the two grabbed her from behind, drag-ged her down to the yard and forced her to sit inside the palan-quin. Then it was lifted into the air and they were off.

Once they were underway, the two bearers ran all the way without stopping once. They were strong and full of vigor. To rest they slowed their pace a bit, but never once did they set the load down. After a fast journey of some twenty miles, the desti-nation turned out to be Sokpo-ri. The litter was deposited at the Changchunok Inn, but it was not as if Pyong-jo was there awaiting its arrival.

The person who pulled Kil-nyo out from the litter was the

proprietress of the inn. This woman, who in her time had gone through countless receptions and farewells with men, for some reason tut-tutted at the sight of Kil-nyo down on the ground. The first favor she accorded Kil-nyo was to offer her a bowl of honey dissolved in hot water. But other kindnesses did not follow.

"You probably have no idea why you've been dragged here, but just be patient and wait."

Speaking in low speech to a total stranger, the proprietress looked to be well into her fifties, though her face was heavily made up. It was the first time since her wedding ceremony that Kil-nyo had been addressed in such a low level of speech, and by a woman who entertained wayfarers in the marketplace.

Aware that something ominous lurked behind this predicament, Kil-nyo first quenched her thirst and then inquired,

"Please, do tell me what this is all about? Why was I dragged here?"

The innkeeper, sitting with her back to Kil-nyo, turned about and with a disapproving look, said,

"What do you mean 'dragged'? We even sent a palanquin out for you, in consideration of the family's standing in the old days, but it obviously was a waste. You needn't know all the details. Until the house is sold, you just stay here with me as a hostage instead of with that creature."

"What creature?"

"That bastard who's always coming and going in a flash, Cha Pyong-jo or whatever he calls himself."

"Where is he now?"

"How should I know where a creature with legs has crawled off to? I don't even know what's happening outside my own fence. If I'm to believe what he's been jabbering, he ought to be off tracking down a broker who can strike a deal for the house."

"Just whose house are you talking about?"

Kil-nyo asked, though she had already guessed.

"How much will be paid for a haunted old house like that, I wonder? You might get a proper price if goblins are in the market, but that place, as you know, is not fit for the living. Even if some blind buyer stumbles into a quick purchase, he'll end up breaking his back to fix it up properly. I'm amazed you managed to go on living there all this time."

A look of sympathy surfaced on the woman's face as she watched Kil-nyo sitting there vacantly, saying not a word.

"You're as simple-minded as me when it comes to the ways of the world. You're lucky to have run into a woman like me whose heart is in the right place. If you had to deal with someone nasty, you'd have gotten plenty of shit all over you. I'm the one to be blamed for having trusted that bastard—I deserve to be cheated. What he's borrowed from me with no security but his appearance comes to three full days of wages for three grown field hands, you know.

"For all I know, the bastard may be tough enough to go on with his dick stuck in a beehive, but never yet've I run across a bastard tough enough to gobble up my money and get away with it. If he sells off the house and sees that I'm paid with full interest, then I'll see to it that you are taken wherever you want to go on a litter like today, but if he's already run away, well, in that case I'm sorry to say that you'll have to work your ass off in my place."

The woman abruptly rose, opened the squeaking door of a closet and removed a satchel with a turtle-shell handle. She hurled it at Kil-nyo.

"Go on and open that damned satchel. It's the same bag that would be brought home by anybody who'd been drafted. Must contain a great deal of money—that's what I thought. I'm so stupid I deserve to die. I'm nearing fifty and I still can't even guess right when it comes to men.

"I don't know whether you and the bastard are blood-relations or just close neighbors, all the same I advise you to be careful in dealing with him. They say when times are troubled, heroes are bound to turn up, but in these days of chaos all I see is a bunch of con men trying to pick people's pockets.

"What a country needs to keep order is somebody strong and

even-tempered. But these days every bastard is going about brandishing his fists, shouting how he alone is in the right, and so it's only natural that the frauds have the upper hand."

The proprietress of Changchunok was still wondering whether Pyong-jo would return, but Kil-nyo knew he'd never be back. To top it all, Kil-nyo had become the owner of this satchel that Pyong-jo had left behind as a pledge for the loan. The matron didn't need to open the satchel to look inside, since it was likely to be filled with rags. As for Kil-nyo, she had neither the courage nor the right to just toss it in the gutter, so she ended up taking it with her to the tiny corner room where the innkeeper put her.

As expected, there was no sign of Pyong-jo. Unable to bear the pressure of his creditor any longer, he probably had offered Kil-nyo to the woman as security for his loans, but perhaps it never occurred to him that she would end up facing such an ordeal. Even if he had thought about it, that was now irrelevant.

Nevertheless, there was one conspicuous fact that proved Kil-nyo was Pyong-jo's woman. It was the satchel. There was one thing the proprietress of Changchunok from the beginning had been very interested to see—would Kil-nyo throw away the satchel or keep it in careful custody.

Ten days had gone by since Pyong-jo failed to appear as promised, but his satchel was still being dusted off each morning and then placed up on the shelf. This confirmation that Kil-nyo was his woman came as a relief to the matron, and this relief led her to neglect the search for Pyong-jo.

After twenty days had passed since Pyong-jo's disappearance from Sokpo-ri, rumors began to be heard that the new owner of the Choi house in Woljon-ri had started renovations. Soon this was confirmed as fact.

Based on these two proven facts that Pyong-jo had vanished and that Kil-nyo was his woman, the innkeeper soon passed beyond the stage of deliberation. She was quick with figures, and instinctively knew how to turn the situation to profit. Three decades of dealing with travelers passing through Sokpo-ri had made her a sensible and resourceful woman. This sensible woman came into Kil-nyo's room one day. Looking around, her gaze came to rest on the satchel laying on the shelf above Kil-nyo's head.

"My lot until now and yours from now on, I say. It's six of one and half a dozen of the other. If you're to make a living on your own, anyway, you need to stop being so quiet and retiring. Don't be shy, learn to open your heart. Silence is not the best policy."

"That's just my nature and it's not an easy thing to change."

"The world won't let you live according to your nature. It's not for nothing that we're all born with two eyes and a nose. Even if you lack the skill to deal with worldly things, if you've been born with some sense of shame, isn't it only right that you do something to pay for your own meals? If you can't earn your own living, why, what's the difference between you and a beast?"

"What am I to do?"

"Use your common sense. Not that I'm unaware you've lived a sheltered life, but don't let it be an excuse to act naive. People are likely to treat a naive person as a half-wit. You may not earn your beef right off, but a woman nearing thirty ought to have some sense of how to earn her daily bread."

What the woman placed in Kil-nyo's hand was a cleaning rag. In charge of the kitchen at Changchunok was another woman about the same age as the proprietress. This woman was kindly and never gave Kil-nyo a hard time. Whenever she noticed that Kil-nyo was overburdened, she'd quietly take some of her tasks on herself.

As days passed, Kil-nyo got used to the kitchen work, and came to rather like the free and open talk exchanged with Chidongtaek, which was the name the other woman used. Chidongtaek knew the family from which Kil-nyo had come. She used to live in little hamlet below Ilwolsan, some thirty miles of valleys and streams away from Sokpo-ri.

She'd chosen to come down to the market town because of a

feeble hope that she might come upon some news of her son, who'd not been heard from since being drafted into the army. Every night she laid down beside Kil-nyo her sleep was troubled, punctuated by moans as though she were in pain.

Knowing Kil-nyo's origin, Chidongtaek made a point of addressing her in an honorific form of speech even when they were alone. From the beginning Kil-nyo asked her not to, but she wouldn't hear of it.

Word that strangers had taken up residence at the Choi house in Woljon-ri came to Kil-nyo through Chidongtaek, who'd picked up the story in the marketplace. On market days around closing time, Chidongtaek sometimes would suddenly drop whatever she was doing and, like a sleepwalker, out she'd go for several circuits of the market.

On some occasions she abruptly went out while in the midst of kindling a fire for the rice pot, on others she'd leave while the laundry needed to be rinsed. More than once she was severely admonished by the innkeeper, yet this habit of hers never changed.

Kil-nyo did not know how much longer she was expected to remain a maidservant at Changchunok to settle Pyong-jo's debt. She had never inquired into the details. It was mainly the kindness of Chidongtaek that helped her to endure the hardship of working and hold out until the following February, deep in winter.

One day toward the end of February, Kil-nyo had finished washing the dishes late in the evening and was getting ready for bed when Chidongtaek said,

"Ma'am, I went to the pottery shop in the market this afternoon and ran into a suspicious character there."

"These days it's pretty common to see people acting suspiciously."

"No, this was different. He looked quite a bit younger than me.... I was just walking into the potter's when this unshaven man waved at me. Looked like he'd been following me."

"Maybe he was somebody you knew in the old days."

"Nope. When he spoke to me in a low voice, he was asking about you, ma'am."

"About me?"

"That's right."

"Who did he say he was?"

"Well, he asked about you, but didn't say a word about himself."

"What did he want to know?"

"First, he asked if I was living at Changchunok. I said I was, it just slipped out. Then he tugged at my sleeve for me to follow him to a quiet corner of the shop. I was a bit uneasy, but it seemed unlikely he wanted to flirt with an old hag like me, so I followed him.

"The man asked me the same question several times, like he wanted to be sure I really was staying at Changchunok—I kept saying I was. After a while he finally asked me whether a certain woman, a daughter-in-law of the Woljon-ri Choi's, wasn't living at the same place."

"What did you say?"

"I said 'Nope'. Isn't that what you've been telling me all the time you want me to say? I put on an act, shaking my head and waving my hand, but I don't think he believed me. So I said to him, if he didn't believe me he could come along to Changchunok with me and see for himself. Only then did he seem a little more convinced."

"What did he look like?"

"On the tall side, stubble of a beard like I said, a full and deep voice—I'd bet he's a rough one. He looked like a peddler to me, but then he could've been a farmer—I couldn't tell what he was."

"You didn't even give your names to each other?"

"I pestered him to tell me who he was, and he did say he was from Woljon-ri, but from his looks I wouldn't buy that."

"You should have followed him!"

"Followed him?! I was ready to run away from him before he started interrogating me with even more questions. I was a nervous wreck, afraid I might let the wrong thing slip."

"What did he look like?"

"I told you he didn't look much like a man from Woljon-ri. You know it's the custom for villagers to clean up and dress neatly on market days. What that man had on was a long coat, at least in name, but the collar was filthy and you could tell he'd been trudging around the countryside on foot."

It could have been Chom-gae. Nobody but Chom-gae would be trying in secret to track her down. Pyong-jo wouldn't have used such a clumsy approach to find her, and a villager from Woljon-ri would've come straight to Changchunok to have a peek in the yard.

Couldn't it have been Chom-gae, born an outcast butcher, who'd been raising the baby she abandoned in the slaughterhouse? But then what would have led him to search for her when he'd left Woljon-ri precisely to avoid her? Had he dropped by Woljon-ri, found her gone and decided to search in secret? Kil-nyo sat motionless with her eyes locked on the lamp, totally lost in thought.

"You're certainly a strange sort, ma'am," said Chidongtaek, who had a pillow in her arms and was looking for a place to lie down.

"You must have eyes that pick out only strange people."

"But you are, ma'am. Ever since you slipped out of that house with only the clothes on your back, you've never gone back even once."

"I've already left that house behind, you know."

"Even so, you could go back and bring back some of your things, you know, clothes or kitchen utensils or sewing stuff, something. The owner here couldn't have stopped you from doing that, could she?"

A twist of fate that wouldn't even allow Kil-nyo to go back to Woljon-ri to fetch her personal things—this was beyond Chidongtaek's comprehension. But if ever Kil-nyo had gone back for such a purpose, news of her relationship with Pyong-jo instantly would have spread through the village. Rumors may already have been rampant because of the sale of the house. That was why Kil-nyo couldn't even think about setting foot back in Woljon-ri.

Although Sokpo-ri was a mere twenty miles away from the house, the road wound over the mountain. She had not the slightest desire to go back to retrieve her own things, but that she'd failed to bring her mother-in-law's mortuary tablet along, that was one thing that bothered her. She could only hope that the people who bought the house would be decent enough not to mishandle the mortuary tablet of someone else's ancestor.

The people who lived in Woljon-ri probably wouldn't gossip too loudly about Kil-nyo for fear of tarnishing the village's name, but it seemed likely they would have heard Kil-nyo was working as a kitchen maid at Changchunok, so close was the place.

Some of the villagers were bound to be peddlers, and no matter how careful she'd been to hide herself from strangers, somebody must have caught sight of Kil-nyo working out in the yard of Changchunok Inn. So, if Chom-gae had been after news of Kil-nyo, it couldn't have been too difficult to find her.

Now Kil-nyo couldn't understand why she'd felt so heartbroken to learn that Chidongtaek had flatly refused to tell Chom-gae of her presence. Her disappearance from Woljon-ri would've been a relief for him, but he was somebody she should have met, even if only for a moment.

"Why didn't you tell me about this earlier?"

"Have you guessed who it was?"

"No, not really."

"Then, forget about it, ma'am."

'I should,' Kil-nyo said to herself. All the same, she made up her mind to leave Sokpo-ri. She had never before felt such a keen pain at the disgrace the people of Woljon-ri would have to go through because of her shameful conduct. A woman who long ago should have left was still living in such a place, resigned to spending the winter there.

"Chidongtaek, please help me find a way to leave this place."

At this, Chidongtaek sprang up from her bed,

"What do you mean, 'leave this place'? Where will you go?"

"It doesn't matter where. No one but us will know of it, and you'll help me out of here, won't you?"

"I've made a big mistake, haven't I? What's this nonsense you're spouting?"

"It's only now that I'm speaking of it, but even a good person like you must have guessed the bind I'm in. It's not that I want to escape this hardship, but I just can't stay here any monger. Now that the winter is nearly over, I'll have to be getting ready to go."

"I knew all along, ma'am, that you weren't the sort of person who'd be staying here with me long. Still, this is all so sudden I can't make head or tail of it."

"If I tarry any longer, even greater disgrace will await me."

Just then Chidongtaek gave a swift sidelong glance at the satchel up on the shelf overhead. She hadn't pried into Kil-nyo's relationship with Cha Pyong-jo, but she guessed that the owner of that satchel must be the one responsible for her wretched predicament.

"It's been a consolation to have you with me... all the same, what could I possibly do to help you?"

"There must be some way. You know far better than I about the world and you're much more experienced. It's thanks to you that I managed this life as a maid up to now without too many mishaps."

"In the middle of winter, where could you head for...."

"I've got to leave, my mind is made up."

"If life was that way, with everything at our beck and call, I for one wouldn't have been separated from my son, and I wouldn't be eking out a living as a washerwoman and cook."

Kil-nyo's insistence upon leaving led Chidongtaek to ruminate upon her own misfortunes, and this made it hard for Kil-nyo to go any further with her own problems. However, Chidongtaek hadn't forgotten Kil-nyo's plea.

There was a man who for a couple of months had been staying at Changchunok Inn on market days. He was a truck driver who carried fish inland from the coast. The truck was the kind that you started with a funnel of burning coal, it was slow as the devil and both the driver and his helper were often coated with soot.

Still, any sort of automobile was a rare spectacle in Sokpo-ri, and this man's arrival in town always drew a swarming crowd. The driver wasn't as crude as one might have inferred from the job, in fact, he was on the delicate side. Chidongtaek was on good enough terms with him to trade jokes. When he smiled, the corners of his eyes were full of fine wrinkles, and when he slept at Changchunok he always bathed, even if there was no hot water, saying he shouldn't soil the bed.

Once when the driver had spent the night at Changchunok, Chidongtaek hinted that Kil-nyo should go in the evening to see him in his room. She found him sitting alone, and when she stuck her face inside the door he moved back and waved for her to enter. When she hesitated, seemingly reluctant to come in, he said,

"Don't worry, do come in. Chidongtaek told me of your situation."

Only then did Kil-nyo suspect what had been going on and plucking up her courage, she entered the room.

"I've noticed you other times when I was here, and from the first I sensed you weren't cut out for kitchen work at an inn like this."

"I'm wondering what Chidongtaek told you."

"She said you wanted to sneak out of here. So I decided to help you any way I can."

"I'm not in a position to stay on here for very long."

"Naturally. What's the point of rotting away as a drudge in a joint like this? Well, then, where is it you're off to?"

"Nowhere in particular in mind. This is awfully close to my in-law's place, and I need to get at least forty or fifty miles from these parts."

"Where are you from originally?"

"Hamyang."

"Want to go there?"

"I'll have to think it over, I need some time. It's been nearly ten years since I spoke with my family there."

"I'm heading out tonight. If you want a ride, wait till I leave and then meet me at the warehouse at the far end of Sokpo-ri, about a half hour later. There space on the truck, and I can take you fifty or a hundred miles from here, it's up to you."

"I don't even have any money to pay you."

"Don't you worry about that sort of thing."

The driver rose abruptly and walked out. In spite of herself, Kil-nyo looked up at the shelf for the satchel. It was gone, turtle-shell handle and all. Who could have taken it? Had the driver taken it when he left just now? But she surely would have noticed.

She distinctly remembered seeing the satchel laying on the top shelf just a moment earlier when she had come into the room. Be that as it may, it was nowhere in sight now. Kil-nyo had an uncanny feeling of despair, as if she was tumbling from a cliff.

What had held her captive at Changchunok for over four months had not been the innkeeper's menacing threats, nor had it been the consolations of good-natured Chidongtaek. Seemingly forgetful of the pact with the driver, Kil-nyo flew across the backyard and dashed into the kitchen.

"Chidongtaek, the satchel's disappeared!"

Chidongtaek glanced up at Kil-nyo's bloodless face and then went on with her work of tending the fire, tut-tutting as she said,

"That bag, I knew you'd be half-crazy looking for it. It was sent out with the driver's helper, so you can stop glaring at me like you want to eat me for dinner."

"I didn't ask you to do that."

"You wouldn't be able to carry that bag with you when you walk out of here, and anyway I thought it ought to go onto the truck now, that way you can't change your mind."

With this, Chidongtaek reached under her apron and checked the contents of one of her pockets. Never before had she carried such a sum around. She had figured right—now that she thought the satchel was on the truck, Kil-nyo had no choice but to go through with the plan.

But hadn't the satchel still been on the top shelf when the driver was in the room? To make sure she had not overlooked anything in the excitement, Kil-nyo went back to the corner room. Still no satchel. Had it been a phantom?

When she turned around, Chidongtaek was standing by the back door of the kitchen, gesturing for her to shoo. As Kil-nyo hastened out the unlocked door and fled Changchunok, Chidongtaek once more reached down under her apron to recheck the payment Mr. Chi, the driver, had given her for services rendered.

When Kil-nyo reached the appointed place the truck was already there. A young man, the helper, rushed over to Kil-nyo and helped her up to the seat beside the driver. Then, shovel in hand, he climbed up behind the driver's seat where the stoking funnel was.

The satchel was lying next to the driver's seat. She gave it a few stealthy caresses. The truck's engine already was warmed up and soon they started rolling along the rough dirt road. Dusk had fallen and outside the window naked birch trees passed by, staggering like drunks.

"About sixty miles from here is a place called Yongdok. We'll be there before dawn tomorrow."

Said the driver, spitting into his hands and clutching the steering wheel firmly. After about an hour of choppy driving, the truck came onto an upward grade where the hills of Hwangjangjae started. From the point where the incline began, there was a continual exchange of shouts between the driver and the stoker who was tending the boiler fire in back.

The truck lurched laboriously up the hill, a step at a time like a pregnant beast, emitting enormous belches from time to time.

"This hill is known far and wide as the roughest climb in these parts. There're plenty of wild animals nearby, too, you often run into wildcats."

Kil-nyo made no reply to the driver. Just when they were all sick and tired of the climb, the truck halted. It was too dark to see anything clearly, but they seemed to have reached the very crest of Hwangjangjae. Mr. Chi struggled with the gearshift a few times, pumped the throttle and then, cocking his head this way and that, called back to his helper. The young man jumped down and came around to the driver's seat as Mr. Chi moved over closer to Kil-nyo.

"Press down the brake with all your might. The instant you let it up, you and the truck will roll lickety-split down the hill, and every bone in your body'll be broken. So stay alert, don't even blink!"

The helper nodded and the driver tapped Kil-nyo on her shoulder, saying,

"Get on down, please. I need you to give me a hand."

Kil-nyo got down from the truck and stood in the raspy wind on the side of the hill. As it scratched through the trees the wind howled like a beast, and the air felt colder than ice.

After a few minutes under the truck Mr. Chi craned his neck out and motioned for Kil-nyo to crawl underneath. She had no choice but to do as told in order to move on from that hilltop as soon as possible. Mr. Chi handed her a piece of iron that looked like the pendulum of a clock and said,

"Even if the sky falls on you, you must hold this tight. It's connected to the brake up front, so if you let go of it, both of us will be run over and crushed to death, crushed like cornmeal, understand?"

"Yes, I see. I'll hold it tight."

Having handed her the piece of iron, Mr. Chi crawled downwards and then suddenly started to take off her underclothes. A roll of thunder came into Kil-nyo's ears once more. That deep sound of thunder, as if huge boulders were cascading down Kalmoesan, was approaching from the distance. The urgent cry of a man came from below.

"If you let go, we'll both be crushed! You hear?"

Kil-nyo couldn't loosen her grasp. Even if it was just a ploy he'd concocted to rape her, nothing in the world was trustworthy any more, as far as she was concerned. The less you trust · something, the more strongly you should hold onto it, right? Kil-nyo mustered all of her strength and held the iron tighter than ever.

A sharp pain ran down her back and it felt like her abdomen was being pierced with jagged stones. Her body writhed, but she clutched the piece of iron so tight that it was drenched in sweat. Before Kil-nyo's eyes floated the image of Chidongtaek's doleful face, Chidongtaek who'd waved her away in such a hurry.

Despite the icy north wind, she could feel hot breathing all over her face. After some time went by, Mr. Chi covered her with her skirt and crawled out from under the truck. He fastened up his pants and then cleared his throat.

"Now you can let go and come on out. Come on now, hurry up. Don't just lay there holding it like an idiot!"

Behind Mr. Chi as he bent over to urge her out was the young helper, urinating with abandon, his back to the truck.

Three Men

After raping Kil-nyo in that sly and treacherous way, Chi Sang-mo dropped her in a forlorn hamlet called Wonjon at the foot of Hwangjangjae. It was only about fifty miles away from the Choi house. The distance was not that far, but the high stone barrier of Hwangjangjae was mighty imposing, and people on either side lived very different ways.

There was little likelihood that Kil-nyo would run into villagers from Woljon-ri here. Peddlers with familiar faces might occasionally cross the mountain to go to market, but they'd scarcely meet Kil-nyo tucked away out of sight in a tiny hamlet like this.

After satisfying his carnal hunger, collecting the fare for the lift from Sokpo-ri, Chi Sang-mo had practically dragged Kil-nyo to this place. She looked totally exhausted and her heart was crushed like a squashed fruit when he dumped her at a small village tavern on the road.

An old hag with a spotted face was running the place all alone. Too old to get about very well, she retired the very next day, handing over all the kitchen work to Kil-nyo, along with the ladle and the earthen pots of rice wine that made up the trade.

When it first opened, this little tavern had targeted travelers passing along the Hwangjangjae road, but the earnings were barely enough to feed one mouth. Unlike in the old days, traffic was light and the flow of peddlers had fallen to a trickle.

Eyes trained on the crossroads all day long, she'd be lucky to have half a dozen strangers poke their heads in for a few swallows of rice wine to cut the dust, and that would be a good day. Kil-nyo had never imagined herself as a winehouse woman, but there was nothing else for her to do.

Strung from the pasteboard thin earthen walls were radishes and bundles of herbs the old lady had picked herself in the fields. The only utensils in the kitchen were a few chipped wine bowls. Atop the soot-caked kitchen counter was a decrepit wooden meal table, full of nails where cracks and joints had been mended. The doorway into the kitchen was covered with a filthy, sticky straw mat suspended from wooden hangers.

Her disease already seeped into the marrow, the old hag already had one foot in the grave and in fact had been awaiting an outsider to help her prepare for her departure for the beyond. It happened that the old woman had not a single relation, close or distant, in the world.

Even in broad daylight, weasels would sneak in and out through the holes in the walls, and at night the horrible sound of famished rats gnawing the furniture made it impossible to sleep soundly. Long plagued by asthma, the old hag frequently disturbed Kil-nyo's rest by kicking away the thin blanket with which she covered her bird-like chest.

With the dawn, the hacking of her coughs would subside, and the hag used the early hours to pelt Kil-nyo with pleas and threats whenever it seemed she might just get up and leave the tavern without looking back. Kil-nyo knew that if she had run away in the dark to live in hiding from the people in Woljon-ri, she could hardly have come upon a better spot than this.

With her awful fate she never would be able to dream of a life of luxury under a husband's protection, so she thought she might as well consider herself lucky to have run into the old hag. All the same, it seems to be in the nature of the human heart to defy any full knowledge of oneself.

More than once each day, the face of Chi Sang-mo would float before Kil-nyo's mind, and often she'd stop in the middle of work, imagining that she'd heard the dull, panting sound of the steamer truck far away, slowly creeping up the hill.

Could she entertain any feelings of warmth for a treacherous character who'd raped a widow, a daughter-in-law of a respectable clan, on a deserted road in the depths of night? She couldn't begin to fathom her own heart, a heart that seemed to miss that beast of a creature.

Was there a trace of doubt, a wavering between repulsion and affection, just because of the mercy he had shown in finding her a place to stay, shabby though it was, when he might just as well have dumped her on the road?

After ten days of confused indecision had passed, one evening at twilight Kil-nyo caught sight of the tallish, lank figure of Chi Sang-mo walking up into the front yard of the tavern. Even if a wretched destiny was responsible for everything that had happened, a woman who had twice been violated by strangers should have learned to conceal her feelings. But at the sight of Chi Sang-mo, Kil-nyo felt like her face had caught fire.

Hurriedly, she let down the straw mat which she'd propped away from the kitchen doorway with an A-frame staff. She heard footsteps crossing the yard and presently Chi Sang-mo's oil-smudged face popped inside the kitchen. An awkward grin on his face, he spoke to Kil-nyo, who was pretending to be mashing potatoes,

"Life's tough, eh? How has life been treating you, is it bearable?"

Kil-nyo said nothing.

"Come on out now, hurry. I've brought a few things for the house."

As if her legs had gone to sleep, Kil-nyo couldn't budge an inch. Chi put his hand under her arm and almost dragged her out. On the floor lay a bundle wrapped in a kerchief. It was a couple of little pots and ricebowls inside a brass basin. The moment Kil-nyo saw them, she was reminded of the times before she was married when the sight of shining new brassware in a shop window used to make her heart beat faster.

Grabbing her trembling hand and placing it on top of the bundle, Chi Sang-mo said,

"Well, I've got a wife with a hot temper who's always got her eye on me. For you, this must be like getting struck by lightning in your sleep. But then a woman is an animal unable to change its lot on its own.

"My behavior was pretty low, I admit it, but if I felt nothing for you from the start, I wouldn't have stuck my head under your belly. Think of yourself as a frog fallen on the hill and stay put here. It just happens I dropped you on a road I'm always traveling, so I won't let you go hungry for men."

Kil-nyo made no reply, but his words, that a woman can't change on her own, came piercing into her heart. In a way she thought herself fortunate to have been raped by Sang-mo—otherwise she would have felt like she'd been dropped from the sky onto the edge of an abyss, with nobody to turn to in this foreign place.

Once her mind was made up to accept her lot, a rush of thoughts flowed through her head. As the old proverb went: "What's a spoonful after a bowl?" How could contact with another man leave any scar of damnation to a body already robbed of chastity? The status of a sinful woman was already branded on her back, so what difference could it possibly make even if she decided to live with this man? Who would praise her for guarding her virtue and leading a chaste life in this strange place?

Would she not be better off with a man of her own to lean on, to protect her wretched body from all the strangers who were coming and going around there? But she'd be intruding between a well-married couple, and being a concubine was extremely unpleasant somehow, as disgusting as if she'd left the toilet without wiping off her bottom.

Fortunately, he said he'd only be dropping by when his route happened through Hwangjangjae, so it seemed neither of them would have to suffer from any great heartbreak. Since she was no tart peddling her body for a living, wasn't it justifiable to keep seeing a man with whom she'd already mixed flesh?

Watching Chi Sang-mo filling the brass basin with water and cleaning the grease off his hands, Kil-nyo decided to regard his call as a considerate gesture on his part. Though he was not meant to be her man, Kil-nyo still felt a certain joy in making a meal for a man. Tears gathered in her eyes as she raked out the ashes and set kindling in the hearth.

"A woman is no fun when she's as quiet as you."

So spoke Chi Sang-mo as he lit a hand-rolled cigarette, having eaten his fill. Kil-nyo stayed silent.

"It's a headache if she's narrow-minded, bad tempered and nosy, but it's no better to be glum and spiritless all day long like you. Are you still mad at me?"

"If so, I blame it on my fate. Who else can I blame?"

"If not for me, you're the sort of person who'd have let yourself rot as a kitchen maid at Changchunok. In the end, after all the hardships, you'd probably end up an old maid lying cold on a straw mat. You should learn to show your feelings. Enduring everything alone won't take you very far in this wild, rough world."

Tugged awake by this reprimand, Kil-nyo changed the subject.

"It's only rumors I've picked up from travelers, but they say the world outside is helter skelter."

"Whether the world is helter skelter or not is nothing to me. Some bastards claim to be the rightists, others to be the leftists, and both kinds are gone wild like mad dogs under lightning, but there's no way to tell which bastards are which, the he-ravens from the she-ravens.

"To make it worse, if you go to the big cities the whole world is under the thumb of western bastards now, they all reek, and you won't even be able to tell East from West. That's how crazy the world is today."

"I'm frightened."

"Now you're talking. well, if that's how it is, think of this place as a paradise and stay put here for the rest of your life."

"Which side have you joined?"

"You're slow, aren't you? Do I look like a man who'd join either side? I'm not one to go looking for disaster. Lots of people have been dying like dogs! Do you take me for one of those half-wits?"

Chi Sang-mo was roaring at the top of his voice, refusing to mix with the world in its perilous state, and Kil-nyo was greatly relieved to hear this. Surprised that there was still a corner of her heart in which she could care for a man's safety, Kil-nyo took off her clothes on her own and for the first time in ages gave herself up to a man's embrace.

The sweet, dreamlike night had flown, and at the crack of dawn Chi Sang-mo got in the truck parked alongside the road and drove away from Wonjon.

From time to time, just as Kil-nyo was about to give up waiting for him, Chi Sang-mo would appear out of the blue and stay overnight with her. Unfamiliar things, scarce in a mountain valley, often fell into her hands through him.

The old woman who had long seemed on the brink of death barely managed to drag her life out through the long winter, and the following spring she reluctantly drew her last breath. Some men from the village who had become acquainted with Kil-nyo helped her with the burial.

After that, Kil-nyo was all alone once more, just as she had been at the Choi house in Woljon-ri. Apart from her temperament, grown tougher due to the rough days she'd been through, there was no noticeable change in her. There was, however, one startling change of which the neighbors knew nothing. When the old lady died, Kil-nyo had not had her period for three months.

A fortnight or so after the old woman's burial, Chi Sang-mo stopped in. His visit delighted Kil-nyo more than ever. Back when the old lady had been running the tavern herself, Chi was one of the regulars. He told Kil-nyo for the first time that the old hag used to pester him to find her a proper widow to whom she could leave the place.

At the news of her death, Chi felt down and got himself drunk that night. Kil-nyo couldn't tell the man she was pregnant when he'd drunk himself silly. She wavered until she saw him getting ready to leave the next morning. As he was putting his shoes on, looking down with swollen eyes, she said in a low voice,

"Can't you drop in a bit oftener?"

His hands froze in the midst of tying his shoes, and Chi stared at her with bloodshot eyes. He jeered,

"My, my, even a madame in a mountain village, if she plays the role long enough, has to grow thick skin. Who taught you to be a coquette?"

Had he been a thoughtful man, he easily would've sensed the change in her, but some men who have lived long enough are simple-minded as children. So Kil-nyo told herself as she said,

"Nobody taught me, it's just something natural with this life I'm living. But I've got something important to tell you, so do come by within a few weeks, even if you have to make an excuse."

"If the right cargo comes along...would I avoid this route?"

"Don't joke like that, please. It's not easy for me, what I have to tell you."

"If you're lonesome, why not get yourself a maid, that'd lighten your work, too."

"It's not that I'm lonely, and I don't need an extra hand. As I said, there's something important I want to tell you."

"All right. It's not that I don't come because I don't want to. So stop nagging."

To avoid an ugly scene with him so irritable, Kil-nyo had barely opened her heart before she saw him leave. Despite what he said, however, two weeks passed and there was no sign of Chi Sang-mo.

Kil-nyo's heart was sinking. What did she know, after all, about this man called Chi Sang-mo? She knew his name, but it might have been just a name he'd thrown at her on the spur of the moment. In that case she had no way to find out his real name. She'd been told he had a home and a family in the port of Kanggu, but she'd never been there and his wife and children were total strangers to Kil-nyo.

Even if she'd considered Chi Sang-mo as her husband, he could easily deny any tie. Not a soul who knew Kil-nyo would go out of his way to testify to their relationship. Besides, she was in no position to press her rights and to go checking the inns where Chi regularly stopped in an effort to track down his whereabouts.

Because she had somebody else's husband on loan, Kil-nyo couldn't even complain. Who would lend an ear to the laments of a sinful woman? A month went by, and still Chi Sang-mo did not come. Trusting in the man's good heart, Kil-nyo refused to believe he was the sort who'd jilt a woman. Whether she'd keep the child or be done with it, she had to talk with the father first.

If the month of delivery arrived in his absence, she couldn't see how that wretched fate could be escaped. Each day was full of the dreariness of waiting. She was growing painfully impatient when one day a stranger walked up into the front yard.

Though the man was clothed in a tattered western suit, she could tell at a glance that he wasn't one of the peddlers who often passed through Hwangjangjae. After exchanging greetings with Kil-nyo, he said he was a man from the county office.

From where Kil-nyo stood, anybody from the county government was a high and mighty personage. He was tall and gaunt, and the skeptical eyes flashing from behind his spectacles made it difficult for her to look him in the face. For a long while he peered at Kil-nyo, who was crouching in a corner, a respectful distance away, then he said,

"Is this tavern letting you make ends meet?"

"Barely keeping the spiders from spinning a web over my mouth, sir."

"Do you have any children?"

"...."

"Before you came here to live, I understand you used to live over the pass in Sokpo-ri."

"...."

"You're not very talkative, uh? That's a sight, an innkeeper who's not talking your ear off."

"There's no need to be talkative to eke out a living here. The travelers are hungry for food, not for conversation, sir."

"Not bad at comebacks, I see. Well, I've had my share of trouble in tracking you down, so don't be too rash with me."

The man was not exactly standing on ceremony, but neither was he downright rude. Kil-nyo found it hard to guess the purpose of his call. For a high official from the county office to treat a tavernkeeper in a mountain village as a nobody was to be expected. The man sat there, staring vacantly at the distant slopes for a while, and then he opened his mouth again,

"Ma'am, you know Mr. Cha Pyong-jo, don't you?"

Kil-nyo's heart dropped to her feet with a thud. Jarred out of her wits, she grew tense and looked up at the man. What a shock! Never had she imagined that Cha Pyong-jo could be so well connected.

"Mr. Cha Pyong-jo, sir?" Kil-nyo asked, wondering if there might have been two men with that name.

"I hope you won't deny the fact that you know Mr. Cha Pyong-jo. Since I got the order to search you out, I've rummaged through all the family registers in the district. It's a good thing you didn't use a false name, or I could have been in a hell of a fix."

"I know nobody by that name, sir."

"Your denial is so strong it's as good as an admission that you know Mr. Cha."

"I sure don't have anything to do with that man, Mister or not."

"This world is a mystery to me. At a time when lots of people would give an arm and a leg to hook up with a man of power and position like Mr. Cha Pyong-jo, here you are, knowing him and flatly denying the fact. I don't know whether you and he are relations or close friends or what, but I do know he's very eager to find you and has taken a lot of trouble with the search. Is it that you have some kind of grudge toward him?"

"I'm no enemy of his, nor a friend. I'm afraid you've got the wrong person, sir."

Kil-nyo knew only too well that it was pointless to keep on insisting she didn't know him. Her tail had already been stepped on, and it was too late to try to conceal her identity. But she still had no idea why Cha Pyong-jo was looking for her.

If he'd swallowed the proceeds of the Choi house in Woljon-ri, wouldn't that have been enough to burn off whatever bad karma was between the two of them? When she'd been planted at Changchunok as a kitchen servant to repay Cha's debt, hadn't she paid for her immorality and for the crime of deserting the newborn baby?

Now, with Cha Pyong-jo searching for her, it looked as though her account had not been settled. Should she try to escape the reckoning, or should she meet it head on once and for all? Neither way would be an easy choice. For she couldn't just leave Wonjon until Chi Sang-mo came back. To flee from Cha would mean she was running away from Chi as well.

Besides, once she left the tavern, where could she possibly find work? Fortunately, the man from the county office hadn't dragged her off by force. If he'd tried, she probably would have fought tooth and nail, even if he had her by the throat.

She was determined to hold out at Wonjon to the bitter end, but once the sun had set and the moon was shining out in the yard, she collapsed onto the floor, totally exhausted. The moonlight pouring in spilled all over her dress, and her heart seemed as shrunken as a dog skin in boiling water.

She crept out into the kitchen, stirred the earthen jar of rice wine, and drank a whole bowl. She'd never touched a drop in her life until that moment. How thirsty she was! She gulped down several bowls in a row, came back into the other room and laid down flat on her back with limbs spread.

As she looked overhead, the ceiling began to whirl and then descended right onto her forehead. Burdened with a disgraceful past—what did she have to show the world to justify her miserable life?

Even when she fell asleep she kept tossing from the thirst. The sound of footsteps outside roused her. A man's voice was asking for the innkeeper. She leapt up and saw the door ajar and her blanket lying crumpled at her feet. She had been so drunk she had no recollection of having taken the blanket down from the shelf.

She opened the door and looked outside. The moon was setting, meaning it was past three in the morning. Two men were standing with their backs to her. She knew at once they were not ordinary mountain villagers. They looked to be in their mid-twenties, and judging from their western suits Kil-nyo guessed they were from the city. But what had brought them way out here in the depths of night?

"Who are you?"

"Travelers passing through. Do you have a room?"

"We just sell wine here, no overnight rooms."

"That's no way to treat travelers stranded in the middle of the night. We're strangers here and can't go knocking on just anybody's door. Have a heart, and let us have a room here. We'll be out by sunrise."

"As I said, we've no rooms here."

"This is too heartless, and way up here in the mountains. There's no strength left in us, we can't walk any farther."

Only then did Kil-nyo realize that the two men were indeed in a grave predicament. The one who'd been doing all the talking was standing erect, but the second man was leaning on his friend and looked about to collapse. Even if she did throw them out, they wouldn't have made it to the gate.

The moonlight was dim, but she could tell from their looks that they must have been walking all night from a distant village. She went back into the kitchen, drank a bowl of cold water to ease her burning thirst, and then led the men to a room. After handing them a mattress and a quilt, she was about to leave when one of the men called out,

"Ma'am."

Instead of answering, Kil-nyo turned back around. A couple

of bills were lying in the man's hand. For some reason she was reluctant to take the money. The man grabbed her hand and pressed the money inside.

"We'll be leaving before dawn. But there's one more favor I must ask—it's very important."

"What is it?"

"If anyone asks about us later, you don't know us and you never saw us. And don't ever let anybody know we spent the night here."

"How is it you trust me?"

"What's to stop a man from trusting someone? Besides, we're in a very tough spot, and we sure can't ask the animals for help, can we?"

His tone was mild and courteous, but there was a certain threat lurking beneath his words. After one of the men plopped down on the mattress, he lit the lamp and only then were their faces revealed clearly. Judging from their features and small, white hands they had to be sons of well-to-do families in the big city. What could possibly have brought them into this wretched situation, she wondered?

"There's one more thing, ma'am."

"Tell me, please."

"We haven't eaten for two days. Could you make a couple of bowls of gruel without the neighbors noticing?"

"Then you should put out the light first. This is the first time travelers have stayed here overnight."

The man hastily extinguished the lamp while Gilnyo went into the kitchen. She fumbled around in the dark for the utensils, made some rice gruel and brought it to them.

The next morning when Kil-nyo opened the door there was no trace of the two men. The gate was open and a pair of shoes had been left behind under the steps. The one must have carried the other on his back. The quilt she'd given them was folded and replaced on the shelf. When she took it down and unfolded it, she noticed one corner had been torn and some of the padding removed. Then she caught a faint whiff of blood.

That very afternoon, as fate would have it, she met the two young men again. A band of·dozen fierce-looking men walked up to the tavern bearing two makeshift stretchers. On them were two dead bodies covered with straw mats. Blood from the corpses was still running down onto the stretchers.

The menacing young men with murderous eyes washed the blood off their sickles and rakes and then sat down on the edge of the step like a row of swallows. They said they were starved and wanted some soup and vegetables. The feet of the two dead men were sticking out from under the straw mats. One pair of feet was clad in leather shoes, the other was bare, the naked soles upturned to face the sky.

One of the young men, ruggedly built with black sideburns, turned to Kil-nyo, who was squatting on the step with her eyes riveted upon the stretchers.

"Those bastards, you know them, don't you?"

"What do you mean?"

Kil-nyo protested, hastily turning away from his glance and hiding her quaking hands under her apron.

"You do know them, but you're pretending not to."

"I haven't even seen their faces, so how can you say I know them, sir?"

"Shall I show you their faces?"

"Why should I look at them?"

"Because you flatly deny knowing them."

"I haven't even asked who the living are, and I don't see why I should be asked to look at the faces of the dead."

"Stop this nonsense and talk straight. Don't worry, even if you are one of them, the calamity won't come as far as you."

"Whether the calamity reaches me isn't the point. You seem bound and determined to blame me, an innocent person, and that's evil."

"There's no doubt those bastards stayed here last night and set out this morning. Are you gonna tell me there're other inns besides this one on this side of Hwangjangjae?"

Just then Kil-nyo caught sight of the old worn pair of shoes she'd tossed up under the floor.

"You're right about that, this is the only tavern in these parts, but they could've stayed at a private house, or in some stranger's barn. What do you gain, I wonder, by pressing somebody who knows nothing of this business? You seem to be dying to see me put to shame."

"Since you insist I won't press you any longer. But if you want to stay in this business the rest of your life, you'd better start being more particular about your customers before you take them in. If anything else like this happens..., we won't just let you go next time."

"To be sure who my customers are is beyond my power."

"You can tell right off the bastards doing the work of the leftists."

What he meant by that Kil-nyo hadn't any idea at first. All she knew was that the people who were supposed to be the leftists lived in hiding and were always being chased, and the others didn't have to be on the run.

Once they finished their meals the men picked up the stretchers and left the tavern for the main road. After they were out of sight Kil-nyo rushed over and retrieved the old shoes from under the floor, hiding them under her skirt as she took them inside.

The shoes looked unusually large somehow and, strangely enough, it occurred to her that they seemed hungry. She thought she should either take them far way and get rid of them or else burn them in secret. But for some reason she hesitated to do either.

She couldn't say why. Not a single word had passed between her and the owner, and what trivial contact there had been between them was merely that he'd stayed there in the tavern for a few hours, being cared for by his friend. Then he was gone. Yet, she felt a deep sorrow in a corner of her heart.

For several days afterward Kil-nyo often paused in the middle of working and got lost in thought. She felt she had to leave. But to do so was no easy matter. As with disposing of the shoes, she just could not make up her mind. Until she gave up on Chi Sang-mo's return, there was nothing to do but stay put where she was, waiting.

It occurred to her, too, that relatives of the two young men who'd been killed like dogs might fumble their way to her tavern. Not knowing whether their remains had been burnt or cast into some ravine, she figured the least she could do was hand over to the survivors the pair of shoes, the only trace of them left.

If Cha Pyong-jo had the power to send his men all the way out here in the mountains, wherever she might go she wouldn't be able to hide. However she looked at the situation she couldn't just leave, and the more she pondered the more reasons she came up with to stay put.

Another ten days passed. She was startled by the sound of every gust of wind across the wall, and ran to the door if even a dog happened by. There was still no sign of Chi Sang-mo. Neither did the bespectacled man reappear with word of Cha Pyong-jo.

Perhaps she was waiting to hear from them both. She knew only too well that whichever one happened to step through the gate, she was fated to deal with him. If that meant she was a slut, she couldn't help it. But over and over again she told herself that even if she never saw Chi again, she'd not do to his seed what she'd done to the child fathered by Cha. She would not harm what was growing within her. She told herself that a woman's lot once twisted is beyond her power to change.

That night Shin Kil-nyo heard the howl of the wind. But it was a different sound than the one she usually heard. She was sitting alone in her room, and all at once she knew there was someone outside the gate. She opened the door. As the light poured out into the yard, she dimly perceived the feet of a man standing on the other side of the gate. Her heart plummeted.

The man standing there was neither Cha Pyong-jo nor Chi Sang-mo. Even in the darkness Kil-nyo immediately knew who it was. Who in the world but Hwang Chom-gae would loiter outside her house, not daring to walk straight into the yard?

Before she knew what she was doing she was already out in the yard. When she reached the gate, lamp in hand, Chom-gae made a deep bow. There was no doubt it was Chom-gae, though he looked starved and seemed barely able to stand. His clothes were so ragged he could easily have been taken for a beggar.

The stubble on his chin and his fleshless cheeks made him look hideous, but his eyes were surprisingly clear and shining bright. Kil-nyo was tongue-tied at first, but then cried out,

"Who's this?"

"It's Chom-gae, ma'am."

As he spoke, tears streamed down his cheeks.

"My word, am I dreaming?"

"Ma'am, please put out the lamp."

Kil-nyo grabbed him by the hand and at the same time blew out the lamp. Chom-gae bolted the gate tightly and turned around. He was so exhausted he could barely walk. As she hurried to prepare some food for him, he propped himself up against the wall, seemingly about to faint. Even in such a sorry state, he kept asking Kil-nyo in a muffled voice to be wary of the light. Each time he spoke it made her tremble with fear.

She stopped cooking the rice and added more water to make a thin gruel. Chom-gae had a few spoonfuls and then, unable to sit up any longer, he stretched out on the floor.

"How long has it been since you ate?"

Only after she repeated the question did he finally reply,

"It's five days, I think."

"Just what's this all about? How did you find me here, and why are you in this awful condition? You act like you're being chased, is that it?"

A vague grin came to Chom-gae lips for an instant.

"You haven't changed much, ma'am. You still have the same beauty you had in the old days, ma'am."

"Don't call me ma'am. I'm no longer the daughter-in-law of the Choi family. As you can see, I sell wine and food to travelers."

"I've known you were living here for some time."

"Not too many people know that, so how could you know?"

"I found out at Changchunok in Sokpo-ri."

"Changchunok?"

"From the kitchen maid, I mean. The one called Chidongtaek. She hinted you were living here thanks to her skill at matchmaking. That evil woman was certainly greedy, too."

"You mean she demanded money to reveal where I was?"

"Without money there was no way to get any information. They say that the bear does the tricks but the Chinaman gets the money. She pretends to be naive and good, but her heart is black-through and through. You can't imagine how sly she was, pretending to do me a favor by slipping a word on your whereabouts."

"How could she? How much did you have to pay?"

"That's history. We can't go ask her to cough it up now. It doesn't matter now that I've found your place. The world is all calculating, it's only natural to run into such women. Without her, how could I ever find you?"

It had been Chi Sang-mo, no doubt, who'd leaked the fact she was running a tavern at the foot of Hwangjangjae. If he'd told Chidongtaek about taking her as a concubine, why hadn't he been back the past few months? Kil-nyo decided to ask no more question of Chom-gae, who seemed about to pass out.

"How's your wife doing with you out on your own in strange places?"

"She's doing all right, ma'am."

"It's not just your wife, there're children to care for. What about the little one you spoke of... he must be old enough to be very cute...."

Chom-gae, who'd nearly gone to sleep, opened his eyes wide and struggled to sit up. He stared hard at Kil-nyo.

"To bring him up right... to save him from suffering because his father was a lowborn butcher... that was why I left home, ma'am."

"What nonsense are you talking? You mean you don't know

that a boy growing up with no father around surely'll be mocked as illegitimate?"

"How could I not know—people call any ill-bred kid a bastard? But I didn't want him to be branded as the son of an outcast. In the end, that wish was so strong I had to leave my family. I wanted to do what I could, so when he's old enough to understand the world would be changed, a world without lords and outcasts, no rich and no poor people.

"I hoped he would never know of his father's origin. When such a world arrives, it'll be like a paradise for him. I hear there's a world where everyone, whatever his origin, can be successful if only he's able. They even say there's a world where the sons of the oppressed are a rank above the sons of the ones who call themselves nobles. Right now I'm running, always hiding and chased, but when that world comes, even if I drop dead with my face in a ploughed field, my son will live as a free man, never knowing his father was a butcher."

Kil-nyo at first was deeply touched and then felt helpless. Her eyes came to rest upon the pair of shoes she'd placed on the shelf next to the satchel. It was then that she finally grasped what Chom-gae had said about living on the run and in hiding. Only then did she realize why he was worried about the light as they came in from outside.

Suddenly, the sound of thunder, as loud as if a mountain were crumbling down, was heard. That sound of rolling thunder she longed to wipe from her life, that sound she never wanted to hear again—it had returned. She opened the door. It was pitch black outside and the night wind blowing through the valley rushed into the room. In the distance, the mountain peak stood darker than darkness itself. She saw a few stars shining in the sky and wondered where the thunder had come from. A piercing pain ran through her heart.

"What's the boy's name?"

"We named him Chun-bok. Got the name from a famous fortuneteller. My wife is a very tough woman, she won't let him grow up hungry even if they are living among strangers."

"That a boy's father, who should be home for his son's sake, must for that very reason lead the life of a vagabond... that I'll never understand. Is that the way of the world? I've lived half my aimless life, but I'll never be able to understand that."

"Right now if they caught me I'd be stoned me to death. But if I survive this crisis, a day will surely come when I can watch Chun-bok live a free life in a decent world."

Was Chun-bok not her very own child, the baby she'd abandoned at birth? So Kil-nyo asked herself. Yet she knew she no longer had any right even to ask. Even if she had, Chom-gae would not be likely to give her an affirmative answer.

She couldn't figure out what his real motive was for going out of his way to find her. Whether he had wanted to track down the mother of the boy, or just had come for refuge in time of danger, it seemed certain he had willingly left his family so his presence would not damage his son's future.

Before such a man who had freely sacrificed himself for the sake of his son, how could she possibly come forth with a wretched claim of motherhood? A woman who'd abandoned her own flesh and blood, she was living without worrying about bread and shelter, while the woman who'd taken on the burden of raising the child was wandering around among strangers, half dead from hunger and cold, all for the sake of the boy.

If that was how things were, she told herself, the time had come for her to make a quick decision. The bloodthirsty faces of the young toughs who'd stopped by about a month before flashed in front of her eyes. Then she recalled the man with black sideburns who'd threatened her. Once more her trembling hands were concealed under her skirt.

She moved Chom-gae, who'd fallen asleep up against the wall, over to the warmer part of the room. As she rubbed and kneaded him from head to toe, she saw that his health was so poor that he'd be needing a long rest and plenty of care.

For three days Chom-gae stayed in bed and took his meals lying down. When he returned to his senses, the most he could manage was to make a trip to the outhouse under cover of darkness. Because he hadn't eaten for so long, his stomach was ailing and he frequently threw up.

Kil-nyo was chilled to the bone with worry and impatiently waited for his condition to improve. What if Chi Sang-mo showed up suddenly? What possible explanation could she give? How could she resist Cha Pyong-jo's men if they turned up to drag her off?

And if the murderous young men came back looking for Chom-gae? Wasn't what Chom-gae called "paradise" nothing other than what they called "Leftism"? What sort of creature was this thing that led so many people to be tortured? All the same, Kil-nyo made no attempt to understand it. Men folks in general were like that—unpredictable, naive and full of silly ideas. They'd even try to tie farts together, so to speak.

For the five days Chom-gae spent recuperating at the tavern Kil-nyo kept the place closed on the pretext that she was ill. Travelers stopped by in vain, and she ceased going out to work in the neighborhood for extra money. On the evening of the sixth day Chom-gae quietly got up and started putting on his socks. As she was clearing away an empty bowl, Kil-nyo asked in a dubious voice,

"Where do you think you're going?"

"Yes."

"What do you mean 'yes'? Well, where are you going?"

"It's high time I was off. If I stay here long enough you'll get yourself in trouble. Just this afternoon four men came by the gate and glared at you before leaving, didn't they?"

"You can't leave yet. I won't allow it, not until you're fit to travel."

"It's not so much because of those who're chasing me, there's something I gotta do... that's why I need to leave now."

"But I say you're not...."

"People are waiting for me. I have to see them so I can live freely, even for a short while. There's a limit to going on living under your breath. By sheer luck I ran into you, and I'm much better now, so I've got to leave before lightning strikes you."

All of a sudden Kil-nyo grabbed Chom-gae by the waist and fell to the floor.

"You can't! You'll be caught if you leave now. Tomorrow I'll go out and check how things are around here. Wait until then, please."

"You really shouldn't do this, ma'am. If I stay here, both you and I will be murdered. My death is something already decided, but yours'd be a worthless death."

Finished putting on his socks, Chom-gae stood up.

"Who are these people you have to go see, anyway, and where are you headed?"

"I can't tell you that. But things won't be smooth."

"If you insist I can't stop you. But take me along."

"Take you along? No, ma'am, don't be crazy. You know very well I'm not going out for a walk."

"Take me, please."

"It's out of the question, ma'am. Besides, I can see you're pregnant and it's simply impossible. Please, stay here and have a safe delivery. There is one favor I'd like to ask."

"Favor?"

"Please, keep his belly full of mother's milk. That way when he grows up he'll recognize his own mother."

At these last words, Kil-nyo's hand fell limply from Chom-gae's waist. All the energy in her body seemed to have been drained in an instant and she sat down exhausted. Keeping a close watch through the window, Chom-gae moved to the door and was stepping down into the yard.

"Wait a minute, please."

Said Kil-nyo, springing up and taking the pair of shoes down from the shelf. The worn shoes were gray with dust. She wiped them clean with the hem of her skirt.

"Wear these shoes, please."

Even in the darkness a look of astonishment was visible on the face of Chom-gae, who had been practically piecing his old ones together. Before he knew what he was doing, he had accepted the shoes from Kil-nyo, asking,

"What about their owner?"

"There isn't one."

"That can't be. These soles are good for five hundred miles of walking. I can't take them ma'am."

"I said there's no owner."

"Even so, these are too good for me. Besides, you weren't keeping these with me in mind."

"I did have you in mind when I kept them."

"I guess these dark spots on the sides are blood stains."

"Give them to me."

Kil-nyo snatched the shoes from his hands and pulled his feet forward to put them on for him. His feet turned out to be bigger than the shoes, but once they'd been forced on, they weren't bad for walking after all.

Run far away, run far, far away and live, Kil-nyo kept saying to herself. With these you could run a thousand miles without wearing out the soles. Take them off if you cross a stream, put them back if you're on a rocky road, and run far, far away for your life—this was Kil-nyo's prayer as Chom-gae moved out through the gate, his gait uncertain due to the unfamiliar shoes.

If only he'd turned around and opened his arms for just once, she'd decided she would drop everything and follow him. But Chom-gae must have guessed, for without once looking back he vanished into the grayness of the dark night, heading toward the towering peaks of Hwangjangjae.

The winter of that year had flown. In early March, as spring was slowly approaching, Kil-nyo felt that the hour she'd been awaiting was at hand. Outside the dawn was feebly breaking. She crawled on her stomach over to the door and opened it. There was no sign of anyone at the gate.

She was expecting a sudden push on the gate, and to see Chi Sang-mo walking in rubbing his hands, but beyond the door was only the grayness of the dawn. She hurriedly straightened her clothes and went to the kitchen. Despite the cramps afflicting her, she put the water jar on her head and went out to the well.

With the water she'd drawn she filled the tub and sat down in it. As she was rubbing her throat she heard a rooster crowing outside. She scrubbed the dirt from her body until her fingerprints were almost worn away. By the time she got out of the tub, the pains in her abdomen were shooting all the way up into her throat, and her forehead was drenched with a cold sweat. She went into her room and put on clean clothes.

As she hung a skein of yarn over the door handle and lay down on her side, the sweat was pouring down. She knew she needed the help of a midwife. But then she thought of the faces of the women who'd been out when she'd gone to the well.

At the sight of her waddling, nine months pregnant, they'd almost jeered, shortly replying to her greeting and turning away to whisper among themselves. Pouting looks and mocking gossip she provoked. She remembered telling herself not to expect any help from them, not even at childbirth.

She had no reason to isolate herself from the neighbors, nor did she have the nerve to do so. A woman making a living by running a winehouse might be shunned for no particular reason, but since the day when the two corpses had been brought there things were worse. The local idlers and gamblers who used to drop by now and then all of a sudden stopped coming, as though by agreement.

With bulging eyes, she glared at the ceiling and at the satchel with its tortoise-shell handle up there on the shelf. Her spine felt like it was turning to liquid from the pain, and she pulled at the yarn so hard that the door handle was about to drop off. Never in her entire life had she felt so utterly alone.

She knew that brandishing a ten-foot pole in all directions would bring not a soul to help her, yet she'd never imagined that she would be thrown into a situation as wretched and pitiable as this. The ceiling and the shelf overhead seemed first to be falling down on her and then to be soaring off into space.

As she desperately tried to stay conscious, a roll of thunder resounded from far away. The same ear-shattering sound she'd heard at the time of her first childbirth had returned, grabbing her by the neck and shaking her all over. At that moment she heard a rustle of footsteps outside the gate and then lost consciousness.

When she came back to her senses, she could hear dry firewood breaking. Someone was making a fire in the kitchen. Startled, she looked to her side and there was a newborn baby lying wrapped in a clean new blouse. She quickly lifted up the blouse and saw that it was a girl. Someone was in the kitchen, but she lacked the strength to get up and open the door. She gave up looking around the room and shut her eyes again.

"You seem to be recovering now. Well, I've made some seaweed soup."

The woman who shook her awake was an old hag from the village who told fortunes and performed shamanistic ceremonies for the sick. Kil-nyo peered into her face for a long time as she brought the bowl of pungent soup right up under her chin. It smelled like river water. The old woman dipped the spoon in the soup and looked over dolefully at the sleeping baby, saying,

"For a woman flown in from outside I thought you were decent and good-natured, but seeing what happened here today it looks like you're not so good-natured after all. This is not a village where people hate each other, and you should let others know if you're about to give birth. No matter how independent and willful you are, you can't expect to cut the umbilical cord with your own hand."

"It all happened so suddenly, there was no time to go for help. I don't know how to thank you...."

"When I got here, there was blood all over the room. The mother was unconscious and the baby was rolling about wrapped in the umbilical cord.... People like us who live in a mountain village should stick together and take care of each other. Nobody can stand alone, you know. It's not that I can't understand what you have in mind.

"The women around here are ignorant of the world outside. They don't have the brains to show any sympathy for the hard lot that brought you in here. If they gave you the cold shoulder, treated you with contempt as a woman who sells wine to suck the money from idle men's pockets, well, that shouldn't surprise you. You can't go on living with your back to the neighbors, oppressed by such things. Neighbors are supposed to share their happiness and sorrow among themselves, so if you look, you're bound to find a friend among the hedgehogs."

"It's probably my shyness that made the neighbors frown on me. But I've never blamed anybody in particular, and I never made up my mind to keep away from the neighbors. Living here as a woman in a place frequented by strangers, where even dead bodies come and go, I figured I better just mind my own business. Maybe that was why they look askance at me."

"Woman or man, you can't afford to be a loner, not if you have any sense. Even if they give you a hard time, you should be thick-skinned enough to take it. No bastard can spit in a smiling face. There are times for a woman to lead a solitary life, but there are times too for a woman to be open and friendly. You can hang your pride on a hanger and take it down when you go to bed at night."

"I'll bear that in mind. You showed up just when I fainted— you saved the lives of my daughter and me."

The old shaman looked at the mother and the infant in turn and reluctantly said,

"I can care for you a while until you're better, but... looks like the child's father is nowhere to be seen."

"It seems that way now, but he should be coming before long. I should be hanging a length of hemp on the gate so he'll know of the birth when he gets here.

"I've already seen to that."

The old woman had hung a piece of hemp rope on the gate, but it didn't seem to have kept the evil spirits away, for the baby soon was stricken with a bad fever. The top of her head was matted with black hair, but within five days after delivery the baby's face was splotched with red sores and her urine was reddish in color. She was constipated and wouldn't suckle either.

The old woman went out and brought back some Chinese medicine. It helped with some of the symptoms, but the little girl never recovered the strength to suck like a normal newborn.

About two weeks after the birth, a stranger appeared outside the gate while the old woman was in the kitchen kindling a fire. The sun was slowly setting and dusk was on its way. The man was wearing an old suit and a felt hat pulled well down on his head. His shoes looked too big for his feet.

At the sight of him, the old woman had a hunch and rushed outside. As he peered through the fence, she said,

"I don't know who you are, but we aren't serving travelers just now. There's a woman here who just had a baby."

The man made a gesture of doffing his felt hat and replied,

"I know. I saw the rope on the gate."

"It's still five, six days before the three weeks is up."

"Is that so? This is the only tavern at the foot of Hwangjangjae, eh?"

"Yes, but are you a relation of the woman of the house? The father of the child maybe?"

"No, not me. I was just wondering if I'd found the right place."

"Speak up, tell me who you're after. I'm in the middle of building a fire."

"I have to see the woman who lives here before I say any more."

Having carefully looked the man over during the conversation, the old woman guessed that despite his ragged clothes he was certainly no lunatic. Still, she couldn't very well invite him in without knowing why he had come.

Meanwhile Kil-nyo, curious about the voices outside, had opened the door to take a look. She could tell instinctively that he was no wayfarer and no panhandler begging for food. She saw the shining eyes under the brim of his hat, and she recognized the gleam in those eyes.

It was the same gleam she'd seen in the eyes of those two young men who were brought back dead. And hadn't Chom-gae's eyes been the same, too? She felt as though a rock was crushing down on her heart. Hurriedly she smoothed her

clothes and said to the old woman in a low tone,
"Please, show him in to the upper room."
Startled at hearing this, the old woman dashed back inside
and whispered,
"For some reason he sends a chill up my spine. Have you seen
that glint in his eyes?"
"How could I miss it? But his eyes are no different than anybody else's."
"That light in his eyes is not a good sign. There's murder in
those eyes. It hasn't yet been three weeks, and to bring in such
an ominous character would be courting evil."
"We'll worry about it when it happens. Now, hurry and bring
him in, please."
Kil-nyo waited until she had led him inside, and then went
over to the room. Her face was still swollen and puffy from the
childbirth. As she crossed the hall to the upper room, Kil-nyo
saw the man's shoes neatly set on the step. She was so shocked
at the sight that she clutched at her heart just to keep breathing.
Her racing heart would not calm down.
In the meantime, the man in the room kept clearing his throat
to let his presence be known. Her hand trembled at the
doorknob. Could it be possible? For a second she regretted having allowed him in the house. But the even sound of his coughs
made her gravitate to the room despite her dread. She found
herself hesitantly opening the door, and before she knew what
she was doing one of her feet was already across the threshold.
The man was sitting with legs crossed, and after a hint of a
bow he resumed his former posture. His glance paused a while
upon her bloated face and then shifted to her trembling hands
tucked inside of her skirt.
"I'm sorry to cause you inconvenience by showing up so
abruptly."
Kil-nyo read his face quickly. He looked haggard and his
cheeks were deeply sunken. Although she had some idea of
what to expect, her heart sank all over again. As she remained
speechless, he waited a bit before opening his mouth again,

"It wasn't easy for me to find you here. I'm a stranger in these parts, never been around here before. I'm from a town very far from here. At first I wasn't sure, but in the end I decided to go on and find you." '

"I'm not sure what business brought you here, but my place is open to all and a visit from a stranger is soon known all over the village."

"I won't be staying long. I'm not even going to stay the night."

"It's already getting dark...."

"Even so, I must leave."

"Tell me where you're from, please."

"Where I'm from is of no importance. What I'm going to tell you is something I was strictly forbidden to let you know by the person involved, but I couldn't just let it pass so I took it on myself to come here to see you. After hearing me, I don't even know whether you'll do anything or just let it go in one ear and out the other."

"Please, what's this all about?"

"You know a man by the name of Hwang Chom-gae, don't you?"

She had expected this, so she merely nodded, looking straight into his eyes.

"I was lucky enough to have some friends looking after me on the outside, so I was released after a while, but Mr. Hwang is still in prison, going through hell."

"What do you mean prison?"

"I can't say much about the charges. Even among people arrested and taken in together, even those suffering the same ordeals, they know nothing about the others. Nobody knows who's on what side, and when somebody walks out of prison you don't know whether they're to be executed or transferred to another lockup."

"Why was he arrested in the first place? You must have some news about it."

"Can't be sure, but it seems he was deeply involved with the leftists. He was brought in a fortnight after me and we were in the same cell. Every few days he was taken out and given the electric torture, each time he came back he just collapsed senseless. He barely came to when the rooster crowed the next day.

"Even in his sleep, he always seemed to be seeing things and your name was often on his lips as he jabbered. I got curious and asked him about it, but he clammed up tight. Just a day or two before I was released he finally opened up a bit and told me a few things."

"Where is that place?"

"Andong, that's what they call it."

"When did you last see him?"

"Only three days ago."

"He's still alive then?"

"Then were interrogating him for the names of the leftist leadership, I think, but he wouldn't open his mouth. He's strong and tough, maybe it was his rough origins, but he seemed to endure the torture better than the others. Everybody's endurance has its limits, though.

"He seemed gloomy about his own chances, and when I left the place he took off his shoes and made me wear them, even though I tried to refuse. He kept murmuring, 'go far away, go far, far away.' In wretched shape, he was. I couldn't stand to look at him.

"Never in my days have I run into a man as alone as he was. Right before parting with him I was determined to get some answers. I demanded he give me the names of relatives or friends who might be able to help him from the outside, but he gave none. You seemed to be about the only one likely to know him, and that's why I came here."

Except for a bit at the beginning, Kil-nyo couldn't make much sense out of the man's words. She was transfixed by his eyes and by his sunken face, hollow as an empty water jar. The cavernous old house at Woljon-ri suddenly popped into her mind, followed by the pale face of her old mother-in-law, Pak, who'd drawn her last breath just after Chom-gae announced he was leaving the village for good.

The man fumbled in the pocket of his worn-out suit and removed a cigarette butt. He patted it fondly, then put it in his mouth and struck a match. An enigmatic smile appeared on his face, which until then had been tense and uneasy. Perhaps it was the pride he felt at having tracked down the woman called Shin Kil-nyo, or maybe he felt relieved at being able to share with her the burden he'd been bearing alone for the sake of Chom-gae.

An awkward silence reigned in the room for a while. He sat there without once taking his eyes from her face, as if he were intent on reading the slightest change in her expression.

"You don't look well."

"This is no grand house, but you are a guest and I'd like you to stay for dinner before you go."

The man did not answer. He had expected something else from her, perhaps. The thin, self-satisfied smile vanished, replaced by a disappointed look. Drawing the ashtray toward him and extinguishing the butt with a trembling hand, he quietly said,

"No, I can't accept your hospitality. I have to leave now. I may catch a ride of some sort if I head south."

Kil-nyo made a few attempts to change his mind, but he only became more firmly resolved to go. She gave up. The mountain's shadow already had already crept down to the steps and the evening wind could be heard blowing against the wall, but the man got up to leave.

It took him a long time to tie his shoelaces, and once he'd laced up those huge shoes he banged his heels on the step a few times. Kil-nyo got the unspoken message of his behavior, but she didn't want to detain him any longer. She was fed up. What a pointless thing, to try and hold onto a man....

The next morning Kil-nyo fastened the baby on her back and busied herself preparing to head out. There was no way to bolt the gate, of course. To let people see the place was untended she made a breach in the hedgerow. Without any clear plan, she decided to head over Hwangjangjae and set off.

Toward the top of the hill she managed to get a lift from a passing truck. She feared it might take her no farther than the market at Sokpo-ri, but luckily the truck was headed beyond to another town called Imdong across the next ridge. There she got off and got a ride with another truck bound for Andong. When she finally reached Andong, it was past eleven that night.

Several times on the way to Andong she took out a crumpled sheet of paper on which a map had been scrawled. She spent the night in an inn, and the next morning she went out in search of a corrugated-metal warehouse. She found it on a blind alley in the midst of a few private houses.

Judging from the thick, whitish scum in the drainage ditches nearby, the structure must have been used for salt storage during the Japanese colonial period. She did not dare to approach the building, and just peered at it from a distance. Somehow the air around the place seemed ominous and suffocating.

She crouched down beside a wall and again removed the map from her pocket and compared it with the neighborhood. It was the right place, all right, no doubt about it. That dark warehouse was where Chom-gae was locked up.

When the man who came to see her at Hwangjangjae took his leave, she had walked after him to the main road. He had turned around only once, saying,

"I'm not sure I should tell you this, it might just make you worry more."

A bit weary of his preliminaries, she'd replied,

"If there's something you haven't told me, let me hear it, please."

"Mr. Hwang has lost his sight in one eye. It was because of the horrible torture."

Nevertheless, Kil-nyo could not picture a grotesque Chom-gae, disfigured by the loss of an eye. All she could see in her mind was that face with both eyes open wide and shining.

The baby was wailing at the top of her voice. To try to soothe her, Kil-nyo sought help at the house nearest to the warehouse. She pushed open the unlocked plywood gate and stepped inside the courtyard, calling out for the owner. A man about forty stuck his head out from a shed. He spoke first,

"Come in, please."

Still trying to calm the fretting baby, she approached the shed, coming directly to the point,

"I'm a stranger passing through here. I was wondering if you have a room I can use for a while?"

The man, who had been sharpening a sickle on a whetstone, did not even bother to look at her face. Glancing over quickly at the train of her skirt, his voice grew gruff, unlike his initial welcome, as he muttered,

"Go straight up the main road and you'll find some decent inns."

She didn't know what to say.

"Is there some secret reason you'd rather stay in a private house?"

"No special reason, I don't have much cash and I don't feel comfortable in those inns where rough types are always going in and out."

"No need to make up excuses. Why don't you jsut own up and admit you've got a relative being held in that salt house?"

" . . . ."

"It's the crime not the man that we hate. Prisoners' relatives often come to me to rent a room."

"Do you have a room to rent?"

The owner of the house, his expression cordial once more, showed Kil-nyo a room in the back of the house. It wasn't too small, and it was set off from the rest of the house, just right for someone with a crying baby. And if you stood on tiptoes, you could look directly over the fence at the warehouse.

Kil-nyo was peering over at the metal building, thinking what a coincidence it was for her to find a place so near, when the man standing behind her bluntly said,

"Nothing good will come of just glaring at the place."

It sounded as though his remark might have some deep ulterior meaning, but then again it might have been insignificant. Kil-nyo paid for ten days in advance, and it was agreed she would take meals with the family.

It was the middle of the day, but no sooner had she sat down than her fatigue overtook her and she fell into a deep sleep. Whenever the baby stirred she gave it her breast to suck and fell back asleep before the infant did.

The following day, Kil-nyo stayed inside the room, skipping meals. Awakened by the noise of trucks far off on the main road, she found herself lying there exhausted in an unfamiliar room. What if Chi Sang-mo had stopped by the tavern in the meantime? She regretted she hadn't left a note for him with the old midwife.

It wasn't that the thought had not occurred to her, but she had been hesitant, and in the end she concluded it would be better not to leave any message behind. It now seemed a strange decision, even to herself. She was obsessed by the thought that she wouldn't be seeing Chi Sang-mo again for a very long time.

Since she remained confident he would never just abandon her, this time it was truer to say it was she who was leaving him behind. This meant, too, that a certain feeling for Chom-gae had finally sprouted inside her, a feeling that went beyond gratitude for his rescue and loving care of her baby. She was aware of this vague feeling, and began to realize it was what had led her to go off without leaving any message for Chi Sang-mo.

The night was deep. From afar came the sound of dogs howling. The noise went on for a long time. It almost sounded like the wails of someone in insufferable pain. A man in terrible agony, whose intestines were melting, would probably sound like that.

Unable to listen any longer to those screams lacking any trace of human dignity, Kil-nyo pulled the quilt over her head. But the sound pierced through the it, and the howling dogs seemed stitched into every square of the quilt. Their tongues licked at her eardrums.

From the ceiling descended the visage of Chom-gae, eyes wide as the eyes of the wooden guardians at a temple gate, descending right onto her own face. Only then did she asmit to herself that the howls were muffled screams from a human throat.

All along she'd known very well that people were imprisoned there in the salt warehouse—that was precisely why she was where she was. She couldn't help wondering how she'd could have told herself it was dogs howling, and not the agonized voice of a human being.

Abruptly she sat up. A cold sweat enveloped her body, but she was oblivious to it. She unbolted the door and left the house. The starlight was pouring down with such radiance that every rise and fall in the road was clearly visible.

Like a child hopping over a chain of rocks to ford a stream, she made her way toward the salt house. Outside of it, firewood was stacked high. There was no sign of people. The wails from inside were gradually subsiding, replaced by a hiccoughing sound.

Never before had she heard a grown man hiccough like a child does after an outburst of crying. What could it have been that had rooted out every trace of manliness from him? However much grandeur one possessed, however lofty one's station in life, nobody could just peel away a grown man's years as if skinning an animal.

To Kil-nyo, nothing on earth was more valuable than the dignity of a man's age. But now she was witnessing the pathetic sound of a man's dignity being stripped away. She put her ear to the metal wall. Just on the other side of the corrugated tin, the sound of hiccoughs was distinctly audible. Between the gasping came a man's icy voice, cold as the December night,

"Talk straight and you'll be freed at once! If you resist, do you think you'll just die? Do you really believe just killing you would satisfy us? No, never. No way we'll make you into a hero by a worthless death!"

"I never once thought of being a hero, sir."

"You're a special breed then—all you bastards ever babble about is being a hero. Now, tell the truth! You want to be a hero, don't you?!"

"That's pointless for me. I'm the kind who for a meager bowl of rice a day acts like a dog, and you, sir, know it."

"Sir? So you don't want to be my equal, is that it? You're sick and tired of dealing with me, is that what you're saying?"

"Don't beat me, please, I'm begging you. If you don't beat me, I promise I'll follow you the rest of my life. Please, sir, don't beat me, I beg you!"

"Hey, you really are a dog, eh? With every bark you want me to do you a favor, but how come you ignore the favors I ask? That's not fair."

"What can I do for you, sir?"

"You don't know?"

"No, I don't. Don't be unreasonable, please."

"Enough of that shit! You know damn well you're mocking me. And yet it's me that's unreasonable, is that it? You really want to tell me to tell you what I want?"

"...."

"I want to pull out your tongue with my own hands!"

"I don't know."

"I know."

"If you know, why are you doing this to me, sir?"

"I know all you bastards say 'I don't know'. I won't beat you. If that's what you want, I tell you I have the heart to grant it."

Kil-nyo wondered how long this had gone on. For a time there was only silence. The silence was broken by the sound of a cat crying somewhere. This sound, which continued a while, stopped, and then started again, was not coming from anywhere near the salt house.

She saw the lights come on in the house where she'd taken lodging. She rushed over. The baby was awake and crying. As she opened the door, the owner of the house was standing there rocking the baby in his arms. With his eyes, he signaled for the speechless and pale Kil-nyo to sit down. But she stood their motionless, nailed to the spot.

Kil-nyo snatched the baby from the man and put one of her breasts in the child's mouth. The man did not leave, but leaned crouching against the wall.

"Don't rush so, the baby may get an upset stomach. The shape you're in, I'm afraid you may kick the bucket first. The man in the salt house, is he the child's father?"

"...."

"Take care, you can't be going out of your mind with a baby hanging to your neck, not if you want this child to outlive you. Gather your senses and find some way."

"What way could there be?"

"You mean you're just going to linger outside the salt house every night like a crazy woman with nothing in mind? Is that your plan? My neighbors are so used to the sound that to them it's almost music, sometimes it sounds like a flute, or like an owl's cries, and other times it could be just a truck backing up—all sorts of sounds in their ears.

"In the beginning, the people who live around here dreaded nightfall. They trembled and couldn't sleep a wink. Even the rice they ate tasted like sand. But as we gradually got used to the sound, we managed to replace it with whatever we felt like hearing. Not just flute music or the hoots of an owl, these days we can even hear the spring breeze whispering through a valley, or a lullaby sung by an old grandmother. It's a blessing, don't you think? If you're without tricks and have no way to do anything, you should change your habits like my neighbors, change in order to survive."

"What way could I have?"

"If you don't decide one way or another, you'll surely end by going insane. Either you give up for good and just leave this place, or you have to fight for your life. Otherwise, this is a perfect situation to drive anyone insane."

"What do you mean 'insane'? Why do you keep saying that?"

"I don't say it for no reason. I've seen a woman go insane with my own eyes, that's why. She, too, went to the salt house every night and stayed outside there until morning. During the days, she just slept, soaked in a cold sweat. In the end she started showing signs of madness and then vanished into thin air."

"But what could I...."

The man looked about the room as though he was in a stranger's house and murmured quietly,

"If you really look for a way, it's not impossible to find one. As they say, to catch a tiger, you have to go into its cave. I didn't think you came here with no ideas in mind."

"Are you saying there's a way?"

"Maybe. I'll check around and see what I can come up with, and you just be sure to keep this baby quiet at night. The neighbors haven't yet cultivated the talent of turning a baby's bawling into the sound of a flute."

"You already know of a way it seems, am I right?"

"I said I'd look into it, didn't I? If you rush things you can get a bellyache from a glass of water. It's not that I don't sympathize with your impatience, heartless man though I am. But as they say, it's safest to check even a stone bridge before you cross. The more impatient you are, the more cautious you should be. After all, the result is more important than the first step."

Despite this firm undertaking to check on means of helping her, every time Kil-nyo ventured out into the yard to see what was happening, the man was always right there in the shed, sharpening sickles on his whetstone. He knew how impatient she was, but never once did he glance her way as she stood there awaiting some sign. He just went on sharpening at a leisurely pace.

On the back wall of the shed, several more well-honed sickles were already hanging from hooks among other tools. After sharpening for a while, he'd pause to carefully examine the edge with his fingers, then hang the sickle on the board and begin anew with another.

To Kil-nyo, the monotony of his work was so absurd that he seemed to be the one who was losing his mind. But then, had he not expressed a kind concern with her predicament? One thing, however, seemed strange about his routine. The main gate of the house he kept wide open until nightfall, and from where he was in the shed he had a clear view all the way to the main highway as he worked. He often shifted his glance from the whetstone toward the highway. It seemed to her this habit meant he was waiting for somebody.

The link tying the man to her was too weak, however, for Kil-nyo's hope to linger for very long. She could do nothing except spend each day listening to the grinding on the whetstone, and during each sleepless night her ears had to endure the unbearable screaming from prisoners in the salt house.

Could some of those screams have been Chom-gae's? She told herself that the howls she'd heard did not sound like his voice, but at the same time this troubled her. She recalled what the young man had said—that Chom-gae didn't look like he could hold out too long.

That he'd given away the shoes to his friend might have meant he felt he'd already passed the point where barefeet would make any difference. Did it mean his death was already at hand? For Kil-nyo to give up the nightly vigil outside the salt house was not easy, for she desperately wanted to hear Chom-gae's voice, even though at first she had dreaded it.

As she had continued the nightwatches, she had felt a heartache worse than any she had ever experienced. It seemed to rise from the depths of her heart and gradually to fill her throat so that breathing itself became almost impossible. But oddly enough, there was a certain exhilaration in this feeling, too, a feeling of being alive that she'd never felt from being with Chi Sang-mo or Cha Pyong-jo.

An extremely strange affair it was. How strange that she found this inexplicable affection for Hwang Chom-gae within her, an affection that did not only arise from his being the man who'd taken it upon himself to bring up her illegitimate child. Was he not a man ostracized by everyone in this world? What's more, he was a man who was already legally bound to a wife.

On one particular night the man's voice issuing from within the salt house was less dry and crisp, less ominous than usual. A downpour of rain allowed her to conceal the sound of her footsteps, so she'd been able to move closer than before to the building and eavesdrop on the interrogation. There was no sign of beating on this night.

"Wouldn't you like to get out of this stinking warehouse as soon as possible?"

"Yes, sir."

The voice replying was not that of Chom-gae.

"If that's so, the business between us can be wrapped up very simply. Just stop insisting that the organization uses anonymous cells. You may not know the names of all those you've had contacts with, but you have to know at least some of their faces."

"Don't treat me like a spy, please."

"Who said you're a spy?"

"When you speak of 'cells' and 'contacts' that's what you're headed toward, isn't it?"

"Don't speculate, I had no such thing in mind. They say 'knowledge is a curse' and knowing too much seems to be your problem. A schooled man is not necessarily better at gauging the trustworthiness of others. You seem worse off than the ignorant people in that respect."

"I know what trust is, too. But I believe truth and love cannot be found in everyone, only in those who have them to give. A false-hearted man is not likely to recognize a man of love, nor is a trusting man likely to understand the clear conscience of an unjust man."

"No use dragging out pointless arguments. Even if you refuse to confess, we had enough evidence to arrest you, didn't we? If you deny even that, you're a hopeless fool. If you are a so-called intellectual, you should be able to justify your conduct whether or not it's within the bounds of the law. If you call yourself an intellectual, and don't wish to tarnish that title, you should be able judge yourself. You don't expect to be treated like that ignoramus, Hwang Chom-gae, who can't even write his own name, do you?"

"Stop your vulgar slandering of Mr. Hwang. He is the one who taught me to open my eyes to love and conscience, and that trust and loyalty among friends has nothing to do with how smart you are or the ideology you spout."

"A lobster taking the side of the crabs, that's the saying for you. You must realize that what you're saying is both logically and practically self-contradictory. The two kinds will never join together, and even if they meet, they are like oil and water. You know better than anybody else how ridiculous it is to address Hwang Chom-gae as 'Mister'. You do realize that, don't you?"

"No, I do not, but one thing is clear. No matter how gentle you are with me, it only makes me weary and I think of nothing but avoiding you, but when I'm with Mr. Hwang, even if he says not a word the whole day, his presence gives me peace of mind. That's the truth."

"Don't try to make fun of me with your sophistry. You and I may disagree about ideology right now, but there's still room for us to communicate. You and Hwang Chom-gae share the same ideology for the present, but you can't even carry on a conversation with him. It's not for nothing that they say 'Birds of a feather flock together.' "

Kil-nyo turned about. So, Chom-gae was still alive after all. She didn't know whether he was being held captive inside that salt house, but the two men had mentioned him more than once in their conversation. If he was in there, what could it mean that the whole day passed without a word from Chom-gae? She wondered.

Could he have lost one of his eyes, as her visitor had said? Maybe he'd lost both eyes by now... perhaps the man who said Chom-gae went all day without opening his mouth meant he was blind. Who was this man who kept defending Chom-gae?

When she returned to her room, she found the man of the house sitting there with the light on. It occurred to her that every time she came back from the salt house he always seemed to be there, soothing the baby. And she only now marked the fact that the man's face never showed any indication he'd been awakened from sleep. Whether in the middle of the night or at daybreak, his face always looked dusty, like that of a man just arrived after a long journey. As usual, his eyes shone brightly and his expression was as cool and collected as ever. Like always, he sat leaning against the wall as he spoke:

"Can't shake that habit of yours, it seems. Stop wasting time on futile visits and listen good. I'm aware you've been keeping a close eye on me, too. So, how much do you have on you?"

"What are you talking about?"

"I knew from the first that you've been guarding some cash. You needn't worry, though. I'm not about to rob you and leave you penniless. All I'm saying is, if the money is for saving the life of the child's father, then it's about time you and I had a talk."

His habit of beating around the bush didn't instill much confidence in others. Kil-nyo looked him straight in the eye. There was no glimmer of sincerity in his face that commanded her trust. But she'd reached the point where there was nobody upon whom she could rely. In other words, she could no longer afford the luxury of questioning anyone's trustworthiness.

Even if he was going to snatch everything she had and disappear overnight, Kil-nyo would gladly bear the consequences. Her predicament no longer left open the possibility of reasoned deliberation, or so it seemed to her. She took a diaper from the bundle and removed the money from its hiding place, then pushed it over to him.

It was money she'd amassed out of all the petty change cast her way by wayfarers who'd stopped in at the tavern. She hadn't saved it with any special purpose in mind, and certainly not in the hopes of building a fortune. As a single woman she'd had little use for the money, and it simply went unspent and slowly piled up. When she set out from home, she'd emptied the earthen jar where her savings were kept and stuck the money in a diaper. When it occurred to her that this cash, until then useless, might actually be exchangable for a man's life, she felt proud of herself, for the first time, at having survived all her misfortunes.

To the man, who was counting out the cash on his knees, Kil-nyo asked,

"There's one thing I'd like to know."

"What's that?"

"It's just something I overheard from outside the salt storage, but it seems Hwang Chom-gae is respected by those who're under interrogation."

"That's possible."

"But he can't read, doesn't even know the alphabet, and is no man of great character. And he's from the lowest class. Still, I heard a man who sounded very well schooled speak up in defense of Chom-gae when the interrogator slighted him."

"Isn't that the way men's affairs go? Dignity and nobility of nature are no monopolies of the educated. You, for instance, seem to be well bred—your looks and carriage say so—but here you are married to a lowborn man, even raising his child, and now you're giving up all your money to save his life.

"You needn't care so much what others think, look into your own heart and you'll find an answer. Whether a man buckles under when faced with a life or death crisis, that's when it becomes clear whether he possesses dignity or not.

"Among all the so-called intellectual bastards there's not one who doesn't know how to curry favor with the powerful for selfish ends, and not one of them will stand up when a righteous voice needs to be heard. That's a legacy the Japanese bestowed upon us. I don't know who that man was, but if he paid respect to Hwang so-and-so, it was probably because Hwang so-and-so was no coward."

"What could it be that's more precious than one's life...? After you die, isn't it all in vain, whether one was lofty or base?"

"I don't know how to answer that, either. But there must be something more precious than life, otherwise those people could never endure all the suffering they've been through."

The man of the house abruptly grabbed the money and rose. Kil-nyo rotated her head so as not to see the man's back as he walked out of the room. Instead, she held the baby tightly in her arms. The child woke from sleep and began searching with her mouth for a nipple. Kil-nyo was extremely nervous and her pounding heart caused her hands to tremble so much that she couldn't even feed the baby properly.

"No need to be so anxious about something that may turn out to be nothing." That was what the man had said to Kil-nyo as he was leaving, and she repeated the same thing over and over again to herself.

He advised her not to be too impatient and just to wait for a while, but she couldn't bring herself to ask whether "for a while" meant a few days or a few months. The man still never left the house. As always, he spent his days crouching over the grindstone in the shed, whetting sickles. For someone about to rescue a man who'd fallen into a great peril, his expression and behavior were all too resigned.

It was cloudy the whole day and toward dusk it began to rain. The downpour slowly took away what little warmth there was in the room, and around ten that night it grew so cold that the baby's lips took on a bluish cast. Just then that Kil-nyo heard footsteps approaching through the backyard. The owner of the house cleared his throat before walking into her room.

"Looks like Hwang so-and-so is being transferred to the salt house tonight."

"Transferred?"

"I mean, he's coming here from somewhere else."

"What time?"

"Should be after eleven."

"What am I to do?"

"Don't go out."

"What do you mean? Why, then, are you telling me this?"

"Because if you hang around the salt house tonight, it might ruin our plan. Most relatives, once they catch sight of their wretched loved ones, lose their senses and go wild without a thought for the consequences."

"I see. I'll stay here."

It was after midnight when a three-quarter ton truck appeared. Through the rain, the barely audible rumble of the truck reached Kil-nyo's ears. To keep the baby quiet, she'd been breast-feeding her for hours. From the sound she could tell that the truck was coming closer, not rapidly but not unusually slowly, either.

It was not very far from the main highway to the salt storage building, but the makeshift road, built along the dike of a rice paddy, was covered with deep mud after the deluge. The driver kept muttering to himself as the truck squirmed along the waterlogged road. Almost hysterically, he kept hitting the accelerator and the brake in turn, trying to keep from getting stuck.

The truck settled into a rut, and the driver got out to check the tires, which were sunk down in the muck. He went back to the driver's seat and raced the motor a few times, grinding the gears in an attempt to get underway again. The truck wouldn't budge. The stretch of road ahead was in terrible shape, with gaping holes here and there. Whether the damage was due to the heavy rains wasn't easy to say, but from there on the road looked to be impassable without repairs.

In the bed of the truck, beneath the canvas, were sitting seven men. Rain was pouring down through cracks in the canvas and the cold was so severe that the passengers were all doubled over, their heads between their knees. When the truck lurched violently, their shoulders would bump together or their noses would almost hit the bed of the truck. Then they'd struggle to regain their balance and they resumed the same posture, but not one of them made any effort to exchange a word with the others.

One of the seven men was wearing a quilted outfit coated with blood and dirt stains. Others were youths in thin, summerish shirts that were torn open to reveal their bare chests. Another, skinny as a stick, was dressed in a ragged western suit. His eyes were tightly shut, and he stayed motionless even though raindrops kept striking the bridge of his nose. Clotted blood made his hands and face almost unrecognizable.

One man was swollen up like a balloon, and yet another was so haggard and wasted that it seemed he'd keel over dead at a tap on his shoulder. Then there was the seventh man. He wore a felt hat pulled down over his forehead, and under the brim of the hat his eyes were shining bright. His face was extremely thin, but unlike the others he had no visible scars on his face. A closer look would have revealed that one of his hands was tightly clutching the end of two ropes by which he was bound to two of the other men.

Each time the truck jerked, the men in the back pawed the air to try to balance themselves, and each time the felt hat watched over the six prisoners with an icy glare. When it was clear that the truck was stuck, the driver got out and walked around to the back, sticking his head in and reporting to the felt hat in a complaining tone,

"Can't get it to move, sir. The road is full of deep holes all of a sudden."

The felt hat looked contemptuously at the driver and replied,

"What do you mean the road is suddenly full of holes? It was fine just a fortnight ago."

"It was all right then. I don't know if it's the rain or some bastard has wrecked the road on purpose, but either way we can't go on."

"That can't be. Try to fix it somehow."

"We're in big trouble. How a road that was decent only a few weeks ago could've gone to hell like this is beyond me."

"Are you just going to stand there pissing and moaning? We haven't come all this way to be turned back this close to our destination."

"You'll have to come down and help push the truck."

"Nonsense! I'm guarding these six bastards on my own, you know that, no? Go to the town and bring back some men or do it yourself, I don't care. I have to stay right here where I am."

"It'll work out fine if you order these men down and have them push the truck a little ways...."

"Impossible."

The driver walked toward town, berating the felt hat under his breath the whole way. Before reaching a populated area, he ran into three men with umbrellas walking toward him. Wiping away the water streaming over his forehead with the back of his hand, the driver spoke to them in a hopeful voice,

"You live around here, don't you?"

"That's right."

"My truck is stuck in the muck over there, can you give us a hand? Among the three men was the owner of the house where Kil-nyo was staying. He stepped forward and asked,

"Where's the truck?"

The driver peered at the man's face for a while in the darkness and then pointed the way. The four of them walked over toward the truck. The back wheels were sunk deeply in a muddy hole and the front of the truck was visibly inclining upward. The driver led the three men to the back of the truck and in the loudest possible voice yelled directions on how to extricate the tires from the mud.

"How many people are inside?," asked the owner of the house.

"Seven."

"This is not gong to be easy. Why do we have to try to pull the truck free with so many grown men sitting inside?"

"They can't get out."

"If so, they'll have to wait until the rain stops. This whole area is waterlogged, and if you don't do something soon the truck is liable to slide over on its side."

Without asking permission from the driver, the man of the house pulled the canvas flap aside and stuck his head inside the back of the truck. He looked about until his glance came to rest upon the man in the felt hat. At that moment the man seemed to nod slightly. The other six men were paying no attention and so didn't notice this behavior by the two men. After taking another look at the passengers, the man of the house said,

"Unless you get on down, there's no way this truck will be moving until the rain's stopped. The wheels are stuck too deep."

Then the felt hat, totally ignoring what had just been said, savagely cast back the canvas and yelled to the driver, who stood a few steps away,

"Look here, do we really have to get down? Or are we to spend the night here?"

"What did I tell you? I said you'd have to get out, didn't I?", the driver replied in an irritated voice.

"If anything goes wrong, you should take responsibility."

"What's going to go wrong? All you have to do is have the men get down, stand them to one side, and then put them back on the truck once we're clear of the mud."

"You drivers are all good at chattering."

"Don't speak ill of drivers. You think I do this job because I'm in love with it? If I hadn't smashed a decent car into a ditch and been left with nothing else to turn to, I wouldn't be doing this kind of shit."

"Must you show off you nasty temper again?"

"Why shouldn't I have a nasty temper, I've been away from my family for over a year now? A ghost of some bastard who died without ever riding in a car must have taken over my life to fulfill his wish, shit."

"All right. Everybody out."

Once decided, the felt hat ordered the six men down from the truck in a low, icy voice. He loosened the ropes a little, one man at a time. The felt hat got down first, followed by the others, who slowly crawled off the bed of the truck, their hands bound at abdomen level. They ignored the downpour as they slowly climbed down in good order.

The felt hat didn't take his eyes off them once until all six were standing in a line on the road. Then he ordered them several steps away from the truck on one side, and aimed a ferocious snarl at the driver,

"Don't you dare screw up, hurry and let's be done with this!"

It was pitch dark on all sides. By the time picks and shovels were rounded up to begin the work, the rain had grown even heavier. Everyone was drenched to the bones. Even after considerable digging, the truck still wouldn't budge an inch. In the end, the prisoners had to join in the work.

When they were ordered to lend a hand, the man of the house

sidled up to the one the felt hat had shortly before pointed out with a jut of his chin. In the bustle of trying to push the truck free, he pulled a blade from his belt and cut through the rope tying the man's wrists to his waist. The prisoner pointed out by the felt hat was Hwang Chom-gae.

Realizing that his bonds had been severed, Chom-gae quickly concealed himself to one side of the truck, out of sight of the others. From there he crawled toward the dike, only a few meters below where the truck stood. There were only two ways to run—to the front or the back of the truck. But with the headlights burning, his flight would soon be revealed if he ran to the front. And if he ran the other way, that would likely attract the attention of the workers and the felt hat.

His fellow prisoners must have noticed he was missing, but they would no doubt pretend nothing was wrong. Just then, the man of the house shouted from behind the truck,

"Hey, driver, come on back here!"

At this outburst, the driver shut off the motor and got down from the cab, loosing a stream of long-stifled curses. Chom-gae seized the moment and dashed toward the village. Whether he got caught, or got a bullet in the back of his head, that he left to the will of Heaven. He had no choice but to run for his life.

Within a few minutes Chom-gae reached the house. The gate was closed but not bolted. When he rushed into the yard he found no sign of people. All was quiet as he crossed the yard and entered the shed. It was so dark that he couldn't see more than two steps ahead, but he did manage to see the tools hanging on the wall.

Even in that moment of crisis, the implements that used to hang in the Choi's stable at Woljon-ri flashed into Chom-gae's mind. He quickly snatched a scythe from its hook. If the felt hat dashed in with a gun aimed at him, he'd have to hurl the scythe at him. Even if it meant committing murder, and living as a fugitive the rest of his life, fate had allowed him no alternatives.

He held his breath, listening for the slightest sound from outside the gate. From afar he heard the motor of the truck start up, and then the sound as it slowly got underway. Not long after the truck moved out away beyond the fence, the owner of the house walked into the yard, his shoulders drooping.

The instant he was through the gate he bolted it. Then, as if he'd been right on Chom-gae's heels, he came straight to the shed and helped Chom-gae up from where he lay on his stomach. They hadn't moved more than a few steps toward the kitchen when the piercing sound of sirens blowing reached their ears. Chom-gae froze. The man of the house said,

"Looks like they know you're gone. But this is a good place to hide. They say the darkest spot is under the candlestick, don't they? Let's try to believe it."

"But they have to know I couldn't have gone far."

"Even so, you won't get away if you try to make a run for it now. Let's leave it to Heaven. If we try to escape from here now, it'll be the end of both of us."

"Who are you, anyway?"

"Introductions can wait until we see whether we'll survive."

They went into the kitchen, where the stench of garbage and sewage was almost unbearable. A few ears of corn were hanging from the sooty ceiling, dripping rainwater. They walked out of the kitchen through the door leading to the back part of the house. Sitting in disarray on the terrace were earthen jars of all sizes.

The man of the house took the lid off of a huge jar, directing Chom-gae to it with his chin. Once Chom-gae had crawled inside he replaced the lid. Footsteps and excited voices were heard just outside the gate and Chom-gae dared not breathe.

The owner of the house sat himself down in the room and lit a pipe. When shouts from outside ordered him to open up, he took his time going to unbolt the gate. Two young men dressed in western suits stood there pointing guns at him, and one of them snarled,

"The bastard's jumped into your house, right?"

The man of the house looked blankly at the two agitated men.

"You saw him, didn't you?!"

"I could make more sense out of thunder on a clear day than what you're saying. What brings you here anyway?"

"You're one of the men who helped get the truck out of the mud just now, aren't you?"

"Sure enough. They begged me to lend a hand, so what's wrong with that?"

"Nothing's wrong with that, but one of the bastards being moved took advantage of the confusion to escape."

"Escaped? But we saw them all hopping back up on the truck and then we went home. That's all."

"We think you're an accomplice. The prisoner's ropes had been cut."

"What are you talking about, accomplice?"

"I mean you had a hand in his escape!"

"You need bait for fishing, even fishing for an innocent man. You round up bystanders to do hard work in this cold rain, and then, instead of paying us for helping you out, you make an innocent man out to be some kind of a criminal and try to arrest me! I don't know what all this stuff about accomplices is about, but I had nothing to do with it!"

The man of the house had just turned around, as though he were too weary to argue any longer, when the order "Search the house!" rolled forth. The two pursuers were brandishing flashlights, and every time the beam paused on the face of the owner, he pursed his lips in an expression of contempt.

As they hurriedly searched through the house, the two young men looked more and more disappointed. One of them, who was constantly shaking the water off the visor of his hat, muttered,

"Should've searched them all thoroughly when they were loaded on the truck for transfer. Or, he might have found a piece of metal scrap in the truck. The real mistake was to let them down from the truck at all."

"The driver, isn't he a suspect, too?"

"Can't blame him. Not much he could do when the wheels got stuck in the mud. It wasn't like he'd deliberately chosen the route."

"Maybe he dropped a shard of metal in the truck."

"It's possible, but we can't arrest him with no evidence."

"The bastard's already vanished into thin air. Must be damn fast on his feet, and he's not even able-bodied, either."

"Our worst blunder was that the shortness of the distance made us overconfident. He could be pretty far away by now. The search orders are already out and there's a chance the others will bring him in."

One of the young men pointed his finger at the man of the house, who was sitting down puffing on his pipe, and said,

"If you see anybody suspicious, you better report it to us right away."

"You needn't worry, at the first sound of 'comm' in 'communists', I'll be on my way to let you know. But let's get clear about one thing."

"What?"

"Stop harrassing innocent citizens just because you've got an emergency on your hands. A single word from your mouth can make our hearts drop like a rock, you know that, don't you?"

The two young men gave cursory nods at these words from the man of the house, who was almost at the point of raising his voice. As they headed toward the gate to leave, their rifles were slung over their shoulders with the muzzles aiming at the ground. The householder sat there and smoked without stirring until no trace of their footsteps could be heard and the only sound in his ears was that of the falling rain.

Not until he was sure that the coast was clear did he head out to the backyard, take the lid off the jar and help Chom-gae out. Then, instead of leading him to the room where Kil-nyo was staying, he took Chom-gae to the main room and had him change out of his wet clothes.

"God, this is terrible. I'm amazed you're still alive."

So spoke the man of the house at the sight of the caked blood on Chom-gae's abdomen and the serpentine lacerations on his chest and back.

"What next?"

"Let's wait a bit. You can hide here for at least ten days or so. Remember, one false step will take you straight to hell. If I play my cards right they won't suspect this place for a while."

"To hear you so confident is music to my ears, but who are you, anyway, to take such trouble for me? You're risking your own life, isn't that true?"

"I've done nothing to risk my life. And don't try too hard to find out my name. I'm no ideologue, not a communist, nor am I a spy. Whatever happens, I'm content just to lead the life of a citizen. One thing I should make clear is that this whole thing was not my idea, what I did was as a favor to somebody else."

"What do you mean, 'favor'?"

"Care for a smoke?"

"Yes, thanks."

Chom-gae, barely able to keep his balance as he sat up, half snatched the pipe that the man of the house had loaded with leaf tobacco. Once it was lit for him, Chom-gae took a ravenous puff until his cheeks went hollow. Then he peered about the room and asked,

"How come the house is dead quiet?"

"Not long ago I had my family moved elsewhere. But we're not the only ones keeping the place quiet right now."

"Then you have other worries, too, eh?"

"Quick of you to catch my drift, but no need to be too alarmed. It's your family who's here."

"My family?"

"That's right."

Glaring through the darkness into the man's face, Chom-gae put down the pipe and in a tone of utter disbelief said,

"I have no family any more, and even if I once did, it's been more than two years since I left them, and they had no way of knowing what became of me."

"You needn't deny it now. They're right here, staying in the back room of this house, so why don't you go on back and see them? Remember, though, you better be quiet as a pair of cats or there'll be hell to pay."

"I'll go all right, but nine chances out of ten you've mistaken me for somebody else. Even if my wife had gotten word of me, she's too ignorant to have found me all the way down here."

The man of the house motioned for Chom-gae to sit down and then left. The rain had slackened somewhat, and first light was already slowly breaking. A few minutes later the side door opened and from the yard a woman cradling a baby in her arms came into the room.

When the door opened Chom-gae saw that it was a woman entering the room, but he didn't recognize her, even when she sat down before him and grabbed his hands. Since losing one of his eyes, he'd been having trouble discerning faces. Chom-gae cocked his head slightly to avoid looking at the other person head on. When the sharp voice of Shin Kil-nyo reached his eardrums he knew it was her.

"Can it really be you?"

Startled by her voice, he cried,

"Why, what in the world brought you here, ma'am?"

Oblivious to the question, Kil-nyo was carefully scrutinizing his appearance. His hair was disheveled and he was clad in a thin jacket. But he was not the Chom-gae of old. He was nothing but skin and bones, and the wound around his lost eye looked like a squashed cake due to lack of medical attention.

The cuffs of his shirt and jacket were hardened with dirt and dried blood. His trousers still gave forth a fishy stench of blood. Kil-nyo laid the baby down on the floor and went into the kitchen to make a fire. As she arranged the kindling tears kept falling onto her skirt.

Meantime, the two men's voices drifted out from the room. Chom-gae's was barely audible. Kil-nyo hastily filled a big basin with water and took it in, asking the man of the house to leave so she could undress Chom-gae. He resisted like a little child, but with no strength left he could not withstand Kil-nyo's willfulness. After removing his shirt, she took of his ragged pants. Once he was stark naked, she started to wash him with a hot towel. Not a single spot on his skin was unmarred, and the tears in Kil-nyo's eyes made it hard for her to see as she cleaned his body. How could such a strong and sturdy man have become such a wreck? Chom-gae kept demanding his clothes, but Kil-nyo went ahead all the way to his feet before she dressed him in some clothes borrowed from the owner of the house.

"Just what happened to you, ma'am?"

"That can wait till later."

"How come you're always so courteous with me?"

"Now that the whole world is enlightened, there's no such thing as low or high birth any longer. No need to talk about it."

"I see you've had a healthy baby, but you don't look well. Did you rush here before you were recovered from the childbirth?"

" . . . . "

"I'm wondering how you found out about my predicament. I never sent any message."

"I said that can wait till later. First, we've got to figure out a way to get away from this place."

Kil-nyo fetched a dirty pillow and placed it under his head. Chom-gae laid down and she put the baby beside him. Outside the sun was shining brightly and the man of the house was sharpening blades in the shed as always. Like a wife might to her husband lying beside her in bed, she told him in a soft voice,

"Every night I went to the salt house and listened in on the interrogations inside. I had no idea who was being questioned, but from time to time I heard your name mentioned."

"I don't know why they'd be talking about me."

"I didn't catch it all, but a few days ago the interrogator was questioning a very well-schooled man."

"Not questioning but torturing, I guess."

"There's nothing stubborner than a man's will to survive, I think. To me it seems there are lots of people in this world who'd be better off dead than...."

"Don't say such things, ma'am. You've got to live long enough to see the world changed for the better. I want to live. I won't welcome death until I've seen a brighter world, even with only one eye."

"This prisoner that the interrogator called 'sir' spoke of you with great respect, and he got very upset when the interrogator talked ill of you."

"Among those arrested with me there were quite a few learned men."

"It was a mystery to me why those gentlemen thought so highly of you. I know it's not right to look down on others, but you can't even read and to deal with their sort would be beyond your power, let alone to be revered by them."

"You don't understand, ma'am."

"What do you mean?"

"After I lost my eye and passed out, I thought I was dying for sure. That I'd refused to talk the whole time until then seemed a total waste, worth nothing. I decided to confess. That was when those admirers of mine who shared my cell took to persuading me. They said I shouldn't."

"Why not?"

"If I confessed, they said, I'd surely lose my other eye, too. That was their argument. But I said I didn't care anymore whether I ever saw their bright, new world. Then the older man they took as their leader stuck a dagger in my side. It'd never occurred to me that they could've snuck a dagger into the cell. If I talked, I'd leave the prison feet first—that's what he promised me.

"After that, every time I was taken out to be tortured, they told me if I held out they'd find some way to get me out of prison alive, but if I ever revealed the inner secrets he'd make sure I was cut into pieces that very night.

"Those well-educated admirers of mine, when we were in the same cell they never let me sleep at all. They took turns keeping me awake, shoving me around the floor whenever I started to nod off. It was a relief to be taken out for interrogation, though I could barely control myself because of the complete lack of sleep.

"Half the time, I couldn't make heads or tails out of the interrogator's questions. Maybe he thought I had guts, but that was never my intention. Even if the interrogators were lying when they said they wanted to release me, I wanted to believe them. When the other men in my cell found out that I didn't confess, they started to address me as 'sir' or 'Mister Hwang'.

"They gave me the best seat in the cell, and the word was spread all over the prison that 'Even after losing an eye, Mister Hwang is not caving in.' Whenever I left the cell, the other prisoners shouted 'Mr. Hwang! Mr. Hwang!', clapping their hands or pounding the floor.

"I didn't have the slightest idea what was going on. All I knew was that to be worthy of their outbreaks I was supposed to doze in front of the interrogators, laying myself open to all sorts of torture. Then I'd return half-dead to my cell and be kept awake so I could doze again the next day."

The sound of a whistle was heard, followed by the rustle of footsteps as somebody moved by just outside the wall. There was tension for a moment, but then the whistling and other noises abruptly ceased. From the shed the sound of sickles being sharpened droned on. The baby began to fuss. How, Kilnyo wondered, could so many sounds be distinguished?

The evening before she'd been able despite the rain to make out the faint rumble of the truck engine as it came closer to the house. There had been no sound of passing vehicles since. Pulling the truck out of the mud created a big commotion and she'd heard the men who'd come in search of Chom-gae, but no longer could she recall what their voices sounded like.

Now, all of a sudden, every single sound was so crystal clear that she could visualize everything going on in the area surrounding the house. Maybe earlier she had been too tense to hear such things, she told herself. She set the baby down and got to her feet. Opening the door, she stepped down into the backyard.

On the steps were a pair of mud-caked work shoes. As she shook the mud off of them, she was startled because they seemed familiar, but she couldn't tell where she'd seen that pair of shoes before. They were too small for Chom-gae. Tears well-ed up in her eyes as she stared down at them. She lifted her head and turned her gaze absent-mindedly toward the salt house, its vague outlines barely visible under the dense cover of fog.

Chains

There was nowhere to go. Hunger might have been eased somewhat by sleep, and road weariness might have been dealt with by a rest every so often. But how much more wretched than being poor it was to be a healthy soul with no place to call home and nowhere at all to go. For Kil-nyo this was not just a decision to be made, it was a fall into despair.

Every place she had been she had left footsteps behind, but looking back, all those places seemed a million miles away. They had been frightful, ugly places, and to return to any of them would have been like trudging to forbidding zones at the ends of the earth.

Woljon-ri and Sokpo-ri would greet her with jeers and sneers. In the little hamlet of Wonjon, suspicions had likely been snowballing since she left, and Cha Pyong-jo's bait would be there if she returned. As for her own family in Hamyang, there she would be sure to hit a thick wall of heartlessness and unrelenting reproaches.

All the same, she had no excuse to stay where she was much longer. She meant to take her leave, but she lacked a destination. Maybe she had grown so accustomed to partings that she had been deliberating avoiding settling down with anyone new. Becoming inured to farewells may have stemmed partly from her helplessness in the face of worldly matters, but it stemmed too from the insane turmoil of an age that refused to let her stand on her own two feet.

One thing was clear—the indescribable loneliness and the deep feeling of peril that were wrenching her body into knots every second, these she had to deal with alone if she was to survive at all. When a person is unable to struggle through the shadows of suffering, it's a relief to know that suicide is a way out that can be chosen. Whatever the consequences turn out to be, it at least offers a chance to gaze back at the way one has traveled along the precipice of despair.

Kil-nyo felt she was perched on the edge of that precipice. Yet she had found many others gathered on the same cliff—the man of the house, Chom-gae, the other prisoners in the salt house, and the tiny baby whose life was totally dependent on her.

This discovery was no trifling consolation to Kil-nyo. It helped her to see that she, too, had a dream of the future. To bring up the little baby until she could walk on her own, and to have the chance to see her son, Chunbok, someday—these were hopes that gave her a reason to live, even when she had no place to turn to.

Kil-nyo brushed all the dirt off the pair of shoes that she'd found sitting on the back step. Inside the shoes she noticed distinct imprints of feet that could not have been Chom-gae's. Those traces were not unfamiliar. She knew they had to be Chi Sang-mo's.

Without her knowledge, Chi had walked through the valley of despair more than once, as the marks in these shoes testified. That his footprints were not yet erased showed he had been around there not long before. It was something totally unexpected. That he never had showed any sign of involvement with Chom-gae made the whole mess even more terrifying to Kil-nyo.

She clearly recalled what Chi Sang-mo had said—some bastards say they're rightists and others say they're leftists, but all of them are jumping about like they've been struck by lightning and he had no intention of venturing out on the perilously thin ice of world politics.

To her, these shoes meant that Chi Sang-mo was loitering about in the shadows somewhere nearby, and that surely would lead to some unforeseeable misfortune for her. She told herself she had to do everything in her power to drive him as far away as possible. That meant she had to find him before he found her. If the order was reversed, she'd be stuck deeper in the mire than she already was.

A bitter smile came to Kil-nyo's lips. Even to herself she seemed a strange woman, a woman beyond comprehension. She could make no sense out of what she was about to do—track down a man she once had waited for with longing, but now here she was trying to avoid him at all costs. She picked up the worn old shoes and placed them on a wooden chest sitting up on a shelf. Then she sat back down next to Chom-gae, who was still lying there half-senseless. As she fed the child, she nonchalantly asked,

"Those shoes don't look like they fit you. For a long journey, there's nothing more important than a good pair of shoes...."

"To me, shoes are a luxury. In the old days, I always went barefoot—shoes seemed too cumbersome."

"When you were young and healthy that'd do, but you better wear them now. By the way, where did you get this pair?"

As Chom-gae flashed a glance at Kil-nyo, a thin smile appeared on his lips.

"Stole 'em."

"Hard as life is these days, I'm surprised you came across a pair of shoes worth stealing."

"It was something no prisoner would dream of, but during the transfer I saw them laying in the bed of the truck. I'd given my shoes to a man who was released from prison some time ago. When I saw this pair in the truck, I was seized by an impulse to have them.

"Ordinarily, shoes would strike me as useless, even a whole pile of them. But once I had snatched these and stuffed them inside my coat, it gave me a strong urge to go on living—an urge as strong as a burning flame. Thinking back on it now, maybe it was a good omen that I'd be running into you. In times like these with shoes so scarce, I wonder why someone would've left them laying there...."

"They must have belonged to somebody...."

"I bet they were the truck driver's. Later I saw him hopping about barefoot in the mud. Still, I was scared out of my wits that he'd notice they were gone. Without these shoes, I couldn't have made a run for it like I did."

"In a way, then, he saved your life. Not just because of the shoes; he was the one who brought you here, though it's true he was paid to drive the truck."

"That wasn't how it was."

"What do you mean?"

"From the way he kept sparring with the big shot in charge of the transfer, it was clear enough he'd been drafted for the job on account of some trouble he'd gotten into. There was sure something fishy about the way he acted, but the story behind it was a mystery to me. Men are killed like flies these days, and he must've done something to fall into that fix. He must have had some bad luck, no doubt."

"Whatever his situation was, it'd be nice to run into him again to repay him for helping you out. We have little enough, but we shouldn't be stingy in showing our gratitude."

"Nobody'll deny what you say, but there's about as much chance of seeing him again as there is of a pig sprouting wings. Maybe they'll scapegoat him for losing me. And if they transfer others here, the security will be tighter than ever, you can count on that."

To Kil-nyo it was utterly astonishing that Chi Sang-mo could have been behind the escape of Hwang Chom-gae. But then, as Chom-gae said, in these days when men were dying like dogs, it'd come as no surprise if Chi Sang-mo had met a cruel demise. Nor was an unjust fate looming before Chom-gae and Sang-mo alone, the same was happening to people all over the country. Such being the general state of things, Chom-gae couldn't be blamed for the ill-starred destiny of others.

Cuddling her baby, who was desperately suckling at a milkless breast, Kil-nyo walked out to the front yard. The sun had been down for a while and in the distance the mountains were slowly submerging into the darkness. The man of the house was not in the shed and she was about to turn back when he abruptly appeared from the direction of the outhouse.

"Where do you think you're going?"

His voice had a surly edge.

"I wasn't going anywhere."

"You should stay put in the house, then. I've told you a thousand times not to leave your room. If you don't have any common sense, you should at least do as you're told."

"There's something important I have to tell you."

"All the more reason to stay inside. The yard around my outhouse is like a marketplace. Come on, follow me."

Kil-nyo left a nipple in the baby's mouth as the two of them sat crouching against the back wall. The man had already half-guessed what she was going to say, and spoke first:

"It's too early. Don't be impatient, just wait a while longer. To work for the communist party in the South is not as easy as flipping your palm. You seem a good-hearted woman, but you're too impatient, that's the problem."

"There's a man I've got to find."

"Who?"

"The truck driver who transferred the man inside."

"Now that is a problem, all right. I can't make heads or tails of this nonsense you're spouting. What in the world would you do if you found him? Is it revenge you're after?"

"No, not revenge. I just mean to get word of his whereabouts. He's saved a life, so how could I dare think ill of him? I should try to repay him for helping us."

"Busybodies don't know when to quit, and that's a saying made for you. Even if you feel bound to show your thanks, what you're saying is crazy. In our fix we have to keep wary at each second. If you just keep that gratitude in your heart, you'll run into him someday, I'm certain. You've got to be sensible or you're headed for a catastrophe."

"All I want to know is where he's staying. And the only one in the house who can dare to go out is you, right?"

"It's beyond me what you have in mind, but I don't have to leave the house to ask after him. As far as I know, he was hauled off by the man in charge of the transfer. It was his bad luck to get hooked up by chance with the scum of the earth."

"But he didn't do anything wrong."

"When the world goes to the dogs, there's no shortage of slander and false accusations. For a man with guts it's better to roll in the dogshit than to just let it be poured all over you."

Kil-nyo pulled the baby's head up from slipping down under her breasts and closed her eyes. That familiar sound of rolling thunder that had crashed down the hillside at Woljon-ri was rapidly approaching from the distance. Suddenly the baby burst into a shriek and spit up all the milk she'd swallowed. The owner of the house instantly reached over from where he sat and muffled the baby's wail. Seeing that Kil-nyo was oblivious to the baby's crying, he snatched the blanketed infant and rushed it into the back room

At that very moment, heavy footsteps could be heard moving along the outside of the wall towards the gate. The door was slightly ajar, and three men in western suits with rifles slung over their shoulders kicked it open and walked into the yard.

They called out for the owner of the house, but the tone of their voices was less abrasive than that of the two young men who'd come in from the rain to search the place a few nights before. The man of the house handed the baby over to Kil-nyo, who'd followed him inside, and then he walked out into the front yard, not hurrying at all.

"Are you Pak Sok-ho?"

Surveying the three men with a critical eye, the man of the house replied in a resigned voice,

"Yes, what's this all about?"

"How long have you lived here?"

The man of the house adopted a puzzled expression and said,

"Let me see... I'm awful dull with arithmetic, so if you rush me it'll take even longer to get it right."

"Unless you're an idiot, it shouldn't be too hard to spit it out. How long have you lived here?"

"That's why I told you I'm clumsy with figures."

"We heard it's been over ten years since you slipped into this area from somewhere, is that true?"

The tone of the young man's voice, at first cordial enough, was growing more skeptical, far from a good portent. Nevertheless, the man of the house kept on responding with non sequiturs.

"Ten years alters even mountains and rivers, that's what they say. So, I can't recall just when it was, but now I'm treated like one of the natives here. We tend to think it's only natural to stay put where you're born, but nature's way is for all living creatures to move about till they find the best place to live. The beasts do it all the time, so there's nothing surprising about my case, is there?"

The young men patiently listened to this long-winded response to their simple question, then one of them said,

"The difference between beasts and humans is that humans don't change their home without a reason. Judging from your ability to argue, it's unlikely you moved here for no reason, like a wandering beast, eh?"

At this the man of the house looked visibly perturbed.

"You've put me on the spot, demanding a clear-cut answer. Well, I don't have one handy at the moment. Had I known I'd be pressed like this, I would've written up something for the occasion, but you've taken me by surprise. Back when I was helping a peddler, we moved about by donkey cart from one market to the next, and when I used to make my living as a laborer I went wherever I could find work. I wandered all over the country before ending up here, and after a few months as a day-laborer I decided to settle down.

"So, despite what you say, there was no special reason for my home being here. And I don't think I'm unusual, quite a few people's lives go the same way, don't you think? How come, with things in such a mess, you are going around trying to root out the pasts of innocent people who never had anything to hide from anybody?"

"You talk too much. That makes you suspicious, don't you think?"

"Speaking of suspicious, to me you are the ones who're suspicious. If I talk little you insult me by calling me a mute, and if my replies make sense you accuse me of an ideological offense—so, if you look at the thing fair and square, which of us is suspicious, you or me? Let stop somebody passing on the street and ask his opinion."

"Why did you send your family away and stay here all by yourself? Besides, from dawn to dusk all you do is sharpen useless tools. Is that what you call living a logical life? You're either waiting for some convicts to be transferred, or plotting with others to help some of those bastards escape, that's what you have in mind, isn't it? You may not show it, but we've scared you all right, haven't we?"

"You must have come here knowing quite well that I've no such idea, even if I could do it."

"This woman in your house, what's she to you? Stop beating around the bush, you'd better speak up straight."

"If you suspect me of lying, what's the point of asking so many questions? Why not ask the woman herself? Then you'll have a simple answer for your question, right off."

"Just keep on being uncooperative and we'll take you in for a real taste of interrogation. If you cooperate, though, you'll be living a much better life. Now, tell us, who is she?"

"She's no blood relation of mine. Just drifted in here looking for some work to eke out a living. She was in such pathetic shape that I temporarily let her have a place to stay. She has a baby and I didn't have the heart to just throw her out on the street."

As questions and answers were exchanged, the three young men from time to time sent glances toward the main room where Chom-gae was sleeping and toward the path leading to the back room. Unlike the previous visit, this time they made no search of the house. The man of the house had succeeded through his snide retorts and non sequiturs in focusing their suspicions upon himself at the risk of arrest.

That night Chom-gae realized how experienced the man of the house was in dealing with the powers that be. Had those three officers inadvertantly opened the door to the main room, the whole house would have instantly been reduced to a smoking ruin, not to mention the fate Chom-gae would have faced. Nevertheless, the owner of the house had never been caught without a rejoinder in dealing with them.

The three men's footsteps were heard as they exited through the gate and moved away. Within a few seconds, the gate had been locked and the man of the house appeared in the back room.

"You have to leave tonight."

" .... "

"In your situation it make's no difference when you leave, there's nowhere you're heading anyway. Those guys sniffed something suspicious here, so from now on every day you stay would be like walking on thin ice. It's best for you to get as far away as possible, before they happen on some evidence and rush back here."

"To leave is something I'm ready to do, but the baby's feverish and Mr. Hwang is still in no condition to travel, so I feel beaten before we even start."

"Even when you're totally alone, if you make a go of it there's bound to be a hill to lean on in this world. You still have your health, so if you swallow your pride and are willing to work, the baby won't starve. It's not unheard of for a widow to bring up a child on milk begged from other women."

"If we're stopped and searched, they're sure to arrest us. What would happen to the baby then?"

"Don't worry. When the world is topsy-turvy, it may be better to act against your better judgment if you want to survive. The fact that you have a baby may even save you from a catastrophe, instead of the baby being in the way. It's not the baby but the father that you should be concerned about. If he's stopped, it'll be the end of him. The eye he's lost is too conspicuous to hide."

"I hadn't thought of that, but it can't be that unusual, there are others who have been crippled by the loss of an eye."

"But that's not much help if your husband is an important leader who's widely known. They'll no doubt be on special alert and searching everywhere for him if he's a notorious rebel."

"He can't be that famous, I know that."

"I hope you're right, because things will be easier then."

"You don't understand. His whole life he's just been a handyman working for others, minding livestock or ploughing the fields. He's had no schooling at all, a common farmer who knows nothing of the world."

"Sounds like you don't know that in the communist party around here, the lower your birth, the higher you're regarded."

"That makes no sense. Where've all the high and mighty gone, then?"

"For you and I to sit here in this room debating about the political big shots is like blind men arguing over the shape of an elephant. You might as well go ahead and get ready for your departure. I'll tell you one trick. Wrap your husband's head with a few towels. If they stop you for questioning, just say in a calm voice that he's come down with the mumps. You never know, you might scare them off as easily as that."

Outside the gate it was already so dark that you couldn't see three steps ahead. Kil-nyo's heart was just as dark as they set off, not knowing whether to head to the west or to the south. The only thing clear was that to save their necks they had no choice but to leave the house behind.

She had one-eyed Chom-gae lead the way, following with the baby on her back. As dark as it was, it made no difference whether the leader had one eye or two. They couldn't even dream of traveling on the main road, which was occasionally lit by the headlights of passing cars, but had to move through seldom-used alleys and back streets. Even though their progress was slow, it seemed they could cover ten or fifteen miles by dawn.

In all events, they wouldn't have dared to flee except in the middle of the night. When they stumbled on the sharp edge of a stone, her kneecaps were pierced to the marrow with pain. They were startled out of their wits when they turned a corner and ran up upon a menacing old tree.

Fatigue grew overwhelming, especially when they heard dogs barking as they passed by small hamlets. They rarely spoke and just lumbered on heedlessly through the bushes liked dumb animals. The farther they got from Andong, the heavier Kil-nyo's heart grew.

She regretted not having tried harder to find out what happened to Chi Sang-mo after his arrest. If the man of the house, whose name she later learned was Pak Sok-ho, had gone out of his way to check on the matter, she would have had some notion of what Chi might be going through. But there had been no time to persuade Pak.

Even if she had cared to divulge to Pak the whole sordid story of her life, there just hadn't been time. She felt she'd fallen into a fate like that of an unskilled seamstress whose doomed forever to go on mending. All the same, she could not remain indifferent to Chi's fate. They had mixed flesh and she was now carrying his baby on her back.

She had not been able to ignore Chom-gae when he was in great hardship, and now it seemed that Chi had been arrested for his part in Chom-gae's escape. To blame Chom-gae would be pointless, though, and no good could possibly come of it. When her thoughts reached this point, it began vaguely to dawn on Kil-nyo where her destination should be.

As day began to break, the mountains in the distance slowly revealed themselves in dark gray. Their stomachs, already empty when they set off from the house of Pak Sok-ho, by this time were aching from hunger. Their only hope to get any food was to stop before the sun was up at one of the remote farmhouses on the way and beg for a handout. But Kil-nyo had no idea where they were.

Along one of the main roads, they could at least have spotted a landmark of some kind. But nothing like that was to be expected up in the mountains. Exhausted, she paused to watch the thin fog envelope the mountain valley, propping herself against a mudbank beside a field.

An old farmer came into sight walking towards them, two buckets hanging from a staff on his shoulders. Chom-gae, his pants down, at once leapt to the ground and crouched in the grass. Kil-nyo moved higher up onto the bank and sat there with her face turned away. Without exchanging a word, each of them had something in mind.

The old farmer was about to pass by Kil-nyo, but then he turned back, saying,

"Looks like you've been walking all night."

Kil-nyo pointed with her chin to Chom-gae, who was pulling up his pants as he got to his feet, replying,

"My husband's not well, so we tried to save some steps by taking a shortcut, but with no moon on a strange road we ended up getting lost."

"On a moonless night you should use the stars to find your way. It's a pity, a woman of your age and you never learned to tell directions from the stars."

"I figured it'd be easier to count on the road under our feet than the stars in the sky, but I was wrong. Now that it's light we ought to be looking for the main road."

"From here it'll still be more than five miles before a main road comes into sight."

"How far to the closest village?"

"A good fifteen miles at least. Seems you two sure enough are lost way back here in these hills. But you can't expect to see too well at night on empty stomachs."

At this expression of concern from the farmer Kil-nyo felt much relieved. When they left she'd hoped to put at least ten or twelve miles between them and Andong, and she was happy to hear they'd traveled that and then some. Mountain people were renowned for their hospitality to passing strangers.

The farmer gave the once over to Kil-nyo, who despite the arduous journey was a rather nice-looking woman. At the sight of Chom-gae approaching toward the bank the old man tut-tut-ted,

"I don't know what you've been through, but it's a pity you have to be on the road with a man in that shape. Looks like he's got the mumps."

"With him in that condition we couldn't even ask to stay with our relatives, so we hurried on our way and ended up lost. What he has is so contagious we can't very well stop in a village, so now we don't even have any way to get a meal."

"Your heart, thinking of others first, is as nice as your looks. I'll send my wife to bring you a bite to eat, meantime, you can take a rest under the big tree down here at the mouth of the village. Bringing a man with mumps in there may cause a commotion, so just bear with it, even if you don't get much of a welcome."

Kil-nyo and Chom-gae, who'd been watching the farmer put the buckets back on his shoulder, got to their feet and headed toward the big tree the farmer had pointed out. They could have gone on despite the hunger, but Kil-nyo needed to eat for the baby's sake. It seemed foolish to go on when food was offered.

When the farmer's wife appeared with a potful of rice, Kil-nyo bantered with her to find out the shortest way to Yochon, also asking the way to Andong just to allay any possible suspicion.

In the mountains there were quite a few people who had reason to avoid the big cities—trespassers who hunted for gin-seng and medicinal herbs and woodcutters who felled trees illegally—so Chom-gae didn't have to worry much about concealing his identity.

It was exactly five days after leaving Andong that they reached a small hamlet from which Sangju was supposed to be right under their noses. The shortcut had taken them at least twice as long as the journey would've taken if they could have traveled the main road.

Now they were far enough away to venture into the village, with Chom-gae pretending he was suffering from a bad eye ailment. With food no longer so hard to come by through begging, they even grew a bit secure. The only thing that might strike some people as suspicious was the fact that a rough character like Chom-gae with a peasant's build and a grotesque face made a rather unlikely husband for a good-looking woman like Kil-nyo. Though not suspected as fugitives, they often attracted jeers for that very reason.

One day they reached a village around dusk and managed to get the use of a room in the outbuildings of the local notables, a quite well-to-do family. There was no furniture, only a strawmat for the floor, but for the first time in ages they could sleep with blankets over their bellies.

Like cotton soaked in water, Kil-nyo felt fatigue in every fiber of her being. She was too tired even to open her mouth. She must have fallen asleep, for when she woke with a start she found Chom-gae massaging her legs. Surprised at first, she nearly pulled herself away, but then she decided to stay still.

Chom-gae evidently had been touching her for some time, but in sleep she hadn't been aware of it. His hands were kneading her calves, and then once or twice they hesitantly moved up above the knees to her thighs and then back down. She could feel a slight tremor in his hands.

Kil-nyo felt her heartbeat growing irregular. The draft moving in from the crack of the door was not terribly chilly, and from this she guessed it must have been a little past midnight. There was enough moonlight in the room to see fairly well, and she couldn't readily gauge Chom-gae's intentions. He had lit the lamp. Even in the dark, he was not the sort of man who would force himself upon her. Not so much because he was a good-natured man, but more because of the wall between them that would never let him treat her like someone he found languishing in a winehouse.

Even so, Kil-nyo's heart was skipping beats. She told herself to be resolute, but despite everything she grasped Chom-gae's hands as they fumbled around her abdomen. This time it was Chom-gae who was startled out of his wits. For a second he just stared at her with a blank look. But she did not loosen her grip.

It was a sufficient signal for a new kind of relationship to have been born then and there. If she only released his hands, Chom-gae's body would have naturally fallen on hers. But Chom-gae pulled back his hands and said,

"Sorry to wake you, ma'am. You were talking in your sleep and seemed restless, so I turned on the light and found you soaked with a cold sweat. I was kneading your legs hoping to ease the fatigue of the journey."

Kil-nyo gulped to moisten her burning throat and replied,

"You needn't worry about me. Try to get some sleep yourself. You must be just as tired from the long trip. Your hands are burning hot, are you sure you don't have a fever?"

"Fever? No, ma'am. Here, see for yourself, I'm quite all right."

This time Chom-gae took hold of her hands. It was not just to prove he had no fever, it seemed. Maybe he was trying to undo the embarrassment she must have felt. Kil-nyo wiped her forehead with her sleeve and, rearranging her skirt to cover her abdomen, sat up. She looked down at her side to find the baby fast asleep.

"It was my fault to wake you up, ma'am."

"No, I was just too beat to stay awake."

Chom-gae peered up at the ceiling for a while and then his eyes came to rest upon the lighted lamp.

"We've been running up to here, and for now we can breathe a little easier and not worry about getting nabbed, I reckon."

"They're not likely to forget about you so easily. It's too soon to feel safe."

"I can't go on running the rest of my life."

Judging from the way he spat out these words, Kil-nyo knew there was something unsaid behind them. But she felt sick at heart, not knowing what it was he had in mind.

"I've been meaning to speak up, and now that we've made it

this far, I think we'll have to part here. There's only so long we can go on pretending to be man and wife. We're from different classes—it's plain to see from the way we look and the way we act. Everybody notices it and sooner or later it'll cause suspicion, I'm afraid.

"Besides, with me unable to show my face we've been eating up what little money you'd saved, and at this rate we'll soon end up beggars. Nobody is born to be a beggar, but when you don't have a penny in your pocket, that's how beggars get that way."

Kil-nyo's hands always started to quake when she was at a loss. To steady them, she hastily picked up the sleeping baby and held it in her arms.

"I can't let you go now. I know only too well that you're in no state to look for work, but I'm healthy enough and no matter what I do, cooking or washing or what not, I won't let the three of us starve."

"I've reached a safe place. But I'm such a fool I was slow to see that a place that's safe for me is dangerous for you."

"You mean to say one goes north and the other east from here?"

"It's only because that's what's best for both of us."

"They say even a bull has to have a hill to rub against. You and I are in the same boat, no family and not another soul to depend on in this world. What you're pressing me to do is crazy. Are you telling me you have some secret way to get rid of that scar on your face, that scar that can't be concealed? That man back in Andong told me I had to know myself to survive."

"That's just what I'm saying. Besides, it does no good to argue, and that's what we're doing. The truth is, I'm in no position to go with you where you have a mind to go."

"If you're so good at reading my mind, then tell me where I'm heading."

"I guessed it some time ago."

"Well, don't dawdle, speak up."

"Where the family of that child of yours is living, no doubt. I may be clumsy in dealing with people, but anybody who knows your heart would find it easy to guess what you have in mind."

Kil-nyo had been skeptical when she called his bluff, but upon hearing his answer it was she who was at a loss to reply. Maybe that was what made men so fearful, she thought—men have an uncanny ability, inexplicable even to themselves, that allows them to guess ten steps ahead when a woman takes a single step. As he looked at Kil-nyo, blushing like a little girl caught red-handed, Chom-gae vaguely smiled and said,

"To burden you any longer... nothing good will come of it. Just tell me where it is you're heading, please. Maybe I'll live to see the new world, or maybe I'll be damned and won't, but I'll see you again, that's for certain. Even if we were strangers with no old ties between us, I still'd owe you for my life, this second life I'm living now. So, born again a new man, how could I ever forget you, ma'am?"

"I'm not sure whether it's Kanggu or Pohang where the child's father used to live, I only know it's a port."

"You might as well go looking for a Kim in a big city. How can you take to the road with only that to go on?"

"I do know his full name."

"Well, no address is better than a man's full name."

The two of them went to bed, agreeing that further talk could await the next morning. Kil-nyo's racing heart had settled down a bit, and the baby was sound asleep. However she looked at, what Chom-gae said was right. After all, they couldn't live together the rest of their lives, and it would lessen the pain of parting if they went their separate ways when there was a good reason to say good-bye.

It had become clear that both of them had built up their lives so solidly there was just no room for one to interfere with the life of the other. The vicissitudes each had endured separately had made their lives too full to change now. That Kil-nyo already had a destination in mind was proof of it, as was Chom-gae's decision to go his own way at that moment in time.

What was more, Kil-nyo could not even tell the leftists from the rightists, while Chom-gae had already become a leading figure in one party. He still addressed her with the utmost courtesy, but she sensed a wall between them. He had been able gracefully to reject her sexual passion, and he had skillfully evaded her importunity.

All the same, the feeling she had in her heart for Chom-gae had not been damaged in the least, and that was indeed a mystery to her. That feeling, by itself, was enough to point toward an inevitable reunion in the future. Perhaps it was because Chunbok, her own flesh and blood, was lurking beneath that inevitability.

When she awoke the next morning with a start, Chom-gae was not laying beside her. She quickly reached over to check if the spot where he'd slept was still warm, but there was no trace of him. She opened the door, and one of the servants of the house who was sweeping outside cast a glance her way. Seeing her flustered, he imagined what must have happened and said,

"He said he had to leave on some urgent business and left without looking back even once."

The part about not looking back even once might have been the servant's embellishment to convey the message to Kil-nyo, but even so the words struck her with a crash. She knew further inquiries would be pointless, but she moved down onto the step with the baby in her arms and asked,

"When was it?"

The man stopped sweeping and gestured to the village gate, saying,

"It's been at least an hour since he stormed out in a rush, and at that pace he probably made four or five miles by now."

" . . . . "

"Between man and wife, he couldn't have left his family without some assurances, right?"

"Right."

Even after she'd said 'right', Kil-nyo herself was not exactly sure whether it meant 'yes' or 'no'. The sense of loneliness she felt at being on her own yet again was nearly unbearable. But she could not afford to indulge that feeling like an animal licking its wounds. The greater her loneliness, the clearer she could see what had to be done. Perhaps it was a gift unique to her.

As always, she felt no hesitation after encountering a dead end. She lifted the baby, fussy at being roused from sleep, onto her back, and without even asking the servant, headed straight over to the main house. She knew when she first saw it from outside the gate that it had to be the house of a wealthy family. Once inside, the order and spotlessness reminded her of the Choi house in Woljon-ri.

That this clan had maintained their property on such a scale and with such dignity during this time of great turmoil no doubt earned them great respect in the surrounding villages. The mistress of the house, a bit on the stout side, stood scrutinizing Kil-nyo, who had dared to invade the main hall before breakfast in order to seek a job as a charwoman.

"You've the look of a noble about you, but you must have been through a great deal—so drained you seem. People try to hold out on spite alone when life takes a wrong turn, but if you're born a lady you should learn to take care of yourself."

The mistress's words were sympathetic, yet they also conveyed a mild scolding of Kil-nyo for showing signs of her humiliating descent into the lower class.

"The father of your child, did he just take off at dawn and abandon you here?"

"He'd been trying to persuade me that he should head for one of the big cities to find work."

"No breeding to speak of. In your condition, how could you look down on the beasts? Didn't even coax him to stay, so you could remain a good-hearted woman, eh?"

"He'd already set his mind on it, and he wasn't about to change his mind at my pleas. It was just my lot, I'm afraid."

"If you go on letting yourself be tied down to your lot, you'll never be free from hardship. A man and wife have to share the joys and the pains together to keep their lives from falling apart, that's long been known."

Kil-nyo hung her head, anxious to hear the verdict. The mistress of the house summoned the head maid and ordered her to give some sewing work to Kil-nyo. It might have been due to the virtuous nature of the mistress that the kitchen maids and the other women working in the house welcomed an outsider with kindness, giving Kil-nyo no cause for dismay. Whenever Kil-nyo's baby took to crying, they took turns picking up the little one and calming her down. Not one of them ever mocked her for her clumsiness as a seamstress, nor did they report the fact to the mistress.

For the first time in a long while Kil-nyo was fed well enough to belch. Her tasks left her no idle moments, but now that she was at ease in body and mind she seemed to be putting on weight.

That household could not remain totally insulated from the outside world, however. All the goings on in the town or at the marketplace found their way into the kitchen of the house where the passed the lips of the maids.

"Even if I rinse my eyes and look again, I can never tell if a man is a red or a yellow, but those fellows can pick out the reds without a single mistake, just like they were picking weeds in a rice paddy."

"Don't be so foolish, a red isn't born with a brand on his forehead. You shouldn't feel so overjoyed about it, they're doing it to make a living, you know."

Feeling awkward at remaining silent, Kil-nyo decided to join in the gossip and asked,

"What sort of people are being taken away?"

"We're just ignorant women up here in a mountain village, we don't even know the sun's up till it's light outside or the sun's down till its dark. If we try to understand all the ins and outs of such things we'll end up with an ulcer."

"It could happen that an innocent man gets nabbed and beaten to death, don't you think?"

"Like a minnow caught in a net for big fish. They say quite a few people were taken away and tortured, all because of some slander."

"I sure wish they'd stop all this."

"Indeed. Lots of men have run away or disappeared from the village because of it. Some women became widows overnight, poor things."

"If that's the way things are here, must not be any better in the other villages, eh?"

"As a matter of fact, it's been months now since the youngest son of this family disappeared. Everybody knows it, but we all keep our mouths shut and you should, too. Some say he's been seen in the marketplace in town, but we still shush it up.

"One man even said he saw him about a fortnight ago, traveling at night with a one-eyed man. You can never plumb a man's heart. It's beyond me why a son of this family should leave a life of luxury and voluntarily seek out suffering. The youngest son of this house is known far and wide as the handsomest youth in these parts, and what's the world coming to if he's off somewhere in the company of a Cyclops?"

The inner quarters of the yard were quiet, dyed in the twilight of early May. In one corner the servant's little children were absorbed in a game of marbles. Kil-nyo forgot that she was building a fire, and from the kitchen gazed out at the children as they played.

Hearing a woman's scream, Kil-nyo was shaken to see that a burning piece of kindling had rolled out from the hearth and was about to set the hem of her skirt ablaze. Fortunately, the other woman hurriedly fetched a pail of water and quenched the ember, else Kil-nyo might have burned the house to the ground.

The women being as they were, instead of chastising Kil-nyo for her carelessness, once the peril had passed they took to teasing her in a joking way.

"You just about incinerated that mortar of yours, then you'd end up lugging it around without a pestle the rest of your life."

At the burst of laughter from the other two women, the baby on Kil-nyo's back was startled and emitted a piercing shriek. That night Kil-nyo made up her mind to leave the house. It had already been a month and a half since she had taken shelter there, and she was fearful that her presence might bring harm to the innocent. The more she thought about the report that the youngest son of the house had been seen in the company of a one-eyed man, the more sure she grew that it was no coincidence.

The news gave her a vague hope that she would be meeting Chom-gae again, but in such an hour of turmoil such a rendezvous could hardly end happily. Kil-nyo consoled herself with the thought that she should live as openly as the world was closed. The next morning right after breakfast she went into the main room to bid farewell.

The mistress did not seem greatly surprised at the announcement of her departure. It was not the first time she had dealt with a woman who was wandering like a nomad from place to place. She opened her purse and took out some money for Kil-nyo's journey. Just out of courtesy, she might have inquired about Kil-nyo's destination, but she asked no such thing. Perhaps she knew that a woman about to drift away would regard her curiosity as a mere nuisance.

As she left the house, Kil-nyo reminded herself how fortunate it was that she was still healthy. Had she been unable to work, she never would have made it alive as far as she had, nor could she have gathered money to move on, small sum though it was. Providence, it seemed, was on her side. For a woman destined for a hard life to be granted such favors made the present seem one of the most luxurious times she had ever known.

As soon as she reached town, she dipped into her travel money and bought a new pair of shoes. Her heart felt lighter and her step more lively. With money in hand, she decided to catch a ride. On the way to the port city of Kanggu, she constantly kept mulling over the preciousness of money. She had paid the requested fare in advance, but as the car passed along a deserted mountain road she more than once felt a sense of panic lest the driver suddenly pitch her out.

When at last they reached Kanggu, with its pungent fish-market air, she was so relieved she gladly would have handed over her shoes if the driver had asked her to. Once she was standing there at the ocean's edge gazing out at the sea, the future seemed too hazy and remote. Looking up at a row of dwellings hanging on the side of a hill, her heart started to pound at the thought Chi Sang-mo might appear at any moment.

The rest of the day until dusk Kil-nyo spent like someone selling door to door, calling at every single house lined up on the hillside. She carefully scrutinized the faces of the little boys in the alleys and of the little girls playing dolls in the shadows of the earthen walls. She even forgot to eat. Though she was hoping to run into a child resembling Chi Sang-mo, she knew her chances were about as good as catching a fish in a cucumber field.

On the following day she ended up out on the main pier. Along the docks, the traffic was hectic, with boats slipping in and out, trucks whizzing about, and carts full of fish and tackle constantly coming and going.

The mood was different from the hospitality of a mountain hamlet. The women had raucous voices and there were lots of rough-looking men who enjoyed trading wisecracks. Unlike in the mountains, there was no standing on ceremony here, and this made it easier to do some snooping.

For Kil-nyo, who used to think that salt mackerel was the only species of fish, the mere sight of an open air market with all kinds of live seafood was a wonder of wonders. She spent the whole morning absorbed in the spectacle. When she came back to her senses, all the faces she saw on the pier seemed in her fancy to be acquaintances of Chi Sang-mo, somehow or another. But no sooner had they turned their heads than they became total strangers to him.

The first person she managed to speak with was a women in her forties who was gutting fish in one of the quieter corners of the pier. Kil-nyo struck up the conversation but after a few words she herself was the one being questioned. After a ponderous cross-examination, the woman advised Kil-nyo to go check with the fishermen's cooperative, and if that failed, to start asking around among the truck drivers working the docks.

"Birds of a feather flock together," the woman said, and if Kil-nyo gave them a full name and a detailed description, even a dead man would be bound to turn up. Before going to the fishermen's cooperative, Kil-nyo stopped a few truck drivers. Most of them lived there in Kanggu, but they shook their heads at her questions.

It was not until night was falling that a porter, overhearing Kil-nyo's queries, interrupted with a reply. He said he used to be Chi's regular porter whenever he took on loads at the port. He knew the house where Chi and his family lived, but Kil-nyo shooed him away when he started to accompany her there, lest she be compelled by his presence to explain herself to Chi's family.

She led the porter to a house at the head of the pier where ricecakes were sold. She ordered some ricecakes for herself and some soup and wine for him. He seemed to be renowned in the neighborhood as a tippler, and he lived up to his reputation by draining three bowls of wine in the blink of an eye.

The porter was no different than the others in pestering Kil-nyo to disclose her true identity and purpose. She tossed him a village name off the top of her head and said she had come to collect an unpaid debt. The porter paused from drinking, sat the bowl down on the table, and began volubly chuckling. Then, seemingly pleased with himself at having guessed it right, he banged the table with his fist and said,

"I knew it, I say, I knew it! He was a hot-tempered man, all right, and couldn't just pass by when a slimy bastard crossed his path, but he did have one fault—never paid up on his debts."

Fearing that his jeering would get out of control, Kil-nyo hastily added,

"That wasn't the only thing that brought me here. I was on the way to some relatives and remembered he lived here, so I thought I might as well try to find out what's become of him."

"For a woman from a mountain village, you sure are good-hearted. On this pier alone, every other man has loaned money to Chi. The guy has as many debts as a there are dates on a tree. And more than a few were burned by co-signing notes for him, you know."

"Shouldn't talk ill of a man who's not around to defend himself."

This remark, though coming from the mouth of a woman, must have struck the porter as sensible, for at once he grew more sedate and said,

"I didn't mean to slander him, that's just how he was."

"How's his family doing with him away for so long?"

"I don't know the details, but the scuttlebutt around here is that he's set up another family, or gone to the dogs from gambling, or been arrested and hauled off to prison—none of the rumors sound good."

"Bad rumors are bound to pop up when a man's drifting about away from home, but what's this about being thrown in prison? What prison?"

"That, again, was just hearsay. I don't know the source. In this muddle of a world, you never can say about anything."

"How has his family been getting by here, I wonder?"

"Since Sang-mo dropped all contacts with them, his wife came down to the pier to gut fish and mend nets, but there's only so much work a woman can handle. They barely keep the spiders from spinning webs over their mouths, I guess."

"Still, I suppose it's easier to eke out of living in a fishing village than up in the mountains."

"Depends on the person. If you're born lazy, you won't eat three square meals a day even if the table is set for you."

Whether he was jeering at Chi's family or just dropping an idle bromide, Kil-nyo couldn't tell. All the same, she let the conversation draw to a close and started off for the house he had pointed out. She walked a good way along the main street abutting the pier, then turned right and climbed a steep alley toward the row of plastered dwellings lined head to head across the ridge.

In some of the cramped houses she could see strings of fish set out in the yard on bamboo trays to be dried by the sun. The women passing through the alley had sun darkened faces, and they looked stronger and healthier than the womenfolk up in the mountains.

Upon reaching the house singled out by the porter, Kil-nyo craned her neck high to peek over the fence. The house was a cubic structure, with two rooms opposing a soot-stained kitchen. A straw mat hung over the screen door and from a hook outside a coiled pad was being aired out. Dangling from the same metal hook were some dried squid.

Laying in one corner of the yard was a crushed chicken pen, the wire mesh in pitiable condition. The gate in the earthen wall was half-detached and similarly decrepit. Some warped boards had been laid out as a floor in the empty space in front of the house.

Sitting on that floor was a woman in her mid-thirties and a little girl of six or seven. The child was lying stomach down across the woman's knees to have her hair checked for lice. It was already dinner time but there was no sign of smoke from the kitchen hearth.

Kil-nyo felt torn. It seemed she had found the right place, but it was much harder to step through the gate than she ever expected. Oblivious to the fact that someone was lingering outside, the woman was deeply absorbed in the task of catching nits and cracking them between her fingernails. Only an incorrigibly lazy woman would be so slothful at mealtime, yet the pathetic scene moved Kil-nyo almost to tears.

When a woman had lived her whole life dependent on her husband, considering it a blessing, but all at once found herself alone or abandoned, her life would very likely seem unbearably exhausting, even for a clever and tidy soul. Kil-nyo straightened the baby on her back and walked through the gate. Sensing her approach, the woman glanced at Kil-nyo and the little girl slowly got up.

"I'm a traveler passing through and I'm thirsty so I wonder if you can spare a drink of water."

The woman looked Kil-nyo and the baby over, and shifting her eyes to the kitchen, said,

"As for water, there's buckets of that, but looks to me like you're less thirsty than hungry."

"Thanks."

Once inside the kitchen, Kil-nyo could see ˄hat they had nothing to speak of. The ceiling and the joists were coated with black soot and cobwebs hung in every corner. Inside the makeshift cabinet, a few strips of wood nailed together, were some dirty soup bowls, rice bowls, a little bottle of vinegar and so on, all scattered about helter skelter. How could anyone be so careless with eating utensils, Kil-nyo asked herself.

She picked up a bowl so filthy that it stained her fingers and looked down into the water urn. There was barely enough in the bottom to wet one thirsty throat, if that. She rearranged the baby again and went out to the yard with the urn on her head. The woman, still preoccupied with the search for head lice, seemed taken aback at the sight of Kil-nyo heading to fetch water. Kil-nyo spoke first,

"Where's the well?"

"Why, what are you doing?"

"I found the water jar empty and I can't just ignore it and be off."

At first the woman was speechless, but after a pause for thought she said in a slightly accusatory tone,

"I see what you have in mind, but we've no food for an extra mouth. We've been filling our bellies with water and it won't be long before we're bloated."

"If that's how it is, shouldn't you at least keep the water jar full?"

At this the little girl, who'd been still as a corpse on her mother's lap, sprang to her feet and declared she'd show Kil-nyo the way to the well. As the child stepped down from the wooden floor, Kil-nyo noticed she was barefoot.

The little girl briskly led the way with Kil-nyo on her heels.

The well was a good distance off, so far that by the time they got back Kil-nyo was tired and almost out of breath. Only then did the woman brush off a spot beside her and invite Kil-nyo to sit down.

"You're a good sort, sure enough. I thought when you found the water jar empty you'd just walk away. Never expected you'd trouble yourself to go all the way to the well. There was a well nearby not long ago, but it stank so bad they filled it in."

The dirty feet protruding from under her skirt, the disheveled hair that hadn't touched a comb in ages, the rank odor issuing from her mouth, the dried spittle on the corners of her mouth— all this was more than enough to prove that laziness was in her nature. But she was not at all slow in divining the predicament of others, for she said, as if a mind reader,

"I can tell from the way you look that you've fallen into a state where you're drifting with nowhere to go."

Then she heaved a long sigh, thinking of her own unhappy lot, perhaps. Kil-nyo went still further and said,

"These days, when even the rich find living hard, I guess a drifter like me should feel lucky to have made it this far."

"Where are you from originally?"

"Hamyang."

"What about your in-laws?"

"Around Yong-yang, but my husband kicked me out years ago."

The woman took another long look at Kil-nyo, tuttutted and said,

"For a mountain woman you sure look prim and tidy. Must've been some womanizer of a husband to have kicked you out for another woman. If he's a womanizer, you're better off without him. That so-called husband of mine walked out and I haven't heard a word from him for the past six months. If I heard for sure he'd dropped dead, then at least I could do something to change my lot. What sort of widow am I? I'm stuck, can't escape and can't make a move at all."

The talk about changing her lot she probably spat out without thinking, just as an outburst of pent up resentment. All the same, the complaint did not become her when she was doing nothing to care for herself. But in her own pathetic condition how could she dare criticize others, Kil-nyo said to herself. Gazing at the little girl who was playing with the baby, Kil-nyo asked,

"Is she your only child?"

"Why, no. I've got a boy who came into this world because I didn't know what's what. With nothing to eat at home, he's gone in the morning as soon as his eyes are open. The kids all go down to the seaside to hang around and they only come home after dark. Down there they gather seaweed from the beach, or pick up the tiny cuttlefish thrown away on the docks, that way they dull the edge of the hunger."

"How is it you've had no word of your husband all this time?"

"Damned if I know what he's up to. I've heard different things—some say he landed in prison, others that he was crippled in an accident. I even heard that he crossed the 38th parallel."

"The 38th parallel? What do you mean?"

"I'd be the last one on earth to know what that's all about. I've never been near it and sure never crossed it myself. They're all talking about it, so I guess there must be such a thing."

"Once you cross that line you can never come back?"

"I suppose if you can cross it one way, you can cross it the other, too. He's a born drifter, else why the hell would he have become a truck driver, out of all the hundreds and thousands of jobs a man can do? A man who'll wander here and there and end up dropping dead in some stranger's field, that what he is. We were supposed to be a good match, according to the horoscopes, you know, so I went ahead and married him. And now look at me, all alone at my age with half my life ahead, with no future is it any wonder I'm a total wreck?"

"Just blame fate and calm down a bit. Even if your lot is wretched, you can't just sit down here and starve."

"That's why I've been sitting here exhausted day in, day out.

I thought of doing myself in, but I couldn't kill myself what with the children. If I just sit here waiting for a creature who never sent a word for the past six months my heart will burst. But how can I change my lot? I'm already fast becoming a grandma and no man is going to give me a second look...."

For a time the woman was on the verge of crying, and finally she did stretch out both legs and emit a wail. But the sound of her weeping was not terribly loud since she was weak from lack of food.

"If you mean to bemoan your fate, there's hardly a woman alive who can't go on forever about the wretchedness of her life. It's best if you just calm down and start thinking of ways to survive. There's got to be a good reason for your husband's being silent for so long. Instead of wasting away blaming him, you should do something to feed the children while he's gone."

Chi Sang-mo found this stranger, this woman who'd drifted in out of nowhere in search of a drink of water, a real consolation for her ailing heart. There was nothing to arouse any suspicion in Kil-nyo's behavior, and that made it easier for Chi's wife to spill out her miseries.

Just then the boy returned from the shore, and a chill ocean wind rose as dusk settled in. The two women went on talking, and Chi's wife said she would consider it a favor if Kil-nyo stayed longer to chat, especially since she had nowhere to go for the night. Kil-nyo had secretly been hoping for such an invitation, and ingratiated herself by avowing she would never forget the kindness that had spared her a cold night on the street.

After a meal of thin gruel, the women sat up late that night talking, but nothing had changed from the afternoon. The whereabouts of Chi Sang-mo was still a mystery, which meant that Kil-nyo had traveled all this way in vain. She had no choice but lean on the family until news of him came. But to lean on this family was but wishful thinking, and Kil-nyo knew that, lazy as this woman was, it was she who would have to be responsible for feeding all of them.

At daybreak the next morning Kil-nyo went down to the pier

before the others awoke. She spent all the money left from the trip and with it bought enough rice to feed five mouths for a week. At seeing Kil-nyo walk into the house with the baby on her back and a sack of grain balanced on her head, Chi's wife was visibly astonished. She made a great fuss, babbling on and on how lucky she was to have met such a benevolent person coming from the northeast.

The children, awakened by all the commotion, opened the door into the kitchen and soon were hovering anxiously about as the rice was cooked, drumming the floor with their feet. Witnessing this spectacle, Kil-nyo was gratified she had not revealed who she was and relieved at being able to stay with the family for the time being at least.

From that day on, Kil-nyo coaxed Chi's wife into going down with her to the pier each day. The few coins tossed their way as wages for odd jobs were not nearly enough to buy food for the family. Chi's wife was lazy all right, but she had an outstanding knack at stealing things, stuffing this and that into her pockets or under her skirt.

Sooner or later this talent at theft would be discovered and Chi's wife would find herself barred from the pier, but as long as they were in imminent danger of starving this skill made a far from negligible contribution to their daily bread. When they came home after a day's work, out from her clothes would come two or three fresh fish still smelling of salt-water.

Kil-nyo started to reprimand the woman, but was halted by an overwhelming sense of compassion. Looking at the way the children and the both of them relished the soup made from these fish, she could not bring herself to denounce the stealing. Instead, she told herself it was justified as a means to survive at a time like this.

While they were out at the pier, however, she was constantly worried that lightning might strike them at any moment. Before long she learned that the other women who worked as fish gutters did the same thing rather openly, but when Chi's wife did it Kil-nyo felt her neck stiffen with foreboding. It struck her as yet another hardship to be endured for the sins she had committed, and she decided to concentrate on tough ways to eke out their tough existences.

Besides, what they called "wages" were absurd—mere token payments that indicated no real concern for the workers. The idea was not to compensate but to steal the labor of others. To try to live on such wages alone meant starvation. Kil-nyo gritted her teeth and made no attempt to protest the unfairness of it.

Within a month after beginning work on the pier she became a fishmonger. The selling was on a trifling scale, but even though she sometimes waited hours for a buyer to select one of the fish spread out on the board in front of her, and even when she had to carry her goods to neighboring villages in search of a sale, at least she could hope for a bit of cash at day's end as long as her haggling was in good form. Kil-nyo thought herself lucky to be able to put not only barley but sometimes rice into five mouths. In the meantime, she had kept her ears open for any news of Chi Sang-mo that might float by on the docks, but no word came.

Two months passed from the day Kil-nyo took up lodgings with the Chi family, and they had managed to set aside in the corner a few bushels of grain. The two women often ran their hands through this cache. The sooty kitchen walls and ceiling got a fresh coat of white paint and the broken gate was rehung.

About this time a peculiar rumor circulated on the docks, a rumor that soon was confirmed. The sound of gunfire had not reachèd the village, but word had it that war had broken out. "War" was a word that the two women had never before had occasion to use. Because they could not understand why anyone would wish to wound and trample over others, this news left them mystified to no end.

Damp Firewood

About a month after the outbreak of war, Kil-nyo decided to head out to see her own family in Hamyang. Once resolved to leave Chi's house, she had no other place to go. There was no plausible excuse for her to stay on with Chi's family any longer. Unless she meant to be a servant to that lazy woman and her children the rest of her days, Kil-nyo thought she better leave before becoming too deeply attached to them.

It was odd how all the travails she had endured to support them no longer seemed to matter once she decided to go. Her heart overflowed not with memories of sacrifice, but with the anguish of parting.

The war was to blame. Being slapped in the face and cursed by strangers was no longer anything new to Kil-nyo—she had come to accept it as part of her life in a cruel world. But even for a toughened soul like her, the war was an unspeakable monster.

The bustling crowds at the fish market were shrinking with each passing day, and the fishermen were pulling out with their vessels. Only the men with the smallest boats continued to sail out to nearby islands to fish or to harvest seaweed. At night, the sea lay silent as a sleeping monster and the folk around the pier were restless and anxious. When the sun came up, the dock was as still as a corpse while the waves whipped at it without warning.

The busybodies who had been forever meddling in others'

business and the fixers who were never at a loss to solve problems—they all had disappeared without a trace. People scattered in all directions. One day when forlorn touch-me-nots were starting to bloom here and there along the back alleys above the docks, Kil-nyo finally made up her mind to leave. That evening she just blurted out her intention,

"I've got to be off."

Chi's wife, busy working on some tangerine-sized potatoes, looked up at Kil-nyo and then hurriedly lowered her glance, saying,

"Well, you're no exception. You've got to go somewhere with the war on the way."

At this half-hearted response showing no recognition of her intentions, Kil-nyo found herself at a loss for words. Still, the notion of taking Chi's family with her in search of sanctuary seemed no help to either of them. In fact, that would only make matters worse, Kil-nyo told herself.

The hiatus in the conversation made Chi's wife feel awkward. She stopped peeling potatoes and pushed away the gourd she was using as a bowl, then said,

"Now that you're leaving, where are you meaning to go?"

"I was hoping to hear some news down at the pier."

"When you're in the main room the mother-in-law is always right, and when you're in the kitchen the daughter-in-law is always right—that's just how things are. Who can you believe in the midst of this chaos, eh?"

"I ran into a refugee from Kang-won-do. He said lots of people were killed there, he saw them killed, he said."

"You don't have to go all the way to Kang-won-do to see people killed."

"I wasn't by myself when he told about it. He said some of them were shot down by the North Korean army. They had some kind of cannons that can slaughter that can kill lots of people at once. He said they make big holes in the ground."

"Not much unusual about people being shot to death in a war. How the world went to the dogs like this is beyond me, but I can't believe they'd bother to shoot down women who do nothing but go down to the pier every day to gut fish."

"It's not that simple. I've seen plenty in my day."

"You always talk like you know everything when you don't—that's your problem. Nobody is going to lift a gun if it doesn't pay. For women like you and me who live from hand to mouth year round, this very spot is a refuge. if you're so smart, how come you don't know that the only ones heading for the hills are those that claimed to be better than everybody else, huh?"

"Well, I've got to leave."

"Don't be foolish. Don't stir up trouble, just stay here quietly like a snail in the mud."

"My mind is made up."

There was no immediate response, and when Kil-nyo looked up Chi's wife was staring straight into her eyes. She seemed to be at a loss to speak. Then all at once she burst out crying with such abandon that Kil-nyo didn't dare to stop her. As delirious women do, she cried buckets of tears at the top of her voice.

The children in the other room were jarred awake like hatching swallows menaced by a snake. Pressing their small heads to her breast, Chi's wife let out another wail, this time leading into a lengthy lament:

"I knew it'd come to this! I knew you'd leave us behind! Now how are we going to live? I'm cursed by fate! I was going to live with you, like your wife, like your own sister, and now it's like being hit by lightning!"

The children burst out crying, too, and Kil-nyo coaxed them into the other room, then brought a glass of water in to Chi's wife. She tried to calm her down by rubbing her back, but the woman was not about to stop weeping. Not until eleven that night did Chi's wife finally recover her composure a bit. The potatoes she'd cooked for dinner sat between them as another altercation flared up.

"You're leaving, you say, but where can you go in troubled times like these?"

The eyes of Chi's wife were swollen and even her voice

seemed tear-drenched.

"I'm thinking of going to my family."

"If that's so I suppose I shouldn't try to stop you, but what makes you think your own family will provide a safer place than this?"

"I'm not going there to seek shelter, but to be with my parents."

"If you love your family so much, how come you didn't head there in the first place? Why've you been drifting around strange places, like you were asking for trouble?"

The lament had turned into jeering.

"I thought I could make it on my own if I tried hard enough, but I've come to the point where I can't afford to be choosy. It's been six years since I was in touch with my family. Even if I became a hard-hearted and willful woman, it's only natural to keep some feeling for them after all this time.

"With things so up in the air, the least I can do for my parents is to see them again. If they're still alive, I'll chop up the wet firewood and make their dinner with my own hands. Having lost my husband I don't doubt they'll greet me with cold eyes when I walk through the gate, but I can't help this urge to hurry there. I won't be content till I see the white sheet that covers the firewood out behind our old house."

"Nothing greedy about it. The wish is only natural for animals like us. All very proper, I know, but now I've become like a beast with a broken leg. You've been such a comfort up to now."

"I'm grateful for all you've done for me. We're not blood kin, but maybe we'll meet again some day, if fate says so."

"We will, I'm sure, we should. Even if the bombs start falling from right overhead, I'm not budging an inch from right here."

After all the wailing and gnashing of teeth, Chi's wife unexpectedly seemed resigned to Kil-nyo's departure. Whether she had just given up in the face of Kil-nyo's resolve or had concocted some plan for living on her own, Kil-nyo could not say.

In actuality, there was an ulterior motive behind Chi's wife's decision to give up on persuading Kil-nyo to stay. Kil-nyo knew that even on the edge of starvation this woman, like a dog who always shits under a rice basket, somehow had managed to carry on a love affair with a loafer who sponged off others at the fish market. More than once, Kil-nyo had seen her steal out of the house in the dead of night, only to drag herself back around dawn.

Kil-nyo had asked where she had gone, but each time Chi's wife evaded the question, mumbling something about having gone to the outhouse or out to gather some news. At first Kil-nyo was taken in, but later, seeing how the woman sprawled down and dropped off to sleep the moment she reached home, she started to look like someone just back from a wild orgy.

Kil-nyo had blushed, thinking that beauty is indeed in the eyes of the beholder. It seemed there actually existed a man who'd care to share a bed with a woman like that. Sometimes Kil-nyo had an urge to follow her when she snuck out at night, but this impulse she managed to stifle.

The pot calling the kettle black, Kil-nyo told herself. She had been a loose woman, too, and certainly had no grounds to dig into the dark side of another, nor to accuse others of promiscuity.

One thing still bothered her, however. She was afraid that good-for-nothing of a man might creep into the house after her departure and squander the grain they had saved on gambling—that precious grain that had cost them so much in pain and humiliation. But if this bothered her so much, she might as well stay with this family for good. In the end, Kil-nyo only hinted at her concern with an offhand remark.

"That grain we've saved is worth its weight in gold. I heard that refugees sometimes are willing to trade gold for food. You know well enough that if it should be stolen, you and the children will starve. When I'm gone, it won't be easy to make it last through this war, even if you count out every single kernel to stretch it over time."

"Well, with you gone the pile's not going to get any bigger, is it? It'll be used up in time, that's for sure."

"I'm not going to make it any less, am I? All I mean is, if a woman sets her mind in the wrong place, the whole family can end up begging in the street."

At this, Chi's wife flinched, then instantly mounted a counter-attack, jeering,

"It's more than a few who'll be out on the streets in wartime. For somebody who's picking up and leaving, you sure are gener-ous with advice."

After this display of pouting, Kil-nyo thought twice about say-ing anything further. Good medicine is bitter, and Kil-nyo only meant well by saying she should be watchful for the children's sake, but if the woman saw it as a taste of arsenic, why should she even try?

That night when everyone was asleep, Kil-nyo wrapped the baby on her back and walked out of the house. Around dawn a constant rumble and crackle of gunfire came echoing over the mountainside. To Kil-nyo, the artillery sound was very like a roll of thunder.

Once down at the pier, she paused for a while. There was no chance to get a ride, so she decided to head off toward Pohang on foot. From there, she planned to go through Yongchon and Taegu, then on through Koryong and Kochang to reach Hamyang. If any means of transportation was available, she had enough money for the fare. But on the way to Pohang, there were only army trucks—not even a single ox cart was in sight.

For a long walk, nothing would have been more welcome than company, but the few travelers she encountered were all men, and all of them were in a great rush, as though they were half out of their minds. She was too scared to strike up a conver-sation with any of them.

At Pohang she bought some soup and rice for breakfast, then set off for An-gang by way of Yonil. She reached An-gang before nightfall, but her knees were aching so badly she could not take another step. After catching a few winks of sleep in a crowded inn, she woke up with a pain between her thighs from a boil that seemed to have erupted from the long walk.

She had no choice but to go on walking all the way to Yongchon, but once there she had the good luck to catch a ride to Taegu on a truck. When she arrived there, the streets were swarming with refugees. The mere sight made her heart plummet. Until then she had only half convinced herself that there really was a war raging.

There was no reason for her to linger in Taegu among those aimless crowds, but it was the first time she had ever been in a big city and it was not easy for her to find the right road to Koryong. Almost the whole day was wasted asking for directions as she peeked up into every alley as if to catch a mouse on a deserted island.

More from a desire to escape the confusion than from a longing to reach Hamyang, she kept on walking despite the boil that hurt with each step she took. After countless stops for directions, she finally found herself on the outskirts of Taegu.

There was a guardpost on every streetcorner and any questionable looking male was stopped and interrogated by the soldiers. Without high hopes, Kil-nyo made a plea to the soldiers and, surprisingly enough, they located a truck scheduled to depart for Kochang and put her aboard.

Five days after leaving the port of Kanggu, Kil-nyo arrived in Hamyang. From there to Tunchon, the village where her parents lived, was about eight miles. Not until she had made it all the way to Hamyang did she stop to reflect upon what a wretch she had become.

With a war on, nobody dared to ridicule others for their appearance, but the body under her rags was a shambles and she could scarcely conceal the baby on her back. Her parents had long known that her husband had passed away without leaving a child behind. And here she was carrying a baby bearing no resemblance to the Choi family.

The trials Kil-nyo suffered after leaving Woljon-ri were visibly etched into her face. The mark of baseness could not be concealed. The only thing she could hope to hide from her parents was the relationship with Cha Pyong-jo, for that had left no visible trace.

Nevertheless, there would be no denying her wantonness and she had no excuses for her past. She ended up loitering a whole week in Hamyang, hesitating to face her family. In the meantime, the town fell into enemy hands.

Upon waking in an inn one morning, she learned that the Northern army had occupied the town overnight. Dawn was breaking but it was still dark outside when someone knocked at the door of her room. Startled, she opened it to find the innkeeper, a man in his fifties, stooping down outside. In a whisper, he said,

"Ma'am, if you're up, come on out, please."

His voice was quaking with the fear of uncertainty. In a reflex, Kil-nyo bent over to pick up the baby, but he motioned her to come out alone. She laid the baby back down and covered it, then followed the man out into the alley. Even in the dim light of dawn over the fence she could see people's heads passing by.

The main road was busy. The soldiers lining both sides of the road in preparation for a march were wearing different uniforms than the soldiers who were stopping travelers in Taegu. At this sight of a strange army, Kil-nyo felt a cold chill run down her spine. The sound of thunder came into her ears.

The mountains were far off, yet the violent roll of thunder lingered in her ears for a long while. People who seemed to have been dragged from their beds were out on the street holding torches to light the way for the passing troops.

"Hold that light higher!"

From somewhere in the dark, a young harsh voice rang out and the people moved closer to the street. The number of torches increased as clusters of two and three joined. The torch-bearers were mostly old men, but those on the march, whenever their faces were revealed in the light, seemed almost all to be young.

The faces of the soldiers were half-hidden by strange-looking helmets that covered their ears. A few of them gave a friendly wave to the people lining the street, but most wore a stony expression and just briskly marched on, seemingly wary of their surroundings.

The innkeeper tugged Kil-nyo's sleeve from behind. Remember that her baby was alone, she followed him back inside. The man trembled like a leaf as he stood next to her. To calm him down, she grasped his hands, but she was shaking, too.

When she finally managed to calm herself down, she picked up the baby and cradled her in her arms. The little one was not heavy to begin with, but at that moment Kil-nyo felt like she was holding air.

"The war's brought us all to ruin, after all. What can we do now? There's nowhere left to run."

"Where in the world did they come from?"

"Probably the ones drafted from the villages up north. They're the ones people call 'the Reds'."

"It's funny how they look no different from us."

"Yeh, I thought they had horns like devils. I'd have been less surprised if they were horned beasts. Somehow its even scarier to see them looking just like us."

At these words from the innkeeper, Chom-gae's face flashed into Kil-nyo's mind.

"You have to hide somewhere, anywhere."

"I heard they don't kill common citizens."

"How do you know what to believe at a time like this? Even though you may not be hauled off to be tortured, you might get killed by the bombs that'll be falling."

"Why try to run when there's nowhere those airplanes can't go?"

"But they're not likely to drop bombs on some village way back in the hills. If you hang about a big town like this, you might get drafted for war labor and die for nothing."

"They have no use for an old man like me. Don't worry about me. Get yourself ready to go. Judging from your speech, you must be from these parts. I've been wondering why you've been staying in this inn so long. Anyway, we're going to close this place."

"They say all the roads out of here are blocked and whichever way you turn you'll hear gunfire."

"Maybe I should get my family ready to hide in the mountains, like you said."

Tunchon was eight miles off, and even if you left at sunrise and walked at a brisk pace it would take a few hours to get there. Kil-nyo spent the rest of the day helping the innkeeper pack up his things for his family's departure, and only as night fell did she finally set out. By the time she reached Tunchon it was so dark she could see no more than a few feet in front of her face.

Had it been peacetime, the villagers immediately would have recognized Kil-nyo, whose appearance was quite conspicuous. As it was, however, this remote village tucked back away both from the sea and from the main cities was boiling with strangers of all sorts. It was as though the war had washed all the rotten fish up there in Hamyang.

Tunchon, the hamlet itself, was perched there on the mountainside as quietly as ever. In the distance you could see Pallyong pass, where the Chirisan range of mountains all at once seemed to drop from sheer exhaustion on their way toward Cholla-do. The storm squalls that blew over Chirisan's Chonwangbong often spent themselves over Tunchon, the winds dead tired out after hammering the stone face of the mountain.

There were about forty dwellings in the village, all clustered together. The house belonging to Kil-nyo's parents stood toward the far end, with the gate facing east. Inside, to the right was a stable and a shed and to the left alongside a fence was the outhouse and a neatly cultivated flowerbed. Beyond, facing the gate as you entered, stood a wall.

Vegetables had been planted in two plots within the yard, one on the far side of the well and another nearby, separated by a terrace of soy-jars. The house itself stood in the center of all this, with a small open space in front. The kitchen was on the left as you entered, and to the right across a wooden-slatted hall were the main room and a second small room used by Kil-nyo's father.

In the back corner of the house was one more small room with its own side door to the yard. Outside the main room, the house was trimmed with a wooden deck broad enough for one person to lie down on. On hot summer days Kil-nyo's father often used to nap there.

One thing had changed since Kil-nyo had married and left her family behind. A peculiar looking structure was standing across from the outhouse at one corner of the vegetable garden. It had a sort of a hearth inside that looked to be a fireplace used to heat the space inside. From the pair of men's white rubber shoes neatly placed on the step outside this shack of a room, Kil-nyo guessed that her father must be staying there.

Though by this time her parents were over seventy, they had always had the reputation of a couple that lived in perfect harmony. It was beyond Kil-nyo how their loving bond could have been shattered so badly that they were living apart.

Outside the war was raging, but within these walls all was a quiet as a mouse. Only one of the three rooms of the house was illuminated, and there was no sign at all of anyone moving about inside. The only thing disturbing the silence was an occasional flutter of night birds by the wooden fence. No human shadow was visible in the lit room.

Because the gate was ajar and the house seemed dead still, Kil-nyo thought her parents might be away at one of the neighbor's. Whether they were in or not, she could wait outside no longer. From the first glimpse of her old home through the darkness, Kil-nyo had felt all of the suffocating tension she had been bearing for so long begin slowly to melt away.

She felt so drained that it was hard just to stand upright on her own. Reminding herself how far she had walked, she called out in a low voice,

"Mother?"

Only after repeating her call a few times did she detect some signs of movement in the main room. Her mother appeared in the doorway with a candle in her hand and looked out. It was plain to see that the old woman was having trouble getting around. Her back was bent as she strained to crawl part way out onto the wooden deck and stared vacantly into the darkness. She was unable to come any closer, but evidently was able to see that the only person standing in the yard was a young woman, and asked,

"Who on earth can it be at this hour?"

"Mother, it's me."

The old lady seemed to recognize the voice, though she had not been able to make out the face. She leaned forward with some difficulty, bracing herself on the edge of the floor, saying,

"Whoever you are... come a little closer, please."

As she approached the wooden floor, Kil-nyo shifted the baby on her back and it began to fuss. For a moment the old woman squinted at her, then whispered abruptly,

"Hurry in."

The old woman's voice was muffled, but Kil-nyo could hear the tremble of trepidation in it. As Kil-nyo stepped up toward the room, her mother added,

"Bring in your shoes with you."

Kil-nyo picked up her shoes, went inside the room and sat down on the floor. Her mother's eyes were riveted on her the whole time. Perhaps she still could not believe that her daughter had actually paid a visit. After unbinding the baby and cradling it in her arms, Kil-nyo looked her mother in the face to find tears welling up in the old woman's eyes. She, too, felt like she would burst into tears at any moment. But the next words from her mother made her uneasy.

"You shouldn't make a scene. Your father'll be coming back soon."

Silence reigned for a time, but nothing could stop the tears from streaming down Kil-nyo's cheeks. From the first, there had been something odd about her mother's behavior. For someone setting eyes on her daughter again after ten long years of separation, her reception had been too icy. Even if she was a daughter who had sullied the family name, Kil-nyo's mother could at least have held her hand. But she had not, and she had not even glanced at the baby. The only thing she asked was,

"Where are you coming from?"

"From a port called Kanggu."

Kil-nyo could see now that her mother could hardly move at all from the waist down. The old lady pulled herself swiftly over to the window and took down the lamp so that it would cast no shadows on the paper in the windows.

"If we'd passed each other in a city street somewhere, I probably would have passed you by without recognizing you. I've heard news of you from time to time, but I never thought you'd turn up here looking like a bag of bones."

These words her mother uttered one by one, then leaned back against the wall and wept. Even then she covered her mouth with one hand to keep her crying from being heard. All this made it look like she wanted no trace of Kil-nyo's homecoming to remain once she was gone.

In truth there were many reasons why Kil-nyo's family would not welcome her visit. Their village was not large, but the Shin family for generations had enjoyed a reputation for impeccable integrity. One reason Kil-nyo had been matched with a man from as far away as Hamyang had been pressure from others in the Shin clan, who were greatly concerned about preserving the dignity of the family line.

Kil-nyo more than once had tried to prepare herself for a cold reception from her family, but she had never imagined her mother would actually be so unkind. Even if she found her father remarried and a stepmother at home to greet her, the welcome would have been warmer than this.

Still, when all was said, she told herself, a cold reception was what she deserved. She ought to consider herself lucky to have found a sanctuary from the wet chill of the night. If her mother by hurrying her inside had only meant to conceal her presence, then she would soon have to leave. Kil-nyo smiled bitterly, thinking she would have been better off staying in Kanggu with Chi's family. She regretted that the crazy idea of coming here had ever occurred to her.

"I expected you to pop up sooner or later, but this is no place for you to linger for very long."

At this Kil-nyo knew she was not welcome, and the time had come to recover her wits. She unbuttoned the front of her blouse and unceremoniously began to breast-feed the baby, saying in an irritated tone,

"No need to worry, I wasn't planning to stay here long anyway. Whether you care about me or not, I don't know how you can be so heartless at seeing your own flesh and blood. You're not the stern father, you're my mother...."

"Quiet down. Your voice shouldn't be heard outside this house."

"Even strangers won't kick out visitor once they've been invited inside. I'm so stupid it never occurred to me I'd be thrown out of my own house. You can disown me if you want, but at least let me stay here long enough to have a good look at you before I leave."

"Judging from that smart mouth of yours, you've been through a lot out in that world out there."

Unsure whether to take this as a reproach or just a mild complaint, Kil-nyo was finding her mother more and more hateful.

"You, you've lived your seventy years here in this greenhouse without ever needing to know anything about what goes on outside the fence. But my fate was cruel, and I've had no chance to age gracefully. I've had to roll in the world's shit."

"Don't blame me. The worse your fate, the more you need to guard your dignity. If you have no self-respect yourself, you can't expect others to respect you."

"If life ran as smoothly as you say I never would have been like I am now. For years now, it's been all I could do to stay alive. I never could afford to be choosy, so there's not much dignity left in the way I speak and act. Just think of me as a traveler who needs to stop here for the night. Stop worrying yourself over me."

"The child you're holding doesn't look too healthy. You

haven't been feeding it on the milk of other women, have you?"

"Don't worry about the child. How many babies live in luxury now that the war's on?"

There seemed no chance that the two of them would be reconciled. The thought that they might go on arguing like that until the next morning when she had to leave made Kil-nyo feel terribly sad. Then someone was heard out by the gate. Announcing his entrance by clearing his throat, Mr. Shin Hyon-jik unlocked the gate and started slowly across the yard to his abode. Kil-nyo's mother waited until no more footsteps could be heard and then said,

"Help me up. Once I'm on my feet, I can make it to the outhouse on my own."

The old lady meant to go and speak with her husband. Hesitantly, she rose with her daughter's aid and went out. A few minutes later, Kil-nyo's father came into the room, his wife leaning on him for support. His glance barely paused on Kil-nyo before his eyes froze on the face of the sleeping baby. His hands were visibly quaking.

"Maybe you had to work as a maid among strangers, but it was still wrong to show up here. I knew you'd come back someday, but I was hoping you wouldn't."

It was the same old voice, but his hair had turned white as snow, his face was gnarled with wrinkles and his cheeks drooped.

"I know all about the straight path a widow should follow, but once I ended up drifting all over my wandering steps somehow led me back to my old family."

"You don't look like you're going to drop dead any minute, so what's this nonsense about 'wandering steps' leading you here? You have some nerve to say that, but I can see through you."

"I don't know what you're talking about, father. I didn't come here with any bad motives."

"Whatever your motives, you're old enough to know that one false step could mean the death of the whole Shin clan. Blame fate for your wretched condition if you want, but I don't know how you can act so senselessly. How can you burden us this way when we're barely surviving?"

Her father's words were at once comprehensible and incomprehensible, nonetheless, to Kil-nyo they sounded cold-hearted. It would have been easier to endure if he had simply slapped her face instead of going on with roundabout reproaches.

"Heed what your mother says and try not to bring any more disgrace onto this family. Look at the state we've fallen to. And don't even think about stepping into this house again. Even when your mother and I have set off for the other world, there'll be no call for you to show your face at the gate of this house."

Leaving those words behind, her father headed out to his room in back of the house. Her mother, who'd been gazing at the lamplight, said in a low tone,

"The man in the back room, did he know you were going to come today?"

"I don't understand mother, who do you mean? Who would know I was coming here?"

"Then, you're saying he doesn't know?"

"Just what are you talking about, mother?"

"It does no good to deny it. We may be old and ignorant of things outside, but even we can see that all this was prearranged."

"Mother, stop going on like this and tell me exactly what this is all about. Who's in the back room, anyway?"

The old woman looked aghast and the words that came out of her mouth were the last thing Kil-nyo ever expected to hear.

"He seems to be the father of the child you're holding there in your arms."

"This child's father?!"

"Why, did that baby drop out of the sky? I don't believe you've been nursing somebody else's child that you picked up somewhere."

"So, there's a man back there now?"

"It's already been five days since he walked in using your

name. He's hiding out. With all this commotion, I'm beginning to wonder whether he's just pretending he doesn't know you're here."

No doubt it had to be Chi Sang-mo. So, he had come all the way to Hamyang to hide in her parents' house. In spite of everything, Kil-nyo couldn't help feeling a bittersweet mixture of joy and sorrow.

She could understand why he had come to Tunchon instead of going back home to Kanggu. He had no way of knowing all the hardships she had endured in Kanggu. It was probably awkwardness that led him to stay silent even after her arrival. Only now did Kil-nyo understand what her mother and father had been talking about and why her reception had been so cold.

No wonder they had mistaken her motives for showing up at this point in time, for it must have looked as if she and Chi had arranged a rendezvous when she arrived only five days after his appearance in Tunchon. If her ailing mother had hidden him in the back room and served his meals it meant he was on the run.

The village had fallen into enemy hands, so it was obvious he had been on the rightwing side. In that case it had been a wise decision for him to head for a remote mountain village instead of to an open port like Kanggu where he would soon be discovered. It was an extra burden for her old parents, but she could not think of a better place to hide out.

"We heard you couldn't manage the life of a faithful widow and had taken to the road to change your lot. Maybe that was your destiny, but you can only go so far, dragging the Shin family name through the muck. War or no war, you can't imagine how it outraged your father when you brought a man into your parents' house.

"Besides, that man of yours used to be a high official in these parts, and if shows his face they'll drag him off and beat him to death before he knows what's what. You may say your father and I have lived long enough. But if we're beaten to death for hiding that man, there'll be no peace on the way to the other world. In the old days we Shins were great landlords, but we've lost everything and now to make it worse there's this extra headache. Every day we're walking on thin ice, that's the truth."

" . . . ."

"Once a woman changes her lot, it's likely to get easier to change it again. In my seventy years there were times I joined the crowd in jeering at fallen women, and I never dreamed my own family would meet with those jeers, not in my old age. But that's how things stand. I want you to talk with that man and see to it no more disgrace falls on your father."

Kil-nyo had been shocked at her cold reception, but now that she knew the whole situation she couldn't help thinking she deserved the harsh treatment. She felt in no position to make any demands. After a few days at the most she would have to go and leave them in peace.

Filial piety was no longer something in her power to give, yet she at least had to try to avoid bringing further shame on the family. In any case, she thought she better see Chi Sang-mo, who'd snuck into the house under cover of her name. She sat the baby down on the floor and went to the back room.

In a space barely large enough to lie down in, a man was sitting on the floor. As Kil-nyo opened the door and put one foot across the threshold he clutched her by the hand and jerked her towards him. Trying to keep her balance at the same time she was pulling her hand out of his grip, Kil-nyo caught sight of the man's face in the dark room. For an instant her gaze locked upon him, and then she fell down in a faint. A big hand, not that of Chi Sang-mo but of Cha Pyong-jo, covered her mouth.

He kept striking her on the cheeks and shaking her shoulders until she recovered her senses. After the initial shock, Kil-nyo again looked at him, but it was still Cha Pyong-jo. His mouth was covered by an overgrown black beard and his sunken eyes seemed miles away.

Only then did she recall her mother's words—that the man had been a high official in that region. Back when she was expecting to see Chi Sang-mo, she paid no attention to that absurd talk about his being a high official. Now that the man had turned out to be Cha Pyong-jo, everything made sense. She could well understand why he needed to hide. Kil-nyo was still silent, trying to recover her composure, when Cha said,

"If this war hadn't broken out, I might never have seen you again. Well, I figured you'd probably come back to your parents' place, but I didn't know if my guess would turn out right."

What a shock! What had become of all his past power and glory? Years before he had talked down to Kil-nyo as though she were nobody, but now he addressed her more politely. Unlike in the old days, he now looked like a learned and even somewhat distinguished man. His eyes lacked the vicious arrogance of those days and his voice was powerless.

At first, his humility seemed attributable to the fact he was living off of her family, but it turned out there were other reasons.

"I couldn't join the group that moved southward. I missed the chance because I took my sweet time finishing up the work at hand around here. Suddenly the North's army appeared right under my nose and scared me out of my wits. If they caught me, they'd execute me on the spot.

"They say when you're in deep trouble some way out will turn up. Well, it dawned on me that your parents were living close by. There was no time to stand on ceremony or to save face. I was so desperate I'd have jumped in the first house I could find to hide in, and it was lucky for me I remembered your hometown. It was like falling off a cliff and then latching on to a branch of an old tree.

"I know what there was between us was so vile you wanted to erase it from your life, but somehow I felt your parents wouldn't turn me in. So I showed up here and begged them to save my life for your sake."

"You came to the wrong place. I can't stay here more than two days myself, and as for you.... My family is not what they once were, we used to be landlords, so the communists will soon be nosing around here. This is no place for you or me to be staying for very long."

"As a stranger I don't expect a welcome from your parents, but you're their own flesh and blood and I can't understand what harm your presence could do them?"

"Blood relation or not, a person is bound to be treated as they deserve. I thought they were harsh to me at first, but the more I think of it, the way they've treated me is natural enough."

"I'm to blame for that, I suppose. But I've come to the point where I have no choice. I'll put up with humiliation and disgrace if that's what it takes to survive. More than a few people would remember my face."

No solution was in sight. Kil-nyo's father would doubtlessly be watched as a reactionary element, and now here he was, providing a hiding place for Cha Pyong-jo, feeding him and even carrying out his bodily waste. To top it all, she makes an appearance before his eyes. But Kil-nyo could not just kick Cha out of the house. Not only might he be killed on sight, if his hideout was ever revealed the whole clan might face execution.

Despite her longstanding grudge, Kil-nyo did not have the heart to cast out a man whose fate was bound up with her own father's. If all of this was in retribution for her past sins, she had no choice but to leave and to take Cha with her.

Despite the predicament he was in, Cha must have been curious about Kil-nyo's situation, for he asked,

"I've been wondering about that baby I heard fussing a while ago...."

"I'd have thought that man you sent out to track me down would have filled you in on everything about me. Nothing good will come of sniffing around in the mire I've fallen into. It was beyond the power of a simple woman like me to change the fate that befell me, so I had to find a man to lean on. Maybe barrenness better befits an ill-starred woman, but like they say—a vicious brute of a dog doesn't pass a day without getting bruised on the nose—so here I am with this poor unfortunate child."

Cha lifted the corner of the mattress up from the floor, pulled out a dusty cigarette butt and lit it. He looked as pitiful as a rain-drenched rooster.

"That's a fact, I did send out a man a few times to check up on you, but I meant no harm. If you were getting by all on your own, I suppose I meant to find some way to help you out. Anyway, you can see the awful shape I'm in now. Instead of being able to help you, I'm a burden yet again. I've met a lot of people in my day, but every time you and I cross paths things instantly seem to take a turn for the worse. It's a mystery to me why we seem to bring trouble to each other."

"I don't see it that way. I'm the one who must have been a burden to you back in those days."

"It's good of you to try to be sympathetic."

"A lot of good it does to be consoled by a woman who's barely surviving midst the jeers of the crowd."

"You say that, but you're a woman who learned early the right way to live an honest life. You have something a man like me will never have, even if I tried the rest of my life. For you this world is already like a heaven, and then there's a second heaven ahead."

"I'm not destined for paradise, so I guess I do babble on, trying to tell myself that this life is already a paradise."

Kil-nyo's mother must have thought their conversation was going too long, for from the main room came the sound of the old woman clearing her throat.

"Mother thinks you are the father of the baby lying in the other room."

"I don't doubt she does."

Kil-nyo returned to the main room. Her mother uttered not a word of reproach, nor did she make any inquiries about Kil-nyo's plans for the future. Unsure whether her mother meant to leave the decision up to Cha and her, or whether she was just struggling to maintain some equanimity in an impossible situation, Kil-nyo lay awake the whole night, vigilantly listening for any hint of a sound from outside the gate.

As dawn broke the window shone grayish white. But for piercing echoes of gunfire somewhere nearby, all was as still as in the moment just before a thunderclap. For Kil-nyo, the uncanny silence was an omen of evil to come. It was the same suffocating silence that always hung in the air when in the past her fate took an abrupt twist.

She looked over at her mother sitting with her back to the wall, asleep. Her emaciated form was clearly revealed in the early morning light. The ramie blouse hanging over her scrawny shoulders looked wet as though she had been out in a deluge, and the knotty hands resting on her knees trembled from time to time.

How could she have let her health deteriorate so badly she could hardly move her legs? A daughter could hardly pose this question to her mother after passing the night in her company. How heartbreaking it must have been for a mother to be unable to give a warm welcome.

Kil-nyo laid the baby down and quietly crept into the kitchen. Before her sister-in-law had left to follow her husband to another town, the things in the kitchen had always been impeccably clean, and the shelves used to be shiny enough to make a cat slip and fall. The hearth never grew cold in those days, and the water jar never lacked fresh water from the spring.

There was no chance for soot to blacken the walls and ceiling, and there was always a tasty aroma in the air. Back then, when neighbors stopped by on windy days to get some embers to kindle their fires, her Kil-nyo's sister-in-law used to make fun of the visitors, asking if they were wandering beasts who had no souls.

The kitchen was no longer the same. Now it was in disorder, chilly and unclean. Little wonder, for all the work had been left to her old mother who could barely get about. Kil-nyo felt dread at the sight of her family slipping slowly into ruin, just like the Choi household back in Woljon-ri.

The people who dwelt here were skin and bones, but out behind the house a big, well-fed rat could be seen. As it waddled toward the sewer at the back of the yard it paused every few steps, furtively stealing a look back at Kil-nyo before continuing its leisurely stroll.

Through the open kitchen door, she could see one corner of

the terrace of soy jars. There was no sign of life from her father's room or from the room in the back where Cha Pyong-jo was hiding. Kil-nyo squatted down in front of the hearth and poked through the ashes. There was one piece of wood still glowing. Hastily, she stoked some twigs inside and fanned the fire back to life. Then she poured some water into the pot.

The smell of the burning wood touched the tip of her nose. The odor of the kitchen hearth was tinged with the smell of home and kindred. In the smoke of clover tinder was the aroma of cooking potatoes, and in the smoke of pine kindling was the fragrance of vegetables and rice porridge.

As mealtimes approached her sister-in-law used to call to Kil-nyo: "Sis, let's make something to eat!" In those words, "make something to eat," there had been a certain inexplicable joy. It was less the contentment that comes from a full belly than the pride and accomplishment one felt in the course of the mysterious process that began with rice sacks in the barn and ended with steaming bowls on a well set table.

When the bowls and dishes came back empty from her father's meal table, surreptitious looks were exchanged between Kil-nyo and her sister-in-law to share their secret triumph. This strong bond between kin sharing hearth and food had seemed invulnerable, but with the coming of war it was shattered, spat upon and violated like everything else. How was it possible to be so utterly lonely? Even on that morning when she awoke to discover Chom-gae gone Kil-nyo had not felt half as broken-hearted as she did now.

She went to the outhouse and on the way paused to look inside one of the storage urns. Taking the lid off, she found the jar was half full of barley meal. Several worm-like bugs, sensing the presence of an intruder, scattered in a flash to the sides of the urn. From the fact that barley and not rice was on hand, it was plain to see that life was far from bountiful for the old couple.

Even in better times, Kil-nyo's father had suffered from stomach ailments whenever barley was mixed into his rice. Now that he was no longer in a position to be choosy, doom could not be far in the future.

Just at that moment Kil-nyo heard the sound of footsteps entering the front yard. It was still quite early in the morning, but the sound was that of a man unmindful of waking anyone. She caught a glimpse of two men and immediately dropped what she was doing and rushed into the kitchen to hide.

Kil-nyo peeked out though a crack in the door into the front yard. The murderous look in the eyes of these strangers was one she had seen too many times before. One of them was unusually tall and the other was short and thin. Their appearances were peculiar in that the tall one was wearing a filthy beret pulled down almost over his eyes, and the short one had his pushed so far up his whole forehead was showing. The boots of both were buffed to an extremely shiny gloss.

The tall man went straight to the side door of the house and plopped down. The short one started pacing off the distance from the west side of the yard to the east, stretching each step to compensate for his diminutive build. When Kil-nyo was small, after the harvest they used to thresh the grain in the yard, and on those occasions the workers used the same method to mark off dimensions.

The short man stopped after he reached the wall on the east end of the yard. From his pocket he took out a handkerchief and frantically buffed his boots for a second to remove any dust from the sparkling shine. It was a ludicrous sight to see. Why, Kil-nyo wondered, do men pay so much attention to their shoes?

She recalled the days when she was running the tavern at Hwangjangjae, and the two dusty pairs of shoes on the feet of the corpses of those two young men. And she remembered as well the shoes worn by Chom-gae's ex-cellmate when he paid her a call. For Kil-nyo, men's shoes were truly fearful things. They were something like the unexploded bomb people said was supposed to be laying hidden somewhere on the outskirts of the village. Now that unexploded bomb was set to go off.

"Shin Hyon-jik."

In a low but authoritative tone of voice the tall man perched on the deck called out Kil-nyo's father's name. Having uttered the name with no preliminaries of any kind, the man sprang up and fixed a glare upon the main room where Kil-nyo's mother lay in bed. As if to test whether they were in full contact with the ground, he stomped the soles of his boots where he stood. Then he adjusted the red armband wrapped around his left sleeve.

After calling out the name the man said nothing for a while. He did not look very concerned at the lack of any response to his call. The sudden appearance of these two men seemed at odds with the tense atmosphere of the house. There was no stifling the anxiety she felt, but from the very first Kil-nyo could not help finding the behavior of the two absurd.

Nevertheless, this absurd conduct on the part of the two men was full of self-confidence. That made it strange and different somehow. At a time when the whole village was robbed of energy and just limping along, the masculinity and confidence in their behavior elicited a certain fear in onlookers—they reminded one of a wild boar on a rampage after being wounded by an artless hunter.

"Shin Hyon-jik."

The tall man called out the name once more. Then he raided his hands from his belt and moved his beret slightly up.

"Come out."

This order he spat out as crisply as if fitting a square lid upon a square box. Only then did Kil-nyo realize why the tall man was saving his breath and speaking so sparely. These men had come to arrest her father. A chill oppressed her heart as though she had gulped down a chunk of ice.

Yet, there was something about the short man's behavior that came as a relief. While the other was calling out her father's name and summoning him, the short man had not looked in his direction even once. From the beginning, he just kept on pacing back and forth from one end of the yard to the other.

Given that the two of them had obviously come on the same mission, the difference in the way they were acting was for Kil-nyo a puzzling sight. She noticed something else about the short man's appearance. Unlike the tall one, he was carrying a rifle. It seemed too big for him—the rifle was almost as tall as he was, yet as he adjusted the sling the gun moved on his shoulder so effortlessly it seemed as much a part of him as one of his arms. The butt looked like it would drag on the ground but it never did.

The reason Kil-nyo felt a bit relieved despite being fearstruck had to do with that rifle. Stuck in the mouth of the long barrel was a fresh cosmos blossom. The flowers had barely started to bloom—God only knows where he had picked it up.

Each time the short man adjusted the sling of his rifle, the cosmos blossom flopped this way and that. This was the sight that allowed Kil-nyo to feel hope. The tall man paid no attention to what the other was doing, nor did he criticize him in any way. Each seemed indifferent to the other.

The drama in the yard was moving on to a new act, however. After straightening his armband one more time, the tall man abruptly opened the door of the room where Kil-nyo's mother was sick in bed. He paused for a second until his eyes could adjust to the darkness of the room, then turned away to avoid the sight of the old woman.

"You'd better get up."

As if speaking to an equal, the man used a familiar mode of speech. He wore a thin smile at the corners of his lips.

"Who are you?"

It took quite a while for Kil-nyo's mother to raise herself to a sitting position in her sweaty smelling bed, but the man waited patiently and did nothing to hurry her.

"You don't need to know who I am."

Whether or not the man had thought twice after seeing how old she was, his voice had changed to a much more deferential tone. He went out onto the wooden floor outside and sat down. Taking a good look around the room, he asked,

"Shin Hyon-jik, where is he?"

"I'm not a well woman, and I've been bedridden for months.

I've no idea what's going on outside the fence."

"So, you've been in bed for months, eh?"

"That's right. Can't you tell by the way I look?"

"You may be right about being sick, but I can see you're clear-headed enough. Sure you're not exaggerating your illness?"

"It's nice to hear that I seem well in spirit, but it's a pity I can't move about more freely."

"A bedridden person ought to have better ears. Besides, Shin Hyon-jik is the man of this house, so don't lie and say you don't know where he is. Not even a three-year-old would believe that."

"I said I didn't know about the world outside, but I never said I don't know what goes on inside these walls. Did I say anything about not knowing where my husband is? You shouldn't judge others just any way you please."

"Got a point there. Well, I didn't expect you to be such a smooth talker. Now, where did you hide him?"

"Hide him?"

"If he's not hiding, tell him to come out here now."

"What wife would dare to order her husband to come out or to go in? We've been married fifty years, but it's been a few years since we shared a room, and I don't concern myself with his comings and goings. He's not in the habit of reporting them to me, either."

These replies from Kil-nyo's mother would strike anyone as reasonable enough. Where she summoned the energy was a mystery, but she managed to enunciate every word clearly and come up with bold answers that more or less fit the need.

The man at first had been sitting erect but by now was leaning over the threshold of the room, twisting forward so as not to miss a word as the old woman spoke in a soft voice. He seemed irritated by the situation but with some difficulty he was suppressing his anger. In the kitchen, Kil-nyo was growing uneasy, afraid lest the man's attitude suddenly change and a flood of curses be loosed upon her mother.

The man seemed to grasp, however, that patience, though

hard to maintain, was the best weapon to use if he meant for his interrogation to bear fruit.

"Auntie...."

"What nonsense to call an old hag like me 'Auntie' when I can't even keep my balance."

"Very well, then, grandma, are you telling me you don't care whether Shin Hyon-jik is in this house or not, and you don't care where in the house he stays?"

"You could say that."

"You're lying."

"I've told you no lies."

"Do you think I don't know there's a boa coiled up in your heart? What you mean is, we're free to search the place if we don't believe you. But this boldness can only mean you've hidden him somewhere you think we'll be unlikely to uncover. You're trying to raise a fog by making up stories about not being on good terms, but however good or bad your marriage is, handing over your husband to be arrested isn't like lending a hoe to your neighbor, is it?"

At that moment, the short man ceased his pacing back and forth across the yard. He glared fiercely at his companion and spat out,

"Hey, you! You gonna act like a fool?"

His dialect made it clear he was not from any of the nearby villages. It was not Kil-nyo's mother but the tall man who was shocked by this outburst. For a while he just gaped at his comrade in the yard, greatly perplexed. It was obvious he was at a loss to understand why the short man had suddenly snapped at him.

"Arrest Shin Hyon-jik? Whose bitch told you to do that?"

At this, a regretful look appeared on the face of the tall man, who seemed to realize the nature of his careless blunder. The short man, a stare riveted on the other, said,

"Understand, comrade?"

"I understand, chairman."

"Comrade, comrade."

"Yes, comrade chairman."

Having once again pulled up the sling of his rifle, the short man walked briskly over to the gate and then turned back around.

"Grandma, you heard him, didn't you? We did not come her to take him in."

"If you don't intend to arrest him, I wonder why you're so eager to find him."

"All we want is to escort him over to our place and have him give us some advice. If we meant to arrest him, do you think we'd come here and try to persuade you like this? You don't think we lack manpower or information, do you? I hope you realize that nothing good will come of it if you interfere with our mission. At your age, you should have the sense to size up the situation. Let me have a word with Shin Hyon-jik."

"Here I am."

These words slammed like a rock into the back of Kil-nyo's head. Out of the blue, her father revealed himself and now was walking out into the yard. Kil-nyo was not the only one startled. The two men gawked as old Mr. Shin stepped toward them in rubber shoes.

They never expected finding him would be this easy. For a pair who had been expecting to stay several days at this house in order to root out his hiding place, the sudden presence of the old man must have seemed too good to be true. Upon arriving at the house, Shin unhesitantly reached past the tall man and closed the sliding door of the main room.

"My wife is not well. You shouldn't pick out a sick person to argue with, should you?"

While the tall man continued to gape in disbelief at Kil-nyo's father, the short man plucked the cosmos bloom out of the barrel of his rifle and stuck it in his mouth. He nibbled the stem and the petals whirled around and around. The flower in his mouth, the short man approached the side of the house. He stared at old Shin for a moment before opening his mouth.

"So you're Shin Hyon-jik?"

The flower fell from the man's mouth to the ground.
"That's right."
"Let's go."
The short man was standing behind Mr. Shin and the tall one stepped forward and held him by the arm. Kil-nyo's father turned around and said,
"I'll be back, dear."
Just then the side door to the kitchen slid open. Though Kil-nyo's mother looked haggard and weak, her voice was forceful.
"Stay right where you are."
She meant to stop Kil-nyo from making a scene by coming out of the kitchen and trying to follow her father.
"Nothing terrible will befall him. Our family has been in ruins for a long time, and your father never hooked himself up with any political business, right or left. He's no different than any run-of-the-mill farmer."
Kil-nyo watched as the rifle barrel passed through the alley, jutting up before the thatched roofs.
"The baby must've been seen, and it's odd they never asked whose child it was."
As Kil-nyo's mother spoke, she gestured with her chin toward the baby sleeping in the corner. Then she laid down on the floor, exhausted. Kil-nyo hurried to the back room. Cha Pyong-jo could not possibly have missed all the commotion outside. He, in fact, must have been the most anxious of all of them, not old Shin Hyon-jik who had gone off with them of his own free will. Cha looked up as she entered the room.
"They took my father away."
"I know."
"I'm awfully worried. Nobody would expect him to live a life of luxury in wartime, but he's old and weak and who knows what sort of hard time he's in for... to think of it makes me shudder."
"It's something I never expected. If they meant to arrest him, I can't understand why they didn't do it at the outset. Why wait till now? I guess his name was given to them by somebody else they'd taken in, that must be it."

"What can they hope to get out of father?"

"In their eyes, your father is still a landlord, that's why."

It was the last thing Kil-nyo had expected to hear out of the mouth of Cha, something more jarring than the arrest of her father. Even if it was the reason for taking him away, that Cha Pyong-jo had blurted it out that way meant he must have known something about her family's downfall.

"We were a well-to-do family once... but that's ancient history now. You can see for yourself we don't even have food to live on. Father never harmed a flea in his whole life. I can't think of anyone who'd bear him a grudge or have any reason to seek revenge.

"Maybe he gives an impression of being a stern and strict character, but when times were bad he was foolish and soft-hearted enough to borrow money to pay the field hands he'd hired. Even if somebody wanted to slander my father, there are no pretexts for planting suspicions. He knew this himself, and that's why he's felt he didn't have to run away or hide, even with the war on."

"It's been years since you last saw your family. You can't be so certain about your father when you have no idea what's happened while you've been away. No man can live in complete isolation, the world intrudes everyday to harass him, and going through ordeals like that, a man may very well change his way of thinking. It's not for nothing that people say: 'Every morning brings a change of heart.'

"You haven't lived half your life yet, but by now you should know better. Even if your father has a heart of gold in the eyes of his own flesh and blood, to others who know him he might have quite another reputation. Look at me, will you. Who on earth would've thought I'd fall this far?"

"That your lot'd change overnight, or that my father would be in this predicament—I expected none of this. You would certainly go on prospering, that's what I thought. But even though I've been on bad terms with my parents for years, I can't believe my father has anything to do with the wickedness going on in this world."

"How you can say that is a mystery to me when you and your family haven't seen each other for years. You're old enough to tell wheat from rye, and what you're saying strikes me as far from sensible."

"Maybe I can't distinguish rye from wheat, but I do know the kind of man my father is."

"Don't drag this on. What grounds do you have for being so sure?"

"I'm his daughter, that's grounds enough. A wife may not be able to fathom her husband's innermost thoughts, but a daughter understands her father, you can't deny that. Not just me, even simpletons are able to judge the character of their own fathers."

Just then Kil-nyo heard the sound of scratching at the door. When she opened it, she found her mother there. The old woman had crawled there from her room.

"A woman should have nimble hands, but if her tongue moves faster than her fingers she's in for a tough life. Everyone says we're living in an enlightened world, but I've never seen a loud-mouthed woman with the good fortune to serve her husband and him alone. The worse your lot, the less you should wag your tongue."

Kil-nyo's mother was more heartbroken than she was, yet the daughter was far from pleased by her mother's unfaltering stoicism. They say a married couple, once they've turned their backs on each other, become total strangers, never having been blood relations. But given that her parents were still together, Kil-nyo's mother was closer to her father than she herself.

Whether she liked it or not, her parents shared a kind of a fortress that to her was impenetrable, despite being their own child. Wondering what the real story behind her father's arrest could be, Kil-nyo opened the door to the kitchen. It was midsummer, but she felt chilly.

All at once she was plagued by regret at not having followed her father to see him once more before those men hauled him away. Why had she followed her mother's order so unthinkingly? Had she been too terrified to take a single step? She had no reason to fear the two young men, yet she had been more afraid than anyone else that her presence would be discovered. That was the truth.

The fear she felt was not fear that they would take her away. Cha Pyong-jo was probably the reason—she must have feared that discovery of her would lead to a revelation of his presence. She recalled how Cha had spoken almost jeeringly of her father's apprehension, as if there must have been a good reason to arrest him. Was it not possible that her father had surrendered as a diversion, to protect Cha? Had her mother guessed this intention and so ordered her to stay inside the kitchen?

There was not a single clue to her father's motivation anywhere in the house. The two men who had put him under arrest now found themselves searching for the key to the same puzzle. Old Shin Hyon-jik himself could not figure out why they wanted him. After they took him away, he spent two days and nights without anyone asking him a single question.

At the front of the district office, a structure built under the Japanese occupation, hung an unfamiliar sign reading "People's Committee". Shin had walked all the way there from his house that day without being prodded to hurry. But they had not led him inside the building with that sign. Instead, they steered him to the left and took him into a small office next door, an annex that used to house a copy room and the night watchman in the old days. There they left Mr. Shin.

Quite a few people were moving busily about, absorbed in various tasks, but none of them paid any attention to Shin. Of the twenty people within those walls and windows, not one showed the least interest, hostile or kindly, at the sudden appearance of the old man. This cold indifference left Shin greatly cowed.

They put him in a tiny room that reeked of urine. Footsteps were heard from time to time on the other side of the thin walls. He stayed there alone, confined in a storeroom housing old mats and broken furniture. The stench of urine coming from the other side of a paper-thin wall subsided at night, but in the early morning it suddenly came back, aroused like a hornet's nest to torture old Shin's nose. Grubs crawled up through the dirt foundations of the place, and flies buzzed in by way of cracks in the door, buzzing constantly as they orbited in that cramped space.

That he had been confined there was not so unusual, but the behavior of the men who had brought him in was strange. Through two whole days in that storeroom, not even once did anybody so much as open the door. From time to time Shin took a peek out through a crack, but there was no guard nearby and no sign of anybody watching the place.

Nights were the same. With a prisoner inside, they might at least have stuck some sort of food through the door at mealtimes. Maybe Mr. Shin in their eyes was a parasite unworthy of normal rations, but even a prisoner needed to eat, that was the basic point.

If this went on, he might starve to death without anybody knowing. To die in oblivion that way was far more dreadful than just being killed. In a word, the total indifference of his captors was more terrifying to Shin than two days of torture would have been. By the end of the second day, he was numb to the stink. His limbs felt like they had atrophied and become insensible to pain. To him his body seemed to have been changed into one huge eyeball, for all he could do was peer out through the crack of the door at the corner of the main building.

After these two endless days of isolation the third night finally brought the sound of footsteps approaching the door of the storeroom. At first, the man who unbolted and opened the door was not recognized by Shin. Pointing his flashlight here and there, the man finally spotted old Shin's head where he was crouched against the wall in one corner, more dead than alive, his eyes glazed over.

"Are you all right?"

Asked the man in a tremulous voice, as if shocked at Shin's appearance. Then, reassured by signs of movement in the old man's hands and feet, he spoke once more,

"Stand up, please. I'll give you a hand."

Only then did the voice strike Shin as familiar. It was the tall man who had led him away from home. The man grasped Shin under his arm and helped him to his feet. The two of them were anything but friends, but the warm touch of another human being overwhelmed old Shin and brought tears to his eyes. He was grateful merely because they had not forgotten him after all. Had he not been of a mind to oppose them all along, the old man might have embraced him.

The tall man helped Shin all the way over to the main building and took him inside a large room. Two brightly lit lamps hung overhead and a conference table stood in the center of the room, but nobody was there when they walked in.

"You'll soon meet our comrade from party headquarters."

Leaving these words in his wake, the tall man left the room. Shin's attention gravitated to one of the walls that was entirely covered with written posters—declarations of some sort.

"The Korean Communist Party fights for radical progress for the life of the working classes including laborers, soldiers, slumdwellers and intelligentsia, by protecting their political, economic and social interests. We shall fight to the end to achieve the complete liberation of the Choson race, to eradicate all remnants of feudalism and to open the path to free and democratic development.

"We fight to establish a revolutionary, democratic people's government that respects the interests of the working classes. We take upon ourselves the duty of mankind, with the final aim of establishing a communist society without class distinctions, free of oppression, and overcoming deprivation by the only means possible—the complete liberation of the Choson laboring masses through a dictatorship of the proletariat. Long live the liberation of the proletariat! Long live the establishment of the Choson People's Republic! Long live the formation of a unified democratic government!"

"Eat this."

Shin realized somebody had come in and was standing beside him.

"Do you think you can join in our revolutionary mission?"

Shin looked up at the man who had posed this quite unexpected question. The speaker used standard Seoul pronunciations, yet his intonation had an unmistakable tinge of Kyongsang-do dialect. He had personally brought in a bowl of soup and placed it right under Shin's nose. Then, the man quietly took a seat about three chairs away.

"As you can see, I'm too old to join in your fight."

"But you do have the will, you mean?"

"What good is will when there's no strength left in the body? Besides, I haven't eaten for days and I barely have the energy to answer your questions as it is."

"My arrival was delayed. You belonged to the landlord class, did you not?"

"A class, is that what you call it? It's true a large estate was handed down to me from my ancestors, my choice had nothing to do with it, and I did lead a comfortable life for a time. But that was long gone when the Northern Army came down here and I'm at the point now where I can barely scratch out a living with some help from my neighbors."

"What do you mean 'came down'? Where do you think we came down from?"

"Well, I didn't go up north, so I have no choice but to say you came down south."

"The Choson Communist Party is a natural growth, it's not an organization formed in any particular location, north or south."

"If you say so. I've had nothing to do with all of that from the beginning."

"The truth is, I myself am the son of a landlord. Our family too owned a great deal of land. But in the north, according to the decree of the Communist Party, all of the land has been nationalized during the process of democratic revolution. This mission was fulfilled by dividing the land among the farmers in proportion to their labor power and family size. The land held by the Japanese imperialists and the traitors of our race was unconditionally confiscated.

"As for the holdings of Choson landlords, the property of the great landowners and the moneylenders was confiscated first. We also took over the land held by the temples, the schools and the clan groups, in order to finish the task of redistribution. But you, Mr. Shin, you disposed of your land as you pleased, with no regard for our revolutionary mission, didn't you? That you sold you land before the Communist Party undertook its mission does not mean you're not a counter-revolutionary element, not necessarily. The class consciousness of a landlord is still alive in you."

"It's true I wasn't thinking of your plans when I sold my land. But before I met you right here today, nobody ever made any claim to that land, and nobody cared what I did with it. I'm seventy years old and just marking time until I'm summoned for the journey to the other world. If I hadn't followed the way things were done I never would've lived to see today, would I?"

The man fumbled through the pockets of his jacket, took out some cigarettes and offered one to Shin.

"Will it be all right to smoke with your empty stomach?"

"I feel better now that there are people around. For two days I was completely abandoned, and being isolated was worse than starving."

"There's too much to be done within a very short time, and I'm afraid our short-handedness made us neglect you. I myself arrived here behind schedule because I had to stop in to see my family on the way."

"I appreciate your effort to see me in person, but I hope you're not expecting to get anything out of me. I have no property left, and I'm too feeble to do you much good. I'm no more than a decrepit old good-for-nothing."

"That's not true. There is something you can help us with. You don't think we brought you here for no reason, do you?"

The man lit the cigarette that was dangling from Shin's mouth. The latter felt that the other was more relaxed now than when he had first walked into the room. Shin tried to read his expression as he leaned over to light the cigarette, but the face bore no message."   •

"You seem to have been raised in quite an aristocratic family," said Shin quietly as he took a puff. The man said nothing. He ceased fumbling with the cigarette pack and placed it back in his pocket. Then he looked up absent-mindedly at the writing posted on the wall. With his back to Shin, the man quietly said,

"I'm from Sangju."

"Sangju is renowned for its fertile land, great fields that from ancient times let people enjoy affluence. There are lots of historic sites there, aren't there?"

"You have a daughter who was married away, don't you?"

The man's gaze was still riveted on the wall.

"That's right."

"Where is she now?"

"If you know I have a daughter I'm not very proud of, you must also know it's been six or seven years since she took to drifting about without bothering to contact her own family. Am I not right?"

"Right you are. That's what we thought. But what interests us is not you daughter's whereabouts but her husband's, a man by the name of Cha Pyong-jo. We want to know where he is."

"The family in Yong-yang my daughter married into is named Choi. After she was widowed, she severed just about all ties with us. If you yourself were raised in Sangju, you must know that parents by custom do not take back a married daughter, even if she's widowed. Well, the same custom is followed in these parts. All we heard was a rumor that she took up with some bastard when she was living at the Choi house and ran off with him, but I have no idea what kind of man he was, not to mention his name."

"Well, that man is Cha Pyong-jo and he happened to hold a high office in a neighboring town. That reactionary missed his chance to flee and he was seen here in Hamyang. The crucial fact is that after being seen here he just up and disappeared.

"We know he has no relations around here. If he does, you are the only one it could be, right Mr. Shin? If we had word he'd been sighted elsewhere, why would we bother to bring you here? We're certain you hid him. And I'm telling you the only way you'll walk out of here alive is by telling us where he's holed up."

The cigarette in his mouth was almost burning his lip, and Shin told himself that never before in his life had he faced such a clear-cut decision. His life was at stake and one step forwards or backwards would tell all.

Until then he had lived a kind and generous life, like someone living in a room in which the light filtering through the rice paper window never got too bright or too dim. Even if there had been crises from time to time, he had always managed to deal with them in a moderate way. He never had doubted that moderation was the most natural path for a man's life. If caught in the middle of an argument, he would nod first to one side and then to the other, thinking that was the way to leave antagonism behind.

He had never been a clever man, and so ended up poor, yet through seventy long years of life he had committed no grave blunders in his relations with other people. The choice now presented to him by his interrogator could not have been more unwelcome to Shin. All hope vanished as he realized that there was not an inch of room for him to escape his dire dilemma.

The man was practically asking him to give up his right hand or else to give up his left. This much he had more or less guessed some time ago, but now that he was face to face with this man, Shin found the burden of it all too heavy to bear.

Just then the tall man rushed into the room. He hurriedly moved about, pulling down all the window shades, extinguishing the overhead lamp and dimming the kerosene lamp in front of Shin. When the flame was reduced to a flicker, he put a shade over the lamp and then walked out. The room was totally dark except for a thin streak of light falling right on the chin of old Shin.

Shin felt even more wretched, sitting there with that tiny spot of light trained on his face. It was unforgivable for that man sitting there in silence, gaze never wandering, to have placed him in such a hopeless fix. The most absurd part was that there was absolutely no way he could condemn the man.

Shin was not so ignorant of the world that he could not have come up with excuses of some sort if summoned before the Lord of Hades himself. Not once in all his years had he been in a situation where he found himself utterly at a loss to say anything. The words the man then spat at him underscored the point.

"Cha Pyong-jo is nobody worth throwing away your one and only life for. Maybe you don't know much about him, but I have heard some things about the conduct of that reactionary through personal channels."

That a father must care for his own flesh and blood is something even the beasts know. Besides, at his age, how could he expect to keep any human dignity if he let his lips flap?

"You, a total stranger, know at least something about my daughter's doings, while I, her father—in name at least—am completely in the dark. Go on, spit in my face. I deserve it."

"One thing's clear. You can hold out if you insist. But we'll ferret out that reactionary, whatever the cost."

"It's none of my business."

"I'm a busy man. It's too bad you wouldn't let me treat you well."

Without pressing further, the man abruptly rose from his chair and walked out of the room, slamming the door behind him. Shin felt fortunate that he had gone, but it seemed he would be sent back to where he was. Only then did Shin hasten to eat from the bowl of gruel sitting in front of him. A little while after he finished eating, the tall man came back into the room. Unlike earlier, he was rather rough as he escorted Shin back to the storeroom and bolted the door from outside.

The man said to have come from the party headquarters to interrogate him may not have learned anything, but at least Shin had managed to get enough food to ease his hunger pains for a day or so.

"I'll never allow my dear grandson to grow up fatherless."

So Shin said to himself as he sat crouching with his back against the wall. He was at once surprised and proud to discover in himself this resolve to guard the future of his grandchild, even if he was none too fond of the baby's mother, his wayward daughter. He consoled himself with the thought that no abominable tortures had been inflicted on him and his ordeal, after all, had not been so unbearable.

Back at the house, however, Cha Pyong-jo was having very different feelings—and the difference was one of foreboding. At the end of the third day after old Shin's arrest, Cha began to sense the cold grip of anxiety slowly tightening around his throat. He was all nerves. Even the sound of a tomcat walking by outside was a torment, to say nothing of the insomnia.

At night he shivered from an unaccountable chill, and the least noise at the gate made him quake with fright, lest someone creep up behind him and drive an ax into his skull. On top of it all, he felt indignant at the fact that there was nobody to turn to for comfort or help in escaping his fix.

The more he thought about his predicament, the more he seemed like a duck's egg cast into a swamp. There was nobody to utter a kind word in his behalf and not a soul was there to give him a pat on the head. He felt like an insect, a grub stranded there in that tiny prison of a room.

From the moment Shin was hauled off by those two men, Cha Pyong-jo had been plummeting into a bottomless pit. He was certain that Shin would reveal his hideout before long. The men who claimed to be party members would not rest until they had tracked him down. Even the temporary workers at the district office were said to have been arrested, so a man like him who had governed a whole district was bound to be rooted out.

His execution would be a big triumph for all the people who were screaming at the top of their lungs for pressing ahead with their revolutionary mission. There was nobody better for a show trial. They would drag him before the People's Court and parade him past the crowd to a spectacle of a public execution.

Old Shin had certainly not been taken away to be converted or to be punished. If that had been it, three days would not have passed with the family receiving no word. When Kil-nyo entered Cha's room with a bowl of gruel, he clutched her by the wrist and pulled her down to him, saying,

"Listen, dear, I must get out of here!"

"Where do you mean to go?"

"If I stay any longer, I'll end up dying like a dog. They say right below the lamp is the darkest spot, but I'm not the only one who's heard that. The Reds know that, too, I mean. Besides, it's suspicious that your father's still not been brought home."

"I've been making inquiries about my father, and it seems they haven't been torturing him."

"That's exactly my point. The bastards don't arrest people to wine and dine them, do they? The fact that he's not been tortured must mean he's given them some kind of information, don't you think so?"

"Father's not an man who gives in easily, not like you might think. If he was going to tell them where you're hiding, he would have done it right off, not after holding out for four days."

"You don't understand. He's hesitating for your sake. It's only a matter of time before he talks. He's just taken a step back from confessing because he's worried that you'll face hardships in the future if he talks. The bastards are not torturing your father because they're in no hurry, for one thing, and they must think he'll soon give in."

"So you'll leave, you say? Nonsense. You won't be able to take a single step. This house is being watched from all sides, and not even our close relations dare to come anywhere near here."

"I must go. Otherwise it'll mean death for many."

"If you must, then you must go alone. You don't expect me to leave when I'm to blame for my father's arrest, do you?"

At this Cha snorted, rolled his eyes toward the ceiling and replied with a jeer,

"Don't make me laugh. For somebody so deeply concerned about her parents, you managed to cut all ties and live as you pleased for long enough."

"I didn't keep in touch because I didn't want them to be sneered at by others in our family, not out of any lack of respect for them. You say I lived as I pleased, but that was more because I was ignorant and couldn't change my fate. What do you gain by digging up my past to berate me with at a time like this?"

"My anger made me poke at a sore spot, didn't it? Well, it's obvious that this is no place for the two of us to linger any longer. So why don't we stop quarreling and come up with some plan to sneak out of here?"

"Even if this place turned to quicksand, I can't leave now. I know my parents are ashamed of me and I'm not welcome here, but this is no time for me to abandon them, whatever you say."

"Enough babbling. You put on a kind-hearted act, but in fact you'd be the first to sin. Don't take what I say lightly or I'll put a torch to this house, you can count on that."

What could have caused such a change in Cha's attitude, Kil-nyo wondered. A cold sweat ran down her spine. She had run across all sorts of people in her life, but nobody was as hard to fathom as this man. Was he just oblivious to the fact that she had a baby to feed, and so had to get at least one decent meal a day? Not that she expected compassion from him, but anyone could see that the four people in the house were barely surviving, sleeping each night with a Sword of Damocles just overhead and poised to fall.

How could he spout all those awful things? Was he the only one who had fallen into a hopeless situation? Perhaps he had enough strength left to burn down the house, but there were two others there who could not even make it to the outhouse on their own.

Kil-nyo could not say whether his notion of fleeing with her meant he still felt some longing to be with her, or whether he merely thought she would make good camouflage for his escape. She saw little point in asking his intentions, yet the predicament was far too serious for her readily to consent to what he had in mind. Above all, it was certain that their next meal would exhaust the stores of food in the house.

The whole thing seemed like it might be some sort of punishment. No, it was punishment, it had to be. No matter how hateful Cha Pyong-jo became, it was he who had fathered her first child. She told herself that all these humiliations at his hands were deserved, for she, a so-called mother, had abandoned that baby. What sin could possibly compare with that of a woman who deserts a defenseless baby, her own flesh and blood? Not even a hedgehog would do such a thing.

All at once tears streamed from her eyes, not because she was hurt by Cha's harsh words, but because she felt all the mistreatment was deserved. If it was not she who had changed her lot, the change was also beyond her power to undo.

"You feel suffocated, but you have to endure it. You're not the only one going through this, we all have to endure it. I don't think the world can go on like this for long."

"No, we can't wait. We've got to go now. This is no time to be worrying about what others might say, and it's surely no time to drag out that rubbish about respect for your parents. If we don't leave now, we'll be killed like dogs, like dogs, I say!"

Cha was shouting and waving his arms like a man who's lost his mind. Kil-nyo noticed beads of sweat all over his forehead. She grasped him by the hand and said,

"Calm down, please. If you don't, we'll all be dead sooner than you think, all of us at one blow."

"What do you mean, 'all of us'? I'll survive at all costs. You don't think I'll let them slaughter me like a dog, do you? I'll not go easily!"

"That's why you have to calm yourself down. They'll hear your voice even outside the fence."

Once Cha's frantic rage had subsided, Kil-nyo went to the main room. Her mother was constantly bedridden, but she kept a steady watch on the baby lying beside her. Whenever the little one stirred and fussed, the old woman had a way of immediately guessing the problem and soon put things aright.

Ever since her husband was dragged away to the People's Committee, Kil-nyo's mother had grown even quieter than usual. Nevertheless, no change was detectable in the way she cared for the baby. That she said not a word to her own daughter about her husband's fix was hard to accept, no matter how skeptical she was about her daughter's character. Kil-nyo, however, knew why her mother was so cold.

The old woman knew that Cha Pyong-jo was responsible for her husband being arrested. From the very beginning, she knew that as long as Cha stayed in the back room of the house, her husband could not come home. She knew, also, that it would be fruitless to try to get her husband released, so she decided not even to mention that possibility. Talking about such things would only make her feel worse.

Kil-nyo's mother guessed that it might be a long time before her husband could return home. She knew he was not the kind of man who would let his own offspring fall into the muck. When he was arrested, the two of them had not exchanged a word, but in an instant she had divined his intention.

"Mother, there's somewhere I need to go."

" . . . ."

"I'll be back in four days."

"Aren't you afraid to be out and around with the Northern Army all over the place?"

But there was no conviction in these words. The old woman had no idea where Kil-nyo planned to go, but she did know why she wanted to leave. No more secrets were left.

"I heard the Northern soldiers don't abuse womenfolk for no reason. I made up some buckwheat curd so you can eat something while I'm gone."

"You'll die if you go out there."

"If it's my fate to die, I suppose I'll die even if I go on sitting in this house."

"Sounds like you've got me in mind, saying that."

"Don't be so feeble-minded, please. Why would I possibly

want to say mean things to you? I've been racking my brain to find some way to save all of our lives."

"I know you've been out on your own long enough to have guts and maybe you're shrewd in your own way, but I also know men's heads are being sliced off like radish greens nowadays."

"I may not be worldwise, mother, but I know it's not peacetime and I won't be reckless."

"With a war on, you'll run into plenty of men on the road who are starved for women. Treatment of strangers has no doubt gone to the dogs. Besides, jets are dropping big bombs on the cities, that's what they say. A clever man would know how to take care of himself, but you won't."

"Don't worry so. I'll manage to look after myself on my own."

"So, is that how you got to where you are, by taking care of yourself? If you must go, leave the baby here with me."

"Don't tell the man in the back I've left until I'm gone."

"He'll have a fit, I'm sure."

"Reproach him. Talk some sense into him, please."

"In my seventy years I've done many things that deserved reproach from others, but I've never felt I was in a place to reproach anybody. Human bondage is like a vine that strangles a tree, they say. I never once thought the world would bring a bondage as evil as this."

A Silver Ring

The following morning at daybreak Kil-nyo set off from the house. She walked at such a fast clip that in no time she was out of Hamyang. As her mother had advised, she left the baby behind. By leaving alone, she meant to reassure her mother and Cha Pyong-jo that she would be back, but more importantly she had figured by traveling alone she could make a round trip to Kanggu and back within four days. If anything happened on the road, at least the child's life would be spared.

The road would be familiar, she told herself, since she had traveled it once before. Reaching Koryong, however, she found the safe part of the journey at an end. From Koryong to Taegu the road was blocked. Having no alternative, Kil-nyo went up to Songju and after five long days made her way via Waegwan to An-gang.

Along the road, whenever passers-by heard her declare she was headed for Kanggu, they shook their heads and muttered that the war had a way of driving people out of their minds. She herself was beginning to worry. In leaving so rashly she had thought only of her prior journey. Now she hated herself for ever having come up with the idea.

Still, there was no place to pause, and from where she was to Kanggu was not nearly as far as the way back to Hamyang. Nobody on the road paid her any mind, yet there was plenty to see. Humans, so seldom seen back home of late, were overflowing the highways.

At first, it occurred to her to look up some of her relatives to seek help from them. But her mother had said, "Planning to ask our relations for a helping hand? It's been ages since they turned their backs on us." At any rate, she had dropped that idea, for she could not bear the shameful thought of presenting herself before them to beg for aid. Perhaps they would give some food, but she knew humiliation would be handed out more generously.

That was what she feared most. Besides, once she started contacting kin, sooner or later Cha Pyong-jo's presence in the house would be uncovered. But by the time she arrived in An-gang, five days after her departure, she wished she had gone to see her relatives. One with nothing to protect has nothing to fear. After sinking as low as she had, why was she was so afraid of the scorn of her relatives? She could not say.

To Kil-nyo, the strange thing was that she was not at all frightened of the constant bursts of gunfire around her or even of the bombs that shook the mountains. The people traveling in the opposite direction could not have cared less about anyone's scornful reproaches, but they were terrified by the sounds of guns and artillery.

When she came upon these people who could never have understood her feelings, and whose road led the opposite way from hers, she saw herself more than ever before as a person running against the tide of the world. It was a mystery to her why the paths she found natural always seemed to take her on different roads than those traveled by others. It was as inexplicable as if an apple in her hand suddenly changed into a peach or a melon, though her hand was no hand of a wizard.

This sense of estrangement grew still stronger on the sixth day when she finally reached the port of Kanggu. She had left Hamyang under a vague expectation that Chi Sang-mo would have returned to his home. That she waited until dusk before going to his house was due to a desire to spare him embarrassment if he had returned.

To her great surprise, the main room of the house was brightly lit. Most private houses dimmed their lights at night, she had thought, to keep from being spotted by bombers overhead. The lights in Chi's house were brighter than those in other dwellings nearby, and for a few moments she just leaned against the wall, looking.

She again regretted having set out on this trip to Kanggu. From the light in the house, she detected a strong odor of betrayal. The man's voice she heard coming from the room was the voice of Chi Sang-mo, of that she was certain. She felt an impulse to rush inside.

What a shock it would be for all of them. The children, having no cause to be shocked, would nonetheless be pleasantly surprised to see her again. The wife who had been so reluctant to let her go would greet her with confusion, and Chi would be amazed just to see her still alive and well.

Kil-nyo reached back to check the baby, but her hands touched only air. Only then did she remind herself that it had already been nearly a week since she left her child behind in Hamyang. She chided herself for not having brought the baby along. The infant would have been a good excuse for bursting into the brightly lit room.

Not until the next morning, however, did she meet Chi Sang-mo out in front of the office of the Fishermen's Cooperative. She had gone down to the pier to find someone who would deliver a message asking him to meet her away from his house.

The pier was bustling with an unusual vitality. The ominous stillness of just before the outbreak of war was gone. Kil-nyo saw quite a few fishermen mending their nets and here and there boats were getting ready to head out to sea. Nevertheless, a vague scent of conspiracy seemed to hang in the air over the lively pier, an air not unlike that she detected in Chi's brightly lit house the night before.

As luck would have it, it was Chi Sang-mo who spotted Kil-nyo first. A man in work clothes, reeking of fish, walked up to her and pointed in the direction of the Fishermen's Cooperative. They passed through an office where several men were bent over their desks and arrived at a room used by the night watchmen. Waiting there was Chi Sang-mo, seated in a chair. When Kil-nyo came into the room, he saw bewilderment in her face and grinned.

"What's this all about? I thought I'd never see you again."

Since the previous night Kil-nyo had been clenching her jaws, but now that she was face to face with the man, she could not help but burst into tears.

"Uh, uh. Stop this silliness and sit down here."

Said Chi, lighting a cigarette and pointing at the chair across from him, on the other side of an ashtray. The offered seat was only a few steps away from him, but Kil-nyo felt like she was tumbling off a cliff. There was something suspicious in the way Chi was acting, but she could not say exactly what it was. She managed to fumble her way over to the chair and sat down, like a little bird perched on the edge of a precipice.

"I've only been back a few days."

Chi did not look very different from the refugees Kil-nyo had seen on the road to Kanggu. He was starting his story at the end instead of the beginning. What the two of them had in mind seemed as unlike as apples and oranges. She would have liked to have started by asking him where he'd been all this time, but he had a different intention, evidently. She was having a hard time stifling another outburst of weeping.

"Where have you been all this time?"

"Well, I know you stayed with my family for a while. My wife's babbling was pretty incoherent, but I gathered it must have been you."

"I never gave her my real name."

"I know. You did the right thing. If you had, my wife wouldn't have given me a moment of peace. She's a real nag, and I'm a busy man."

"Where are we now?"

"Here? This used to be the Fishermen's Cooperative in the old days, but we've taken it over."

"What do you mean?"

"You're a dense one, eh? Just because a war broke out, it doesn't mean a person has to hide at home and go hungry, just watching what others are doing. To survive you have to fish for something, right? The reactionaries who used to play so high and mighty are all hiding now, and somebody has to be here to put the fishery business back on its feet, so here we are, as you see."

"Reactionaries?"

"Just yesterday those bastards were feasting on our blood, and now that their lives are threatened every last one of them has run away. Not long ago I used to think that all the endless bounty of the ocean belonged to them alone. But with the world changed like it is, now I know that the ocean is mine. Never able to see, my whole life I was forever kowtowing—well, can you imagine a man more foolish than that?"

"You'll come to a bad end if you keep on like this."

Chi Sang-mo abruptly lowered his voice. He gave a quick glance out through the window and said,

"Look here, I'm not a leftist and I'm not a rightist. I'm in a position to be both, so why should I be foolish enough to choose only one side? A businessman ought to keep both his hands and use them wisely. Stick out the right hand to those bastards who want to see the right one, and give the left hand to those who want to see the left.

"I've seen too many cases, I can tell you, when a stupid man who claimed to lead a righteous life met a worthless death because he hesitated between the right and left hands. We weren't born with two hands for nothing. I'm a busy man."

"I'm staying now back with my parents in Hamyang."

"I'm not surprised. Where else could you go? You might think I'm a dangerous man, but that would be a mistake. Even if the world is turned upside down again, everything's negotiable and I'll be in a position to run the fishing business on this pier. Then, I'll put my left hand back in my pocket and stick out my right hand, that's all. I tell you I'm a busy man these days."

"Are your children all right? They aren't going hungry, I hope."

"Stop talking nonsense. You show up out of the blue and now you're trying to ridicule me, or what? Have you seen many fathers letting their children starve? There's a saying that the money you earn out at sea is too precious to spend on your own kids. Still, who'd sit back and let his own children go without food? Never you mind, they'll eat to their heart's content, just you wait and see."

"You look to me like a little boy playing with the family's best china plates. There's time to stop and think before you decide to go one way or the other. What's the point of all this rush?"

"I'm a busy man, so stick to the point. What brought you here, anyway?"

At these words from Chi, Kil-nyo no longer had the energy to go on talking with him. Why in the world had she hurried all that way? She wondered, but then she knew why. She had come to see the father of the baby she was bringing up.

She was not welcome here, it was true, but she saw that Chi was not in his right mind. Besides, whatever the details might have been, he had been the one who had helped Hwang Chom-gae to escape from Andong. A truck driver might not be the lowest station in life, but he probably had been scorned often enough by pretentious big shots. Who knows, maybe he was acting like a madman now to get revenge against those sorts of people.

"You're not going to ask about me at all, are you?"

"About how you've been doing up to now, you mean? The past is done, what's the point? I'm sure a woman with your willfulness has managed everything just fine."

"My family is totally ruined, and I'm not worried at all about myself, but raising a little baby is not so easy...."

Kil-nyo's voice died out before she could finish what she was saying. Chi Sang-mo all at once was enraged, and shouted,

"Hold on one minute! You want money from me on account of that lousy fling we once had, is that it? Listen, even a dumb beast looks around before taking a shit, understand? Do you actually think that I, in my present position, can be bothered with a woman like you? All my time and energy have to be invested in the great mission that's been entrusted to hundreds of workers on this pier. If you came here with the idea of shaking me down for money, you made a serious miscalculation, and I mean it!"

Chi sprang up from his chair. Kil-nyo could not understand how things had taken such a wrong turn and changed him into a totally different person. And she did not know how to head all this off. She felt dizzy for a moment and, forgetting where she was, grasped at his trouser leg, pleading,

"Please, just listen to one thing, I won't keep you long."

"Let go of me! If you don't, I'll shoot you!"

Chi stamped out and slammed the door behind him.

In a daze, Kil-nyo ran all the way back to the pier. When she recovered her senses, she found to her surprise that she was standing on the dock staring out at the sea. A few notes of paper money were in her hand—at first she wondered where they came from, then she vaguely recalled that on the way out of the office someone had walked up to her and thrust the money into her hand. It was barely enough for the trip back to Hamyang.

Now the only thing left for her to do was to go back to her parents' house. But after coming all this way, she asked herself if she shouldn't at least pay a visit to Chi's wife and children. That she had been treated badly did not justify her becoming low and mean herself. They might not welcome her there, either, but the sight of the children would give her some comfort, she thought.

Besides, she recalled that the wife, though lax and lazy, was not so bad at heart. Even if she was not overjoyed to see Kil-nyo again, she at least would offer a little rest before the long return journey. She might utter a reproach, upbraiding Kil-nyo for making such a trip during wartime, but if she left without seeing them Kil-nyo thought she would feel guilty later.

What with the hard times and humiliation they had endured

together working as fishmongers, the wife would be unlikely to slight her. Even if by chance she turned out to be unfriendly, Kil-nyo was not going to be crushed by the consequences. She had just been treated most cruelly by the father of her baby, so it would cause her no special grief to get a cold reception from a woman who, when all was said, was a total stranger.

Kil-nyo climbed the steep hill and stood in front of Chi Sang-mo's house. The woman was sitting by herself on the wooden deck, eating lunch. She had put a spoonful of barley in her mouth and was about to follow it with a piece of *kimchi* when she caught sight of Kil-nyo outside the gate, standing there like a withered pumpkin blossom. Hastily swallowing, she grinned at the visitor just as her husband had. Then, gesturing to the spot beside her, she said,

"Have a seat."

After scratching her heel with the handle of the brass spoon in her hand, she repeated,

"Come on in and sit down."

She did not welcome Kil-nyo with open arms, but on the other hand she did not seem hostile, either. Watching the visitor sit down, she asked, greatly startled,

"My! Where in the world is your baby?"

"I left it behind."

"Well, well, for a second I thought you'd lost her, recklessly wandering about in wartime."

"How could you think such a thing..."

"Well, it's sure nice to see you again after all this time, but I don't know what brought you here. At first I wasn't even sure it was you, but come to think of it, this really is a big surprise."

"You're right, it has been a long while since I left here. It's hard to believe our paths would cross again in this world."

The woman put the spoon into the gourd full of *kimchi* beside her, and chuckled, nudging Kil-nyo's side and pointing down toward the pier with her chin.

"Turned out that creature didn't forget his way back to the nest where his little ones were. When he showed up out of the blue, I almost had a heart attack, taking him for a ghost or something."

"You mean the father of your children?"

"Who else? For a while, I couldn't even let the neighbors know he was back. They would have been shocked, too. They say if you live long enough you'll even get to see your mother-in-law drop dead and this was no different. It was like lightning from a cloudless sky, you know."

"What do you mean, 'lightning'? What could be better than his safe return?"

"Who said it wasn't good to have him back? Thank heavens for that, but I'm telling you I almost had a heart attack. As luck would have it, I happened to be at home, else I probably would've been on the way to the other world then and there."

"How could anybody be expected to stay home day and night? You might've been out visiting the neighbors."

All at once the woman interrupted, lowering her voice to say,

"You're so dim-witted, dear. I mean it was in the middle of the night. If it'd been broad daylight with lots of people about, why the hell would I get so scared? You're so slow, you don't understand a thing."

Still, Kil-nyo could not see why, of all the things in the world, the woman had brought up her trysts with the bum from the pier. She must have guessed that Kil-nyo had figured out something like that was going on when they were living together, but her motive for making such a big deal out of it was a mystery. Especially with her long lost husband now back home, you would think she would avoid dragging out that unsavory affair, but the woman seemingly thought otherwise.

Unless Chi's wife meant to probe into how much Kil-nyo knew about the whole thing, her manner of talking about was indeed odd. In her husband's absence, she was going over her own shameful misdeeds, as though she were gossiping about the misdemeanors of a neighbor. It was the behavior of a crazy woman, or of a woman asking for trouble.

Kil-nyo found all of it most perplexing, but she managed to

feign innocence and said,

"I don't understand what you're talking about. You broke your back working to feed the children, sleeping in an empty bed every night while you waited for a husband who didn't even send word of himself for so long—who could find fault with you?"

"Don't pretend you don't know."

"Pretend? What am I pretending? It's beyond me what you're going on about."

"Do you mean to tell me you didn't know I was sneaking down to the pier and back in the middle of the night?"

"As long as I live, I'll never forget the hard times we had down on that pier. But you were always with me, weren't you? Just what are you talking about?"

Only now did the woman look somewhat relieved, and as if her mouth was full, she mumbled,

"Well, never mind what I said, I didn't mean to argue with you."

"Since your husband came back it seems to me your hot temper has cooled a bit."

"I've been harassed every night—he wants to make up for all the time he was away—so that must have got me raving such nonsense."

"By the way, where are the children?"

The woman pointed down toward the pier, and nonchalantly said,

"Down there."

"Down where?"

"They're busy as little monkeys, running around and learning songs—something about Changbaeksan and Amnokkang, I never know what's what."

"Who took them?"

"The soldiers of the Northern Army came by, calling them 'Comrade Niece' and 'Comrade Nephew', and led them off. Whether they mean to turn the little ones into a bunch of good-for-nothings or just have some fun teaching them songs, I can't ever figure out what they have in mind."

"Children should be raised by their own mother."

"That's the pot calling the kettle black for you. What about you, leaving your baby behind while you traipse about the countryside?"

She had a point. Suddenly, Kil-nyo came back to her senses. She could not understand why she was loitering there for so long. As though to slake a lingering desire, Kil-nyo lifted a bowl of water sitting next to the rice pot and drank to her heart's content.

"My, I'm such a scatterbrain. You must not have eaten lunch yet, right?"

"I had a bite down at the pier."

"Are there still women hawking fish on the docks?"

"The world may be a different place, but there's still no way to survive without eating. Nobody is an exception. Well, I better be going now."

"Going? Where to?"

"I didn't leave Hamyang to come here. This was on the way, so I couldn't just pass by."

And why the tears yet again? Kil-nyo had been gritting her teeth to conceal her pathetic state, but the tears kept welling up in her eyes. She left without looking back, and not until she was through the gate did she wipe away the tears with her sleeve. She wondered how there could still be any tears left inside her.

The goddess of motherhood was a heartless deity. How grateful she would have been if that deity had saved her from going on weeping. But the goddess must have still found in Kil-nyo a frail woman. What heartlessness it was to have kept her from telling Chi Sang-mo that she had given birth to his child. It had not been Kil-nyo's own spinelessness, but the sheer heartlessness of that spirit that had closed her lips.

Emerging from the alley, Kil-nyo was heading onto the main road when she heard someone running after her from behind. She turned back to discover the clumsy wife of Chi breathlessly running toward her, arms flailing and her skirt dragging in the dirt.

"You must be stone deaf or something. I've been yelling after you time and again but you never looked back."

"Why, what's wrong?"

It took some time for the woman to recover her breath, then she grabbed Kil-nyo's hand and shoved something in it. It was a silver ring.

"Only after you'd gone did it occur to me you must be short of travel money. If you sell this you can get enough to cover your needs for a few days. Don't think you owe me anything, just take it. It's not much, but it'll be of some use, and I'll feel a little better if you have it."

"How can I...."

"Stop loitering here in the middle of the road and be on your way. I see your baby fussing for her mama, you poor thing...."

Dropping these parting words, the other woman was the one who now turned and walked away without looking back. Kil-nyo had thought of her as a sloppy and lazy character, but now she thought the woman must be good-hearted and that was what earned her the blessing of having a husband who did not abandon her.

Even in peacetime to lead a comfortable life was far from easy. Especially now, when the fields were laid waste, to lead a decent life was even harder. In the best of times, it would be no small matter to give away a treasure of a ring you had kept all your life to help another pay for a journey. Thinking the woman had hurried off so she would not see her crying, Kil-nyo, too, turned away.

Along the way she was frightened out of her wits more than once by jets in the sky overhead. She was hungry most of the time because she only ate when she could beg food for free. Fortunately, she was able to shorten the trip by two days by walking through the nights, seldom pausing even to sleep.

The sun was nearly down when at last she arrived back in Hamyang. After the journey, Kil-nyo was skin and bones and her clothes were little better than rags. She pushed open the gate and mindlessly walked in to find the whole house a wreck. Murderous looking men wearing red armbands were busily ransacking the house.

What little furniture there had been in the main room had been thrown into the yard along with all the kitchenware. As the men rushed about they kicked things out of their way. Kil-nyo's mother, the baby held tightly in her arms, was sitting there absent-mindedly watching the house being turned inside out.

Among the men running amok, Kil-nyo spotted one who looked familiar. It was the short man who had come there when her father was arrested and taken away. She recognized him first, but he was the one who spoke to her. A cigar was in his mouth as he emerged from the outbuilding where her father had been staying. There was nothing out of the ordinary about the man's behavior. As soon as he saw Kil-nyo come into the yard, he rushed over to her and, pulling the cigar out of his mouth, said,

"You're the daughter of this family, aren't you?"

As if to leave her no time to fabricate any alibis, he went on immediately,

"You are Shin Kil-nyo, correct?"

Through the wide-open door Kil-nyo could see her mother sitting in the room, patting the baby's back. She felt a sense of relief at the sight.

"I am the daughter."

"Where have you been to hide Cha Pyong-jo?"

Her mother was shaking her head.

"Hide who? I have no idea what you're talking about."

"Cha Pyong-jo. You know that reactionary, don't you?"

As Kil-nyo moved over to the edge of the wooden floor and sat down, the man summoned the others from inside to come out into the front yard. After sending them outside, he continued,

"Cha Pyong-jo is your husband, isn't he?"

" .... "

"Isn't he?"

"Yes."

"Where is he?"

"I've been gone for eight days to get some food and just got back."

"You're lying."

"I swear on my ancestors' name."

"Swear on their name? You think that'll save you? I'll kill you."

"...."

"Listen, comrade, if you mean to lie, you better do a better job than that. You say you've been gone for eight days in search of food, then how come you're coming back here empty-handed?"

"I failed."

"You didn't just walk out of here on a whim, did you? You had a plan. And here you are, eight days later, with nothing but empty hands. Where did you hide that bastard?"

"I never hid anybody."

"Very well. Show me some proof, then. You've got to have some evidence that you actually went out to get food."

Proof. Who could have had more proof than she. But when pressed, Kil-nyo could come up with not a single piece of evidence to satisfy him. Like a crow pecking away at a hatching in its own nest, she had swallowed every bit of proof there ever was.

If she had not, all those ragged bits and pieces of half a lifetime would have given her not a moment of relief. In a way, her whole life until then had been one endless series of struggles to bury the signs and clues of her past—to forget all of it. For there was not a single trace of her past about which she could feel proud.

All the same, the monumental efforts she had made were all melting into air. To conceal the results of her coupling with Cha, she had abandoned a newborn baby. But Hwang Chom-gae was still around to testify to that. And the second baby, a child still without a name, was there to evidence her tie to Chi Sang-mo. As if all this was not enough evidence, her wretched fate now had become an incurable disease of some kind, penetrating to her very marrow.

Compared to all these traces of her shameful past ordeals, what the short man was requesting was a mere trifle. Still, as the man said, whether her whole family lived or died depended on her coming up with that trifling bit of evidence.

What would her mother expect her to do, Kil-nyo wondered. Would she want her to produce something showing she had hidden Cha away? Or would she accept the evidence that her daughter had gone off to see yet another man? Ultimately, however, the one in control of this desperate predicament was not Kil-nyo, but the short man.

She fumbled through the folds of her skirt, took out the silver ring and laid it down on the edge of the floor. The man looked down at the ring.

"What's this?"

"A silver ring, what else?"

"You know what I meant."

Kil-nyo knew.

"The family I went to see gave this to me. Times are so bad they must have been reluctant to give away any food. They told me to sell this for my trip back."

The short man picked up the ring. He rubbed it against his pants and held it up in the air. However long he examined it, the ring was not going to turn into a precious jewel. Still, he went on rotating the tarnished ring this way and that in the twilight. Then he put it to his mouth and left a tooth-mark on the edge of the ring. Abruptly, he said,

"Try it on."

"What?"

"You have to prove it's not your own ring."

Kil-nyo felt her heart sink. Why had she not thought of trying it on these past four days? Since leaving Kanggu, her only thought had been to get back home as soon as possible. In fact, the ring was not on her mind during the journey. If only she had slipped it onto her finger just once, she would not have felt so utterly helpless now.

If it hadn't fit her finger, she could now smile secretly to herself. What's more, if it hadn't been the right size for the ring finger of her right hand, she might have tried her left hand, too. What Chi had said flashed back into her mind: show your left hand to the bastards who like left hands, and if you run into a bastard who likes the right, put your left hand in your pocket and stick out your right.

It had been only four days before when she had heard those words from Chi Sang-mo. At the time, she'd paid them little heed, but now she'd fallen into a fix she could neither ignore nor escape. A dead end it was, for she had not the slightest idea whether the man wanted her right hand or her left.

Chi must have been the kind of man who could figure things out before he chose which hand to offer. But she, a woman who knew no better, waited in vain for a revelation. In any event, there was no time to dwell on such things, and to stick out your left hand to another would be unseemly. If the lifeline of the whole family depended on which hand she now extended, she might as well stick out both of them.

The short man stared at the two hands held out before him. Now it was he who had to choose. Suddenly he raised his left hand and slapped down her right hand.

"Take that away. No woman wears rings on her right hand."

Then, like a blacksmith's helper working at a bellows, he tried the ring on every finger, slipping it on and off of each with astonishing speed. It fit none of them. A look of embarrassment replaced the expression of confident anticipation that only a minute before had been visible on the man's face. Disappointed, he briefly glanced at Kil-nyo and muttered to himself,

"Well, seems the reactionary sneaked out of here at dawn today, after all."

It was not until much later, long after the short man was gone, that Kil-nyo realized he had taken the ring with him.

"Close the gate and come in, dear."

Her mother spoke in a soft voice. But Kil-nyo went straight inside and took the baby from her mother. The child was just as she had left her. Hurriedly, Kil-nyo put a nipple in the baby's mouth, but the baby's lips wandered around the mound of the breast as if she had forgotten how to suck.

"He left the house this morning at dawn."

"Left? How did it come to that?"

"He started crying."

"I beg your pardon?"

"Last night he seemed to get frantic. Well, I'm bedridden and just waiting for my last breath and I feel like going crazy sometimes, too. So, it's no wonder he, an able-bodied man, couldn't stand being cooped up in a coffin of a room any longer. I thought he'd calm down after a while and change his mind, but there was no sign of him this morning, and I checked his room and found the door wide open."

"How could it be possible…?"

"He's ungrateful. Either he mistook the intention of your father, who practically volunteered to be taken in, or he was just too suspicious. He must be out of his mind."

"I have to go and find him."

"No, you can't."

"He wasn't in his right mind when he left, and I can't just sit and watch like it was a fire across the river."

"Is your father's predicament a fire across the river to you? Are you going to put on a hat before your hair is done?"

Everything her mother said was invariably right, whatever the situation. So it was always Kil-nyo who ended up tongue-tied after a few exchanges in any argument with her mother. The old woman went straight to the point, like she was swatting flies. And now she nailed her point yet again just to make doubly sure.

"When I was in labor, your father never left my side and it was he who delivered you."

Once she had sealed Kil-nyo's mouth, her mother flopped down on the floor, moaning in pain. Kil-nyo went out to latch the gate, the baby in her arms. The sun was not yet all the way down, but everything was as quiet as beneath the ocean. Not a sound was to be heard from the surrounding areas.

She propped the baby up on her back and started retrieving the furniture and other things scattered around the yard. Then she headed to the back of the house and looked in the vacant room. The small space, too cramped for a five-foot man even to turn around in, gaped like a barn stall after the cow has been slaughtered.

She had never found Cha Pyong-jo to her liking, yet in her mind she must have depended on him more than on her own father. She had not thought to go look at her father's room after he was hauled off, but now she could not resist having a peek at the room where Cha had stayed.

That night Kil-nyo went to the District Office that had been converted into the headquarters of the local People's Committee. The light that always used to stay burning in the old days was out. She took the baby with her, just in case she was caught in the act of spying into the building.

She scanned the area from a distance but did not dare to approach the building. Even though there was no light outside, there were two guards posted at the front and back of the place. She was trying to determine the likeliest place where her father might be confined, but the whole time she was thinking about Cha. Where could he have gone?

That they had come in the afternoon to search the house for him meant he had made it through the whole day without being caught. But where could he have hidden himself? Nobody was likely to welcome a perfect stranger, and even a close friend would be hard put to hide someone if it meant risking his own neck. That was clear enough from the way Kil-nyo's so-called relatives had turned their backs on her family, despite their hardships.

Had he worn proper shoes when he set out? Whatever could have possessed her to head off on that trip to Kanggu? If not for that, she might have been able to dissuade Cha from leaving. A peculiar sound was approaching from the distance. It was thunder, intermittently heard as it rolled through a series of valleys.

Or was it? Could it have been the sound of bombs falling from a jet high above? Or artillery pounding another village somewhere? It was neither bombers nor artillery. It was a roll of thunder, there was no mistaking that. Kil-nyo peered up at the night sky. Only when she realized that not a single star was shining did she notice how very stuffy the air had become.

"A deluge is coming."

She murmured to herself, turning to look at the baby asleep on her back. She recalled the downpours back when she was keeping vigil outside the salt storehouse in Andong. Now that Cha had flown and they were convinced she had not gone away to help him find a hideout, Kil-nyo saw no reason why they should hold her father any longer.

They should have known better than to expect Cha to surrender himself just because they were holding Kil-nyo's father. Perhaps they never expected that. All the same, Kil-nyo could not simply turn back around and head for the house. For she had a feeling Cha would suddenly materialize out of the darkness, right in front of her face.

The sound of thunder repeatedly faded and returned but never quite made it all the way to where she was. There would be a serious downpour before the night was through, no doubt. Would the rain help Cha Pyong-jo or hinder him? After all, it had been raining hard on the night Hwang Chom-gae made his escape while being transferred.

She wondered why she had not thought of it earlier. If only Cha had taken off with his shoes well-tied, he should have covered a good fifteen miles by sundown. In the rain he could walk a long, long way without worrying about his footsteps being heard. Just then, the thunder took a giant step and was rumbling much closer, just around the bend.

Kil-nyo could not recall exactly when it started, but it seemed there was one thing she always wanted of all the men she had ever known. It was true of Hwang Chom-gae and of Chi Sangmo too—she had urged them to go a long, long way off—to go far, far away. And now here she was, praying the same prayer for Cha Pyong-jo.

"I wonder what it means," she murmured to herself, "when I say they should go far, far away." She turned around to look at the baby on her back. A raindrop splattered on her forehead. If they were caught in a deluge, the baby would surely catch pneumonia. Kil-nyo hurried back to the house. By the time she got there, the rain was pouring down.

"Ma'am."

As she was about to push open the gate, Kil-nyo thought she heard something of the kind. Then she caught sight of a good-sized man standing in the rain at one side of the gate. She was startled, but instantly recognized the man who had spoken. It was Hwang Chom-gae. Still, she asked,

"Who's there?"

"It's me."

A match was struck and the face above the flickering light was that of Chom-gae.

"No lights were on and there was no sign of anybody inside, so I've just been waiting out here."

In those times people rarely spoke in their true voices, especially at night. But Chom-gae spoke in an undisguised voice, unchanged from years before.

"What's happened? Why have you come?"

"Nothing happened. It didn't take me too much trouble to find you, ma'am."

"Let's hurry inside."

Kil-nyo led him to the room her father had been using and lit the lamp. Chom-gae made the customary deep bow, and said,

"Better screen the door with a blanket or something, ma'am. These days the bombers can't tell the civilians from the revolutionary forces. We'll be a target if that light is seen."

She hastily took a blanket down from the shelf and in the meantime Chom-gae picked up the baby from the floor. Kil-nyo looked over at the one-eyed man.

"Just what brings you here?"

"There's plenty of time to tell you later. Right now, I'm so relieved to see for myself that you and the baby are both safe and well. I've been trying to find you all this time, and I guessed you'd end up here in Hamyang with your folks sooner or later."

"I never thought I'd see you again here...."

"I can understand you being dressed like that, but your face looks pretty awful. I guess nobody finds it easy to stay healthy in times like these."

"You haven't been going hungry, I hope."

"Not at all, in fact I've been eating to my heart's content, three square meals a day, all thanks to our honorable leader. But from what I've heard I know times have been hard for you."

"Tell me what's been going on with you."

"No hurry about that, I'll tell you in good time."

Only then did Kil-nyo carefully look him over. His clothes were not much different from those of the men who had hauled her father away, except there was no armband over his sleeve. His skin was darkened by the sun but his cheeks were not as sunken as when she last saw him. Chom-gae pulled a cigarette from his pocket and stuck it in his mouth.

"You've got to watch out for yourself. Nobody's in their right mind, and one false step will get you killed like a dog. It's a good thing I happened by here."

Kil-nyo remembered what Chom-gae had once said about the coming of a better world. She recalled, too, that at a time when everybody else was talking in whispers, his voice had no tremor of hesitation. Nobody envies the guard at a granary, but for the bundle of keys in his hand. Likewise, at that moment was less delighted at seeing Chom-gae alive and well than at the possibility he had a set of keys in his pocket.

She found him frightening because all the neighbors and all the refugees passing through the area were keeping their voices low, and those on the rampage all had voices that were abnormally loud. At that very moment Chom-gae lowered his voice as he said,

"I'd like to help you out, of course, but it's not in my power. I came here to see you only because I wanted to find out how you were. Don't misunderstand."

He seemed to have been reading her mind. Through the rain Kil-nyo heard something—it made her uneasy. It could only be her mother calling out for her. The old woman had to be worried, hearing a stranger's footsteps but not seeing anyone come in. Kil-nyo picked up the baby and said,

"I'll leave the little one with my mother and be back shortly."

Her mother was up from bed.

"Who's the stranger?"

"There might be a chance to save father."

A light appeared in her mother's face that had not been seen for a long while. But she must have felt less than relieved at the vagueness of Kil-nyo's remark, for she immediately asked,

"What do you mean 'might be'?"

"This man was a neighbor back in Yongyang; did work at my in-laws' house. It looks like he's got connections with someone in the Northern Army now."

"Connections?"

Her mother's hands were quaking as she took the baby in her arms.

"Lucky for us to run into somebody like that, good luck, indeed."

"It is lucky. I never thought I'd see him here. He's a good man and can be trusted."

"I don't care if he's a northerner or a southerner, beggars can't be choosers. You must get him to help. Implore him, get down on your knees and beg. For your father's sake, a daughter's got to do what she can."

Kil-nyo went out onto the wooden deck. The drone of the rain was dismal. No lights could be seen in any houses nearby. Her mother's words were still echoing in her ears. It was all she could do to keep from weeping. It had been an endless day for her. After trudging for miles to get home, there had been not a moment's rest since she arrived, and the night now was deepening.

As Kil-nyo sat down, Chom-gae spoke again, rubbing his

hands roughly together,

"It's beyond my power to promise anything, but if I can't help free your father, my stupidity will be to blame. But there's one thing I have to know, and you better tell me the truth."

"What is it?"

"Cha Pyong-jo was hiding in this house. Is that right?"

"Yes, it is."

Chom-gae heaved a long sigh. Then, rubbing his hands together again, he said,

"This is not the time for such a grave blunder. Hiding a man who should be standing before a People's Court, it's not like you offered a meal to a stranger passing by—you must be aware how things stand."

"I've no special attachment to him, and I even loathe him sometimes, but I can't just ignore him since our pasts are bound together, you know that, don't you? Besides, he was already here before I arrived."

"This is no time for feeling duty-bound. A shovel may not be able to finish a job when a trowel would have done at the start— that's a saying for this case. Your father was once a landlord, that already put him on the wrong side, and then, to top everything, he hid a reactionary bloodsucker who held a high post in the southern government! Well, with things like this you don't think there's any hope to save your father, do you? Unless they're a bunch of simpletons, I don't doubt they'll find a way to vent their rage."

"The man walked in on his own and walked out the same way. That's how things stand."

"You should've turned the bastard in, he deserved to be stoned to death. You should've informed, I say."

"Maybe I never lived a life of luxury, but until now I've managed to survive without ever informing on anyone. So if there was a blunder, I have to say that was it."

"The way you talk, it sounds like you're reproaching me, is that it?"

"No, I never meant it that way."

Streaks of rain were blowing in through the door and wetting the threshold. There were still no lights to be seen, but a convoy of vehicles was heard passing down the main road in the distance. The bombing had been much more intense and more frequent of late, and the blackout was strictly enforced for vehicles as well as dwellings.

The Northern forces which had been sparse were getting more conspicuously numerous. Unlike in the early stage of the war, the Northern soldiers wore gloomy faces as they marched through heading northwards. Shouts of "Long Live the People's Republic" were faintly heard from afar. Kil-nyo felt a sudden chill penetrate to the marrow of her bones. That endless day did not seem to be over yet.

Just then Chom-gae opened his mouth,

"Suppose you're in a jam where you're about to be dragged off and thrown to a tiger, or else thrown to a wolf. What'd pass through you mind then, ma'am? Wouldn't you think about which of the two you knew more about?

"Since you can't expect good treatment from either, it's only natural to try to lean toward the side that you know a little better. That's why I became a member of the communist party. In the old days, not only was I blessed with nothing to speak of, nobody every thought of me as any better than the dirt between his toes."

"But a new world should be better for everyone, don't you think? Just because it's to your liking doesn't mean it's a better world. I know you're not the only one who's changed."

Kil-nyo let out a deep sigh as she spoke.

"Lots of people have changed."

"The man in Kanggu was a different man, too."

"The father of your baby, you mean?"

"Yes."

"What makes you say that?"

"The way he mistreated me is out of my mind, now, but my heart still aches from the shock of seeing him so utterly changed."

"So, he had the nerve to treat you badly, did he?"

"It was my fault to set out on such a long journey without a second thought when we ran out of food. I wasn't thinking straight, and I shouldn't ever have talked myself into depending on him to begin with...."

"Unbelievable."

"I'm very used to cold receptions by now and I forgot about it right away, but the way he changed still bothers me, I can't help it."

For a long time Hwang Chom-gae was silent. Then, to her surprise, he blurted out,

"The bastard ought to die."

"Don't blame him. It's the times that are unnatural, it's not his fault."

Chom-gae put his hand into his pants pocket and took out a small bundle wrapped in paper. With her eyes Kil-nyo was asking what it was, and Chom-gae said,

"I was told this was yours, so I brought it back to you."

As she expected, it was the silver ring. To Kil-nyo, getting it back was a welcome windfall.

"The interrogator is a comrade of mine from the party headquarters. He's the revolutionary I met in Sangju when I left our village a long time ago. He's from a landlord family, too, and went to Japan to study, but a man of firm conviction, solid to the bone. Thanks to him I was able to learn you'd rejoined your family. He also told me that Cha had vanished. We must catch him at all costs."

Chom-gae abruptly scrambled to his feet. Kil-nyo asked him to stay the night but he would not hear of it. She virtually begged him to see her mother just to be introduced, but he mercilessly refused even that request.

It had not yet been two years since they last saw each other, but during that time Chom-gae had become another person entirely. His behavior struck Kil-nyo as extremely ill-mannered, yet she was in no position to condemn him. He jumped down onto the steps without saying a word about her father's predicament.

When she first had seen him that night, he at least had answered her questions politely, but now as he made his way out through the yard the tone of his voice was downright rude. So brusque was his attitude that Kil-nyo could not even bring herself to say 'good night'.

She made a bit of a fuss looking for an umbrella to give him, but he curtly declined the offer. Instead, he pulled a cap from the back pocket of his pants, smoothed the crease with his hand and put it on. Then announcing his departure he walked out of the house. Kil-nyo begged him to let her walk along with him to where the alley met the main road.

Chom-gae said nothing and just stared straight in Kil-nyo's face for a while. Then he said,

"Because you acted like this, with no dignity at all, even an ignorant bastard like him could treat you like that."

Having spat out these words, Chom-gae went on his way at a rapid gait. Judging from his rough and ruthless behavior, it seemed unlikely he would be paying another visit anytime soon. Before she knew what had happened, Kil-nyo had lost the guard with his keys to the store room. Had she realized how clumsy and tactless she was at the art of persuasion, she never would have invited him inside in the first place.

Yet, on that very same night old Mr. Shin Hyon-jik came home. Kil-nyo had not had the heart to tell her mother had left in an angry mood. She had no choice but to answer her mother's questions with hopeful replies. To tell the truth to an ailing old woman would have been too cruel.

Mother was very excited. The veins on the back of her pale, bony hands were swollen.

"He's coming, your father'll be back without fail!"

Over and over Kil-nyo's mother said that same thing. To her dismay, Kil-nyo realized that if her father did not appear soon, the crush of disappointment might hasten her mother's death.

Utterly drained herself, lacking even the energy to calm her mother down, Kil-nyo fell asleep right where she was sitting, leaning back against the wall. With every joint in her body turning to liquid, she had been afraid that once she laid down, she never would be able to get up again.

Then she stirred, thinking she heard someone knocking at the gate. When there was no response after several knocks, a series of violent kicks followed. Judging from the arrogant and brutal entrance, Kil-nyo felt sure it was the same men who had ransacked the house earlier.

Thinking she was due to reap a harvest of bad karma, Kil-nyo rose. Every muscle and every bone ached. But as soon as she opened the gate she saw standing before her her father, propped up by a stranger. When Kil-nyo rushed toward her father, the stranger pushed her away and walked into the yard, still supporting old Shin. Both men were soaked from the rain, and Kil-nyo could almost sense the chill emanating from the two living forms.

When he reached the middle of the yard, the stranger halted. Pointing to the eaves with his finger, he asked Shin,

"Are you sure this is your house, comrade?"

"Yes, this is it."

The stranger cast a quick glance at the long face of Kil-nyo as she stood back away, then he walked out of the yard without another word. Shin quietly stepped up onto the porch and went through the open floor into the main room.

A set of clean clothes had already been laid out for him in the corner. Clutching her husband's rain-soaked hands, Kil-nyo's mother was weeping. Kil-nyo stayed in the kitchen long enough to let her father change. She was kindling a fire to boil some water for soup when she heard him calling for her to come into the other room.

"I'm not sure even now why they released me all of a sudden, but I know you've suffered plenty."

"...."

"I feel like I've been to the mouth of the nether world, so next time I make the journey it won't be so unfamiliar. For a man at my age, that's not such a bad thing."

To be summoned this way by a father who had not wanted anything to do with her was in itself enough to make Kil-nyo feel ecstatically happy. She knew only too well that the reason her father had stayed away from the main house was not because of any differences with mother, but because he did not want to deal with his wayward daughter.

The old man slipped his arm under the cushion where his wife was lying, and said in a soft voice,

"I've been worried about you, dear."

"They say a rotten chestnut hangs on the tree for three years. I'm counting down my days, but I'll not be closing my eyes for good any time too soon."

"There were times when they were battering me and my face got awful bloody, and other times they beat me with a club, but then they seemed to leave me to have a natural death, so I did my best to hold out as long as I could."

"That headache in the back room started going crazy then he up and disappeared without a word of gratitude."

"That's what I heard. But, then, I guess that's what gave the excuse to let me go. This is something just between us, but I noticed that those bastards were making themselves very busy these last few days—far from normal. Makes me think our Southern Army has begun to advance to the north."

"I won't be able to close my eyes in peace till I see the world put back right side up."

"It won't be long."

After this brief account of his story her father collapsed into sleep. The next morning he couldn't get up. There was no way to bring a decent doctor to see old Shin, and the ended up bringing in a quack, a total illiterate, who examined Shin and then advised the family to feed him a few dogs to regain his strength and make him good as new.

"With this war on and people being killed like dogs, I'm to slaughter a dog to eat? I'd sooner die."

Shin Hyon-jik flatly fefused to follow the doctor's prescription. The latter grew sullen and, picking his teeth, declared,

"Maybe good food is not the most urgent thing right now. It's said the Northern Army dug a huge pit a few days ago and has been burying innocent civilians alive, whole groups of them at a time. If you ask me, you should go find a safe hiding place for yourselves."

The rumor reported by the quack was actually well founded. Kil-nyo, too, had heard people were being indiscriminately killed, and that massacres were underway. She just hoped that Hwang Chom-gae would never join in such atrocities. But there was no sign of him, and not a word of news about him.

In fact, a few days after he visited Kil-nyo, Chom-gae happened to appear in the port town of Kanggu. He had chanced on a supply truck moving on the Northern Army supply route, and was able to get a ride, arriving in Kanggu only two days after leaving Hamyang.

The moment he arrived, he went straight to the headquarters of the People's Committee and asked after the whereabouts of a man named Chi Sang-mo. There were men at work there, but everything was in total disarray. They were civil to Hwang Chom-gae but of little help in directing him to Chi. It took three men half a day just to locate Chi in their files, for nobody there could read Chinese characters.

Once he had obtained Chi's address, Chom-gae set out for his house, not reaching the place until after nine in the evening. Chi was not home. A woman who seemed to be his wife cracked the door only half-open, her hand on the knob poised to slam it shut at any moment. At his inquiry she only barked,

"Gone."

"Where has he gone?"

From this first altercation, the woman struck Chom-gae as far from well mannered. She seemed taken aback at first by Chom-gae's tone, then she opened the door a bit wider, as if to indicate he could look inside if he wished. She said,

"Should a man check in with his wife every time he goes out? I've already told you he's not home—what an odd character you are."

"Enough games, just tell me where he's likely to be found."
"Tell me a place where a two-legged beast can't go. These days, especially, with the bit out of his mouth, there's not a place he doesn't stick his nose into. He's forever doing the opposite of what you want him to do. I've no idea why you're looking for him, but I advise you to stay put in one place. He'll show up on his own when he feels like it, and you'll never track him down by chasing after him."

It was not easy to say whether she meant to defend the man who was supposed to be her husband, or rather to berate him. Then, after carefully scrutinizing Chom-gae's appearance in the dim light shining out from behind her, she abruptly asked,

"Who are you, anyway?"

"He'll know who I'm when he sees me."

"I see you take me lightly just because I'm a woman, but you'll have to at least give me your name so I can tell him you were looking for him, whenever he crawls back here."

For a mere housewife Chom-gae found the woman impertinent and vulgar. Since Chi was not at home, he saw no reason to waste any more time arguing with a garrulous gossip, and in any case he had nothing more to say to her. As he walked away, Chi's wife yelled at his back,

"If it's something urgent, try the docks. God only knows why, but that damned mission of his has to be done after nightfall."

These parting words at least gave Chom-gae some notion where he should check next. He went down to the pier and strode directly into the office of the Fishermen's Cooperative. When he showed his identification, the guard led him out behind the building to the night watchmen's office.

In the room about half a dozen men with bloodshot eyes were sitting in a ring, talking over something. As the door opened their heads instantly spread apart.

"Is one of you a comrade by the name of Chi Sang-mo?"

"Yes. I'm Chi Sang-mo."

Perhaps the man who had brought Chom-gae there made some signal with his eyes, for all the other men in the room hurried out like gamblers surprised by a riad.

"Please, go on in, sir."

The guard from the main office said in a deferential tone.

Startled by the honorific form of address used by the guard, Chi hastily took the cigarette from his mouth and extinguished it in the ashtray. The crash of waves on the shore could be heard through the open window. The air in the room was heavy with the smell of fish mixed with human sweat. Chom-gae sat down in one of the chairs.

"I am from Party Headquarters."

"Ah, I guessed as much, comrade."

"What are you up to here, comrade?"

"As you can see, I'm taking practically no sleep, working through the nights on our revolutionary mission. It's no easy task keeping the fishing boats out at sea and productive."

"Who entrusted you with this mission?"

"Entrusted me? I volunteered upon my return here after some years away from home. Not a single dog was loitering on this pier, so I took it on myself to perform this duty."

"Would you mind closing the window?"

Chom-gae sized up Chi's figure as he sprang up to lower the window.

"This is secret information for your ears only—our People's Liberation Army is presently on the move North for tactical reasons. Will you join us, comrade?"

"Has Pusan been seized?"

"I said it was a tactical move North, didn't I?"

"Then it's not a retreat."

"Of course not."

"In that case, it's not necessary for us to follow the troops to the North, is it?"

"A comrade like you, energetic and enthusiastic, should be out on the front lines instead of sitting here overseeing a few fishing trawlers. What do you say?"

"But this mission I'm working on is on far too big a scale."

"All the same, there are too many people who haven't been

liberated yet."

"It's late and you must be famished, can I offer you a drink of *soju*?"

"No, thanks."

"I, too, have something confidential to tell you. You better not act too haughty with me. I'm a core member of the party and have been given a secret mission."

The moon was shining in the night sky out through the window. As if it had nothing to do with the waves rolling in ceaselessly to the pier, only to break into spray, the moon was hanging high up in a distant quadrant of the heavens, aloof. It had been ages since he had really seen the moon, Chom-gae thought to himself. Then he felt the glance of a self-avowed core member of the party riveted on his forehead. Chi's grinning visage was dimly reflected in a mirror suspended on the wall.

"Do you know a woman named Shin Kil-nyo?"

"Kil-nyo?"

"You met her in an inn at Sokpo-ri a long time ago, isn't that right? And not ten days ago you saw her right here in Kanggu."

"I'm surprised you know so much about the private lives of others. Now that you mention it, I might as well tell you the truth. I know her, sure. But if you know all the past details so well, I don't see any need to make a full report to you. You even know about her visit here a few days back."

"I left Hamyang two days ago."

"Why didn't you say so earlier? It's got nothing to do with our revolutionary mission anyway. As you know, I'm in no position to be bound by a mere woman."

"Do you know that she has a child by you?"

"Women are known to drop a lump of flesh every so often, how the hell would I know whose bastard it is?"

Chi must have found the air in the room somewhat stuffy. He was about to get up and reach over to the window, when a single razor-sharp word came hissing from Chom-gae's mouth.

"Sit!"

"Oh, no...."

Chi saw a butcher's knife flash out from Chom-gae's belt. Chom-gae's hand flew through the air and Chi Sang-mo felt a dull shock between his stomach and his ribcage. As a kind of reflex, Chi grasped at Chom-gae shoulder and pushed with all his might. But Chom-gae did not even bother to shake off that hand. After a long convulsion, the hand became still on its own. The window was still shut, but a chill passed through the room.

"There's not a bastard in this world who has the right to mistreat her. Especially a son of a bitch who fathered her child...."

Once out of the night watchmen's room, Hwang Chom-gae paused to tighten his shoelaces and then continued walking across the yard. The moon in the sky looked much closer.

A Handkerchief

Shin Hyon-jik was arrested again in the dead of night three days after Hamyang was retaken by the Southern Army on its drive northward.

Crickets were chirping loudly beneath the steps that night. Kil-nyo's mother, her heart devastated, refused to shut the door of her room even though she was constantly coughing in the cold draft from outside.

"Look at the stars, they're as bright as the eyes of clever children."

It was past eleven and Kil-nyo was fast asleep with the baby in her arms. Her old mother was lying in bed gazing at the stars and muttering to herself. Her hands folded on her chest were so wizened they looked like two bundles of dry sticks.

Keeping her hands clasped like that on her chest must have been a habit linked to her heart ailment, but to Kil-nyo it was a sign of approaching death. She often went over to her mother and unlocked those hands, laying the old woman's arms down off her chest to either side.

By this time Kil-nyo had taken to furtively checking her mother's breathing first thing each morning when she woke up. The relief was never more than tentative, however, and in Kil-nyo's mind that breathing remained dangerously precarious, like an earthen wall on the verge of collapse in the rainy season.

The unbolted gate swung open and a young man walked in to

the front yard. He glanced into the main room where Kil-nyo's mother was lying, then headed straight for old Shin Hyon-jik's room in the back. As soon as the young man was out of sight around the corner, his mild voice was heard asking,

"Is Mr. Shin in?"

Like a hustler luring a mark into a high-stakes card game, the voice was unusually sugary and polite. Except for the introductions, everything else was beyond the old woman's comprehension. Not long after, she saw her husband, his gait as ghostly as ever, walking away from the house with the stranger.

Shin was taken once more to the District Office building where only a few days before the sign of the People's Committee had been hanging. A contingent of the Southern Army was stationed there. The biggest differences now were that the men in the office no longer had murderous looks on their faces, and bright lights were on all around the building.

One thing, however, was exactly the same as before: you had to be completely truthful in responding to all questions asked. A young officer politely offered Shin a seat on the other side of the table from him. Lively and self-confident, this officer's uniform smelled of sweat. There were no papers or writing materials on the table. After glancing around at the other officers all absorbed in their respective tasks, the interrogator pulled open a drawer and asked,

"Care for a smoke, sir?"

"No, I don't smoke."

The officer closed the drawer.

"Go ahead, don't mind me."

"It doesn't bother you?"

"No, it's fine. I may be an old man, but I'm not that small-minded. I don't want to make things difficult for those who work through the night."

"Well, with your permission, then."

The officer lit a cigarette and went on,

"I'm sorry you have to come here at this hour when you should be in bed asleep. We're under a lot of time pressure, so

I hope you do understand."

With the cigarette his mouth, the officer clasped his fingers together on the table and stared at old Shin.

"You'd think after seventy years of sleeping every night I'd be sick and tired of sleeping, but...."

A faint smile appeared on the officer's lips, and he interrupted, saying,

"You went through hardships under the enemy occupation. I know those bastards took you in and tortured you. I don't know what I can say to console you for those sufferings. However, we plan to take steps to see that you get compensation, so to speak."

"Compensation? You're not by any chance asking me to inform on my neighbors to get revenge, are you? It's true I was a target for the Northern Army and was treated like a fish on a cutting board for a while, but as you can see for yourself I am quite all right now.

"In the first place, my suffering wasn't caused by any of my neighbors squealing. Secondly, you people are only here for the time being, but this is where my family has lived for generations and we hope to go on living here in harmony with our neighbors. I don't want to be the one to accuse others and sow the seeds of discord."

"I understand your situation. What I've heard about you is true—you have an open mind about accepting your neighbors."

"To you, maybe I seem like a spineless half-wit. That's not what worries me. I just don't want any members of my clan to face retaliation in the future."

"That, too, I can understand very well. But the situation we face is not that simple. Even now there are a great number of partisans active behind our lines, and unless we root them out once and for all we'll never know when the war might erupt again. If you're too much attached to trivial things, you might end up losing what's most important—and then it'd be too late. You've got to understand that, sir."

"Wouldn't I, at my age, know that much? But you have to keep in mind that my ordeals under the occupation weren't due to any informers. I've never had an enemy in my life, and you've got to accept what I'm telling you."

"Even if nobody informed on you, somebody must have arrested you."

"He was a stranger I never saw before."

The young officer dropped the cigarette under the table and crushed it under the heel of his boot. Then he got up and went over to a soldier sitting a few tables away. A few minutes later he brought back a short stack of papers. He plopped back down in his chair again and said,

"I have no problem understanding you, sir. This is the file the puppets left behind. It fell into our hands because they had no time to destroy it before they fled. According to this, you were classified as an obstacle to the accomplishment of their revolutionary mission, so you are on the list of those to be executed."

"They never said anything about that to me, nor did they reveal any sign of their intention."

The officer laughed softly and said in a low tone,

"I don't doubt it. There's one rather strange thing, though. Most of the anti-communist fighters on their death lists were either executed or else taken away with them when they retreated. But you, sir, you alone of all those people are alive and well, as you yourself just told me. I was wondering if you can give us some explanation that we can easily understand."

If, indeed, Shin's name appeared on the list of those to be executed, then this officer's question was only natural. But Shin realized he was in a position where he could neither ignore the question nor give him an answer. He'd already guessed they had released him after all the beatings because of the one-eyed man who had come to visit Kil-nyo.

Old Shin did not know the identity of that one-eyed man, but it was plain enough he was either in the Northern Army or one of their sympathizers. But he had never met the man or asked Kil-nyo about him. He had just been thankful to be released and had never tried to delve into the details of the story behind it.

The fact that a Northern collaborator made his release possible was not something he could fell proud of. At the time, he was too desperate to think over what was reasonable or right. He certainly had never expected he would again be bound to deal with the predicament that had made him lose face and forfeit his pride.

He knew, also, that there was an immense difference between the officer's criteria for judging these things and his own. But now he was cornered in such a way that the question could not be evaded. In his own way, the young interrogator was very polite, but the question he raised went right to the point.

Old Shin racked his brain to come up with some kind of explanation, but it was in vain. Then, all of a sudden he grasped that the very politeness of the interrogating officer had been venomous.

"I've no idea how I came out of all that turmoil alive. When they released me, they didn't say a word."

The young officer stared at Mr. Shin for a long while. Then he opened the drawer once again and pulled out another cigarette. A brief sigh escaped his lips.

"If you don't give me a straight answer, I'm afraid you'll be in a hell of a shape. I know you're a good-hearted man, but this is not the sort of case that'll go away just because you're trying to defend somebody else. All we're interested in is the truth, and we've no interest in arresting people just to take revenge. This is not peacetime when you can get by talking nonsense. Under the enemy occupation there were more collaborators than you might think."

Shin responded in a voice that was no less heated.

"See here, don't badger an innocent man. Now that I can live in a free world again, why would I need to evade your questions? If your job is to get to the bottom of the truth, shouldn't you trust the words of an honest man?"

"Was there, by any chance, some sort of deal between you and them? An exchange?"

"Are you that dismayed just because I made it out alive and

free? You act like you're troubled because they didn't execute me."

At these words, the young officer was greatly taken aback, and waving his hands, he hastily added,

"That's not what I meant at all, sir. If there was some misunderstanding, let's clear it up right now. For a man like you to survive the enemy occupation was most fortunate not only for this village but for the nation."

"At my age I'm more used to being pampered like a child than to be harassed with trivial matters—that's my complaint."

"I can understand that, too. Brought in here in the middle of the night, your family must be concerned about you."

"My married daughter came back home to help her old parents in wartime. My wife's been ill, bedridden for months."

"Was anyone in your family harmed?"

"No, thank heavens, we were lucky to come through it all safe."

"Very fortunate. As you know, many families around here lost loved ones or were separated."

"It turned out for the best that we stayed put here in the village. If we'd left and gone on the road as refugees, god only knows what might have befallen us in some strange place...."

"Wait a minute, if you don't mind."

Said the officer, rising from his seat and walking out of the office. Shin looked around. Unlike the last time he was there, it was empty except for one soldier dozing at a corner desk by the window. The clock hanging in the center of the wall had stopped at seven twenty. The bright lights from every side revealed a thick coat of dust on the clock.

The lights were so intense that an insect creeping across the floor would have stood out conspicuously, but the darkness just outside the room was as frightening as the harsh illumination within. The sparse glints of starlight in the sky had dimmed to black. Mr. Shin glanced once more at the clock. He regretted not checking the time before leaving home.

An inexplicable anxiety seized him. Unlike the last time when he fell into enemy hands, it seemed release would not come as easily this time. He tried to compose himself by reflecting that he had only a few years left to live in any case—no hardship in store for him in his remaining days could warrant such dreadful anxiety. But it was no use.

Then old Shin happened to look down underneath the table. Scattered on the floor were some papers that looked like official documents. Some had boot-prints clearly outlined on them, some had been use to wipe up spilled ink, and others had just been crumpled up and tossed down. There were forms with lots of blank spaces, and others of the papers were lists with row after row of tiny, meticulously printed names underlined in red.

Among the documents were a number that bore a round stamp marking them "Top Secret". Though they had been cast away, once picked up from the floor, uncrumpled and laid out on the desk they seemed to promise earthshaking revelations. Whether those documents remained beneath the desk or were placed atop it might decide the difference between heaven and hell, between a man's freedom and his execution. That such power, a power more dreadful than any foe he had faced in his life, could be locked in those papers struck him as comical, somehow.

"Come with me, please."

Shin looked up and saw a tall soldier looming behind the chair where the young interrogator had been sitting. He followed the soldier outside to a dusty three-quarter ton truck standing in the street with its motor running. The soldier pointed to the vehicle.

Seated in the back of the truck were three men, all shabbily dressed and wearing dispirited faces. They were guarded by a soldier with a rifle. Shin could do nothing but climb into the truck as ordered and wedge himself in among the three men. They were licking the newcomer from head to toe with their eyes.

He felt no warmth of compassion from these prospective traveling companions. Nevertheless, he had no excuse to disobey the soldier's order, nor was he in a position to decline the company of the trio.

"Nothing to be afraid of, sir. Please, get on."

The soldier behind him spoke in a benevolent tone, as if doing Shin a favor. The growl of the truck's engine seemed to Shin to be an omen of the cruel treatment he soon would encounter. He wanted to flee at all costs. He turned to face the guard behind him. The stocky soldier was expressionless.

Just as it occurred to Shin that he ought to stop trembling and calm himself by all means, he realized he was, in fact, quaking more uncontrollably with each passing second. Simultaneously, he felt a surge of indignation from deep down inside. Once again he looked over at the prisoners sitting in the truck.

Strangely enough, they were grinning at him. One extended a hand to offer him help in climbing up, but the hand felt as clammy as the hand of a corpse. He could not see why he should have to endure the degradation of being grouped with them. To be released from torture in the clutches of the communists only to end up in this fix was a fate too outrageous to bear.

Despite all his efforts to calm himself, Shin went on trembling. When he managed to vocalize his indignation, the protest was weak and futile. Barely opening his mouth, the old man croaked,

"If you're offering me a ride home, I don't need one. I'm still strong enough to walk a few miles."

The soldier standing behind him said,

"This won't take long."

"What do you mean by that? Where are you taking me?"

"Just following orders."

"What orders? Nobody asked me about going anywhere."

"You're a stubborn old man, aren't you?"

The soldier muttered as if to himself, then casually lifted the old man up onto the truck. The three others squeezed over to make room for him to sit. The bed of the truck was covered with a straw mat. After a few hiccoughs and belches from the engine, the truck sped off down the road away from the district office.

Three days passed with no word of Mr. Shin's whereabouts. "Your father must be possessed by a wandering demon. Snatched out of the house, bundled off with strangers...."

As she said this on the morning of the third day, Kil-nyo's mother's breaking voice was punctuated with coughs.

"You should have asked where they were going. You knew he's not the type to go off and kill time in a gambling den somewhere."

"What more could I wish than to find out that's where he is, gambling somewhere right this minute? I had a bad feeling he'd been taken away for some dreadful reason."

"Taken away? What has he ever done to make them take him away?"

"I know, but if I had some clue what's happened, I wouldn't just lie here in bed, no matter how sick I am. It's my fault, after all, for not giving him a decent daughter."

Her mother seemed to have said this in order to prick Kil-nyo's conscience. Tired and sickened by these complaints from the old woman, Kil-nyo left the house and headed for the district office, where it was said the army was taking people for interrogation.

In front of the building was an empty truck that seemed to be waiting to be loaded with passengers. Outside the front door of the office stood a soldier with a gun at his side. Through the window she could see several other soldiers busily moving about, thumbing through papers and answering phones.

For quite a while Kil-nyo stayed there next to the parked truck, hesitating to approach the guard. In the end it was he who took notice of her. After aiming a few inquiring glances at her, he motioned for her to come closer.

"What brings you here?"

"I'm trying to find out what's happened to my father."

"Your father? What's his job?"

"...."

"What's his name?"

"Mr. Shin Hyon-jik."

"And what was the problem with him?"

"Three days ago he left the house in the middle of the night and we haven't heard from him since."

"Did someone say he came here?"

"No, but I thought if I came here I might be able to locate him."

"Is that so?"

The soldier peered at Kil-nyo for a time, and then out of the blue asked,

"Are you married?"

It was an absurd question, but Kil-nyo did not want to spoil a chance to speak with him, so she courteously replied,

"Yes, a long, long time ago."

"You look rather young, though."

The soldier did not smile as he spoke.

"I've been through a lot. To hear you say I look young is flattering, but you must be joking."

"How many children do you have, then?"

It very well might have been an innocent inquiry, but it set Kil-nyo's face ablaze. The soldier must have thought she was blushing out of shyness, for he glanced over toward the office and said,

"Let me see, why don't you wait here a bit?"

For a second he seemed to waver, uncertain whether he could leave his post, and then he vanished into the office. Enough time passed before he reemerged for Kil-nyo to be fed up with the wait. Upon his return, the soldier looked tense and quite disturbed. He adopted a more formal level of speech as he pointed at an officer inside and said,

"You see that officer sitting in the middle? He wants to speak with you, ma'am."

As she approached the officer, he took out a cigarette from the drawer and was about to light it. Kil-nyo made a very deep bow. The solid-looking officer gestured at a wooden chair across the desk from where he sat. Before she had an opportunity to say anything, he asked,

"So, what's your relation to Mr. Shin Hyon-jik?"

"I'm his daughter."

"I see. Well, I suppose he's old enough. And he's the one you're looking for, is that right?"

"Yes."

"I understand. It's only natural for the family to be concerned about him, since you weren't even notified that we'd brought him in here the other night. I apologize for the mistake. It's just that we've been so busy things get overlooked now and then."

"My mother is in bed, in critical condition."

"Critical, eh? I knew someone in the family was unwell, heard it from Mr. Shin. And you couldn't move south because of the patient, wasn't that it?"

"Move south? I don't understand."

"To take refuge down south, I mean."

"From the first me never thought about seeking refuge. Our family has lived here for generations...."

"That's quite all right. I didn't mean to make an issue of the circumstances that kept your family from moving south. What concerns me is this: your father was arrested by the enemy occupation forces and then released, isn't that true?"

"Yes, that's right."

"At the time, didn't you get help from someone in particular?"

"Yes."

"Yes, you did get help or yes, you didn't? Which do you mean? Since your father was from what the enemy called the class of bourgeois landlords, he had to be on their blacklist. Once arrested, it would be impossible for him to be freed without help from somebody. Besides, according to a document that fell into our hands, your father's name was on a death list."

"Where is my father now?"

"He's safe and well. But he's so stubborn that everything he says works against him. That's why I've been waiting patiently for someone from the family to show up voluntarily. I'll tell you right now that your father's release depends entirely on you giving me some straight answers. Do you understand?"

"I do."

"If you do, then we can dispose of this problem easily enough. I'll set your father free. You said just now that he was released from enemy hands with help from someone, didn't you?"

"Yes."

"Whoever it was, you owe them a great deal, since without that help I'm sorry to say your father would not be alive today. Even in the middle of this pandemonium, there's always an exceptional case."

"There was a man by the name of Hwang Chom-gae."

As Kil-nyo related the details of her father's release thanks to Chom-gae's intercession, the officer chain-smoked three cigarettes in a row, his eyes glued on some bent sunflower stalks outside the window. When her story drew to a close, he asked, "I don't suppose you know where Hwang Chom-gae is now, do you?"

"No, I don't."

"I don't doubt it. By this time he's probably well on his way northward, mixed in with the retreating guerillas or in the rear with the stragglers. Didn't he say anything implying he'd be coming back, or to lead you to think so?"

"He just left."

The officer rummaged through his pockets and removed a faded green handkerchief.

"Here, wipe your tears, please. Naturally, your father knows his release was due to Hwang Chom-gae, right?"

"I said nothing to father, but at his age he knows something of how the world works."

"You're not very old yourself, but you're far more open-minded than your father, though he's seen much and has been through a lot. You can go home, now. You have my word."

"We must have father back. Without him, our place is as somber as a house in mourning."

"Please, don't even say such a dreadful thing. I said you have my word, didn't I? You can go back home assured of your father's return."

When she came out of the building, the truck was gone. The guard standing at the door smiled at her and asked, "Did it go well?"

Why she kept weeping, she couldn't say. It was no place to show tears, and she certainly was not seeking to elicit any sympathy from that soldier. There was nothing in the story she told the interrogator that was especially apt to evoke weeping, either. She felt no great indignation or resentment at being wronged, nor was there anything embarrassing about it.

As for the officer, he had made no threats. There had been no jeering, either. He had only sat there listening to her story from start to finish without a single interruption. The strange thing, though, was that what set Kil-nyo to crying was her sense of the officer's sincerity as he listened to her.

The more she tried to stifle her tears, the more abundantly they flowed. All the way home, Kil-nyo kept mopping her eyes until the handkerchief was completely soaked. Not until she reached the gate of the house did she realize she had taken the officer's handkerchief with her.

Her mother had the door open and like a sunflower was facing the sun. The rays of light slicing in left one half of the room shadowed, and the baby was lying near the wall fast asleep. Upon coming in, Kil-nyo hurriedly picked up the infant and cradled her in her arms. Even then the tears were still flowing, but her mother somehow seemed to sense they were tears of relief.

The old woman had an uncanny way of seeing to the bottom of things. A long life and many brushes with adversity had given her the power to fathom the hearts of others. Seeing the awkward look on her mother's face, Kil-nyo said, "They said they'd inform us soon. Father ought to be back within three days."

"It's about time. What fault could they find with your father? He lived his whole life in peace with others, never had an ill word to say about anyone. You can't spit in a smiling face, as they say. Your father will make it back home, I'm sure of that. My, didn't he give me a hard time when I gave birth to a girl!

Like the saying goes, it's the crooked tree that saves the ancestral lands—if not for you, I can't imagine how we ever could've gotten through these troubles."

"Enough old proverbs, mother, please. They weren't persuaded to free father because I had any great influence, but just because he was proved innocent."

"Don't be so fretful. It's all thanks to your going to them and pleading for him. Stubborn as your father is, you don't think I could believe it was his doing, do you?"

"He's not back yet, so it's too soon to feel so assured."

"They wouldn't make a false promise. I'm sure they have better things to do than to hoodwink womenfolk."

"They must have had second thoughts about father's predicament. It's not likely they were moved by anything I said."

"Look outside, dear, a real downpour is on the way, looks like."

The sky, clear and sunny a moment before, was obscured by a cascade of dark clouds. The massive grey thunderhead was rolling in from the direction of the Chirisan peaks. Nothing in the front yard would be harmed by a cloudburst. Kil-nyo's mother reached over and shut the door, for the wind had risen and threatened to drive all the warmth from the room.

Kil-nyo laid a quilt over her mother's legs as she laid back down in bed. The old woman's ribcage was skin and bones, and age spots were mushrooming on her neck. Once more Kil-nyo used the officer's handkerchief to wipe off the tears running down her cheeks.

A stormy wind was heard whipping through the yard. Kil-nyo felt a tremor of a cramp in her midsection, and outside the rain slackened for a moment, as though chased away by the wind. A deathly silence followed. Then a dog was heard barking somewhere not far away.

"It's going to rain cats and dogs, I tell you."

As she spoke, Kil-nyo's mother pulled the quilt up snugly against her chin. Then the daughter felt another tremor in her abdomen. All at once there came a crack like the sound of a huge fire blazing up. It was a bolt of lightning, a portent of thunder on the way, of a thunder greater than any witnessed in the past.

The thunder was taking its time rumbling along the ridges of Chirisan, seemingly building force for a greater impact when it finally struck. With both hands, Kil-nyo shielded the ears of the baby.

"Careful with the baby, dear."

Her mother also sensed the imminence of a clap of thunder. Just that instant an enormous crash of thunder hit, loud enough to open an abyss in the earth right under their noses, and with it a gush of rainy wind burst the door open.

Kil-nyo heard part of the earthen wall collapse just beyond the door. She closed the door again and latched it. Presently the deluge began in earnest. It went on all day and into the night. At times it seemed to slacken, but before you knew it the downpour had resumed with the same force.

Through the darkness voices could be heard shouting something about a flash flood. As dawn drew near, the rain abated gradually until it turned into a spring drizzle. Through the shower appeared old Shin Hyon-jik, walking up to the house with the aid of a youth from the village. Carried by the youth would be more accurate to say, for when he realized he had reached his own gate, Shin insisted that the youth let him down from his back.

"I can't be seen coming into the house like a sack loaded on your back. My wife's inside, and she's been ailing in bed for ages."

"But sir, you're in no condition to walk on your own. Please let me carry you in."

The youth tried in vain to coax the old man. Neither of them was much inclined to tell the family how they had run into one another. When Kil-nyo stuck her arms under her father's armpits to support him, she noticed that his temperature was terribly low.

Every bit of strength had been drained from his body, and he barely could stand, a mere scaffold of bones. As the youth helped him to lie down in his room in the back of the house, Kil-nyo stoked the fire to warm the place as much as she could.

Whether she gathered her own strength or was helped by the youth Kil-nyo could not tell, but her mother had managed to seat herself beside her husband's head by this time.

"How many times have I told you, betrayal is not an honorable thing. You understand, don't you, that I couldn't tell them what I knew, not even if it meant dying in prison, gnawing on a straw mat. In my old age this insignificant life of mine brought me troubles, but that doesn't mean I have to surrender my dignity."

"I don't know who to thank for this help or how we ever could repay them. Kil-nyo's been going high and low, pleading for mercy."

"I was afraid of that, and that's why I sneaked out of the house in the first place. Well, it turned out I only brought myself more troubles."

"How are you feeling?"

"Don't worry about me."

A clean change of clothes had been neatly laid out at the head of the bed, but Shin refused to change. The next day, too, the clean clothes were still laying there where his wife had put them.

"They threatened me, saying I was only posing as an innocent man, but I didn't know anything worth feigning ignorance about. Well, ah, there was something—Kil-nyo had dealt with somebody who'd joined up, you could say, with the Northern Army, but how in the world could I say it with my own lips? Over my dead body.

"Besides, if not for his help, I never could've escaped being executed, and a narrow escape it was. I haven't even thanked him, never gave him a bowl of rice, so how could I, even if I'm a mean, ignorant bastard, inform on my own daughter? Not a chance, not unless I was in a demon's power, or gone stark raving mad."

At that moment Kil-nyo's mother looked back over her shoulder at her and in a barely audible voice said,

"Dear, something's not right with your father. He's delirious, raving like this, no doubt because he's totally exhausted. We better get some meat and help him regain his senses."

"What do you mean raving? Everything he says makes perfect sense."

"No, dear."

Her mother's voice had a sharp edge, like the blade of a razor. Suddenly Kil-nyo noticed that the blanket covering her father was shaking.

"It's not like I have no blood relations, and there're lots of distant relatives and plenty of close friends. All of them are our own race, after all. Go and ask them. What's a piece of meat to them? Life is hard in the countryside, but if they hear I've come back home, they'll swarm here and put together a table fit for a feast. Hurry on, now, go get them."

Old Shin was waving his arms in the air, but a moment later they dropped listlessly onto the blanket. With that, Mr. Shin released his grip on life. The copper mask of the underworld began to settle over his face. As the last feeble convulsions rippled through his arms and hands, the spirit Shin had been governing for seventy long years dispersed into the air. His wife quickly closed his gaping eyes, unfolded his clutched fists, and placed them neatly across his chest.

"All your life you were good at pretending, and now it's the same even as you set off for the other world. In your whole life, was there ever a time that you took me out anywhere? Even on the first visit to our relatives after we married, I practically had to force you to go together. Then, you walked way out ahead of me, like a little boy pouting about something.

"What hardships you went through just to eke out a tough living in this world. Don't be too cruel to the wife you left behind. Stop and rest now and then on your way—it's a long, long road to the other world and a bit of a head start makes no difference, dear."

The old woman turned and looked back at her daughter, who

sat there aghast. Kil-nyo's mother continued,

"He's left without changing his clothes. Inform the neighbors of your father's death. If you must weep, do it silently. And we've got to throw some of father's clothes up over the eaves to summon the departed spirit."

After tossing up some of old Shin's clothes, they received their first uninvited visitor, a keener who lived not far away. This mourner for hire was known as Hadongtaek, since she was a married woman from the village of Hadong. She was renowned far and wide for her keening, thanks to a somber, hoarse voice perfect for a melancholy wail.

Some years before, infected with a flirtatious urge, Hadongtaek had left the village and wandered from tavern to strange tavern in remote provinces, and then she had come back two years before the war broke out. She was barely forty, yet her hair was snow white. At the age of eighteen she had been betrothed to a widower, but within a month and a half she herself became a widow. The stars had not granted her a happy lot.

During the short breaks in her wild keening, Hadongtaek upbraided Kil-nyo, who seemed totally lost, for not having set up a mourning altar or sent for an undertaker to wash and shroud the corpse. Back in Yongyang, Kil-nyo had attended funerals, but now that a death had occurred right under her roof, she could not make heads or tails of the formalities.

Her mother, hands quaking, brought out a shroud and other things she had prepared for her own burial and stored in a special chest in the attic. Two men arrived carrying planks under their arms to take care of the body.

From the hour of her husband's death, Kil-nyo's mother suddenly became almost sprightly, alertly minding little details, such as preparing a basin for cleaning the corpse. Kil-nyo, however, was too distracted at first to notice the change in her mother, and the arriving relatives had not seen her in a long while, so they did not think twice about it.

The way the old lady suddenly recovered her vivacity made it seem her being sick in bed had all along been due to oppression in the face of her husband's energetic life. By the time the undertakers were done washing and shrouding the corpse, the pallbearers arrived with the coffin and relatives distant and close began to appear a few at a time.

Once the clan was assembled, Hadongtaek's keening underwent a metamorphosis and her sheer wails were interspersed with eulogies and laments. From the main room where the deceased was laid came the deep voices of men debating the technicalities of the funeral ritual. Once oppressed by dead silence, the house became as vibrant and raucous as a fish market.

In a household that had not boasted even a handful of meal to make a thin gruel, there now were several big sacks of rice piled up next to the kitchen, condolence gifts to aid the bereaved. Out in the yard, well-doers of both genders had flocked in from the village, men conversing in loud voices and women lending a hand with food, preparing a repast befitting the occasion.

Children were darting about and periodically a group showed up in the kitchen to nibble on the trimmings of the sweet rice dough for the *ttok.* So often had they drawn from the well that the bucket constantly smelled of fresh water.

Around dusk the pallbearers hurriedly set up a tent in the front yard and started to build a bonfire. The children romped about in the mud like unbridled donkeys, and everyone present stuffed themselves like a dog who's just whelped a litter of pups. The only ones not eating were Hadongtaek, who was exhausted from keening, Kil-nyo's mother and Kil-nyo.

Those three, in retrospect, were the ones who had been living under their breath. For them any sort of gathering had meant a short path to extinction, and so they had isolated themselves for a long while.

During the war, even those who had once been very close, sharing joys and sorrows, often kept their distance. Even if they crossed paths on the road, no one dared to utter even an exchange of greetings. Cowed and menaced by unfamiliar phrases like "secret contact" or "forced labor", people decided that the best policy was to steer clear of any contact with their neighbors.

That was why there was such a crowd at Kil-nyo's house, using the funeral of old Shin Hyon-jik as a pretext for a gathering. Had there not been a family with a funeral to face, they probably would have gone right on to singing and dancing, turning the evening festive.

The behavior of Kil-nyo's mother continued to be out of character. Once the mortuary altar had been set up in the main room, she sat there erect with the door wide open, supervising all the female helpers. She had already regained the dignified bearing of the mistress of an honorable house. Nothing in her face showed any sign of a person who had been ailing away for months.

The only thing Kil-nyo's mother did not meddle in was the eating and drinking of the helpers. Everything else she personally orchestrated down to minute details. At the same time, she attended to the arguments going on among the men, unfailingly offering astute advice just in the nick of time.

It was a total mystery to Kil-nyo how a person who had been so sickly, irritable and quick to complain could have suddenly recovered both health and equanimity in the wake of her husband's death. All day long she had been beaming with pride at the bustle in the house and the yard, and not once had there been a glimpse of bad temper on her part. The whole day she maintained a serene countenance, repeating the same thing over and over,

"Thank you, dear. Thank you, indeed."

As nightfall approached, the women who had been working outside began to come into the main room to take a rest. All they talked about was the war and the scars it had left behind, about who had been killed and who tortured. As for the death of Shin, however, nobody brought it up. It was as though everyone had agreed not to let a word slip from their mouths on that.

As far as they knew, the death of Shin was a dreadful consequence of some secret contacts between Kil-nyo and the communists. When Kil-nyo was not around, the women whispered about her, their lips pouting. Even when they worked with her in the kitchen, if Kil-nyo asked them anything, they only gestured with their chins or simply ignored her.

If it had not been her own house, Kil-nyo would have walked out rather than endure the cold shoulder from these women. To reproach them openly was impossible, which made things even worse. After all, they had come to lend a helping hand with her father's funeral.

There was no longer any space for Kil-nyo to step aside, whether she was alone or in the company of others. She knew that by custom women were excluded from making a ritual bow at the funeral altar, but they had even shooed her away from the ceremony when the other women were keening.

She had vaguely guessed that all the coldness and jeering burdening her was due to rumors spread among her relatives. Her father was dead, but she could approach no closer to him now than when he was alive. Ostracized, she stayed in the kitchen until late that night, tending the fire to keep the house well warmed.

That night the body of old Shin was moved out of the house into a corner of the yard near the base of the wall. The shrouding of the corpse went in the usual order, first by steps and finally in its entirety, but Kil-nyo's mother didn't even remove the old clothes from the corpse. Instead, she had the shroud hastily wrapped over them, and then had the undertakers put the corpse straight into the coffin.

Kil-nyo had expected that the body would lie in the house until morning, but her mother had the deceased moved out from the floor of the house to the yard well before dawn. The relatives were livid, protesting that she would turn old Shin's spirit into a aimless vagabond, but in the end the old woman's obstinacy prevailed.

"He lived past sixty so nobody can say he didn't live to a ripe old age. But when you think of it, he didn't meet death at home. He died on the road. When a man dies away from home, you know very well you're not supposed to keep him inside the house for any length of time. Name a single place in Korea where that's not strictly observed!

"In his lifetime, my husband was looked down on in the clan as man without principles. It was because he sold off the fields and mountain land that passed down to him through the generations. But now he's dead, and it's only right to follow the proper rules in his case, isn't it?"

Faced with male relatives who were about to point their fingers at her, Kil-nyo's mother stood up as straight as a bamboo stalk and didn't even blink. At last, Kil-nyo began to understand the source of her old mother's sudden recovery. It was no miraculous rejuvenation and it was no uncanny reprise of youthful exuberance. Rancor had been lifted from a hardened heart.

The old woman had been oppressed by impotent rage, clotted and hardened for years as she endured unending hardships day after day. As she watched her father's body being moved out into the yard for the hideous reason that he had died on the road, Kil-nyo wiped stream after stream of tears from her face.

"A woman who switches from one man to another is bound to get thick-skinned. She's too busy lusting to think of anyone else."

These words were uttered by a woman behind Kil-nyo. No names were mentioned, but Kil-nyo was the only woman in the room who had been with a man besides her husband. The others all had been married off in their teens to men from the village and had spent their whole lives serving their husbands.

Kil-nyo felt pain from the gazes nailed into her back, yet she lacked the nerve to turn around. Why all of a sudden had the subject been brought up? No matter how crude her lot had been, she was still the only child of the deceased in a household in mourning. To say something so ugly in these circumstances made Kil-nyo suppose there must have been a reason, but she had no idea what it might be.

"If you've a mind to, seducing a man is as easy as flipping your palm upside down. A man hungry for women won't spit in a smiling face, that's for sure."

"I'd sooner die of thirst with my tongue stuck in the sand than go begging a strange man for love."

"You don't get it, do you? There's a kind of woman who, once she's had a taste of sex, will stop at nothing to get her fill."

"Even with all the turmoil of the war, they say a man was kept in an attic room to satisfy her lust."

"That insatiable, eh? My, my!"

Kil-nyo looked down at the handkerchief she was using to mop her eyes. It was still the same one, and she thought it must have been the trigger for the scene. Always eager to gossip, the women must have taken the handkerchief for a keepsake Kil-nyo had kept after a love affair with one of soldiers stationed in the village.

Dark green truly was an unusual color for a handkerchief, and it was a most conspicuous and unbecoming object in a house in mourning. Startled, Kil-nyo started to conceal it under her skirt, but instantly changed her mind. She feared it might only kindle worse gossip. That particular handkerchief had only a trivial tale behind it, but it provided a pretext for the gossipmongers to babble on endlessly.

If she tried to refute their jeering, Kil-nyo figured she would only provoke even fiercer verbal assaults. On the other hand, if she tried to hide the handkerchief, it would only confirm their suspicions and she would never be free from their slander. Perhaps the real root of the evil was not the handkerchief, but the kind of life Kil-nyo had been leading until then.

That she had become an irrevocable shame to the family was the thing that hurt her the most. Still, she had no one to blame, and there was nothing to be done except to bear the scorn and accusations of the others.

With the return of the geomancer who had been sent out to identify an auspicious burial site for the deceased, another round of heated debate commenced among the male relatives. The gravediggers stood by with their picks and shovels waiting for the decision.

Even in the matter of locating a clearing the right size for the grave, the men of the clan were divided into two factions. They fought each other tooth and nail as though they never had set eyes on each other. But as soon as the aroma of beef came wafting over from a meal table, they suddenly became jovial and fraternal as if there had never been the slightest controversy.

As the corpse of Mr. Shin was shifted out into the yard, without a full night's rest inside the house, his death, too, was slowly pushed out of the memory of the living. No real attempt was made to hide their indifference to the gravity inherent in death itself, whatever death might imply. This attitude of theirs extended to sorrow and suffering as well.

All their concern was focused on the procedural technicalities of funeral ritual. Meanwhile, the passing of Mr. Shin was something to be discarded and forgotten, like a broken rake. When all was said and done, their prime interest was to maintain to the bitter end whatever point they were committed to defend.

Almost from the hour of Mr. Shin's death and through the night, they had disputed the question whether Kil-nyo, as the sole living issue of the deceased, should be deemed a mourner even though she was female, or whether, on the contrary, she ought to be prohibited from coming anywhere near the ceremonial altar. No conclusion was ever reached.

Each time they exchanged arguments, some insoluble problem arose. On other questions Kil-nyo's mother was generous with advice, but on this particular issue she abstained from any comment at all. The women helping in the kitchen had sensed all this and feigned deafness when spoken to by Kil-nyo.

Feeling her heart about to burst, Kil-nyo walked out through the breach in the wall to get some fresh air by the well at the mouth of the village. She found the bucket and dropped it into the water. Then she drank down half a bucketful of water, so much that the slightest pressure on her stomach would have made her throw up.

She felt cool and refreshed, though her belly was near bursting and had not even room for her to swallow a peach seed. She felt grateful to be able to console herself this way, drinking fresh water and contemplating the moon.

She wondered whether the wisest thing would not be for her just to leave the village then and there. If she simply disappeared, her relatives would no longer need to argue about whether or not she should be cut in half once they had placed her on the cutting board. Besides, the shame and disgrace would end.

All at once, Kil-nyo felt a streak of insanity shoot in an instant through her entire body. The sky was full of bright stars and the moon shone full. If she set out right away, she could cover miles and miles before night fell again.

Almost as a reflex. She started to straighten the baby on her back. Then she realized she was out there all alone. She reached for the handkerchief she had slipped into her belt. It was not something she could cast away, and she could not hide it, but neither was it something she could openly brandish for all to see.

The handkerchief was fated to be hers. In a way it was like herself, a woman unable to run away, yet in no position to stay on, even though her destiny appeared to be to remain.

A Guest

It was the day following the ceremony marking the lapse of three days since the passing of the deceased. The relatives who had assembled from here and there had begun to head off to their various homes. The helpers from the village likewise were looking for pretexts to depart.

The whole house was submerged in an atmosphere of abandonment. It was in utter disarray, like a chicken coop after a weasel has paid a call. The big black pot used to cook rice was coated around the edges with sticky brown grain. The drain was stopped up with vegetable cuttings and shards of pottery.

Unclean dishes and bowls lay scattered about the basin in the kitchen. A scrawny dog was lurking behind one of the large earthen storage jars, waiting for the chance to do his share of the cleaning. Mixed with the breeze blowing across the room through holes in the papered windows was an odor of fish. A few relatives were loitering on, resting on the floor, but once the sun went down they would be setting off for home, too.

Once she had put the baby to sleep, Kil-nyo went into the kitchen. A good-sized rat had hidden himself behind the water urn and was peering at her with a twinkle in his eyes. He did not even bother to run away. There was not a drop of water in the urn.

Kil-nyo took all the kitchen utensils out to the pump in the yard. The ravenous dog that had been crouching behind the storage jars slithered close to the pump and watched her rinsing things in the basin. Though raised under the heel of humans, this dog seemed to have a mind of its own, capable of grasping what went on.

Kil-nyo wondered how long it had been since she started the chore of washing. The candles burning on the mortuary altar were casting patches of radiance onto the ground outside. The dog had stood by for a long time watching, but now it was nowhere in sight, and lights from neighboring houses were dimly seeping over the wall.

It had been some time since Kil-nyo had last heard the voice of her mother calming the restless baby. She thought she heard someone calling through the wind, but she just ignored it, reckoning she must have been mistaken. Then she detected the sound of a small stone dropping right next to her by the pump.

"Ma'am."

Not a soul in the world would have called her "ma'am" except for one—it had to be Hwang Chom-gae. Her heart immediately sank with a thump, and at the same moment she sensed someone's presence outside the wall. Chom-gae was back. Kil-nyo hurried over to the wall. No one was in sight but a man's voice wafted by.

"On the hillside off the road to the next village there's an undertakers' shed. Meet me there."

Kil-nyo walked back to the pump. Her limbs began to tremble and her vision grew cloudy as though muddy water had been splashed in her eyes. Next door a dog kept barking, followed by a man's hoarse shouts to quiet the animal.

The undertakers' shed was a remote spot that people tended to avoid, even in the light of day. By his naming such a place she knew he feared being seen. And that meant Chom-gae had made the trip back in disguise to see her. Kil-nyo put the brass bowls back into the basin and rinsed them over and over, although they were already clean.

Just where had he come from? She remembered the interrogator having said Hwang Chom-gae might have joined a retreating column of guerillas or hooked up with stragglers. Maybe he had never even tried to join the retreat. A man who had become a communist for the sake of his son was not likely to leave his boy behind. Just as this occurred to her, Kil-nyo sprang up with a start like a grasshopper menaced by a serpent. She flung open the gate and went out.

Once outside of the yard, Chom-gae's parting warning came back to her: "Please be careful on the way." But she was not of a mind to look over her shoulder warily as she made her way to the rendezvous at the undertakers'. To herself she kept repeating, "Good thing he didn't head off, he did the right thing, that's for sure."

As the lights of the hamlet receded behind her, she no longer felt the need to conceal the quaking in her hands and feet. Once it was no longer necessary to hide her terror, she soon found it easier to calm herself.

"Over here, ma'am."

Chom-gae was perched on a stack of wood heaped up beside the shed. Kil-nyo recognized him at once and the moment she knew it was him, oddly enough, the violent galloping of her heart subsided and she felt composed. Streams of tears flowed down her cheeks, nevertheless.

Chom-gae offered her the place he had warmed up, and after studying her face for a time, he softly said,

"It worries me to see you looking so unhealthy, even worse than last time I saw you."

" . . . . "

"I heard your father had passed away. Three days ago now. I wanted to head straight here, but it turned out I couldn't. Anyway, even if I'd rushed here, I wouldn't have been fit to pay my respects in front of the mortuary...."

A short sigh escaped his lips and he did not try to finish the sentence. This man who was so worried about Kil-nyo's appearance himself looked a dreadful sight. His clothes were worse than a wandering beggar's and he reeked of sweat.

"Your mother must have fainted more than once during the

funeral. Stop crying now, please. At night, even the slightest sound travels far."

"Just where are you staying now?"

Paying no heed to Kil-nyo's laboriously summoned question, Chom-gae continued,

"If I'd known that was how it was going to end, I never would have exerted my influence to get your father released. I couldn't just let it go, not with his name on the official death list."

"You're certainly not to blame."

"Who else can be blamed but me?"

"This isn't the kind of world where everything that goes wrong can be blamed on somebody in particular."

"You seem to have made up your mind to take pity on me, but there's no doubt my stupidity was the source of all this grief."

"Staying alive's not been easy for you, has it?"

"Eating and drinking are not important, and lack of comforts is no hardship for me, so you shouldn't worry about that."

Constantly chewing on dry weed stems, Chom-gae kept an eye trained on the main road in the distance as he exchanged words with Kil-nyo. Then, as if suddenly remembering something, he asked,

"With your father's death, I wonder if you didn't meet with accusations from your relatives?"

"No, I hadn't done anything for them to blame me. If anything's to be blamed, I guess it's my ill-starred fate."

"I heard you were taken in for questioning, too. Is it true?"

"What do you mean, 'taken in'?"

"Didn't they arrest you?"

"I went in to see them on my own to try to find out where father was, but they never arrested me."

For quite a while Chom-gae said nothing, then with a long sigh he went on,

"There's no use crying over spilt milk now, but you should never go anywhere near them in the future, ma'am."

"Just where've you been staying that you know so much about what I've been doing? Why do you have to keep hiding? How come you won't tell me anything?"

"I've got a mission of grave importance to do. I can't tell you the details, but our mission isn't done yet, not by a long shot. From here on out it's even more crucial. Don't ask any more questions, please."

"Why are you in such wretched shape, and how did you get that knife scar on your face?"

At yet more questions from Kil-nyo, a faint smile came to Chom-gae's face. Through the breeze came what sounded like a few bursts of gunfire.

"There is a world where this ugly face of mine earns me respect. Where in South Korea could I go and be treated like a human being with this scarred cyclops face? Not even becoming a beggar'd be easy, and I'll always be looked down on and laughed at due to my lowly birth. But among our revolutionaries, this hideous face of mine is the very image of the oppression and suffering of the people under imperialism, and this scar is a fruit of carrying out our revolutionary mission. For us, this living proof of struggle against suffering is no less important than a medal of valor.

"Without these badges of courage, I'd be just another nameless guerilla, forever kicked around and scrounging for food. Under my command are men who used to be journalists, teachers, even artists under the imperialists. But none of them has been decorated like me. With no decoration scored into their faces, they work their asses off hoping to earn a medal to pin on their chests. When it comes down to hard work, not one of 'em can match me. In the end, the medals will be mine, too.

"The day is coming when the South'll be liberated and it won't be long. From that day on, these medals won't only allow me to live in plenty, my descendants for three generations will know no want."

Chom-gae stuck his hand inside his jacket and removed from a pocket a bundle about the size of an apple wrapped in a handkerchief.

"All the medals they've given me so far are in here. You've got to keep this, ma'am. I don't need to tell you not to lose them, but you shouldn't let anyone know anything of this, not even your family. A mistake will put you in peril. All the same, I want to leave these with you—and I hope you understand why."

Kil-nyo could not refuse. On the contrary, she felt grateful to Chom-gae for wanting to leave such treasures with her. Whether or not the medals were capable of bestowing luxury on three succeeding generations was beside the point. What she could not doubt was that all the hopes and dreams of a man were contained in those objects, and it was overwhelming for her to think Chom-gae wanted her to have them. Kil-nyo unbuttoned his jacket and slipped her hand against his chest. The man's skin, coarse as an old tree's bark, felt hot on her palm.

"Ma'am, don't. I'm a sinner. I've sinned against you, ma'am, but I couldn't tell you."

"Don't say another word."

"Please, don't do this."

"It's not that I'm full of lustful cravings, or starved for a man and begging you to have me."

"I said no such thing to you, did I, ma'am?"

"Where are you staying now?"

"Chirisan, in the mountains."

"What part of Chirisan?"

"I'll send word later."

"Winter'll soon be here, do you mean to stay up there through the winter?"

"I'm just following orders."

"Why not come down into one of the big cities and lose yourself in the throngs?

"I hope that day will come."

Kil-nyo moved her hand onto his belly.

"Are you going to just sit there, stiff as a tree trunk?"

"How could I dare to touch you, ma'am?"

"Don't call me 'ma'am'."

"It won't do."

Beyond the ridge the dark sky was slowly turning to a pale

shade of orange, and sounds of people stirring were beginning to
filter up on the morning breeze.

"Ma'am, I've got to be going now."

"Not today. Why did you call me out here?"

"When I thought about your father dying, and the hard times
you must have gone through, I just had to come and see you.
You do understand how I feel, don't you?"

"Of course I do."

The coldness at the tip of her fingers when she first thrust her
hand next to his belly had changed to heat. His breath reached
her nostrils bearing a sweet scent like ripe persimmon. The next
moment Chom-gae's hand hungrily fumbled through her underclothes. His other hand, groping under her blouse, grasped at
her peach-like breasts. Kil-nyo felt tiny clumps of dry grass
pricking the bare skin of her bottom.

"In a sordid place like this... beside a mortician's shed. Might
as well be at the funerary altar of a house in mourning. Besides,
you just lost your father...."

"I don't know when I'll see you again, so how can I be choosy
about the place? And there's no waiting till the period of mourning is over."

"I'm truly a sinner."

Kil-nyo covered his mouth with her hand. As she felt his flesh
touch her abdomen, she clutched at his broad, stony shoulders
with all her might. From an elderberry tree a few steps away, a
cuckoo sang in a melancholy tone. What had irradiated the sky
a deep orange could only be a tower of flames in the distance.
An isolated village some three or four miles off seemed to be
ablaze.

The fire rose higher and higher until it devoured all the surrounding darkness, turning the entire horizon bright orange.
There could have been shrieks to be heard, but the couple was
oblivious. After pulling up his pants and refastening his belt,
Chom-gae said in a muffled voice,

"Ma'am, it's time for me to go. In a place as shabby as this...."

"I asked you not to call me 'ma'am', didn't I?"

Kil-nyo put back on the underwear hanging crumpled from one of her ankles.

"Never, never give anybody reason to suspect we met here tonight. It won't hurt me, but you'll have hell to pay again. And, no matter what disaster befalls you, you must stay put in this village. If you go to a big city, there'll be no way in the world for me to find you."

"Where could I go? There's nowhere for me to go, and I don't intend ever to go against your wishes."

"I'm off now."

"Stay just a minute longer, please."

"I can't. I must be at the meeting point when my comrades get there. If I don't show, they'll move on without me."

"Is it close by?"

"I'll have to walk a few miles before running into them."

Chom-gae sprang up. All of a sudden her field of visions seemed to blacken. He was not a man to be held back. She did not know what to make of all the talk about finishing his revolutionary mission, but she knew it was no family matter and thought it would not be right for her to detain him because they had just made love.

Chom-gae had already set off and was trudging through the darkness some steps away. She was left with the handkerchief full of medals lying on her skirt. Kil-nyo grabbed it. As she started walking in the opposite direction from the way he had disappeared, the tears that had been so plentiful of late began to fall once again.

"You're a woman, not to mention a woman in mourning who hardly should be out and about, so where've you been at this hour of the night?"

Her mother saw the dry grass on Kil-nyo's skirt. She handed the crying baby over to her daughter, then muttered as if to herself,

"I won't question you, but I don't want to believe you were by some chance out flirting with some stranger. ...it was just an unseemly thought I had for a fleeting moment, I hope."

As promised, Kil-nyo's mother said not another word about her excursion. The door had been left ajar and she gazed out at the flames beyond the hills which had begun to subside. The next morning rumors about the mysterious conflagration raced around the village.

Guerillas, it was said, had mounted a night attack on the remote hamlet of Shiritgol and left it in flames. The village elder had been skewered with bamboo spears right in front of his family and the other villagers, and his house was torched. All the cattle and grain of the village had been seized, and five innocent youths had been taken off into the mountains, with little hope for their return.

One of the five had later been found near a creek a few miles from the hamlet, impaled on a tree stump with all his guts spilt out. They said some among the guerillas spoke a northen dialect, but many were locals and they seemed to know every detail about each household in the village down to the size of each family's harvest.

When ordered to cough up everything, the villagers had no way to refuse, and if they attempted to resist, they only would end up being kicked and beaten. Barking dogs were shot on the spot, and one brave youth who set off running to warn a neighboring village was run down by guerillas and killed with spears.

The villagers found it impossible to determine the number of the guerillas, for at one moment there seemed to be about thirty, but then a few minutes later they suddenly seemed to have mushroomed into a force of a hundred. One of the leaders gathered the villagers together and delivered a long harangue, the main point of which was that the South would soon be liberated and that the villagers should be patient and wait for that day.

At first, some of the people in the village refused to cooperate and a few in fact dared openly to defy them, but before long everyone was so terrified by the reckless killing that they voluntarily brought their cows from the barns and handed them over, bridles and all, to the guerillas. The whole thing took about two hours, and in the meantime some villagers were being dragged off as the others cowered and quaked, helplessly watching the house of the elder burn beneath the night sky.

If anyone made a move toward trying to put out the fire, a black gun muzzle was jabbed against his chest. So the village elder's residence was reduced to embers without a single bowl being salvaged.

The ominous tale sent a ripple of shock through the village where Kil-nyo lived, which lay a mere seven miles from the scene. There was no law guaranteeing that the guerillas would not find Tunchon to their liking and conduct another raid. Under their breath, people were saying the time had arrived to leave the isolated village and head for a city, yet no resolution was forthcoming.

"It's all thanks to that accursed mountain."

Chirisan, long known as a sanctuary for guerillas, stood shrouded in grey fog, looking aloof.

"It's like they say: if you don't like the temple you should steer clear of the monks. We can't very well move the mountain, so what choice do we have but to leave ourselves? For generations we've lived peacefully with the mountain at our backs, but now it's turned upon us... there's no telling whether it's the mountain or us the people who's gone wrong...."

All the same, none of the villagers immediately packed up their belongings and headed for the city. They were people who never once in their lives had thought of sowing seeds among strange people in a strange place. That was why the catastrophe visited upon the inhabitants of Shiritgol had struck them like a bolt out of the blue.

Those who had family in one of the cities might seek refuge there in time of crisis. Others, however, had no relations to lean on outside the village and so had nowhere to go, not even if their whole clan faced annihilation. When all was said, there was only the mountain to blame. Still, Chirisan was no monster that had descended from the sky to block their way.

It had been there thousands of years before their ancestors were born, and it was they who had tied their lifelines to it, curing all kinds of ills with the herbs gathered on its slopes. Senseless and ludicrous it would be, therefore, to cast any blame on the mountain. It was especially true for Kil-nyo, because she knew that somewhere up among those ridges Hwang Chom-gae was hiding.

Whenever she glanced up to see mist veiling the peaks or dark clouds rolling by, a heavy weight burdened her heart. As long as the mountain loomed there, she felt half-confident of his safety. It was a secret consolation known to not another soul, but in this secret solace a threat lurked.

The threat arose from the fact that the guerillas who raided Shiritgol had been so thoroughly informed of the ins and outs of every household. They knew how many sacks of rice were in this house, and how many bushels of barley had been harvested by that. Not even the best sorceress could have come up with exact figures such as they had.

There must have been a spy in the village, people said, who had kept in contact with the guerillas. He must have been gathering information and reporting everything to them. This was quite troubling news that gave her neighbors yet another headache. People started bolting their gates and avoiding all outings.

There were times, however, when people were taken off somewhere and brought back beaten half to death. There were other times when well-dressed men, a ferocious look in their eyes, called at the house of the village elder, talking for hours behind locked doors. Unable to predict who might be the target of a pointing finger, people held their breath whenever such conclaves were held at the elder's.

With the fall of night, groups of the brawnier men of the village took turns standing guard. Nevertheless, the fear and trepidation enveloping the hearts of the villagers was diminished not a bit. One day a man walked into Kil-nyo's house unannounced. He was finely dressed, somewhere in his fifties, wearing a fierce look. This clean-shaven man removed an identification card from his wallet and flashed it at Kil-nyo, saying,

"I'm afraid you must go with me to town."

He did not say where in town, but around the village when people spoke of "going to town" they normally meant the seat of the county administration, which was a good ten mile walk.

Her first thought was: "So, my time is up at last." But even if she accompanied the man to town, she had nothing to say. Just then she recalled Chom-gae's admonition not to leave the village, whatever happened. She was carrying the baby on her back, but thought twice and decided to go alone. If the baby was with her, she was afraid the temptation not to return might be too hard to resist.

While Kil-nyo changed her clothes for the trip, her mother, who had been sitting on the cold floor before the funerary altar, said not a word to the man. Even when she was handed the blanketed infant, she remained silent.

The man's car was waiting at the mouth of the village. Little children were flocking all around it, and when they caught sight of Kil-nyo walking beside the stranger, they looked at her with doleful eyes as if they were parting for the last time. As the car started up the children scattered like flies in all directions.

When they arrived at the county office, Kil-nyo was escorted to a warehouse-like building that had lights burning even though it was midday.

"The journey must've been hard for you, eh?"

Said the man who brought her in. He looked to be over thirty, with dark, very bushy eyebrows. The general impression made by this man was a bit more humane than the other man who had brought Kil-nyo there.

"We should have gone to see you instead of bringing you all the way down here, please accept my apologies."

The man was a smooth talker, and seemed eager to allay her nervousness, but his efforts did little good. She took out a handkerchief and wiped the perspiration running down the nape of her neck. It was not hot inside the warehouse. Indeed, it was a

bit chilly, yet she kept on sweating. Then the man spoke again,
"You know Mr. Cha Pyong-jo, ma'am, don't you? As I understand it, not only do you know him, the two of you have a very
special relationship."

"What?"

"Mr. Cha personally gave us a ring and asked us to find out
how you're doing and make a report back to him. But we've
been so busy we had no time to look you up until now. Besides,
we thought you might find a visit from us something of a bother,
so we decided to bring you down here instead, just to check up
on your welfare."

"Where is he now?"

"Well, he's staying in Taegu."

"How could it be possible that...."

"We heard about it, too. He said if he hadn't been able to hide
in your house, the bastards would surely have executed him and
he'd be on his way to the other world by now. You are a very
special woman, I can see that, now that you're here in person.

You strike me as a bashful woman, unable to say things
straight out, not to mention lacking guts. I wonder how you had
that much courage and audacity in you? Under the occupation it
was hard enough to save one's own neck, yet somehow you managed to shelter a man those bastards were hunting down with all
their forces. They meant to find him at all costs. I hate to remind
you of this, but I gather your father died from the torture he suffered in their hands, isn't that right?"

"That's not true. My father passed away because of some
things I senselessly said."

"Had we known earlier, we would've come by to offer our
condolences. I hope you can forgive us for that neglect of our
duty due to our hectic schedule."

"You shouldn't say that, it's not right."

"It's a good thing Mr. Cha phoned us, otherwise your patri-
otic struggle and its fruit might have been buried without recognition. By the way, how's life been in your household?"

"I don't know of a family that's not having a hard time nowadays."

"You're right. These are hard times, not just for you alone, but for all of us. In your case, however, we can't simply leave you suffering, and we'll see to it within a few days. You can rest assured on that. And now, I find it difficult to say this, but there's one we need you to cooperate on."

This word "cooperate" was not commonly heard around the house. In fact, Kil-nyo could not recall using the word once in all her life.

"It's your cooperation we need, and the thing is...."

The man kept repeating that unfamiliar word.

"I'm sure I don't have to tell you this, ma'am, but the guerillas are on the rampage all over the country, and you probably heard that they raided a village near yours a few days ago. Of course, we're planning a punitive expedition on a grand scale, but the guerilla tactics those sons of bitches use present some difficulties. They're what they call Mao Tse-tung tactics, and it makes wiping they away in one fell swoop very difficult.

"That's why we'll have to absorb some minor casualties until we can root them out completely. And now we have reliable information that the bastards have some secret contacts in the villages. This guerilla band is made up of stragglers who failed to get away when the path of retreat northward was blocked.

"They took away some of the young village men and dyed them red through brainwashing. These young men, who don't know the first thing about real communism, are the ones who've been making secret contacts with their relatives in the village. Until we sever these ties, it'd be pointless to carry out a punitive strike. You understand what I'm saying, don't you?"

"I do."

"That's why we need your cooperation. According to our sources, there's one making secret contacts with the guerillas right in your neighborhood."

"There's nobody like that around where I live. Those people think there's nobody lower than a stoolpigeon or informer, even in trivial matters, so how could they possibly think of such...."

"My point precisely. Spies are always generous about trivial bickerings among their neighbors, for their eyes are on bigger things. A man of dark designs will never meddle in disputes among children over a bigger piece of cake."

"I know nobody like that."

"Naturally. If you did, you already would have told us who the impure element is. What we're asking you is to keep an eye on your neighbors from now on. Unless we can expose the red elements with open channels to the communists, there'll be no peace for us. You must know more than you think, otherwise you could never have kept Mr. Cha hidden under the nose of the enemy at the risk of your own life."

For some reason the man emitted a voluble laugh. Then he continued,

"Personally, I feel very sorry to have had to bring you in here for this important task. But it's something only you and I know about, so when you go back you mustn't let a word about it slip to anyone."

Kil-nyo felt all the tension that had been compressing her body instantly melt away. She could not clearly grasp what sort of cooperation the man wanted, but from his cordial attitude and amiable tone she was sure no interrogation or beating was in store for her.

The people in the village would think she had been taken away for a serious beating and was in a fix from which no easy extrication was possible. It was not that they held any special grudge toward her, but that was what had happened to most of the people suspected of being red elements. And now, when she showed up intact without a scratch, how happy her mother would be and how surprised the neighbors. Kil-nyo got up from her seat, feeling so grateful she would not have minded caressing the cheeks of this young man.

Outside the warehouse the sunlight was blinding. Kil-nyo had an urge to embrace an armful of sunrays, as if a hail of pure gold was falling. Yet by the time she got out of the car at the entrance to her village, all she had left was that mysterious word, cooperation. Of all the things the man had said, that had been the most awe-inspiring and the only one of his words deeply implanted into her brain. Still, she was not at all comfortable with the word.

As she expected, the person most delighted to see her return in good shape was none other than her mother. Looking over the wall at her daughter as she approached, the old woman, who had been vacantly surveying the distant mountains, literally rolled off the porch into the yard. All the two women could do upon being reunited was to weep, holding each others' hands.

"In this time of turmoil, you sure gave birth to a placid child. After a few hiccoughs, she's already bound for dreamland."

As Kil-nyo lifted up the child, her mother hastily inquired, "Was it anything serious?"

"What serious matter would concern me?"

"In any event, they wouldn't have taken you away for nothing. The man who came here to get you looked quite menacing."

"They praised me for offering a hiding place to Cha and for looking after him during the confusion."

"Who do you mean, Cha?"

"I was told he's now in Taegu, and seems he asked them to look after us as a kind of gesture of thanks for what he owes us."

Mother kept quiet for a time and then opened her mouth to say,

"So, that's what it was. That man who was such a headache to us because of his frantic temper and the commotion he aroused turned out not to be so senseless after all. I knew there was something unusual about the way they took you away, how lucky for us!"

"No need to be so grateful, mother. After all, I didn't do anything to deserve punishment from them."

"A kind word alone can be a comfort in this world. So, when did they say he's coming?"

"Seems he just sent word to the county office."

"Just sending word is far from nothing. He must've been of a mind to look after you. Despite the impression he made, he must not be a narrow-minded man. What did they say he's doing in Taegu?"

"They didn't say one way or the other."

"Anyway, it's certain he's made his way back into the world. Had I foreseen things would turn out this way, I'd have been more thoughtful toward him. In any case, we're done envying others, and we, too, can live with our heads held high. No doubt we'll be hearing from him within the next few days."

Mother was right. On the very next morning, a bushel of rice was delivered to the house of the village elder. The elder came along with porters to bring the rice to Kil-nyo's house, but when she asked what it was all about, he said nothing and only winked at her a few times.

It is true they were all neighbors living in harmony with hearts open to one another, still it was a most unseemly breach of manners for a man to act like a hoodlum and wink at a married woman. Even so, Kil-nyo could not maintain a cold attitude toward a man who had just brought a bushel of rice into a poor house, and the Shin clan had declined too far toward ruin to make an issue of such impertinence.

Besides, the rice was not coming from the tenants on family lands, it was food being doled out to the needy. She realized she was in no position to interrogate him on the source of the gift, nor did she have any energy to spare to argue with the elder over his transgression of decorum.

Once again she recalled Chom-gae's advice never to leave the village. Now that she had given him her body, she could not disobey his words, and if she meant to stay there in the village it would not do to be overly particular. Kil-nyo was dismayed as she stared at the back of the elder as he and the porters hustled back out of the house.

Back into her mind came the good-natured face of the man at the county office, along with his "you can rest assured on that." From the first, Kil-nyo had guessed why the elder refused to reply to her question and instead had only winked.

Three days went by and the village elder came to pay Kil-nyo another visit. It was after dark, past ten o'clock. He declined her mother's persistent invitations to come inside and led Kil-nyo back to his house. There in the guest room was waiting the man she had met at the county office. As she came inside the room his face lit up and he said,

"We've finally reached Mr. Cha on the phone. When I told him we had met with you, I could almost see his face beaming with delight. What's more, we were gravely scolded for not having accorded you a better reception. Indeed, it's an honor to meet someone like you here in this village, ma'am. Mr. Cha kept emphasizing that once we get your cooperation our problems will be over, and I was truly relieved to hear him say so."

The more he flattered her, the uneasier Kil-nyo got. She felt like she was sitting on a cushion full of pins and needles. Only then did the man give her his full name, Kang Sok-gyu. The fact that he was deliberately peeling his identity off one layer at a time frightened Kil-nyo to no end. For it meant he had no intention of leaving before he had reached a definite understanding with her.

Besides, he was addressing her with the utmost courtesy, using only high honorific levels of speech, which Kil-nyo took as a hint that something serious was due to happen at any moment. What scared her was the fact that she was fresh out of pretexts to reject what he might request, which in a smooth tone announced his decisive resolution.

"It's true we're in the dark when it comes to detailed information on this village. Through our ignorance innocent people occasionally get wrongly accused when they are not guilty. That's not at all desirable, is it? What's more, if we earn the resentment of the villagers because of such cases, it'll pour muddy water over our original plan to root out the guerillas.

"To avoid repeating such errors, we must have the cooperation of someone like you. As for your point of view, what could be more rewarding than this? Some may consider you a squealer, but they're the narrow-minded type who can never see the forest for the trees. Our peace and welfare won't be secure till there's no room for the guerillas to step in between the civilians. Don't you agree?"

Every single word the man said was beyond dispute, and that was exactly what left Kil-nyo at a loss to respond. As she was searching for something to say, Kang Sok-gyu abruptly said,

"Mr. Cha told me to ask you if you wouldn't like to come down to Taegu in a few days. If you go, we can furnish you with a car. What do you say?"

"Well, I'm not ready yet...."

"I understand. Taking care of a sick old mother as well as a little baby, it won't be easy for you to make time for a trip. As soon as we make contact with Mr. Cha we'll implore him to pay a visit here. We'll be able to reach him within the next day or two."

"You shouldn't, please. I'm not yet...."

"Don't think twice about it, ma'am. It's also our wish for him to come to this village at least once."

On her way back from the house of the elder, Kil-nyo nearly stumbled and felled more than once. "Whatever happens, you must not leave the village. If you do, I'll never be able to find you." The same phrases kept coming back into her mind. At the same time, she could visualize the face of her mother, who had miraculously recovered her strength since her father's death.

She was somewhat relieved by the thought that her mother was now able to fend for herself, even if she had to be away from home for a while. But she could not just walk out of the house without a word. Moreover, to leave an old mother by herself at a time when the house was in mourning was an unthinkable thing for a grown woman to do. What gossip and recriminations there would be from all the relations in the Shin clan! And how devastated would Chom-gae be if he happened to come by only to find her gone? Yet she knew it was impossible to stay in the village any longer.

Unable to sleep even after midnight, Kil-nyo in the end decided to awaken her mother. Surprisingly enough, she was not even sleeping.

"Mother?"

"No need to hide anything from me. Go ahead, tell me."

"It seems.... I'll have to be away for a while."

After a long silence, a startling answer issued from her mother's mouth.

"I'd guessed how troubled you must be. That day when the bushel of rice was delivered here, I reckoned you'd be in difficult straits, that much I guessed."

"Why is life so hard, I wonder...."

"Don't you worry about me. Those hungry days are over and now we've got a whole bushel of rice for meals. I'm not bedridden any longer and have recovered enough strength to move about freely. I'm not going to drop dead within the next few days, as they say."

"I've been thinking it may be best for me to stay away lest I do something that'll bring trouble to others. As a woman who can't even control her own life, I certainly shouldn't meddle with the fate of others. If I commit any more evil deeds, I'm afraid I'll spend the rest of my trifling life being mocked by others."

"You're right. When we try to do something beyond our power, misfortune is bound to follow. What a strange place this world is. Somebody who wants no more than to be left alone, leaving a quiet life of solitude, buried away from the rest of the world, they're the ones who have the hardest time finding a place to hide... isn't that funny?"

"I've got nothing to blame but my own fate. Some live their lives in peace and quiet, with nobody even learning their names until they die a natural death, but I was born destined to be tossed about by the crowd."

"Better watch what you say. It's a grave blunder for a woman to blame everything on her lot. Don't try to blame others or your circumstances. Each one of us in the course of our lives in this world has countless troubles to go through. Why do you think we've been given intelligence and wisdom to go with a perfect body, instead of being simple-minded like lower beings. One thing you should never do, even if you find yourself in hell, is to curse your fate."

The following morning Kil-nyo left the house. Never before in her life had she felt so helpless and forlorn. She could not help expecting Chom-gae's hand to appear at any moment and pull her by the neck. Several times she gazed back at immense Chirisan, but it stood as always in the distance, not moving even an inch.

Because she was carrying a bundle, every woman she met on the road guessed she was on a long journey and showed curiosity about her destination. Each time Kil-nyo said nothing and only smiled. Just as she was leaving, her mother had asked her whether she was headed for Taegu, and Kil-nyo had replied "No" as she headed down the steps.

Kil-nyo had no desire ever to see Cha Pyong-jo again. In fact, she was leaving home because she felt it was more important to avoid Cha, even at the cost of missing the chance to see Chom-gae once more. What Kil-nyo needed now was not money or shelter, but someone to provide some consolation.

After racking her brain through a sleepless night the only person she had been able to come up with was Chi Sang-mo in Kanggu. Naturally, after the cold reception she had received the last time she was there, she had no intention of begging him for help. The people missed and wanted to see again were rather his wife and children.

Even though she was by no means a lively companion, Chi's wife had shared hard times with her in the past and her unpretentious personality made it easier for a woman like Kil-nyo to rely on her. She never snooped around into others' private affairs and was open-minded with everybody. That was one reason the thought of her company was a comfort to Kil-nyo.

Once she had made up her mind to go to Kanggu, the long journey before her was dispiriting. She resolved not to lose her patience. If that man called Kang Kyu-shik somehow forgot about her very existence while she was away, then her main aim would be accomplished. On the way, Kil-nyo told herself to take her time, just as her mother had advised her father in his deathbed.

In her heart of hearts, however, Kil-nyo still had a modicum of hope that Chi Sang-mo would have changed. That she still entertained any lingering sentiment over a relationship that had been over and finished long before seemed pathetic even to her. It was not as though she had any vulgar desire to sleep with him again, but she sincerely hoped to find him there with his heart restored to the right place.

She had practically seduced Chom-gae partly because she knew her relationship with Chi was over, so she trusted she would never allow her emotions to be rekindled even if welcomed by the Chi of old.

The road was familiar, since she had trod the same path both ways before, but it proved not at all easy to get a ride. Though at the outset she had made up her mind not to rush, and to pause for a rest now and then, once she took the first step she grew so impatient that even a brief break made her feel too restless to sit still. What is more, for a shabby woman resembling a beggar with a baby strapped to her back, finding shelter by stopping at the doors of strangers proved to be far from easy.

Six days after leaving Hamyang she arrived in Kanggu. From the moment when the first whiff of salty sea air reached her nose, Kil-nyo found her heart beating more violently than ever. Dusk was approaching, so she headed straight for the house of Chi Sang-mo.

Nobody seemed to be home. She lingered in the yard, making sounds to let her presence be known, but there was no response from within. Judging from the wide open gate and from the refuse—cabbage leaves and fish entrails—piled up in the yard, the house might have been uninhabited.

At one corner of the steps a pair of rubber shoes, seemingly a child's, lay neatly turned upside down. In the kitchen pots and pans were strewn about in disarray, bespeaking the indolence of the woman of the house. Kil-nyo plopped down on the floor, meaning to wait for someone to return home.

As she untied the baby from her back and moved it into her

arms, the door of the main room slowly swung open. One hand on the door handle, a man was lying with his stomach on the floor and craning his neck out. Kil-nyo had never seen him before. At first her heart plummeted, but the next moment she felt relieved that he was not Chi Sang-mo.

For a while, the man just peered at the intruder with sleepy eyes. Oddly enough, he did not ask who she was. Then he glanced about, as if to gauge the time from the sunlight, and slammed the door closed with a bang. Kil-nyo looked back down at the step, but there were no shoes belonging to the man.

She told herself it was easy to guess what sort of man this must be if he could enjoy a leisurely nap even before sundown. Still, she knew that fishermen were known to take afternoon naps now and then after returning to shore from several fatiguing days at sea. But this man did not look like a fisherman. The finely-shaped light-skinned fingers she had seen holding the door handle clearly said: "I am not a fisherman."

As Kil-nyo had anticipated, within a few minutes the man reappeared and showed himself out. His clothing confirmed that he was anything but a fisherman, for though he wore no necktie, he was clad in a crisply pressed snow white shirt and a dark blue suit. In one hand was a glistening pair of black leather shoes that were as shiny as wet seal's skin.

The man set the shoes down on the ground as carefully as if he were a sower planting beans along the edges of a rice field. As he put on his shoes, all of his attention seemed focused on himself, and there was not the least sign that Kil-nyo was in his thoughts, even for an instant. Then he stood up, took a few steps to make sure his feet were settled comfortably in his shoes, and spat out a rather peculiar remark,

"God damn, the flies'll slip off."

Apparently he was admiring the shine on his shoes, and the remark was not directed at Kil-nyo, though uttered in the close presence of an unfamiliar woman. She thought he might simply vanish, so she hastily asked,

"Do you happen to know where Chang-rae's mother is?"

Chang-rae was the oldest child of Chi Sang-mo. The man looked slightly embarrassed at the question, and suppressing a half-grin, replied,

"She'll be back soon. Wait."

Not until the man had long since disappeared did it dawn on Kil-nyo that he might have been the one with whom Chi's wife had been conducting a clandestine affair in days gone by. At that time nothing had been known about the whereabouts of Chi and the wife had been entirely on her own.

Kil-nyo recalled several occasions when she had suppressed an urge to follow the woman after witnessing her midnight outings, from which she came home with her hunger for the other sex gratified. Had the woman parted with that creature and latched on to this, a new man? Kil-nyo wondered.

No matter how cunning, thick-skinned and sex-crazed she might be, no woman could have the gall to bring a lover into her house in broad daylight while her husband was alive and about. That being so, the man who had just walked away must have been one of their relatives. Kil-nyo blushed at the absurd conclusion to which she had leapt.

After laying the baby down inside the room she went over into the kitchen. When she looked down at the hearth, she could not help smiling, for the mess was just like the first time she had come to the house. A rice bowl was laying on one side, licked clean not by a dog but probably by one of the children who had come home to eat and found no adult there.

The half-consumed sticks scattered around the hearth testified to the untidiness of a woman who could not even make a fire properly. A sourish stink of fish and spoiled rice was oozing from the dish basin, proof that nobody had made a trip to the well in some time. The ceiling was blackened with soot and cobwebs were dangling loose like stringy fish guts.

First, Kil-nyo fetched water from the well to refill the water jar, then she scrubbed the kitchen utensils until her fingers hurt and neatly stored them on the shelves. Next, she gathered all the kindling and firewood strewn around the kitchen floor and stacked between a few boards she propped into a box shape. Then she cleared the stopped up drain with an iron poker so that she could be rid of the big basin full of rancid water.

She also discovered a bundle that the lazy woman had thrust out of sight under the side of the house, and opened it to find some filthy laundry, rags and unmentionables. Just then Kil-nyo came upon something else that startled her out of her wits— thrown under the house was a pair of mangled, dust-covered shoes. Carefully, she picked them up. The shoes had belonged to Chi Sang-mo. But, then, they also looked like the pair she had given to Hwang Chom-gae, the same ones that had been on the feet of the man who had visited her at Chom-gae's request back when she was tending the tavern at the foot of Hwangjangjae.

In actuality, they even resembled the pair of muddied shoes on the feet of the young man's corpse that had been borne back to the tavern the day after that man and his companion had spent the night at her place. But given that these shoes had been found cast under the wooden floor of Chi's house, there could be no doubt that they belonged to Chi Sang-mo.

A chill ran through her body, but once again Kil-nyo shook her head resolutely. She brushed the dust off the shoes, as if to dispel an ominous premonition. They were not too worn out to wear, but she figured Chi was probably out somewhere at this very minute talking someone's head off, wearing a new pair of shoes every bit as shiny as those on the feet of the man who had left the house a while before.

Just then she heard a woman's voice from behind,

"Some woman's touch this is. Nobody in sight, but I can certainly tell who's been here."

Standing behind was Chi's wife, with a big wooden platter full of fresh fish balanced on her head. Compared to the old days she looked a bit haggard and dispirited, but her blunt manner was unchanged. Stepping aside as Kil-nyo sprang up, she set the wooden platter on the edge of the porch and opened the door to the main room. She glanced at the sleeping baby and said,

"I thought you might have come alone without the baby, but I can see now that you've not lost your mind and have the child with you. Well, she's really grown, hasn't she?"

Then she cast a look toward the other room and added, while scrutinizing Kil-nyo's expression,

"I had a feeling you'd show up again one of these days. Whether some karma from our past lives does it or we're just meant to cross paths I don't know, but whenever I think about you coming back, you sure manage to make an appearance, it never fails.... Well, how is your own family doing? Nobody hurt in the war, no change?"

"Even if there was, what big changes could there be in a village in the mountains? Where are your children off to?"

"They'll crawl back in here once they're tired and hungry from wandering around. What good would it do to be fastidious bringing up kids born into a family of no standing?"

Kil-nyo marked a real change in the woman. The way she heaved a long sigh as she pulled off her stockings and plopped down on the floor reconfirmed Kil-nyo's surmise that something had gone very wrong.

"After I got here, a man woke from his nap and then walked off from the house," Kil-nyo said.

Only then did the woman's eyes stop moving here and there about the place and settle upon Kil-nyo. Vaguely embarrassed, she replied with a hint of a grin,

"Don't just stand there like a bump on a log, can't you see those fresh fish? Come on, let's make some fish soup with plenty of chopped radishes. Haggling for these wasn't easy, I practically had to snatch them from the vendor."

Leaving these words behind her, she walked inside the room without looking back. Kil-nyo did not even know what the fish in the wooden platter were called, since most of her life had been spent marooned in a mountain village far from the coast. She picked up the fish and carried them to the water basin, thinking she should consider herself lucky at not having been turned away at the door.

Even if Chi Sang-mo tried to throw her out when he came back home, his wife would go out of her way to stand up for her. As for herself, Kil-nyo had long ago given up on having him back, and no humiliation to be expected from him could greatly deepen her sorrow. As she squatted there scaling the fish, a loud burst of wailing broke out from the other room where the baby and Chang-rae's mother were.

Shocked and frightened, Kil-nyo hastened into the room. The baby was crying because of the wailing of the woman, who midst her gasping was shrieking something quite unbelievable,

"What can I do?! That creature dropped dead, and how can I go on living?!"

The woman's face was blotched and drenched from the weeping and by this time the baby was shrieking her lungs out. Kil-nyo grabbed her by both hands and asked,

"What's this all about? Who's dead?"

The woman gulped and blew her nose with the hem of her skirt, replying,

"That creature died."

"What creature?"

"The children's father, who else?"

Chi Sang-mo died? He was no man to go easily. Had he not been rampaging all about like a bull in a china shop, unable to control his own vitality? It was just not possible.

"Calm yourself down, now, and tell me exactly what happened."

"Nothing to tell. All of a sudden, he dropped dead. How could I get the details?"

"How can there be nothing to tell when a man full of life suddenly passes away?"

"If it would change anything for me to repeat the ins and outs of it a thousand times, I'd gladly do it. But things aren't like that. So I just have to stomach it all by myself, and the burden of it has broken my heart."

"You may not think much of me, yet I've come all the way here to see you because I think of you as someone close to me.

So if something is troubling you this much, it's only right for you to lean on me, isn't it?"

"It's not that I don't appreciate that, far from it. I feel the same way about you as you do about me, and that's why the very sight of you made me break down and cry. You see, I've become as pitiful and wretched as I look. Now that this land has been recovered from the enemy, I can tell others with pride that my husband died—even though he was slaughtered like a pig, his throat cut with a knife.

"When the Northern Army was on the rampage in this village, that creature of mine was running about helter skelter, shouting how he was taking over the fishing rights on the pier. With the world turned upside down, he meant to cash in and make a living out of the turmoil. But to turn anything upside down, you've got to have help behind you, and nothing good could come of dashing about with bloodshot eyes.

"They say a crow who mimics a stork's gait will end by tearing his own legs up, and that creature ended up getting knifed by some son of a bitch, not even in his own house, but down on the pier. He dropped dead sitting in his chair, wasn't even able to lift his heels off the ground."

"Is that really the truth?"

"Would I joke about a man's life and death?"

Kil-nyo was stunned. She was right—even if he had been a husband in name only, a wife could not joke at the expense of a man's death. The stranger in the house and the dust-coated shoes began to make sense. Of all places she might have gone, Kil-nyo wondered why she had been drawn to Kanggu as if by gravity. Had some uncanny spirit lured her here to impart this heartrending news?

"A man plotting a scheme that's beyond him won't live to die a natural death. In his own way, he was sure of himself. He thought he had the worldly experience to see through everyone and the guts to carry out his schemes—but whatever he thought, not everyone in the world is a half-wit. Even if the world is turned upside down and inside out a hundred times, a man who points his finger at the innocent and acts against nature will never last."

True, there had been a war raging, but for a man to die far from the front lines was no better than dying a dog's death. Besides, if he had been stabbed to death while raving his service to the communists, such an end could not even be mentioned in public these days. Who would feel any pity at the stabbing of Chi Sang-mo, a man who had been frantic to seize the opportunity of pocketing fishing rights for his own welfare, when countless young men had lost their lives battling for the recovery of their homeland?

"That creature used to laugh at me, scorning me as a illiterate woman who didn't even know which letter of the alphabet is shaped like a sickle. Well, he knew which letter it was, all right, but he sure didn't know anything about sickles. A world turned upside down is bound to be righted again—that creature never had a glimmer of that. He thought everything would stay as simple as it appeared at the moment.

"Those good-for-nothings who were dancing to the same tune as him, not one of them is anywhere in sight, they've all run away. Some of them were taken up north, they say, and some took shelter up in Chirisan or Ilwolsan and became guerillas. Every last one of them is heading for a blood-bath. In a way, that creature of mine was lucky to die early enough to miss all the troubles still going on."

"Anybody listening to you would say you'll be damned for saying that."

"He was dancing a goblin's dance, like a pony with horns on his haunches. Never had an inkling of what the reds were all about. He was so damn sure the reds had come to defend his side and to make him rich. More than once I wasted my breath trying to talk some sense into him, trying to rouse him from his sleep-walking, but his stubbornness was as tough as rawhide, and he just would not heed my warning—besides, he was too far gone by then.

"He was utterly obsessed... couldn't make any sense of what

I was saying. If I'd known it would end this way, I would've hired a shaman to exorcise the evil spirit that'd taken him in its clutches."

"Where did you bury him?"

"Bury? Give me one good reason why I should've wasted money and energy to give that creature a decent burial! He was cremated along with the strawmat they wrapped him in, and his ashes were scattered into the waves. He never gave up his wandering while alive, and right now he's still busy wandering and poking his nose in all four corners of the ocean."

While the two women were absorbed in talking, the children had come in to the room unnoticed. They picked up Kil-nyo's baby, their half-sister, and were enjoying themselves. The baby, who'd been thumping her feet on the wooden floor, was now cackling at the children's funny noises, or pouting on the edge of tears as they made scary faces at her.

Kil-nyo left the room. A gush of briny wind was rushing up over the village from the sea. The fish she'd been in the middle of cleaning still lay there on the cutting board, as though nothing had happened. She lifted the knife, but was unable to slice through the gills.

Just what could be done about it, she asked herself, when it was already in the past, leaving no room for any change. All the same, for Kil-nyo it presented yet another puzzle, a problem she had to take up with no means to solve it. She had no way of foretelling the consequences of Chi's death for the baby and herself. The helplessness she felt was even greater than that which followed her father's death.

However sad she felt, she was in no position to wail out loud like Chi's widow. The most she could do was sit there in front of the dead fish and drop her tears onto the cutting board.

"Is Chang-rae's mother back?"

A man's voice issued from behind where Kil-nyo sat. She hurriedly mopped away her tears with the sleeve of her blouse and turned around. A pair of well-polished black shoes came into view. The man was peering down over her shoulders at the fish on the cutting board, both hands thrust into his pockets.

"Are you a relative of Chang-rae's mother?"

By his inquisitive remark, it was clear he had finally developed a curiosity about her identity.

"No blood relation, but we're close friends. She's inside now."

Kil-nyo had no desire to extend the conversation with the man, so she tried to shoo him on his way by answering, but for some reason he stayed put and cast another casual question to her,

"Where have you come from?"

" ...."

"I asked you a question and you're not a ghost, are you?"

"From Hamyang."

"What brings you here from such a long way off?"

"Came to get some air."

"Even in this pandemonium, I see some people still manage to stay oblivious. Don't you know this is no time for wandering as you please just to get some air? Answer me that."

Fearing any further exchange of words would deteriorate into a scene, Kil-nyo just shut her mouth. The door from the main room abruptly opened and the shrill voice of Chi's wife snapped, not at the man but at Kil-nyo,

"A woman away from home in a strange place ought to be more discreet. You sure shouldn't be so gullible and mellow at the mere sight of a man! The way you act, it's no wonder you're still a roamer."

Kil-nyo did not even look back, but it was the man who seemed to feel awkward. As he hastened into the other room, she picked up the cutting board and went into the kitchen. It seemed the man had slipped his hand under her skirt, for through the side window she heard the woman's voice protesting, "Take that hand away, I say, take it out!"

Kil-nyo then heard the man joining with the children in cooing at the baby. She filled the pot with water and started in making a fire. Suddenly in a flash it came to her that the decision to head for Kanggu had been a mistake. It was her own presence that had reminded Chang-rae's mother of her husband, but in fact she had long since forgotten Chi Sang-mo.

Even while Chi was still alive, the two had by no stretch of the imagination been a happy couple. Perhaps it had not been difficult for her to put him out of her mind altogether. That she had scattered his ashes into the sea perhaps was not so much meant to console his soul as to dissolve the karma that had bound the two of them together in this world. But then, perhaps not.

Kil-nyo reproached herself for entertaining such an ugly notion. She told herself that no woman would conceive such a malicious scheme in the face of her husband's death, no matter how far their married life had been from conjugal bliss. When she herself felt her heart shattered, how much the more sorrow must not she have endured, left alone with his two fatherless children?

By nature Chi's wife was far from subtle and sometimes downright crude. She seldom cared what others might think of her behavior, yet at the bottom of her heart there was a tenderness not so very different from that of any other woman. Kil-nyo cast away the evil designs she had momentarily attributed to Chi's widow.

When Kil-nyo took a meal table full of rice and fish soup into the other room, the hungry children rushed over. But Chang-rae's mother shooed them away by smacking their behinds and pushed the table over to the man. The children, already clutching spoons in their hands, pursued the table on their knees.

As the man emptied his bowl in an ongoing struggle with the children, Chang-rae's mother looked over at Kil-nyo every so often in embarrassment. For their dinner, the two women shared a half bowl of rice.

After eating the man moved to another room and the children went to sleep. The clear sound of the waves lapping the shore seemed so close that the water might have risen all the way to the gate just outside.

"The man in the other room, have you known him for long?"

"Yes."

"He looks reliable...."

Hesitating to go any further with small talk, Kil-nyo was having a hard time continuing her sentence when Chang-rae's mother interrupted, saying,

"He doesn't belong to the same class as an ignorant woman like me. He's a well educated man, has a gift for the language, but unfortunately he's a rotten drunkard. He was just bumming around on the dock and happened to fall in with me. All his life he's been loafing about in gambling dens, and to him work is scarier than a tiger.

"A stepfather of sorts he may be, still it's easier to raise children with a man around the house—except all he's good at is eating and loafing and I've got to be the one putting food on the table. Besides, since all he does every day is take naps and goof off, when night rolls around he doesn't sleep and gives me such a hard time, you know."

Kil-nyo blushed in spite of herself, replying in a low voice,

"He seems to pay too much attention to his own appearance."

"It's not vanity about his looks, but a matter of keeping face. When a man goes out, first and foremost he shouldn't be scorned by others because of his appearance."

Judging from the way Chang-rae's mother went out of her way to defend him, she seemed to be rather deeply drawn to the man. So Kil-nyo changed the subject and said,

"He's a good looking man."

"Well, now, you've got taste when it comes to men, don't you? The creature's three years younger than me, so it's little wonder he's still got his looks."

"But if a hot-blooded man lets himself slow down for too long, his energy'll be gone soon enough and he'll be liable to become but half a man."

"Nonsense. Would a run-down man be clawing my clothes off three times a night? I don't know about other things, but he sure has no lack of energy for that!"

"A man can't live by that alone. He ought to go out and be a breadwinner, otherwise he'll never get the respect befitting a head of a family. Shut up in the house to keep him from womanizing, he'll find a way to vent his anger sooner or later. Then a couple'll break up over any trifling spat."

"Just wait now, one minute you say one thing, the next something else entirely. He's no pony with a bit in his mouth, so how am I supposed to rein him in? It wasn't easy for me to latch onto the man, and now you won't be satisfied till you see us split and shattered to pieces like broken china. Some advice you offer! A woman who can't hold her tongue is headed for a hard lot. You can't eat the cake, so you want to spit on it, is that it?"

"Are we such mortal enemies that I'd try to spoil your happiness? If that was what I had in mind, I would've done so long before now. I better watch who I give advice to from now on, or I'll be in bigger trouble than I think."

Heaving a sigh loud and deep enough to make the floor tremble, Chang-rae's mother said,

"My, my, how've I turned into such a senseless and rash woman? The instant I feel somebody's sticking their nose into my business, I fly off the handle and jump all over the person. I just don't know what's come over me. Maybe it's all just the rancorous heart left to me by that creature of a husband."

"Not to change the subject, but who was it who stabbed him to death? It couldn't have been a man with no name. The pier is always teeming with people, so somebody must've seen something of the crime, and if they did, they must at least have a guess who it could've been."

"All you say is true, but rumor has it that it all happened among those on the Northern side. So, they say it was part of a feud within the same gang while they were on the rampage like madmen, and now that the world's turned topsy-turvy again where can I go to demand a full investigation? Who could I ask? Anyway, I don't know the name of the bastard who was waving the knife. I did get a fair description of his awful face, though."

"A face can't be concealed when a man is out and around. If you mean to track him down, it's better to know his face than his name."

"Even if I managed to find him, what could I do? It'd be like tossing an egg at a rock. All that's left for me to do is to pass my urge for revenge down to the children—they'll have to avenge their father. I was told the bastard's face was ugly as sin, one of his eyes was gone and he had a big knife-scar. Like you said, to look for that kind of face might not be too hard."

"What did you just say?"

"I said with a grotesque face like his, you wouldn't have too much trouble finding him once you decided to hunt."

"You said his face was...."

"As it happened there were several men sitting in the room when this scarred, one-eyed Red opened the door and ordered everybody to leave except my husband. Not long after the two of them started trading words, the others saw the bastard go out. A while later the men who'd been chased out opened the door to find the father of my children collapsed on his belly soaked in his own blood. They felt for his pulse, but he was already gone."

"When did it happen?"

"Around the time the Northern Army started to retreat, I guess it was. If the bastard was really a Red and escaped to the North, I'll have to wait until the country's reunified."

That night Kil-nyo could not sleep a wink. After breakfast, she bade farewell to Chang-rae's mother.

"Thank you for a good night's stay, and good-bye."

Chi's widow, who had been making ready to head down to the pier, could not believe her ears. She had been planning to entrust the house to Kil-nyo and, still half unsure, responded,

"What's that?"

"It's time for me to be on my way."

As Kil-nyo shut the door and stepped down into the yard, the other woman set down her wooden platter and said,

"What a silly woman you are. Where do you think you're going, anyway? I know you're used to the road, but how can you take your leave like this? Last night I was nasty to you without thinking. Is that what's got you feeling so sour? We may be women, but let's not be so narrow-minded—it's not right. Even if you start screaming good-bye, I'm going to keep you here with me for two months at least."

"It wasn't what happened last night. When I left home I didn't plan to stay here long."

"You can't run off. I won't let you. There's nobody else but you to shape him up and break those bad habits. You've got to help me change him before you leave."

"Change who?"

"I mean the children's stepfather, at least in name. Last night I gave a lot of thought to what you said and realized all of it was sensible and on target. But it's too late for me to change him. He sees right through me by now. Talk to him and make him understand, please. You've got to stop him from being a good-for-nothing bum the rest of his life."

Chang-rae's mother was plainly serious and sincere, but Kilnyo could not oblige her plea.

"If a simple, soft-hearted woman like me could change a man's dyed-in-the-wool habits, then I wouldn't mind staying here a few months, but I really can't. I have to meet someone. It's very important."

"So, then, you actually meant what you said. I can't believe it."

"Honestly, I have to go."

"You drop by out of the blue to turn me inside out, and then you're off just like that. Where to now? From your looks, you don't seem likely to have any urgent rendezvous up ahead."

"I do. I'll tell you all about it later when I come back to see you."

"I knew you were cold-hearted, but this time I feel you're toying with me. Go if you want, it's all the same to me. If you're in such a hurry, why did you wait for your mother to bear you, shouldn't you have been your grandmother's child?"

Chang-rae's mother snatched up the wooden fish platter and scurried out through the gate. The thought suddenly flashed through Kil-nyo's mind that this might be the last time she would ever see her, and she felt an urge to run after her to say she'd like to stay on one more day together. But she gritted her teeth and stifled the urge.

Leaving the house, Kil-nyo headed straight to the pier. There was an air of malaise. The fish market was open but it was far more subdued than in the old days. With the war still underway in the northern provinces, it was deemed unsafe for the fishermen to sail out along the coast to ply their trade. Besides, all the decent fishing vessels had been requisitioned by the military, and most of the able-bodied young men were gone, drafted for war service.

Flies were swarming over the decks of motor launches lashed to the docks. Emaciated dogs lounged in the vacant storage yards. Fishermen squatted at the corner of one of the shacks on the pier, their spines curved like shrimp. They chain-smoked as they reminded one another of the horrid scars left behind by the talons of war.

Here and there women sat mending damaged nets, but it was a futile task, since there was no longer any pressing need for nets. A few of the fishermen, unable to endure the privation, secretly sailed out under cover of night and harvested a few fish and perhaps some seaweed just offshore. That was all the fishing being done.

Nevertheless, just as a farmer's eyes fasten on a vegetable garden whenever he looks out through an open door, so those on the pier, whether they were mending nets or conversing in whispers, kept their eyes constantly turned seaward.

Kil-nyo started making inquiries about the few people she knew from the old days when she and Chi's wife had peddled fish there. Some had died or disappeared during the war, but a few she managed to locate. By pleading and pretexts she succeeded in buying some dried seafood from them with the remainder of her traveling money.

She spent all she had down to the last coin with the idea of stretching her paltry funds by reselling the goods on the road inland. The fish and other things she bought had been laid aside

by the vendors due to the uncertainty of the times, but on hearing of her predicament they opened hidden caches to her,
forgetting lost profits.

The baby on her back kept slipping down toward her hips and
struggled to crawl back up a bit. The load balanced on her head
was so heavy she could scarcely move her neck. The seven miles
of road between Kanggu and Yongdok was guarded by stern-vis-
aged soldiers. Every passing traveler was scrutinized with the
utmost skepticism.

Each time Kil-nyo was stopped and searched, her bundle was
thoroughly examined and she was interrogated in minute detail
about the purpose and destination of her journey. Her southern
dialect and the infant on her back made it rather plain she was
a simple woman just trying to survive, so she usually was not
detained for long at the checkpoints.

The soldiers easily enough marked her as a peddlerwoman
from a fishing hamlet leading a hard life, and she escaped the
routine indignity of being searched under her skirts. Those who
were traveling not alone but in clusters of three or four had a
rougher time, more often than not taken into guard posts to
sweat out fuller scrutiny.

Because of the delays on the road, it was approaching ten that
night when Kil-nyo finally arrived at Wonjon village beneath
Hwangjangjae. Whatever impediments might bar her way, this
had been her destination when she set out that same morning.
It was at least thirty miles from Kanggu, and sheer will had carried Kil-nyo all they way to Wonjon before midnight.

Upon her arrival, the place that attracted her attention was
the old place she had once kept as a tavern. Even in the darkness, the sight of the fence around that house made her heart
sink. The tension accumulated through the whole day seemed to
fall away in an instant.

A light was burning inside the house. The lamp had been lit
by a stranger, of course. Yet for a fleeting moment Kil-nyo fan-
cied it was a lamp she herself had left burning upon leaving ages
before. She was roused from this reverie by a man's voice

inside. He was reprimanding a child, it seemed. As soon as she heard his voice, she all at once realized that she and her baby had no place to lay their heads that night.

Kil-nyo stood quietly outside the gate and closely watched the comings and goings inside the house. It was always the same with her—nowhere was there a house she felt free to poke her head inside. Wherever she went, no one ever greeted her by chiding her for not having shown up earlier. Instead, she was always asked 'why she had come. Yet, she herself had never wanted to be a guest.

Being a visitor always meant being a burden on the host. That was not at all her desire, but the whole world was forever treating her like a guest. She had struggled to leave that status behind, but at this very moment she remained nothing else than a guest.

Kil-nyo looked over her shoulder. At the very spot where Chi Sang-mo used to park his truck there was a tank abandoned by the fleeing Northern Army. The metal hulk was sprawled flat on its back, bomb-gutted stomach to the sky.

The wooden porch on the side of the house was unchanged. That was where Chi had relaxed like the man of the house the first time he returned after stranding her there, returned with an armful of kitchenware. Lying there now was an old tattered broom. Kil-nyo hesitated for a time.

Even if she did not identify herself, the hospitality of a mountain hamlet would probably provide her a room for the night. If the owner learned Kil-nyo had once lived in the same house, any reluctance would vanish and he would be likely to accord her a warm welcome. But that was exactly why she was hesitant.

She could see the shadows of the people projected onto the rice-papered window of the room. From time to time the soft voice of a woman was audible defending someone from the man's reproaches. She noticed, too, the light from inside spilling down onto the wooden deck outside. Kil-nyo turned around to leave. For she could not bear to upset the peace shared by an unfamiliar family inside that room.

Even if it had been possible to lodge there for the night, she feared that she would spend the whole night tortured by the spirit of Chi Sang-mo. As she turned her back to the house, the person who came to mind was the old shaman midwife who had aided her in childbirth. As she climbed the steep hill, her legs felt like lead. She was beyond being exhausted.

The old woman was still alive. Looking at her unlit ruin of a hovel from outside the gate, it might have been a dwelling long since abandoned. But Kil-nyo knew nowhere else to go in search of shelter, nor did she have any strength at all left. Without much hope, she called out for the old woman. The door opened instantly, as though she had been expected.

The old woman came outside to the gate, holding the butt of a candle in one hand. For a long while she gazed at Kil-nyo's face in the dim candlelight. Then she quietly murmured,

"A guest has come."

Then the old woman blew out the candle and hastened to help Kil-nyo take down the bundle of dried seafood from her head.

"I'm delighted to see you still up and around."

"No wonder I had such a weird dream last night. That's why my eyes have been glued on the gate all day today, and the dream was fulfilled before midnight."

"There was no light on, but you don't look like you've been sleeping."

"No, I wasn't asleep, but with no means of making money there was no call to waste a candle, eh?"

The old woman fired up a kerosene lamp. Looking more closely at Kil-nyo, she was startled to discover that there was a little baby on her back.

"My, my, my, isn't this the very one who gave you such trouble? What a tough little one! Still alive after all the death and turmoil the war brought us?"

The old woman had a special bond to the baby. She had delivered the child while Kil-nyo was unconscious, and her joy and surprise at seeing the baby well was in some ways as deep or deeper than the feelings of the mother herself. The old woman hungrily took the child from Kil-nyo's arms.

The little one, slumbering from exhaustion, woke up and the shrill voice of the crying baby issued from a house that had long been submerged in a silence as morbid as the stillness of a tomb. But the old woman made no attempt to stop the baby's wailing. She just turned up the wick of the lamp to lighten the room even more.

"None of the bitches around here ever sticks her head in to see me. They don't care if I'm dead or alive. And now the cries of this baby will let them know people live in this house. So my dear little one has just taken revenge on them for my sake."

The old woman was nothing but skin and bones and looked like she would keel over at the first snowfall, but all of a sudden she seemed to have recovered the strength of youth and she held the baby up into the air.

"Now that I've laid eyes on this pretty little thing I could go straight to hell here and now without bearing any grudges. Ever since you two left, all I've been seeing is the face of this little one. I've not been well, either, but I knew, I knew for sure you'd show up before I close my eyes the last time. All my life I never wanted anything beyond my means, but this little troublemaker was an exception—I missed it so much I almost went out of my mind."

"I haven't eaten all day, so I better go and make something to eat."

"Go look in the upper room. There should be some grain in the earthen jar. Since I haven't touched it, there should be plenty of soy sauce and *kimchi* too."

Kil-nyo measured some barley into a black iron pot and kindled a fire for cooking. Not once did the old woman budge an inch from where she was. When Kil-nyo finished making a semblance of supper and carried the meal table into the room, the old lady was still busy showering the baby with laments over all the mistreatment she had suffered from the neighbors. As Kil-nyo sat down to eat, the old woman asked,

"Did you try to stay with your parents all through the war?"

Because her mouth was full, Kil-nyo merely nodded. The old woman continued,

"Then how did you come by the bundle of seafood—it's beyond me. No matter how unsettled the times, no family would kick out there own flesh and blood to roam the roads as a peddler.... In these days of confusion, one false step could easily cost you your life.

"I've no way of knowing what awful slander you went through, or if in a fitful moment you chose to go off like a wandering monk—in any event the course you took is a bit too much, I'm afraid, even for a woman hardened by life."

"If you're so happy to see the baby, why all this picking at me? I may be a common woman, I don't deny I'm ignorant, but it wasn't my ill temper alone that drove me from home, so don't be so hard on me, please."

"A youngster, no matter how excited, shouldn't talk back to an elder. If a woman while young can't control her heated feelings and ends up going against the laws of human nature, she's likely to sink to a sorry state. Show me one creature who wanders the country without ever putting down firm roots and still manages to keep any human decency."

"Some day you'll understand, maybe, but it wasn't my choice to run away from home. I didn't leave on a whim. So don't humiliate me, please."

"Me humiliate you? Nonsense. How in the world could I, lowly and ignorant as a mealworm, dare to humble anyone else? In my situation I'm just thankful I lived through the war."

The old woman might very well have asked after Chi Sangmo, but of all the many things she talked about she never uttered a word about him. It struck Kil-nyo as very strange that she failed to inquire about the man who was most closely connected with the baby and her. But then she recalled that the old woman was a shaman, after all. For her to divine the great misfortune a young woman had endured must not have been too difficult.

Thus it appeared that the woman had guessed all that had

happened to Kil-nyo and was just waiting for her to own up to it herself. Kil-nyo was on the right track, for a little later, when she finished the dishes and went back into the other room to get ready to sleep, the old woman began in a low voice,

"Shall I say one thing you won't be happy to hear? The moment you walked in through the gate, I at once could read a bad omen on your face. There's an evil spirit known as *kopsal*—some folks call it by other names—and this demonic spirit brings murder with it when one blunders into the wrong place, a place governed by venomous spirits. I'm a so-called shaman, and I've done more than a few exorcisms in my time, but a lot of good that does when I'm unable to chase away the evil spirit that's clinging to you."

"I appreciate your trying to awaken me with kind advice, but I'm so exhausted right now I can barely keep my eyes open."

"Go ahead and sleep. Maybe our ancestors were right when they said the good and bad sides of one's fate are entirely in your own mind."

The previous day's thirty mile trek must have drained all of Kil-nyo's strength, for when she awoke the next morning the sun was already well up in the sky. There was no trace of the old woman around the house, and she seemed to have taken the baby when she went out. Kil-nyo opened the kitchen door and from the aroma guessed that the old woman had already made breakfast.

She knew that the old lady owned no land, not even a tiny patch of a garden, but upon her return a while later she was carrying a heavy sack of grain. The baby on her back was for some reason in a jubilant mood, cackling and clapping her hands. The food she probably had borrowed from the neighbors.

Whether the old woman had been widowed at an early age or abandoned by her husband soon after the wedding, nobody seemed to know. All that was known about her was that she came to the village when she was barely twenty and had lived alone ever since, with no relations to speak of.

Back when Kil-nyo was running the tavern, more than once

she had tried to get the old woman to reveal her life story, but the latter never opened her mouth. At the breakfast table, the old woman asked,

"Are you leaving today?"

Kil-nyo had disclosed no such intention, but evidently had guessed as much.

"It's already late morning, and I should be off."

"If you're crossing over Hwangjangjae, you'd better do it while it's still light. Unlike in the old days, there's a steady stream of people traveling over the Pass and the army traffic is heavy these days."

"How did you know I was planning to go over Hwangjangjae?"

"At my age, and a shaman to boot, I should at least be able to tell what a young woman like you has in mind."

"There's somewhere I'd like to go to check something."

The old woman said nothing one way or the other. Then, laying down her spoon, she quietly remarked,

"I've no grounds and no strength to keep you here, but you should listen to me on one thing. Leave the baby here with me."

"What do you mean?"

Kil-nyo put down her spoon, too. What this nonsense was all about she could not say. Had she not firmly resolved to cease sinning, and was that not why she had been carrying the baby on her back every step she took? If she had had a mind to leave the baby behind, she would have left it with her own mother in Hamyang.

"I know this must come as a shock. You're probably wondering how I could dare to say such a thing, or thinking you might've left it with your mother, but not with me. In any event, you'd better follow my advice. That I'm a shaman might bother you, but this is where the baby was born, and traveling in strange places is bad for the little thing."

"I thank you for your concern that the baby might be scorned because of a mother like me, but I'm afraid I just can't do as you say."

"When it comes to this little one, I believe I have some right to meddle for her well being. You might not want to be reminded of it, but when she came into this world, she and I had a very special tie. If I hadn't minded your business then, this baby would never have been born at all."

"Please, don't try to bind me like that. I'll be forever beholding to you for the child's life, and when she grows up I mean to tell her all about you. But I just can't be parted from her at this point."

"Don't be a fool! Was I asking you to leave her here for good? I'm telling you to pick her up on your way back. Whether it takes a week or a fortnight, I won't die before you get back. Can't you understand why I'm pestering you with words you don't want to hear?"

"Why are you?"

"There's a murderous spirit in your face."

"A murderous spirit?"

"Where you're bound is beyond me, but this journey, though you may be disguised as a peddler, is no ordinary one. Now do you see why I'm asking you to leave the baby behind?"

As the old woman said, her special attachment to the baby was not to be taken lightly. If not for her, the child would have gone straight to the graveyard. Considering Kil-nyo's condition at the time, she, too, might have lost her life but for the old woman coming by in the nick of time. Now that she thought of it, Kil-nyo owed the old woman not just her child's life, but her own.

The old woman for them had been a godsend. She had stayed by Kil-nyo's side, nursing her back to health after the birth. When all the other women in the village turned their backs on her, the old woman had volunteered to help her. Remembering that she had never repaid the old woman for what she had done, Kil-nyo was left with nothing to say.

Still, with no companion on the road the little one, her own flesh and blood, had been no small comfort to Kil-nyo. Whenever she was stopped for inspection the baby provided a good pretext, and when she talked to herself she did so with her eyes on the baby. What's more, the bundle of medals given her by Chom-gae was hidden away between the layers of the child's diaper. The guards might be merciless enough to strip search a woman, but they would never stick their fingers inside a little baby's diaper. For that reason alone, Kil-nyo could not even think of leaving the baby behind.

The old woman was too adamant, however, to be put off with words alone. What was still worse was the fact that the old woman was not simply being stubborn, her obstinacy seemed to stem from a definite premonition.

Kil-nyo sat there for a while absorbed in contemplation. Then she took the baby while the old woman went into the kitchen. While she was gone, Kil-nyo removed the pouch of medals from the baby's diaper and put it between her legs. Several times she felt it, remembering Chom-gae's warning that if ever she was found with it, that would be the end of her. She remembered, too, him saying that when the world came he was awaiting, these medals alone would be enough to assure a comfortable life for three generations.

"I'll be back within a month and a half at the longest. Please, look after the baby."

As she took over the child, the old woman said,

"Don't worry yourself. In my old age I may be untidy and slow, but I sure have enough strength to take good care of one little baby. Now you can travel light, that's good, and it's better for the little one, too, since she won't have to share the hardships with you."

A Cuckoo

Not a word more did the old woman say. Perhaps it was because she had already seen through Kil-nyo's resolution. The baby on her back, she left the house ahead of Kil-nyo, seemingly to avoid any tearful parting between mother and child. By the time she had finished packing and come outside, Kil-nyo found no trace of either of them.

Once again she fell into a conundrum, unsure whether she was doing the right thing. She took the bundle down from her head, set it down and then plopped down beside it. The old woman did not reappear. It was as though she had read Kil-nyo's mind. At length Kil-nyo got back to her feet.

There were no longer any guerillas lurking about Hwangjangjae by this time. Inspection of travelers was not very strict, so Kil-nyo managed to transit the Pass without mishap. By a stroke of luck, as she reached the tiny village of Koejong on the far slope of the Pass, she ran into an army truck that had paused for repairs.

"Where you headed?"

Asked a soldier who was sitting on the passenger side of the cab, a cigarette dangling from his mouth. Thanks to this spontaneous offer of a ride, Kil-nyo was able to rest her legs. But the truck lurched so badly and the soldiers in the truck were so fond of cracking jokes at her expense that she was tempted to get off and walk.

Still, the ride was a windfall. The truck would take her at least through Sokpo-ri and maybe even to Andong by nightfall, which was farther than she had hoped to go the first day. Even as she showed irritation in parrying the soldiers' jokes, she was afraid they might ask her to get off. Her audacity amazed them. They said for a woman to travel the roads alone in such times was proof of real courage.

As they came into Andong, one of the soldiers, a tall young man much given to ribald cracks, picked up Kil-nyo's bundle and handed it to her, saying,

"Hope your business goes well."

She felt like bowing in thanks, and even had an urge to kneel on the ground. As the truck sped off, Kil-nyo headed straight for the salt storehouse. It was visible from the main thoroughfare, as was the house of the man named Pak Sok-ho.

According to rumors that had reached her ears, the center of Andong had supposedly been leveled by bombs, but the area around her was undamaged. That alone was enough to quicken her heartbeat. She did not really expect that Pak would still be living in that house, but just in case, even if it was one chance in a thousand, she decided to check and see.

The old stable where Pak used to squat and sharpen sickles was the same as she remembered it. So was the narrow path leading through the yard to the rear of the house. Yet the general atmosphere of the place had changed somehow. It seemed unlikely the man was living here alone as before.

In fact, as Kil-nyo approached the house she came upon a woman who paused from hanging laundry on a clothesline to stare back at her. Because of the bundle on her head, she must instantly have taken Kil-nyo for a peddler. The woman neither welcomed her in nor shooed her away. Ignoring this indifference, Kil-nyo took down her load onto the porch and sat down. Then she casually said,

"My, you scrubbed those so clean and white."

Only after this bit of flattery did the woman condescend to acknowledge Kil-nyo's presence, speaking down to her in a low level of speech,

"Where you from?"

Plainly she had Kil-nyo pegged as a peddler woman from some seaside village and felt superior to her. Kil-nyo, however, was preoccupied with her own plans, and did not care much about the chilliness of her reception. In an ingratiating tone she replied,

"Why, you can tell where I'm from at a glance, can't you? I'm from a backward fishing village."

"I thought as much."

"I've been breaking my back lugging this bundle of dried seafood just to keep myself alive, but with everyone having a hard time of it, I barely make it from day to day."

"It's wartime, remember? People don't even get three square meals a day and here you come with fancy salted fish and such for delicacies. It's hard enough to come up with something as simple as soy sauce."

"You're right about that. And wandering unfamiliar places where I don't know a soul it's not easy to get any buyers. Could you spare a drink of cold water, please?"

After fetching a bowl of water from the kitchen, the woman sat down next to Kil-nyo and said,

"You've got a nice face, but looks like you've been through some rough times."

"I'll say. In the old days I once stayed here in this village for a few months peddling around, and I'm no better off now than I was back then. As I recall, there was a widower living alone in this house...."

As Kil-nyo muttered half to herself, a look of surprise appeared on the woman's face. Then she must be somehow related to Pak Sok-ho, Kil-nyo thought to herself.

"Better watch what you say or you'll endanger yourself."

"Endanger?"

"This is no time for reckless babbling. I don't know what he is to you, but now everybody knows he's a Red."

"A Red?"

"The reddest of all the Reds, they say. Thanks to that son of a bitch, a lot of innocent men around here went through hell. Good thing he was somebody who'd drifted into this place—if he'd been a native, there would've been an even greater disaster."

"No doubt he was captured, right?"

"Captured? I've heard no such thing. We lost our house in the bombing so we moved into this one, but there's an eerieness about it. You can imagine how desperate we had to be to move in here."

"Your family had a farm?"

"No, no. My husband is with the police."

Before she dug herself into an even deeper hole, Kil-nyo wasted no time in taking her leave and heading for the marketplace. She found an inn where she could stay the night. Early the next morning, she sat down in the marketplace with her wares spread out in front of her on a wooden board. As the woman had said, times were so hard that a lot of people did not even have a roof over their heads, but seafood was so hard to come by that she managed to lighten her load by half within two days, pocketing some needed cash.

By the third day, Kil-nyo was ready to move on. Not more than seven or eight miles away where the road forked between Andong and Yechon was a town called Pungsan. Kil-nyo vaguely remembered that there was a lake near Pungsan called Manunji, and that a hamlet alongside that lake was the hometown of Chom-gae's wife, the mother of Chil-rye.

Naturally, Kil-nyo had no reason to expect that Chom-gae's wife, who had been raising the son she herself had abandoned, would be living there in that remote mountain hamlet. Still, she could at least hope it might be possible to find out something about her whereabouts, provided she was still alive somewhere. If there was one person in the world Kil-nyo dreaded meeting, it was Chil-rye's mother. But she could not let that fear stand in the way.

Kil-nyo had no intention to start any kind of negotiations with the woman. She just felt the time had come to confirm that the baby she had abandoned in fact had been raised by Chom-gae's wife. Chom-gae had been very firm on that subject. Even after she had given herself to him, he had said not a word about the boy, who he had given the name Chun-bok.

The very existence of this child was a kind of incarnation of all the sins Kil-nyo had committed in her life. Whether the boy was alive or dead, the consequences of her sinful deed would endure and pursue her into the next life. It was nothing that could be ignored in the hope it would go away by itself.

Indeed, the more she tried to forget the evil deed and its aftermath, the heavier it hung on her heart. Like an acorn passed over with contempt by an eating dog, it would not easily disappear. Just as the inexplicable echo of rolling thunder still pounded in her ears, so the karma of that child would never be lifted from her heart. There was another reason, too, for her to see the child beyond confirming his well being.

Manunji was a big enough lake that when Kil-nyo reached Pungsan and started asking for directions everyone seemed to know where it was. There were several hamlets in the vicinity, however, each of which seemed to have about half a dozen households. Kil-nyo told herself to be patient and just check them all until she happened upon the right one.

When all was said, Kil-nyo knew very little about Chom-gae's wife, just that she had lived in Woljon-ri and was likely to be known as Chil-rye's mother. She had no address and not even a maiden name to ease the search. All the same, her heart raced at the sight of the lake and the thought that she was actually face to face with the hamlets she aimed to check.

Her patience seemed to pay off, for before the day was over she succeeded in finding the house of Chil-rye's mother. It was in the hamlet closest to Manunji, the first she came upon.

The dwelling was a small hut fashioned from earth. An old man, the brother of Chom-gae's wife, lived there, but as luck would have it, he turned out to be blind. After exchanging a few words with him, Kil-nyo could tell the man was not an ordinary commoner. That he had permitted his sister to marry an outcast of the very lowest status was probably due, Kil-nyo guessed, to the very fact that he had lost his vision.

The blind man was living with his wife, whose eyes were bright enough to compensate for his sightlessness, though her wits were on the dim side. He described his sister to Kil-nyo, giving a precise picture down to the most minute detail and his description of Chom-gae was also accurate enough.

As they spoke, whenever his wife butted into the conversation with an inane remark, the blind man fumbled about with his hands and patted hers as he calmed her down with a gentle voice. The wife had suffered a stroke at a young age, which accounted for her slowness, according to the brother-in-law of Chom-gae, but she had a tender heart, he insisted, defending her.

"Since she came back to her own family, I told her to stay on with us, for better or for worse. My pleading with her was shameless, for I thought she'd be a great comfort to a man like me. But she was awfully stubborn, and kept saying she had to go away. I couldn't see the baby they'd adopted, but I felt what he was like.

"It wasn't that I didn't understand why she wanted to go away. The real mother of the baby was living somewhere not far off, and she wanted to avoid any chance of running into her, fearing the mother might come by and demand the baby back. After her girl was born, eight years went by with no sign of another pregnancy, so it looked pretty obvious she wouldn't be having another baby.

Noble or commoner, the wish for an heir to the family name is no different. I couldn't very well hold her here just to keep me company, so in the end I changed my mind and let her go."

Kil-nyo could not admit to him that she was the natural mother of the boy, for she feared the news would make him fall silent.

"Chil-rye's mother always had a heart of gold. I miss the old days when we were friends and neighbors. Since the war I've often wondered how she was, and when I happened to pass through these parts I remembered this was her hometown. So I just came by and I'm lucky to have run into her brother here."

"I heard the rumor my brother-in-law became a communist and was raving all over in the company of Reds. But I had no way to find out if it was true."

"That's something I don't know for sure, either."

"It's against nature, doing that. He should be grateful for being born healthy with two good eyes to see the world around him. He just doesn't know his own place—that's why he took to raving like a madman."

"Since I'm always moving around from place to place as a ped-dler, if I'm ever lucky enough to run into Chil-rye's mother I'll be sure to give her your best."

"I'm sure you will. I've been told she's living in a place called Uisong, but in my condition I'm not fit to travel, you know how it is."

"Uisong's not a small village, is it?"

"It's a place pretty far from here. The village is well known for its Chinese medicine, an herb called *sansuyu*. They tell me that's how she makes her living, picking that herb."

"Even if it's through the grapevine, you seem to be pretty well informed about her."

"I don't have an address, but I figured it wouldn't be so hard to find her if I just can find a village where *sansuyu* is plentiful."

As things turned out, Kil-nyo learned more than she thought she would. She unwrapped her bundle and removed a few salted cod. The blind man felt the fish and thanked Kil-nyo pro-fusely, protesting that he could never repay her kindness. On the pretext of having a long journey ahead, Kil-nyo bid the blind man good-bye.

Her heart had been heavy at having left her baby girl back in Woljon-ri with the old woman, but now she felt almost light-hearted. She decided to retrace her steps through Andong as a shortcut to Uisong. She spent the night at the same inn in the Andong marketplace, and the next morning at dawn managed to hitch a ride on an army truck bound for Uisong.

Upon her arrival in Uisong, she learned that there were a number of villages that made a business of harvesting *sansuyu*. She was steered south until she came to Sagok-myon, where the villages of Chaksung, Shin-ri and Hwajon were all renowned for their *sansuyu*. Those particular villages, unlike others in the region, were cut off from the main roads and could only be reached by hiking up a narrow mountain path for some eight or nine miles. There was no other way to reach them.

Now her task was like catching a mouse on an islet, and all she could do was to comb through those three villages one by one. First she tried the village known as Chaksung, but there was no widow living there with a girl and a boy. Though called a village, Chaksung was not much more than a few houses clustered in two and threes on the hillsides, occupied by slash-and-burn farmers often on the move. To locate someone was anything but easy.

At times, attempts had been made to move the farmers into one of the more populous towns for protection against guerilla raids, but most of them were reluctant to abandon the lives they knew to start all over again in an unfamiliar place.

In fact, they knew little of the war that had ravaged the streets and buildings of the major cities, only what reached them through hearsay. For all practical purposes, the war had left them unaffected. Buried back in the mountains, many of them had never ridden in an automobile, though they had not missed seeing the airplanes that flew by overhead several times a day.

Kil-nyo had not yet come across Chil-rye's mother, but the sight of rows of *sansuyu* being cultivated in every valley and on every slope relieved her somehow, giving her hope that her destination lay at the end of one of those rows. Kil-nyo did not head for the village nearest the road but followed the *sansuyu* path past Shin-ri to Hwajon-ri.

By this time almost a fortnight had passed since Kil-nyo first arrived at the town of Uisong. It was the season when frost begins to form in the mountain pastures before daybreak, and the air was getting quite chilly once the sun went down.

Every now and then the thought of her little girl left behind made her heart ache. At such moments she felt so drained by worries she could not help but plop down on a rock for a little rest. According to the people she had met along the way, there would be no more *sansuyu* beyond the village she was approaching, Hwajon-ri.

Kil-nyo started to panic, fearing that if Chil-rye's mother was not to be found here, she would have no place left to turn. But the woman she sought was there—upon asking the villagers if a woman of such and such description lived there, Kil-nyo was told that she lived in a place called Witjonpung, and it indeed turned out to be so.

Though Chom-gae's wife was living in someone else's house, in a mountain hamlet where there were never enough hands for the work, she managed to make ends meet as a laborer. Since it was the time of year for harvesting *sansuyu*, she could take some of her pay in the herb and dry them to sell, a not inappreciable source of cash.

When Kil-nyo found her, she was laying out *sansuyu* to dry on a straw mat in a corner of the yard. She was quite recognizable; the most conspicuous change was that her teeth were blackened from cracking *sansuyu* berries. She also seemed to have put on a few pounds since Kil-nyo last saw her in Woljon-ri.

When Kil-nyo called out her name, Chil-rye's mother looked up with a start. The two gazed at one another for a long time, both at a loss to say a word.

"It's been a long time."

Kil-nyo said at last, putting her bundle down on the ground and perching on the edge of the porch. Kil-nyo glanced about but could detect no other presence in the house. It appeared Chil-rye's mother was entirely alone there. Her attitude was as icy as a December frost, however, and she hastened to hide her trembling hands under her skirt.

"What brings you here, ma'am?"

"Well, could you let me have a cold drink of water first?"

Chil-rye's mother rushed into the kitchen and returned with a bowl of cold water. After draining the whole bowl in a single gulp, Kil-nyo said,

"It's been nearly a month since I set out to look for you."

"It's good to see you again, ma'am."

"You don't act like it."

"What do you mean? How else could I feel seeing you again, ma'am? I'd have been pleased to see any of our old neighbors, let alone...."

Chil-rye's mother quickly wiped her eyes with the hem of her skirt. Kil-nyo could see she was silently clenching her teeth.

"So, how's your living been here?"

"We get by well enough, but it pains me to see you in such shape—maybe it's the journey that wore you out. Where are you staying now, ma'am?"

"I live way down south in south Kyongsang-do, a town called Hamyang."

As for Chil-rye's mother, she could not show her innermost feelings and welcome Kil-nyo with open arms. Neither did Kil-nyo find it easy openly to ask after the children. She had expected the reunion might be rather awkward, but she never had thought it would be as uncomfortable as this.

"Taken to smoking, have you?"

Kil-nyo said softly as Chil-rye's mother put a cigarette in her mouth.

"Alone at night, I picked up the habit in spite of myself."

"Alone at night? What do you mean?"

"It's been ages since he left."

"But you still hear from him, don't you?"

"He used to send word through others, but ever since we started hearing about the retreat of the Northern Army, there's been not a word from him."

"You mean he never visited you, not even once?"

"Back in the days when the world was turned inside out he did come by a few times, but always sneaking in and out at night like a weasel."

"Do you mean to stay here in this mountain village for long?"

"It all depends on the children's father, ma'am. He said the day would soon come when the world'll be better. When that day comes we'll go live in one of the big cities. There's not a school within ten miles of this place."

"Who can say for sure when the world will change? What's so wrong with this world? Isn't it good enough?"

"What he has in mind is beyond me. I'm just following his strict orders."

"How can you be so senseless? What if he never comes back?"

"He's no child. How could a man fail to return to his own children? He may be a bit slow and that's his fault, but you know as well as me that he's a strong man, willful and able-bodied, so he won't be overcome too easily. And he's not the kind of man who'd abandon his own flesh and blood."

Chil-rye's mother was raising her voice, plainly disturbed at the suggestion Chom-gae might not come back. Kil-nyo looked up at the sun, which already was far along on its arc toward the horizon. Once night fell, Chil-rye's mother could not very well kick her out, and she would have a chance to see Chun-bok. So she decided to bide her time until then.

After a while Chil-rye's mother opened her mouth and in a somewhat subdued voice inquired,

"Judging from the bundle, you're peddling, aren't you?"

"That's right."

"No matter how bad times are, how could you end.up as a peddler, ma'am? The world must be a far sight crazier than I thought."

"I can't afford to worry about keeping face. To live you've got to eat, and I ran out of money so peddling was about all I could do to get a little money. I was dead set on finding you, and I've had my share of trouble on the way here."

"Please, come inside and get some rest."

"No, thanks. I'd rather sit here. It must've been hard for you, with three mouths to feed."

"I've been too busy talking about my problems I didn't even

ask after your parents, I'm sorry. I tried to get news of you, but the last I heard was just that you'd gone back home to your family."

"How could you have heard that sitting way back here in the mountains?"

"The children's father was always checking up on your moves. And now, ma'am, here you are yourself, someone I'd lost track of altogether, and there's no word at all from the children's father...."

"I saw him."

Kil-nyo felt she had to let Chom-gae's wife know, after all. She had meant to wait for the right moment to break the news, but when she saw the desolate expression on the woman's face, she could put it off no longer. For a moment, Chom-gae's wife peered straight into her face. Kil-nyo could see her hands visibly quaking. Tears in her eyes, Chom-gae's wife said,

"I'm such a scatterbrain. For a moment I forgot Hamyang was your hometown, ma'am."

Kil-nyo was puzzled by this remark, and Chom-gae's wife continued,

"The children's father went up into the mountains of Chirisan, I'm told. Hamyang is in the foothills of Chirisan, isn't it? With his good heart, it's only natural for him to look you up when you were so close by, isn't that right?"

Kil-nyo had anticipated Chom-gae's wife would be greatly surprised and would shower her with questions about his visit, its purpose and so forth, but at encountering this rather composed response Kil-nyo felt her own pounding heart calm down. She replied, somewhat vaguely,

"Seems he visited knowing it was where my parents lived, but we were in such different worlds we didn't see each other for long."

"There's not much in the house, but I should fix you something for dinner."

As Chom-gae's wife got up and headed into the kitchen tears were welling up in her eyes. It was already time for supper, but the two children were still nowhere to be seen. The sun had long since slipped down below the mountains, and the lamps would soon be lit, but the children had not appeared. Only then did Kil-nyo realize she had heard not a word of worry from Chil-rye's mother about the little ones.

The night was deepening and from somewhere outside came the sound of a cuckoo. It was not that Kil-nyo failed to fathom what lay in the heart of hearts of this woman, but she could not help being appalled at the merciless treatment Chom-gae's wife had meted out. After all, was she not the natural mother of Chun-bok? Her sins had not altered that fact—but Kil-nyo choked back her indignation.

In actuality, there was not a single thing she could be proud of, no matter how cold the disdain she faced. Who could she dare to criticize when it was she herself who voluntarily severed the natural bond between mother and child? As for Chun-bok, for him it had been a blessing in disguise. All the same, Kil-nyo had to see the child, whatever the cost.

Perhaps coming here was not something she should have done, perhaps it was Hwang Chom-gae who should have come. But Kil-nyo never would have come all the way to this place had she not had faith that it was something entrusted to her by destiny. When it came to masking her unspoken intentions, Kil-nyo was no different than Chom-gae's wife. She kept on telling herself not to be impatient and just wait for the children, but midnight came and still they were nowhere to be seen.

"How cold-hearted you are! So, you've decided not to let me see the child. I wonder if he's eaten supper."

"Don't worry, ma'am. I left him with a family who'll look after him as well as I would."

"I was hoping to have a look at him...."

"I asked my landlady to look after him for a while. I know how terrible blood-ties can be. Chun-bok is still a baby, can't find his way to the bathroom on his own, but if his eyes met yours, he'd surely feel something hot running through his veins, something he never felt before.

"For now, such a meeting might be a great relief for both of you, but you've got to remember it'd drive a nail into his heart that'd cause him nothing but trouble for the rest of his life. Even if you never spoke with him again, he'd always remember the eyes of that woman he met as a little boy. Neither of us can be sure it wouldn't become the root of great misfortunes in his life.

"The instant he learned the woman he met in childhood was his real mother, his life would take a wrong turn. I hope you understand how much my heart is bleeding for you now."

"I understand. I won't pester you anymore. I didn't come here meaning to make waves. I just couldn't stifle a mother's longing to see her own child...."

"You mustn't cry, ma'am."

As she spoke, Chil-rye's mother started weeping, too. The two held each other's hands and cried, then embraced one another shoulder to shoulder. For a long time they wept under their breath like a cuckoo. It was past the season for cuckoos to cry. Living way up in these mountains, maybe they had forgotten the passing of the season and missed the October days when they should have flown southward.

A cuckoo drops its egg in the nest of another bird, living its whole life in solitude and never learning how to build a nest of its own.

"That bird is supposed to bear the spirit of the Chinese Emperor Mangje of the Han Dynasty. It's been crying here the whole summer through and seems lost, unsure which way to fly off."

The next morning Kil-nyo unpacked the pouch full of medals that Chom-gae had entrusted to her.

"What's this?"

Asked Chom-gae's wife, looking inside the pouch.

"I don't rightly know myself. But there's no doubt they're very important. The reason I came here was to give them to the child. The child's father said they should be guarded at all costs and handed down to the next generation, so it's plain they're not something I should keep.

"But the more precious a thing is, the harder it is to hold onto, so you should hide these in a safe place until the child grows old enough to know what they're for. As I understand it, they're medals, decorations of some sort. And if they were given by the Northern Army, then you know they're not something to be treated lightly, understand?"

"Are they really so precious?"

"I know they are to the child's father."

"It's no grain, and no money, either...."

"To him they were treasures worth more than money."

"I don't understand truly."

"I understand no more than you."

"What, why are you getting up? You should have some breakfast before going."

"The longer I loiter, the longer the children will have to stay in a stranger's house."

"You can't leave like this. It's not possible."

"What else can I do if you're doing everything just as you wish?"

Chom-gae's wife pleaded with her to stay a little while longer, but Kil-nyo thrust her aside and left the house. Without a heartless parting, she feared she would not be able to leave at all. But her heart felt like a knife had been run through it, and tears commenced flowing all over again. Chom-gae's wife trailed her outside.

"Can't you guess where the children's father might be?"

"No, I've no way of knowing. I once heard he was in Paemsagol, a mountain village near Namwon, but it was probably just a place he stopped for a short while, and it was some time ago."

Kil-nyo was completely alone now. She had left the rest of the dried seafood with Chil-rye's mother. The baby was not on her back. For the first time in a long while, she was quite solitary. The sense of forlornness she felt was so overwhelming she could not even take a step forward.

She felt neither sorrow nor joy. Her soul seemed to have left her, leaving behind nothing but a shell of flesh. With that thought came a realization she had become a totally worthless being. It occurred to her that the time had come to choose a way to kill herself. Now she stopped to ponder why the old shaman woman had been so pesistent in persuading her to leave the baby behind when she set out on the road.

The old woman had undoubtedly foreseen that Kil-nyo would arrive at her present state, and would never again return to Wonjon. That must have been why she did what she could to try to save at least the baby's life. Having chased off Chil-rye's mother like an enemy when she sought to see her out to the main road, Kil-nyo sat down on a rock and told herself again and again that the time had come to kill herself.

Then all of a sudden she felt an overwhelming desire to see the baby girl she had left behind in Wonjon. It was not the right time to commit suicide, after all. One thing still remained to be done—she had to see Hwang Chom-gae.

Kil-nyo made her way back to the town of Uisong. It was not easy to get a ride, so it ended up taking a whole day to reach Andong. She was so worried that the old woman might vanish with the baby that she was unable to sleep at all that night. Not until the afternoon of the following day was she able get a ride on an army truck bound for Yongdok.

By the time she arrived in Wonjon it was eight in the evening. Rushing to the house of the old shaman woman, she was relieved to see a light burning inside. Practically crashing into the room, she found the old woman feeding some thin gruel to the baby with the utmost care.

Her first impulse was to snatch the child away and hold it to her breast, but a certain serenity in the way the old woman was feeding the baby kept Kil-nyo from acting on her impulse. The old woman slowly raised her eyes to look at Kil-nyo, who was about as unsightly as a half-plucked pheasant.

"Have a seat. Bold and daring you may be, but I don't doubt you've suffered. Don't just stand there, sit down."

Even in the dim light the baby could see her mother was back, and her lips started to twitch as if she'd burst out crying at any moment as she crawled toward Kil-nyo's lap. Kil-nyo held the baby so tight she was almost crushing it. The joyous thrill that coursed through her body at that moment brought every last pore back to life. The smell of the baby caressing her nose made her feel the sheer awe of life. To keep from weeping she clenched her jaws.

"It seems you've made it through a critical moment," murmured the shaman. Then she said,

"They say even a short tongue can spit far. In the same way, even if you've been doomed to blunder, you ought always to keep your heart in the right place. If you try to live any way you please, you won't last a day in this world.

"This baby and me are tied together with a special love even stronger than the love sisters share, but it could never match the love binding a mother to her own child. It's lucky you're not a narrow-minded woman."

"I can't see how I could ever repay you for all you've done for me. At first when you told me to leave the baby behind, I was resentful. I wondered how you could take a mother's love so lightly, and for a while I even suspected some devious motive. But then I suddenly realized I couldn't end my own life leaving this little one behind. And as I rushed back here I was able to get control of my unnatural notions. It's all thanks to your wise precautions—it makes twice now that you've saved my life."

"Why, enough of that already, you're making me embarrassed."

The following day Kil-nyo took her leave of Wonjon. The old woman insisted she needed to recuperate from her trip and tried to make her stay on one more day at least, but Kil-nyo felt she had no choice but to go. Even though she had become used to wandering through unknown regions, the trip back to Hamyang seemed endless.

The road back home had grown more unforgiving than ever. Inspections by the army and the police were stricter than before. Men on the road were forced to strip in the open to be searched. Kil-nyo had become such a veteran at hitching rides on military trucks that her journey was easier than most. Others, men and women alike, would begin to stutter at the approach of soldiers even if they had nothing at all to hide.

Kil-nyo, however, no longer thought twice about self-respect when she happened upon a possible lift. As they say, a beggar who sings in the marketplace knows the secret of making a decent living. When it came to beseeching a ride, Kil-nyo was seldom turned down. Without having to endure any remarkable travails, she arrived in Hamyang three days later.

She waited until after dusk hung low over the village before venturing home. Her mother was still keeping her vigil before the funerary altar, sitting there just as erect as she had been six weeks before. Even so, she must have been terribly anxious about Kil-nyo's return, for at the sight of her daughter and granddaughter she wept softly for a long while.

Kil-nyo reproached herself for having been so cold-hearted. For her to have left a sickly old mother all alone to go off and wander the countryside now struck her as an unforgivable cruelty. Yet, it had not been in vain that her mother had kept a constant lookout for the reappearance of her daughter.

Scattered around Tunchon there were several remote villages separated from each other by five or six miles. While Kil-nyo had been away those villages had been raided by the guerillas and their people mercilessly slaughtered.

"But for some reason those bastards never touched Tunchon. Some say it's a divine blessing, others that they left Tunchon alone because one of their spies lives here and they want to preserve their secret contact."

"A spy for the guerillas in our village? Who in their right mind could say such a crazy thing?"

"People always like to badmouth others, but when you stop to think about it, it's not entirely absurd. There's no other reasonable explanation why we've been spared from the claws of the guerillas, so it's only natural for people to speculate. Even if there's no spy, it's not so hard to believe there might be somebody in the village who's got some close ties with the guerillas."

Kil-nyo ignored this and changed the subject.

"Have you managed all right with nobody around to help you?"

"I slept in a warm room, never went hungry and made my way to the outhouse on my own, so I was no burden to the neighbors. But since you left, the village elder's often come by, asking all kinds of questions about your absence. He's often been prowling around outside the gate, too. That was what worried me.

"Once the guerillas started raiding the other villages, he came by every other day. Every time I sent him away with a flat 'I don't know', but when he finds out you're back he'll rush over here and start questioning you about something. That worries me."

"We shouldn't let him find out I'm back."

"Go take a look in the other room. They brought three bags of rice."

"Three bags of rice?"

"Sent by that man in Taegu, Mr. Cha wasn't it? A truck brought them, drove right up to our gate. They said he'd be stopping by himself one of these days. Seems he made it to a high ranking post. By the way, where have you been all this time?"

"There was a woman I made friends with a while back. I was staying with her family."

"I'm glad you were in good hands and made it back safely. I was so worried, especially for the little one.... There was a cuckoo. No telling where it was hiding, but when spring comes it flies about the forest and cries mournfully day and night. Always living alone, not even building a nest, but dropping an egg into the nest of a lark, a bird known for its beautiful song.

"Do you know why we call rice pancakes made with azalea petals 'cuckoo pancakes'? It's because the redness of the flower petals is supposed to come from blood coughed out by a cuckoo each night."

Kil-nyo was startled to hear from her mother the same thing

the old shaman woman had told her.

"Why cuckoos, of all the birds...."

"I don't know, dear. The notion just came to mind."

Her mother told Kil-nyo to stay put and the old woman herself went outside to bolt the gate. Everything was buried in silence. They burned no lights in the main room where her mother usually stayed. Instead, they lit a lamp out by the funerary altar, being cautious lest the neighbors notice Kil-nyo had returned.

Kil-nyo made up her mind to wait right where she was. Upon first hearing from Chom-gae's wife that he might be somewhere in the mountains near Namwon, Kil-nyo had decided to search for him there. But the more she thought about it, the more it seemed like chasing after the end of a rainbow.

To track down a wanderer through inquiries was impossible enough, but in this case it was out of the question even to ask after Chom-gae. It would be extremely perilous, and so she decided not to jump into the fire with hay on her back.

There was no guarantee she would ever see Chom-gae again, but still she thought it best to stay put there in Tunchon. If what her mother said was right, Chom-gae probably had dropped in at Tunchon a few times while she was away. She did not doubt he was among the guerillas who had raided the neighboring villages. That Tunchon alone had been left intact itself bespoke his presence.

In other words, Kil-nyo knew what everybody else in the village had no way of knowing, but she could say nothing of it out loud. Nevertheless, the circumstances were generating suspicions about the whole village. The inhabitants of Tunchon were painfully uncomfortable at being the only place left alone while all their neighbors were being ravaged by the guerillas. To be under the close and constant surveillance of outsiders only added to their unease.

"Can you guess what it is?"

This abrupt question came from her mother, whom Kil-nyo had thought was asleep.

"What what is, mother?"

"The reason why those bastards steer clear of us, I wonder."

"Shouldn't we just count ourselves lucky?"

"Yes, indeed. But pity is, we can't feel comfortable about it."

"Get some rest now, mother."

"If the baby starts fussing, give her to me."

Kil-nyo gently pushed the baby inside her quilt up towards her mother. Kil-nyo was having trouble sleeping, too. She racked her brain trying to figure out why Chom-gae had stabbed Chi Sang-mo to death.

The question had plagued her constantly. Hundreds of times she tried to answer it, but in vain. She recalled having once told Chom-gae about the cold reception Chi gave her when she visited Kanggu, but that alone could not possibly have cost a man his life. Besides, it had been Chi himself who had given Chom-gae the chance to escape his torturers. She could not imagine what could have led Chom-gae to do him in so suddenly.

Nobody could clear up the mystery except Chom-gae himself. Whatever it may have been, to Kil-nyo the dead man had been the father of her baby, after all. She felt no murderous urge toward Chom-gae, but she needed to know why he had murdered Chi. It was not so much for the sake of Chi Sang-mo as for her own peace of mind. She had to see Chom-gae.

Ten days went by after her return home without Kil-nyo's presence stirring up any suspicion, but there was still no trace of Chom-gae. The season of frost was steadily creeping closer and the wind racing through the naked branches at night was growing stronger and harsher. Since Kil-nyo's return, the village elder had stopped at the house twice to check on her whereabouts.

When Kil-nyo's mother again told him she was still away and had sent no word, the elder said,

"People have heard a baby crying here at night every now and then."

"A baby crying?"

"That's what your neighbors said."

"What nonsense! Are they such fools that they can't tell a baby's bawling from the yowls of a tomcat? Damn them all! Why don't you go tell them they'd be better off minding their own business."

At this irate retort from the old woman, the elder looked taken aback and said in a monotonous tone,

"That's what I say. They'll talk their heads off about anything if it's at somebody else's expense. Anyway, please let me know the minute your daughter shows up. Mr. Cha in Taegu must be really pressing the district office here."

"Pressing? What do you mean?"

"Best I can make out, he's ordered them to find your daughter and bring her on down to Taegu."

"The time will come for her to go there."

Nearly a month had passed with no news of further guerilla raids on the surrounding villages, and the people in Tunchon were feeling a bit relieved. They had heard that the army had mounted a surprise attack up on Chirisan and was now doing its utmost to root out the guerillas.

Earlier, when the guerillas were rampaging over the whole region, quite a few of the young and able-bodied men in the villages had left for larger towns, seeking refuge along with the families of civil servants. But since news came about the start of a punitive expedition into the mountains, many had begun moving back to their home villages and peoples faces were lightening up.

The early winter wind that had been staying up in the distant mountains had descended and was blowing right outside the gates. But many felt thankful they had managed to bring in the harvest and would be able to stay inside their homes with food enough to outwait the snow.

For Kil-nyo, however, the flowing by of these calmer times meant that the hour of Chom-gae's appearance was drawing nearer. In fact, the hour had come, sneaking up right under her nose to stare her right in the face.

It was the night exactly one month after Kil-nyo had come

back home. She had finished up the dishes and laid down to go to bed, but after almost an hour lying there awake she felt restless. The wind was howling more fiercely than usual. With no clock in the house she could not tell the exact hour, but it was past eleven.

For an instant she thought she heard a shriek, but then the sound was gone and in its place there was only the mounting roar of the wind. From the yard came a rustling that might have been dry leaves and refuse rolling before strong gusts. Kil-nyo held the baby tightly in her arms and turned her back to the wall.

Her mother, who had lived seventy long years within earshot of mountain trails, had keener ears. She could pick out from the howl of the wind even the slightest hint of a human presence. If a dog showed up out by the barn and engaged in a staring duel with the cow, or if a weasel was slinking about the henhouse, plotting to snatch a chicken, she had an uncanny way of discerning the intruder. It was a sixth sense developed by the old up in the mountains—even if they could not make out what people were saying right in front of their noses, they could read the distant rustling of the wind.

As she fumbled under the quilt to nudge her daughter in the back, the old woman quietly said,

"Wake up, dear."

On the brink of sleep, Kil-nyo awoke with a start.

"Something's not right outside, I can feel it."

"Did you hear something?"

"No, dear. But go take a look."

"Go where, mother?"

"You'll see if you go and keep your eyes open."

Kil-nyo lifted up the baby in a rush and was about to wrap the child on her back when her mother took her by the hand.

"Leave the baby here."

"I'll take her on my back."

"No, you won't."

Her mother's voice was pointed, brooking no contradiction.

Only then did Kil-nyo realize she had definitely sensed something. Making her way into the yard, Kil-nyo focused all of her attention on the sound of the wind. But she could make out nothing besides the rushing air. After standing there a while, she squatted down by the gate.

A couple of minutes passed, then she heard the faint sound of someone singing—"stains of blood left in the valley of Changbaeksan...."

Kil-nyo's heart began to pound. What she heard was a sign of the coming of Hwang Chom-gae. In spite of herself, she buried her face in her long skirt. Then she slowly drew a dagger out from the folds where she had hidden it, gripping its handle tightly. She opened the gate and walked out onto the path.

The whole village was pitch black with not one light on anywhere. It was too dark even to see an inch ahead, and in that darkness dogs were barking fiercely. The singing suddenly stopped. But soon after, there followed a shrill woman's cry borne on the wind. It sounded like a dying shriek.

Strangely, however, the village had fallen as silent as the bottom of the sea. Yet in that stillness Kil-nyo thought she sensed people moving. Just then a bright light flashed into view somewhere near the house of the village elder. Almost immediately, she detected footsteps only a few feet away, but there was nobody to be seen.

The burning torch stayed where it was, near the old zelkova tree not far from the elder's place. The torch was burning beneath that tree, and as Kil-nyo approached, she could see two men, one holding the torch as the other paced back and forth under the tree.

She could not make out the men's faces, but judging from their movements alone she could tell they were no neighbors of hers. Several more men were waiting in the darkness on the path between the tree and the elder's house. Some had on old-style winter coats, others wore tattered army uniforms, and still others looked to be wearing only rags, but she could see they were all armed.

The men who did not have rifles leaning on their shoulders had bamboo spears in their hands. At that moment Kil-nyo made out a familiar face moving along the path, with some of the armed men pushing him from behind. It was the elder of the village, without a doubt. Already he was covered with blood and his hair was unspeakably disheveled.

Pushed and poked by the bloodthirsty men, the elder was forced to kneel down under the zelkova tree.

"Are you Ma Hak-gi?"

Asked the man who until then had been restlessly pacing back and forth. He was the only one of the guerillas who bore no weapon. Instead, he wore a red armband on one arm. The man holding the torch waved it right under the chin of the elder. Then the man with the armband stepped forward and thrust his face close to the elder, asking again,

"Are you the front man, Ma Hak-gi?"

At that moment, Kil-nyo was stunned as if a rock had crashed into the back of her head. The interrogator was none other then Pak Sok-ho, the man who she had once watched sharpening sickles at the house near the salt storage in Andong. He had been the one who arranged for the escape of Chom-gae during the prisoner transfer.

There was no response from Ma Hak-gi. He looked like he lacked the strength even to pronounce a simple "yes" or "no". Blood kept running down from his shoulder where he had been pierced by a spear, and the man standing behind him had to hold him up so that he would not collapse forward.

"Did you think we'd let a reactionary element like you go instead of executing you?"

The number of torches had grown to four or five. White foam was gathering at the corner of Pak's mouth.

"Please, don't kill me."

The voice was not audible from Kil-nyo where stood, but there was nothing else Ma Hak-gi would have been likely to say.

"Don't kill you? You're asking us not to kill a bloodsucker like you, a man whose been sucking the blood of the people?"

Pak Sok-ho was the one mocking the plea for life, while the man holding the torch was kicking the doomed man. Only then did Kil-nyo notice how many people were watching the atrocious spectacle unfolding beneath the zelkova tree. They were craning their necks over fences when the torches were held high, cringing back out of sight when the lights flashed their way.

Nobody dared approach the tree. They only watched the murderous scene. Suddenly Kil-nyo felt a breath of hot air on the back of her neck and smelled smoke. Pillars of black smoke were streaming into the air over the elder's house. Oddly, there was no sound of wailing from his family. At the sight of the tower of flames shooting up from the house, Pak Sok-ho barked an order aimed at no one in particular,

"Execute him!"

Kil-nyo could see by this time that a length of rope had been tossed over one of the branches of the zelkova. One end had been tied around the neck of Ma Hak-gi. Four men took up the other end of the rope and moved away and the man's body instantly was pulled up to dangle in midair. The only spectators of this cruel ending were the guerillas standing there, rifles and spears in hand.

At last Kil-nyo heard the sound of thunder. She thought it might be the last roll of thunder she would ever hear. The night sky was moonless, but the stars were shining. The rumble might have come from black clouds that even at that moment were loosing a downpour in distant valleys on the far slopes of Chirisan.

Just as her mother had the ability to divine the presence of men from feeble signs carried on the wind, so Kil-nyo by this time could detect the sound of thunder as it rumbled seventy miles away. Some time passed before the lingering echoes of the rolling thunder finally died away.

"This is it, wrap it up."

This firm and decisive order came from beneath the zelkova tree. The voice was unmistakably that of Hwang Chom-gae. He was right underneath the dead body of Ma Hak-gi. Also with a red armband on his arm, Chom-gae stood so close to Pak Sok-ho that their noses almost touched. From where he had suddenly appeared was a mystery.

By now the number of assembled guerillas amounted to thirty or forty. A few more torches were burning, and the area around the zelkova tree was now lit up as bright as day. Standing in a ring under the glaring light, the guerillas were tensely watching the two leaders. After frantically rushing about, they now stood there frozen.

Chom-gae had his back to her, so Kil-nyo could not see the expression on his face, still the way he carried himself was no less imposing and majestic. She recalled how he always hung his head and slouched his shoulders in her presence. But now his chin was held high and he looked like he could impale his chin into the forehead of Pak Sok-ho.

"What do you mean 'wrap it up' with this?"

"I mean this is it, wrap it up."

"Comrade, are you saying we should stop without finishing our revolutionary mission?"

"We've stayed here too long already."

"Just a minute, only a reactionary element could say such a thing."

"Reactionary? Are you saying anyone who suggests pulling out is a reactionary?"

Pak Sok-ho had never stopped whetting sickles back in Andong. All sorts of glistening blades had hung on the earthen wall of his shed. They were already well-sharpened, but he kept taking them off their hooks one at a time to hone them on his whetstone. Then he put them back, but Kil-nyo had never once seen him use any of them.

"We must pull out at once."

"We've already cut all the telephone lines."

"We have to go."

"No, we must not."

This time it was Pak Sok-ho whose voice was determined.

"We can't allow raids and arson any longer."

"I charge you with crimes against the people and call for you to be tried right now."

"I am no reactionary."

Suddenly Pak Sok-ho pulled a pistol out of his belt. It shined like the eyes of the rat that once stared at Kil-nyo from behind the water urn in the kitchen. The torches were being waved slowly higher and higher.

"No bastard who interferes with the accomplishment of our mission will get away with it. And you, you were against this all along for no good reason, right?"

The pistol in Pak's hand was pointed right at the middle of Chom-gae's chest. There did not seem to be any report of the gun, but Chom-gae toppled over sideways like a falling stick. The lapel of his tattered rag of a jacket was fluttering in the wind. Once more the torches rose into the air.

"Darling."

This word slipped from Kil-nyo's mouth before she knew it. It was the first time in her life she had used the word to address a man.